Palgrave Studies in Nineteenth-Century Writing and Culture

General Editor: **Joseph Bristow**, Professor of English, UCLA

Editorial Advisory Board: **Hilary Fraser**, Birkbeck College, University of London; **Josephine McDonagh**, Linacre College, University of Oxford; **Yopie Prins**, University of Michigan; **Lindsay Smith**, University of Sussex; **Margaret D. Stetz**, University of Delaware; **Jenny Bourne Taylor**, University of Sussex

Palgrave Studies in Nineteenth-Century Writing and Culture is a new monograph series that aims to represent the most innovative research on literary works that were produced in the English-speaking world from the time of the Napoleonic Wars to the *fin de siècle*. Attentive to the historical continuities between 'Romantic' and 'Victorian', the series will feature studies that help scholarship to reassess the meaning of these terms during a century marked by diverse cultural, literary, and political movements. The main aim of the series is to look at the increasing influence of types of historicism on our understanding of literary forms and genres. It reflects the shift from critical theory to cultural history that has affected not only the period 1800–1900 but also every field within the discipline of English literature. All titles in the series seek to offer fresh critical perspectives and challenging readings of both canonical and non-canonical writings of this era.

Titles include:

Catherine Maxwell and Patricia Pulham (*editors*)
VERNON LEE
Decadence, Ethics, Aesthetics

David Payne
THE REENCHANTMENT OF NINETEENTH-CENTURY FICTION
Dickens, Thackeray, George Eliot, and Serialization

Ana Parejo Vadillo
WOMEN POETS AND URBAN AESTHETICISM
Passengers of Modernity

Palgrave Studies in Nineteenth-Century Writing and Culture
Series Standing Order ISBN 0–333–97700–9 (hardback)
(*outside North America only*)

You can receive future titles in this series as they are published by placing a standing order. Please contact your bookseller or, in case of difficulty, write to us at the address below with your name and address, the title of the series and the ISBN quoted above.

Customer Services Department, Macmillan Distribution Ltd, Houndmills, Basingstoke, Hampshire RG21 6XS, England

Fictions of British Decadence

High Art, Popular Writing, and the *Fin de Siècle*

Kirsten MacLeod

First published in 2006 by
PALGRAVE MACMILLAN
Houndmills, Basingstoke, Hampshire RG21 6XS and
175 Fifth Avenue, New York, N.Y. 10010
Companies and representatives throughout the world.

PALGRAVE MACMILLAN is the global academic imprint of the Palgrave Macmillan division of St. Martin's Press, LLC and of Palgrave Macmillan Ltd. Macmillan® is a registered trademark in the United States, United Kingdom and other countries. Palgrave is a registered trademark in the European Union and other countries.

ISBN-13: 978–1–4039–9908–5 hardback
ISBN-10: 1–4039–9908–2 hardback

This book is printed on paper suitable for recycling and made from fully managed and sustained forest sources.

A catalogue record for this book is available from the British Library.

Library of Congress Cataloging-in-Publication Data

MacLeod, Kirsten, 1969–
    Fictions of British decadence : high art, popular writing, and the *fin de siècle* / Kirsten MacLeod.
        p. cm. – (Palgrave studies in ninteenth-century writing and culture)
    Includes bibliographical references and index.
    ISBN 1–4039–9908–2 (cloth)
        1. English fiction – 19th century – History and criticism. 2. Decadence (Literary movement) – Great Britain. I. Title. II. Series.

PR878.D372M33 2006
823′.80911—dc22   2005057927

10 9 8 7 6 5 4 3 2 1
15 14 13 12 11 10 09 08 07 06

Printed and bound in Great Britain by
Antony Rowe Ltd, Chippenham and Eastbourne

For Gary, Alec, and Hilary

Contents

Preface and Acknowledgements

In *Fictions of British Decadence: High Art, Popular Writing, and the* Fin de Siècle, I examine largely uncharted territory – the unknown – within a field of study that has, to a great extent, been misrepresented in literary and cultural history – the misknown. The unknown is a significant body of fiction that represented a transition between the plot-driven three-volume Victorian novel and introspective and analytical Modernist fiction. The misknown is the field of British Decadence whose representative figures have been mythologized in many a memoir and literary history as doomed souls, whose histrionics and excesses resulted in a pretentious and overwrought literary output. My aim, then, in the book, is twofold. On the one hand, I illuminate and contextualize this mostly unknown body of Decadent fiction and fiction about Decadence that includes the work of Ernest Dowson, John Davidson, George Moore, Vernon Lee, Marie Corelli, Sarah Grand, Arthur Machen, and M. P. Shiel. On the other hand, in so doing, I revisit the misknowns of British Decadence, opening up the field by re-evaluating the myths that surround some of its central figures and by moving beyond them to consider the role of others generally neglected in histories of the movement. Because of the at once recuperative and revisionist nature of this book, I have provided in the introduction a general outline of the history of and main scholarship on British Decadence which clearly states the knowns and misknowns of Decadence. Though such material will undoubtedly be useful to the undergraduate or beginning researcher, it will be very familiar terrain to scholars well-versed in the area. This overview is a necessary ground-clearing exercise, however, in a study that seeks to change substantially the contours of the field of British Decadence as we know it.

The research for this project has been generously funded by fellowships and research and travel grants from the Social Sciences and Humanities Research Council of Canada, the University of Alberta, and the Province of Alberta. This funding supported research at the British Library, the Colindale Newspaper Library, the Bodleian Library, the Harry Ransom Center, and the Beinecke Library. I am indebted to those who supported me through this project from its inception as a dissertation to its final form: Jo-Ann Wallace, Ted Bishop, Sue Hamilton, Peter Sinnema, Chris Wiesenthal, and Ian Small. I would also like to thank my fellow Victorianists and friends Mary Elizabeth Leighton and Janice Schroeder for their stimulating conversation – about things Victorian and otherwise. A special thanks to Joseph Bristow, the editor of this series, who is a kind, generous, and insightful scholar. Paula Kennedy and others at Palgrave Macmillan have been very helpful.

Preface and Acknowledgements

Introduction

> One had, in the late eighties and early nineties, to be preposterously French. ...
>
> Victor Plarr, *Ernest Dowson* (1914)[1]

The French origins of British Decadence

As Victor Plarr's comments on the Francophilia of the *fin-de-siècle* British literary avant-garde indicate, studies of British Decadence must invariably account for its French origins. Certainly by the time Decadence as an aesthetic practice came into its own in Britain in the 1890s, it had been long established in France, where political and social turbulence throughout the century fostered anxieties about cultural decline. Though technically Decadence did not constitute a movement in France until the 1880s,[2] its exponents in this period traced the roots of the aesthetic in the writings of earlier writers: Charles Baudelaire's *Fleurs du mal* (1857); Théophile Gautier's *Mademosielle de Maupin* (1835) and his poems of the 1850s; the 1860s novels of the Goncourt brothers; and Flaubert's *Salammbô* (1862), *La Tentation de saint Antoine* (1874), and *Trois contes* (1877). In the works of these writers were found elements of style and theme that French writers of the 1880s would come to label Decadent: the insistence on the autonomy of art; a disgust with bourgeois philistinism and utilitarianism; an interest in complexity of form and elaborate and arcane language; a fascination with the perverse, the morbid, and the artificial; a desire for intense experience and a seeking after rare sensations in order to combat a feeling of *ennui* or world-weariness. Inspired by these writers and in revolt against the dominance of Naturalism – a school of fiction led by Emile Zola that dwelt on the sordid aspects of life and took a deterministic view of the fate of the individual and of humanity – the French Decadents of the 1880s developed their own aesthetic.

By far the most important contribution to these efforts was J.-K. Huysmans's 1884 novel, *A Rebours* (*Against Nature* or, *Against the Grain*). In it, Huysmans

1

writes against Naturalism's focus on the family plot,[3] creating a hero who is not only the last of an aristocratic family line but who also disengages himself from social networks. Holed up in a country retreat, Des Esseintes turns his back on nature and on bourgeois culture and attempts to achieve a heightened sense of awareness through the cultivation of artificial pleasures: he sleeps during the day and has almost no contact with people; his dining room is designed like a ship's cabin and is surrounded with an artificial aquarium; his bedroom is monastic; he contemplates his extensive collection of art and literature; he consorts with a female acrobat and a ventriloquist and corrupts a young boy; he has a live tortoise encrusted in gold and precious gems; he conducts various experiments in synaesthesia in an effort to hear colours, taste music, and feel perfumes. Less a traditional narrative than a series of studies, Huysmans's novel also revolts against the more simplistic and direct narrative style of Naturalism,[4] exhibiting instead a highly stylized, mannered, and impressionistic form of writing.

Huysmans's achievements in the novel from the point of view of the development of Decadence, then, were significant. He created the prototypical modern hero 'torn between desire and satiety, hope and disillusionment, aspiration and despair'.[5] This type would be taken up not only by Decadents but by twentieth-century Modernists as well. At the same time, Huysmans developed a signature style for Decadence in his evocative, exotic, and precious use of language. Finally, through his extensive discussions of Des Esseintes's literary and artistic tastes, he provided readers with what Nicholas White has called, an 'alternative literary history' that privileged artists who were obscure and esoteric at that time such as Baudelaire, Mallarmé, Paul Verlaine, Odilon Redon, Tristan Corbière, Jules Barbey d'Aurevilly, and Comte Philippe Villiers de l'Isle-Adam.[6] Huysmans's novel would thus determine the canon of French Decadence.

Decadence in Britain

Though *A Rebours* exerted a profound influence on the development of Decadence in both France and Britain, it is Britain that concerns us here. When the novel was published in the mid 1880s, Aestheticism and Naturalism were the main subjects of controversy in the British literary field. Even if Aestheticism shared many of the same tenets as Decadence – a commitment to art for art's sake, a rejection of bourgeois industrialism and utilitarianism, and a desire for intensity of experience – its force as a resistant aesthetic for the literary élite was, by the 1880s, on the wane. In part, Aestheticism's declining power was a result of its popularity with the middle class, a group against which proponents of the movement sought to define themselves. To add insult to injury, Aestheticism had become the subject of much ridicule and parody, notably in the caricatures of its main proponents, James McNeill Whistler and Oscar Wilde in *Punch* and in Gilbert and

Sullivan's operetta *Patience*. Naturalism, by contrast, was regarded as a new threat by literary and social conservatives who deplored its treatment of unsavoury subjects such as alcoholism and adultery. And yet, despite its apparently subversive force, many among the British literary élite complained that, as an aesthetic, Naturalism was inartistic and unimaginative. For these writers, Huysmans's novel represented the perfect mediation between Naturalism and Aestheticism. Like Naturalism, the Decadent *A Rebours* treated the sordid aspects of life, but moved beyond mundane human vices to engage in a more intellectual fashion with perversion, morbidity, ennui, and spiritual malaise. At the same time, it eschewed the prosaic stylistics of Naturalism for the more ornate, complex, and learned style associated with Aestheticism. These aspects of Huysmans's Decadent style appealed immensely to British writers who were searching for ways to make the novel artistic at a time when literature was becoming increasingly commercialized to meet the demands of a growing mass readership. Many among the literary élite were eulogistic in their praise of the book. George Moore, for example, who had experimented with Naturalism but ultimately found it an aesthetically unappealing mode, was overwhelmed by the beauty of Huysmans's writing. 'Huysmans goes to my soul', he wrote, 'like a gold ornament of Byzantine workmanship' and he called *A Rebours* 'a prodigious book, [a] beautiful mosaic'.[7] Oscar Wilde also loved the book, which he encountered just as he was becoming jaded with Aestheticism and it influenced his move towards the darker Aestheticism of Decadence that he would exhibit in *The Picture of Dorian Gray*, a story much indebted to Huysmans's novel. For his part, Arthur Symons, a leading British theorist and poet of Decadence, declared *A Rebours* 'the breviary of the Decadence', while numerous other British writers of the 1890s expressed similar sentiments.[8]

Huysmans thus served as a major inspiration for the British Decadents as would those Decadent precursors to whom he drew attention in *A Rebours*. Despite their high regard for French writers, however, British Decadents were not without native influences. They regarded Walter Pater, for example, with as much reverence as they did Huysmans. Answering his call 'to burn always with this hard, gem-like flame, to maintain this ecstacy'[9] in a way unanticipated by the somewhat reticent Pater, they used his philosophy to justify their explorations of the abnormal and perverse. Prompted by their interests in Pater, Huysmans, Baudelaire, the Goncourts, Mallarmé, and Flaubert, British writers began to discuss French Decadence in literary and artistic periodicals and to introduce elements of it into their own writing.

This process was necessarily a gradual one due to the prevalence of Francophobia in Britain at this time and to the power of moral crusaders in proscribing certain forms of literature. Though the Francophilic literary avant-garde may have wanted, in Victor Plarr's terms, to be 'preposterously French', many Britons felt that France's literature was a central factor in the nation's decline. A British MP, for example, raised the issue in the House of

Commons in 1888, insisting that pernicious literature had 'overspread the [French] nation like a torrent, and its poison was simply death to a nation'.[10] This discussion in the House of Commons was prompted by the reaction of moral crusaders against the publication of English translations of the Naturalist novels of Emile Zola, Guy de Maupassant and other French writers and led, eventually, to the imprisonment of the publisher for issuing 'obscene' literature, even though these books had been issued in expurgated form. While this action represents a somewhat exceptional example of the forms censorship took in *fin-de-siècle* Britain, writers and publishers were certainly circumscribed in what they could do. Primarily, they were constrained by the circulating libraries and the method by which new novels circulated in the Victorian period. At this time, most novels were initially published in three volumes and were prohibitively expensive for all but the wealthiest people. Cheap, one-volume editions of these novels would not be issued until long after the first appearance of a novel. Most readers thus had access to the newest fiction only through circulating libraries, which bought books at a discounted price from publishers and charged readers a subscription fee. Though cheap original fiction in one-volume was, by the 1880s, becoming increasingly available for readers to buy direct from bookshops and newsstands, the circulating libraries still had a fair amount of influence over the literary market and they took their role as moral watchdogs seriously. They frequently refused to stock books that they felt were not suitable for women and young persons, a policy that represented a serious obstacle for those writers who were trying to expand the purview of literature and to take on more mature subject matter.[11] This issue was much contested in a series of literary debates in the period, including Eliza Lynn Linton, Thomas Hardy, and Walter Besant's 1890 series of essays on 'Candour in English Fiction' in the *New Review* and George Moore's attack on circulating libraries in *Literature at Nurse; or, Circulating Morals* (1885).[12]

Given the British reaction to *expurgated* French Naturalism and the power of the circulating libraries over literary production, it is hardly surprising that Decadence, which exceeded Naturalism in its treatment of vice and moral perversity, should be slow to develop in Britain. The anxieties about pernicious literature, coupled with a largely cautious publishing industry, meant that, despite the eagerness on the part of many among the élite to bring elements of this new French literary import to their own writing, Decadence was slow to emerge in Britain. Beginning in the late 1880s, writers such as George Moore, Havelock Ellis, Richard Le Gallienne, Arthur Symons, and Lionel Johnson introduced Decadence to the British public in critical essays, though many of these were limited to periodicals aimed at an exclusive audience of social progressives, intellectuals, and the literary avant-garde.[13] These essays tended to describe Decadence as a distinctly French phenomenon and sought to provide a precise definition for an audience unfamiliar with its tenets. Emphasizing the style of Decadence as one that focuses on individual parts, rather than the whole, Ellis, Symons, and others tended to downplay subject matter, noting only that such works expressed a pessimistic view of life.

As for attempts to integrate the aesthetic into British literature, it was Moore who was the first to do so. Very early efforts included two volumes of Baudelaire inspired poems, *Flowers of Passion* (1877) and *Pagan Poems* (1881). Though Moore's poems, which touched on lesbianism, incest, and androgyny, met with harsh criticism, in many respects poetry was an easier medium through which to introduce Decadence than fiction, if only because it was a genre with a narrower appeal. Volumes of poetry by largely unknown poets were issued in such small numbers and catered to such a restricted audience that their corrupting potential was regarded as limited in comparison with fiction. As such, poets were subject to less scrutiny than fiction writers when bringing Decadence to poetry. Still, though poetry was perhaps better able than fiction to treat risqué subjects such as passion, lust, ennui, the music hall, prostitutes, absinthe, and opium in the restrictive context of late Victorian publishing, even Decadent poets, as Bruce Gardiner has argued, trod somewhat carefully, drawing on an acceptable 'native tradition' of poetry while bringing to it more 'exotic' French elements.[14]

Despite the greater difficulty of incorporating Decadence into the more popular genre of fiction, writers certainly made attempts to do so. Here, Moore was again a pioneer. Inspired by Huysmans's novel and by the writings of Pater, Moore wrote a series of Decadent novels in the 1880s that aimed to bring psychological depth and stylistic complexity to a study of the exploits of a variety of types of modern young men – the artistic, the morbid, the spiritually and morally bankrupt, and so on.[15] While Moore's novels of this period were significant to the development of British Decadence, they were not sufficiently popular to garner much public attention. It was not, therefore, until the July 1890 publication of Wilde's *Picture of Dorian Gray* in *Lippincott's* magazine that Decadence became widely recognized. Wilde's story, as many scholars have observed, took inspiration from Huysmans's *A Rebours* in its characterization of Dorian's quest for aesthetic and physical stimulation and in its development of a richly ornate prose style. These elements, recognized as imports from the school of French Decadence, were harshly attacked in a critical reception unprecedented for a story issued in a magazine.[16] The publicity surrounding this reception brought awareness of an artistic creed, hitherto unknown beyond the literary community, to the attention of the broader public.

From this point on, Decadence achieved an even greater notoriety than Aestheticism and Naturalism had before it. 'The two or three years after 1891', R. K. R. Thornton argues, 'saw an explosion in the popularity of the word'[17] and Decadence, like Aestheticism before it, was mocked mercilessly in the pages of *Punch* and other magazines. At the same time, more conservative venues focused, as they had in the case of Naturalism, on the potentially corrupting influence of this new form of perniciousness. While pro-Decadent critics such as Symons and Ellis had tried to bring precision to the term in their discussions of the movement, this precision was lost when taken up in popular discourse. Decadence was used loosely by critics to describe everything from Naturalism and Impressionism to Realism and New Woman fiction. At the same time, with the advent of a medical discourse that associated artistic genius with criminality and degeneracy, Decadent writers and artists were increasingly subject to *ad hominem* attacks in which their art was represented as a direct reflection of their own pathological condition.

Despite the revulsion and mockery with which Decadence was greeted, writers were increasingly able, in the 1890s, to treat subject matter hitherto unacceptable in literature. In part, this was a consequence of the emergence of a number of enterprising publishers with an interest in promoting the latest high art trends and in bypassing the circulating libraries by pricing their books to sell directly to readers. Of these firms, the Bodley Head, established by Elkin Mathews and John Lane in 1887, was the most strongly associated with Decadence and drew the greatest amount of negative attention. The Bodley Head published the poetry, fiction, and art of the main figures associated with Decadence including Ernest Dowson, Arthur Symons, John Davidson, Max Beerbohm, Oscar Wilde, Aubrey Beardsley, Arthur Machen, and M. P. Shiel as well as New Woman writers such as George Egerton, who were often considered part of the Decadent coterie. The success of the Bodley Head's magazine, the *Yellow Book*, and its Keynotes series of advanced fiction, as well as the 'log-rolling' efforts of the firm's poets to promote each other, put these writers under increased scrutiny from 1894 on. Through 1894 and 1895, the Bodley Head's publications and its authors were repeatedly identified as Decadent and criticized for being sex-obsessed, lurid, morbid, revolting, nonsensical, cynical, nasty, and self-promoting.[18]

The attacks against Decadence reached a boiling point in early 1895 when the arrest, trial, and prosecution of Oscar Wilde for acts of gross indecency gave counter-Decadents the ammunition they needed to bring down the movement. The press linked Wilde's crimes with his art and used his status as the most high-profile of the Decadents to indict the whole movement. This strategy made life difficult both for those who professed an allegiance to Decadence and for those who had no such allegiance but were guilty by a too close association with its proponents. As a consequence, many of those associated with Decadence tried to disassociate themselves from the movement. Most famously, Arthur Symons, who was working on a book entitled *The Decadent Movement in Literature* changed the title to *The Symbolist Movement in Literature* and in it declared that Decadence had been 'a half-mock interlude' that paved the way for the more serious aesthetic of Symbolism.[19] Along with Symons, Yeats jumped on the Symbolist bandwagon, while others found different ways of reinventing themselves: John Davidson, for example, turned to writing for the theatre, while Ernest Dowson took up translating work and exiled himself in France, M. P. Shiel began writing popular serials for mass-market periodicals, and Arthur Machen became an actor.

Mythologizing British Decadence

The taint of being associated with Decadence, however, as some soon discovered, was hard to remove. If Wilde's trial and prosecution had not dealt enough of a blow to the status of the movement, events in the lives of the Decadents over the next 15 years only worsened the situation. Hubert Crackanthorpe's suicide in 1896, the untimely deaths of Beardsley and Dowson from tuberculosis in 1898 and 1900, Johnson's fall from a barstool and subsequent death in 1902, Symons's mental breakdown in 1908, and John Davidson's suicide in 1909 served as occasions for opponents of Decadence to perpetuate their view that this group of artists were degenerate and suicidal types with little talent. Critic Andrew Lang, for example, commented on the Decadents after Dowson's death in the following terms: 'By kicking holes in his boots, crushing in his hat, and avoiding soap, any young man may achieve a comfortable degree of sordidness, and then, if his verses are immaterial, and his life suicidal, he may regard himself as a decadent indeed.'[20] It was not long before anecdotes, gossip, and stereotyping of the Decadents as drunks, whoremongers, paedophiles, homosexuals, lunatics, and drug addicts clouded a more comprehensive view of the Decadents and their writings. Even one-time proponents of Decadence were not immune to these kinds of characterizations, perhaps as part of a strategy for distancing themselves from a movement that had become so disreputable. Max Beerbohm, for example, drew on stereotypes of Symons, Dowson, Victor Plarr, Theodore Wratislaw, Yeats and others in his story 'Enoch Soames' (1916), representing Soames as a ridiculous figure, a morose, grubby-looking, cigarette-smoking, absinthe-drinking, Catholic Diabolist poet who peppers his conversation with French phrases and who has written two slim volumes of incomprehensible poetry titled *Fungoids* and *Negations*.[21] Even those sympathetic to these writers acquired a distorted view of them that idealized what counter-Decadents vilified, celebrating them in romanticized terms as bohemians, dandies, and martyrs to art who suffered at the hands of a vulgar and unappreciative public. Symons, for example, created powerful life-myths around Dowson and Beardsley as *poètes maudits* – doomed, alienated, and misunderstood geniuses – while a host of memoirs in the 1910s and 1920s glorified the Decadents as wrongfully neglected revolutionaries in arts and letters.[22]

Taken as a whole, these images have served as the foundations for the principal myths of Decadence – the myth of the 'tragic generation', the myth of Decadence as high art, and the myths of Decadents as bohemians and aristocratic dandies. These myths have held a particular allure for the popular imagination in the twenty and twenty-first centuries, notably at the point of our own *fin de siècle* when these artists have been represented as progenitors to pop culture icons such as Andy Warhol, Jim Morrison, David Bowie, and Patti Smith, and have attracted renewed interest among a new generation of absinthe-swilling self-professed bohemians and dandies.[23] The internalization of these myths, however, has not only occurred within popular culture. Scholars and academics have also at times been seduced by their compelling nature. Too often these myths have been taken as the givens of Decadence rather than as the *exaggeration* or *idealization* of truth that myths, by definition, represent.[24] The acceptance of these myths has had a deleterious influence on the representation of Decadence within literary studies. Most problematically, as I shall argue, it has led to misrepresentations and oversimplifications about the contributions of Decadent writers to the literary culture of their day.

The 'tragic generation'

Though the tragic lives of the Decadents had long been exploited when W. B. Yeats offered his own account of the movement in the *Trembling of the Veil* (1922), he produced the most enduring of the characterizations of the movement because his mythologization provided an explanatory narrative for a whole generation of artists as well as for the emergence of Modernism. In his account, Yeats focuses on Wilde and on some of his fellow members of the Rhymers' Club. This club constituted a loosely knit group of poets which, despite its cross-generational composition and the differing poetic aims of its members, was invariably associated with Decadence, no doubt because its Decadent members – Davidson, Dowson, John Gray, and Symons – attracted the most notoriety for the unconventionality of their verse. For Yeats, his 'tragic generation' contemporaries were not talentless degenerates, but rather, as he wrote elsewhere, 'Hamlets of [the] age',[25] martyrs to art who were admirable in their dedication to art and beauty but ultimately 'unstable' and incapable of functioning in a world that failed to live up to their ideals.[26] While art and religion offered consolation to some of them, the 'tragic generation' most often reacted to their disappointment with the world with 'dissipation and despair'.[27] Yeats's characterization of a 'generation' of doomed artists depended necessarily for its rhetorical force on the failure of more than just a handful of poets. As such, he exaggerated the casualties among the Decadents, insisting that 'hardly one of them is still alive' when, in fact, a good number of them, as he well knew, were.[28] Literal truth aside, the myth of the 'tragic generation' was very real for Yeats. At one level, it described, as Karl Beckson indicates, 'the artist's struggle to achieve unity of being in a fragmented world'.[29] On a more personal level, however, it justified and explained his own artistic mission. Yeats's tone throughout the account is predominantly 'there but for the grace of God go I'. Certainly, as Beckson argues, he 'identified himself [with]' his peers and 'saw his own achievement as the product of the same intense struggle which had destroyed' them.[30] Still, his focus on the failings of his peers – Dowson's emotional instability and wantonness, Davidson's intellectual weakness, and Johnson's alcoholism – merely serves to emphasize his own survival. Despite his romantic mythologization of his peers, then, there is no question that Yeats is the hero of his narrative, the 'survivor', as Bruce Gardiner argues, 'alone able to realise [the Club's] aspirations'.[31] As Yeats himself put it in another context, he was able to move beyond the expression of mere impressions to the creation of 'a symbolic language' that represented a more mature aesthetic.[32]

Yeats's myth of the 'tragic generation' has had a significant impact on the shape and emphasis of modern scholarship on Decadence and has led to a distorted view of the movement. The prominence given in the myth to the Rhymers' Club has placed an undue amount of attention on Decadence as a poetic movement despite the fact that, in the 1890s, there was as much, if not more, focus on the Decadence of fiction. At the same time, his account has narrowed attention to a limited range of writers, namely those who conform most strongly to the 'tragic generation' stereotype, particularly Wilde, Dowson, Symons, and Johnson. Meanwhile, other Decadents, who either did not write poetry or did not fit Yeats's stereotypical 'tragic generation' have suffered neglect, notably women who were barred from membership in the Rhymers' Club. Early writing on this literary movement certainly reflects Yeats's biases. Wilde, Johnson, Symons, and Dowson, for example, garner the most attention in noteworthy studies by Barbara Charlesworth, Graham Hough, and R. K. R. Thornton.[33] Literary anthologies are also characterized by a narrow representation of Decadence. The sixth edition of *The Norton Anthology of English Literature* (1993), for example, limits its coverage of those it calls the 'aesthetes' to Wilde (four poems, the preface to *The Picture of Dorian Gray*, an excerpt from 'The Critic as Artist', and *The Importance of Being Earnest*), three poems by Dowson, and one by Francis Thompson, a poet that the editor acknowledges is only 'peripherally' associated with the movement.[34]

If, on the one hand, Yeats's myth of the 'tragic generation' has resulted in a limited representation of Decadence with too strong an emphasis on poetry, it has, on the other, also contributed to a biased view of this poetry. Mythmakers such as Yeats, as Joseph Bristow has argued, have encouraged a conflation between the life and art of these writers to the detriment of their art: 'In their influential view the intoxicating self-destructiveness of this era's characteristic male protagonists expressed a depressive purposelessness of the age, often in antiquated forms and pretentious rhetoric whose excesses supposedly accentuated the superficiality of the fin-de-siècle poet's art.'[35] Such biases have, until very recently, been prevalent in Decadent criticism which seriously undervalues the poetic output of these writers. John Munro, for example, describes the British Decadents as 'irresponsible' because they were not 'concerned with ideal values', and links their aesthetic practice to the fact that many of them 'were confirmed drug-takers, alcoholics, and homosexuals'.[36] Similarly, Charlesworth is concerned with the Decadents' lack of vision, of a 'belief' that might give 'significance to the moment', concluding that they 'failed in their lives and in their art'.[37] For his part, Hough declares them men of 'small talents' and criticizes their lack of 'moral insight'.[38] More recently, Regenia Gagnier has characterized the 'tragic generation' as 'men [who] were either cared for by sisters, intimidated by New Women, or like Johnson, after "four or five glasses of wine," denied "that a gelded man lost anything of intellectual power" '[39] and has linked their personal weaknesses to an aesthetic that she describes as 'paranoid, fearful, conservative, and reactionary'.[40] At the same time, the *Norton Anthology of English Literature* presents Decadence to a whole generation of college and university students as a histrionic, sensationalistic, and male-dominated movement.[41]

Decadence as high art

Despite the distaste registered by these critics for what they regard as the aesthetic and moral inferiority of Decadence, none has questioned its legitimacy as high art. In this respect, they endorse a myth nearly as compelling as that of the 'tragic generation'. Indeed, the notion of Decadence as high art is part of this broader myth promulgated by Yeats in his insistence that his peers were martyrs to art who 'made it a matter of conscience to turn from every kind of money-making that prevented good writing'.[42] The origins of this myth lie with the Decadents themselves who developed it in response to the conditions of literary production in the *fin de siècle*, particularly the increasing commercialization of literature, the expanding periodical press, and the growth of an emerging mass readership hungry for cheap reading matter. These factors, as Andreas Huyssen has argued, created the conditions for the emergence of the 'great divide', a discourse that 'insists on the categorical distinction between high art and mass culture'.[43] Though the Decadents were among the growing number of writers entering the profession at this time who depended on their art for a living (rather than having independent means or the support of a wealthy patron), they despised the middle class and mass readership and resented the idea of catering to popular taste. Those writers who did, Wilde insisted in 'The Soul of Man under Socialism', were 'tradesmen' selling a commodity and not artists.[44] Other Decadents agreed, insisting on the purity of their art and distinguishing themselves from popular writers, particularly women whom many among the male-dominated literary avant-garde associated with cheap, mass-produced reading matter. There is no question that many Decadents did engage in the least lucrative but most symbolically prestigious form of writing – poetry. Unlike their predecessors among the Victorian poets whose narrative and didactic poetry was geared towards a fairly broad audience, the Decadents favoured 'pure poetry', a concept developed from

French poets such as Verlaine, Mallarmé, and Baudelaire. In their creation of pure poetry, they aimed at technical perfection, exploited the musicality of language, sought to capture the intensity of a moment, and catered to a small readership of intellectuals. They sought out avant-garde publishers such as David Nutt and the Bodley Head, who issued beautifully designed limited editions of their work in small print runs. At the same time, more strategically, they perpetuated the image of the economically disinterested martyr to art in their prose writing. Identifying themselves with their subjects, they idealized the plight of the artist in a hostile bourgeois environment. Among the notable contributions to this mythmaking are George Moore's *Confessions of a Young Man* (1888) and *Mike Fletcher* (1889) and Ernest Dowson and Arthur Moore's *Comedy of Masks* (1893) and *Adrian Rome* (1899), John Davidson's *North Wall* (1885), and Arthur Machen's *Hill of Dreams* (written 1895–97; published 1907).[45]

Along with the myth of the 'tragic generation', the myth of Decadence as high art has reinforced the focus on poetry in literary scholarship. Though many Decadents, as I have indicated, wrote prose fiction as well as poetry, it is their poetry, a form of writing that holds a high status in the hierarchy of genres, that garners the most attention. In particular, the myth of Decadence as high art has informed criticism that posits a relationship between the poets of the 1890s and the high Modernists. Again, as with critical approaches that conflate the Decadents' life and art, scholarship that links Decadence to Modernism in a genealogy of high art frequently represents the former as an inferior aesthetic.[46] Thornton, for example, insists that Decadence was unable to 'bring together the real and the ideal' as Symbolism and Modernism did.[47] A similar conception is also held by Hough, Munro, and Charlesworth who claim that a lack of an ideal, belief, or vision mars Decadent poetry. According to these critics, the Modernists have no such lack and are better interpreters of French Symbolist ideas.[48] For such critics, Decadence has very little value in itself and its central importance lies only in relation to what follows it. Thus, Hough insists, 'There is no very strong reason why they [the Decadents] should be read: yet they are not insignificant. They represent a phase through which the poetic sensibility had to pass before it could emerge into new territory.'[49] Though the Decadents themselves sought to perpetuate the myth of their art as 'high art', this myth has, like that of the 'tragic generation', had a negative impact on their status within literary history in which they are characterized as weak precursors to a more vibrant literary movement. Because of this focus on poetry and on the movement's anticipation of a better, more refined aesthetic in a genealogy of high art, scholars have lost sight of the more immediate context of the Decadents' literary production and the important role they played in negotiating between the ideals of high art and the demands of the marketplace at a time when the conditions of literary production, circulation, and reception were undergoing a substantial transformation.

Class myths of Decadence: bohemians and aristocratic dandies

Just as the myth of Decadence as high art was one initiated and perpetuated by artists themselves, so too were the myths of the Decadent as bohemian and aristocratic dandy. In an age that witnessed the commodification of literature and a concomitant fascination with writers and their lives on the part of late-Victorian readers, the Decadents, exploiting the enhanced visibility of the artist, adopted personae that signalled their resistance to Victorian middle-class consumer culture. In so doing, they looked to two models, the bohemian and the dandy. Though the bohemian and the dandy are radically different in class terms – bohemians are represented as poor and garret-dwelling, while dandies, though typically not aristocrats, adopt an aristocratic hauteur – both aimed to shock the bourgeoisie.[50] For this reason, bohemianism and dandyism were attractive to the Decadents. At the most basic level, bohemianism and dandyism informed their dress sense. Thus, on the one hand, writers such as Le Gallienne, Symons, and Yeats attired themselves in Bohemian fashion – long hair, wide-brimmed black hats, flowing ties, capes, and velveteen jackets. On the other hand, Decadents also drew on the dandy tradition that originated with Beau Brummell in Regency England, subsequently gained favour with Barbey d'Aurevilly and Charles Baudelaire in France, and was revived by Wilde, Beerbohm, Beardsley and others in 1890s Britain. The Decadent dandies of the 1890s were immaculately and austerely dressed. High, stiff collars, gloves, silk top hats, canes, boutonnières, frock coats, and tapered trousers were the key elements of the dandy's wardrobe. Eccentric elements were generally limited to a single detail – a green carnation as boutonnière, a brightly coloured waistcoat or set of gloves, and so on. Beerbohm's caricatures have been instrumental in conveying a strong visual sense of the distinctive modes of dress adopted by himself and other Decadents.

In addition to providing resistant modes of dress, bohemianism and dandyism also represented alternative, counter-cultural lifestyles. In their unconventionality and their dedication to the principles of high art, the Decadents were bohemian. In their interest in artificiality, posing and masks, and in the cultivation of esoteric and arcane tastes, they were dandies. In many aspects, however, the interests of bohemians and dandies merged. Thus, the Decadents were both bohemian and dandy in their fascination for the music hall and its female performers, for walking the streets like a *flâneur* and in streetwalkers, and for drugs, alcohol, and sex as a means to escape the drudgery of everyday existence. Bohemianism and dandyism were intrinsic not only to the lifestyles of the Decadents but to their art as well. Moore's *Confessions of a Young Man*, which documents Moore's free-wheeling youthful days in Paris perhaps best exemplifies the Decadent treatment of bohemianism. Wilde's *Picture of Dorian Gray*, by contrast, is a notable representation of Decadent dandyism, particularly in its characterization of Lord Henry and in its depiction of Dorian's quest for pleasure. All in all, the myths of the Decadent as bohemian and dandy were important in constructing alternative anti-bourgeois identities for artists of the 1890s. Both identities situated them firmly outside middle-class culture. On the one hand, as bohemians, they circulated among the poor and working class. On the other hand, as dandies, the Decadents identified themselves with upper-class and aristocratic culture.

Of these two myths, the myth of the Decadent as dandy has had the most significant impact on scholarship. It is primarily due to this myth that Wilde holds such a central position in Decadent scholarship and it is the reason that *The Picture of Dorian Gray* and his plays and essays, all replete with dandy figures, draw more attention than his poetry. At the same time, the allure of the myth of the Decadent dandy accounts for much of the interest in Beerbohm, for he neither conforms to the 'tragic generation' stereotype nor does his work perpetuate the myth of Decadence as high art. If notions of the Decadent dandy have led to certain emphases in literary scholarship, however, they have not been as readily accepted as 'truths' by critics in the way the myths of the 'tragic generation' and Decadence as high art have. After all, it is widely known among scholars (though perhaps less so among the general population) that despite their bohemianism and dandyism and their expressed disdain for the middle class, the Decadents were, almost without exception, of middle-class origin. And yet, despite the seeming hypocrisy of their posturing, until quite recently little effort has been made to examine more carefully the complex class positionings of the Decadents and their relationship to a middle-class audience whom they at once despised and depended upon.

Demythologizing British Decadence

Taken as a whole, the myths of the 'tragic generation', of Decadence as high art, and of the Decadents as bohemians and dandies have limited scholarship in the area to a narrow range of figures and texts, have led to a greater focus on poetry than on fiction, have obscured the class identities of its proponents, and have bred a criticism frequently coloured by a denigration of the movement in moral or aesthetic terms. To be sure, not all Decadent criticism has perpetuated these myths. Indeed, many critics have been invested in overturning the stereotypes attaching to the movement. Notable in this regard is Linda Dowling who, in her 1977 bibliography of Aestheticism and Decadence, complains that these movements have been mired in myth and clichés and calls for an expansion of the 'cast of characters beyond the stereotypical set of ... decadents'.[51] She herself contributed importantly to the demythologization of Decadence in *Language and Decadence in the Victorian Fin de Siècle* (1986), a study that examines both the poetry and prose of a broad range of writers within and without the traditional canon, including Dowson, Beardsley, Davidson, Johnson, Wilde, Symons,

George Moore, Walter Pater, and Arthur Machen. At the same time, she grants Decadence a seriousness of purpose not often attributed to it. Decadence, she argues, is a 'counterpoetics and critique' that 'emerged from a linguistic crisis'.[52] In addition to Dowling, a recent generation of feminist critics has also gone a long way towards moving beyond the stereotype 'tragic generation' by drawing attention to the ways in which women writers such as Vernon Lee, Marie Corelli, Ouida, Alice Meynell, Lucas Malet, Graham R. Tomson, and Sarah Grand participated in, critiqued, and reconceived Decadence.[53]

While some critics have aimed to shift focus away from the 'tragic generation' by identifying other participants in the Decadent movement, others have sought to distance particular figures from the negative stereotype. This approach has informed many single-author studies, biographies, and edited collections of letters. And yet, while these studies extricate their own individual subjects from the myth, many do not challenge the myth itself. J. Benjamin Townsend, for example, describes Davidson's 'hedonism' as 'sterner, more positive and vigorous' than that of Beardsley, Dowson, Symons, and Wilde,[54] thus freeing his subject from the stereotype while leaving the others mired in its oversimplifications. David Cecil does the same with respect to Beerbohm, setting him apart from his peers whose writings he describes as 'a feeble English version of a French phenomenon'.[55] Similarly, Gagnier's negative characterization of the 'tragic generation', mentioned previously, functions in her inquiry to distinguish what she regards as their paranoid and reactionary aesthetic from Wilde's 'engaged protest against Victorian rationality, scientific factuality, and technological progress'.[56]

Despite Gagnier's bias against the 'tragic generation', her research on Wilde has had ground-breaking implications for the disruption of the myth of Decadence as high art. So too has Jonathan Freedman's research on Henry James and Josephine Guy and Ian Small's materialist analysis of Wilde's literary production.[57] These critical studies challenge the myths of Wilde and James as aesthetic purists and dilettantes, arguing instead that they were hard-working writers fully engaged in the processes of commodification and professionalization that characterized the literary field of the 1890s. In addition to these studies of the engagement of particular writers with the literary marketplace, Margaret D. Stetz and Laurel Brake have exposed the commercial nature of the so-called avant-garde venues of British Decadence – the Bodley Head publishing house under John Lane and its house organ, the *Yellow Book* magazine. Lane, they argue, set out to render Decadent 'high art' profitable by appealing to the public's desire for sensationalism.[58] Still other critics have more closely explored the relationship between high art Decadence and popular writing. Talia Schaffer, for example, has boldly and convincingly argued that the origins of the Aesthetic and Decadent novel may be traced to popular women's writing, notably that of Ouida.[59] Focusing on a more masculinist form of fiction, Stephen Arata identifies shared concerns in high art Decadence and popular jingoist fiction of the *fin de siècle*.[60] Finally, David Weir and Brian Stableford have also questioned the strict divide between high art Decadence and the popular, specifically with respect to the relationship between *fin-de-siècle* and Modernist forms. Weir, for example, has argued that the influence of Decadence is found not only in high Modernism but also in a popularized American version developed by writers such as James Huneker and Ben Hecht, while Stableford contends that the Decadent 'heritage' can be traced to the twentieth-century popular and pulp genres of supernatural fiction, science fiction, horror, and fantasy.[61]

Class myths have also been taken up by some critics, though not to the extent of the myth of Decadence as high art. Here Gagnier has, once again, been instrumental. *Idylls of the Marketplace* provides a nuanced analysis of Wilde's manipulation of both his middle-class and upper-class audiences. In addition, she argues that Decadence must be viewed not in terms of 'stylistics', as has traditionally been the case, but rather primarily as a 'rejection of middle-class life'.[62] In making this argument, Gagnier points out that for 1890s critics of Wilde's *Picture of Dorian Gray*, the story's Decadence lay in its complete exclusion of 'the normative values of society' in favour of those of 'idle aristocrats and romantic artists'.[63] Jonathan Freedman and Alan Sinfield also discuss the importance of notions of upper-class and aristocratic culture in the Aesthetes' and Decadents' self-fashioning, while Linda Dowling has explored the Decadent interest in what Yeats called 'the common pleasures of common men'.[64] In their frequenting of music halls, for example, and in their more bohemian pleasures, the Decadents imagined themselves as experiencing the life of the working man in ways that deliberately put them at odds with the middle class that they sought to alienate.

Though indeed much scholarship of the past 20 years has sought to revise our understanding of British Decadence, still, to a large extent, it is focused on Wilde and the 'tragic generation'. No one has yet attempted a full-scale re-evaluation of the movement. In part, this gap in scholarship may be attributed to a certain doubt that Decadence as it manifested itself in Britain constituted anything like a movement. As Dowling observes in her survey of scholarship on the period, many critics have claimed that Decadence is not 'indigenous to English literature'.[65] John Reed is one such critic. Applying a highly specific stylistic definition of Decadence to a range of poetry, fiction, art, and music, he discovers only one British work worthy of the term – Wilde's *Picture of Dorian Gray*.[66] Similarly, Thornton insists that in Britain Decadence 'lack[ed] ... a coherent group of writers who accepted the name and fought for it'.[67] Thornton is correct in his assertion that Decadence in Britain lacked coherence and it is certainly difficult to identify any writer who stood consistently for it. Wilde's *Picture of Dorian Gray* and *Salomé* have been considered Decadent, but what of his other writings? Symons, a poet and theorist of Decadence, would renounce it in favour of Symbolism;

Johnson and Le Gallienne were both ambivalent in their attitude towards Decadence; and, George Moore's engagements with Decadence in the 1870s and 1880s would be overshadowed as he became known primarily as an advocate of realism and the Irish literary revival.

This lack of a significant corpus of work or of a consistent spokesperson constitutes convincing evidence against the existence of a British Decadent movement. And yet, surely this view is counter-intuitive, failing as it does to account for the flavour of so much *fin-de-siècle* British literature and for the lived experience of many who believed that Decadence was pervasive. At the same time, the disavowals of so many of the writers of the 1890s must be treated with suspicion. After all, most of those who renounced Decadence did so in the aftermath of the Wilde trials, when it was a matter of career survival to do so. So too, the absence of a representative number of self-declared British Decadents may be accounted for by a feeling among those who admired French Decadence that their efforts could not live up to their ideal. They knew, quite simply, that the kind of literature being produced in France was unpublishable in Britain, and that to adopt the term to describe themselves was risky at best, career suicide at worst.

None of these explanations proves that there was no Decadence in Britain; only perhaps that there was nothing that could be called a *movement* and that it manifested itself differently in Britain than in France. In fact, a large part of the problem in establishing whether there was something called British Decadence arises from approaching the subject comparatively. In this context, as Brian Stableford argues, British Decadence is but a 'a pale shadow' of its French counterpart.[68] And yet, there was Decadence in Britain, even if it was only Huysmans 'and water', to use an expression current among writers in this period to condemn pale imitations of a superior work. There was no question, as I shall demonstrate, that writers of the period were trying, in modest and cautious terms, to import elements of French Decadence into English literature. There was no question, either, that readers understood much of the literature of the period as Decadent, even if their more sophisticated French counterparts would not have. *Fin-de-siècle* Britain had its own Decadence, a Decadence that must be considered on its own terms as a form conditioned by literary, social, and cultural forces specific to its historical and national context.

Reading British Decadence *à rebours*

The present study – *Fictions of British Decadence: High Art, Popular Writing, and the Fin de Siècle* – draws on recent revisionist scholarship in the area, but aims at a broader illumination of the emergence, development, and legacy of a culturally distinct form of Decadence in Britain. In its approach, it takes its cue from the title of Huysmans's *A Rebours* in that it reads 'against the grain' of received understandings of Decadence. I have been guided in my selection of writers and texts by three intentions: to examine the origins and development of representations of Decadence by both proponents and opponents of the movement from the *fin de siècle* through the Modernist period, to broaden the critical terrain of studies in this area, and to dispel the central myths that have coloured histories of the period.

The first sense in which this study reads *à rebours* received understandings of Decadence is by decentralizing Wilde, who has remained a dominant presence in scholarship as a figurehead for Decadence. Instead, attention is given to George Moore's largely neglected role in the introduction and promotion of Decadence in Britain. At the same time, I allow room for a consideration of lesser-known writers in order to examine the degree to which Wilde is representative of the larger group of writers participating in the movement. Though not central to this study, Wilde nevertheless 'haunts' it, if only because his high-profile status coloured the way his less-famous counterparts would be received. As such, the critical reaction to *The Picture of Dorian Gray* and the controversy surrounding his trials are discussed as defining moments in the reception of Decadence in *fin-de-siècle* Britain that had serious repercussions for other writers.

Second, this study resists the myth of the 'tragic generation'. Thus, like recent recuperative scholarship in the area, it draws attention to forgotten figures associated with the movement. On the one hand, it discusses Arthur Machen and M. P. Shiel, Decadent writers who defied the 'tragic generation' stereotype by living long and productive lives. On the other hand, in its treatment of works by Vernon Lee, Marie Corelli, and Sarah Grand, my discussion builds on the recent recuperation of women writers who engaged, in an often ambivalent manner, with Decadence.[69] At the same time, I challenge the 'tragic generation' image associated with Davidson and Dowson that much revisionist criticism, notably Gagnier's, keeps intact. This image is contrasted in this book with an account of the Decadents, even the so-called tragic ones, as productively and ambitiously involved in the literary marketplace. In questioning the 'tragic generation' stereotype, I also revisit the role Decadents played in the Modernist literary field, both as participants in this field and as figures whom the younger generation of writers either revolted against or aligned themselves with. This examination indicates that the relationship between the two movements is far more vexed than has traditionally been assumed.

Third, I read not so much against as *into* the class myths of Decadence, examining the context in which certain writers fashioned themselves and perpetuated the image of the artist as bohemian and dandy. Constructed through appropriation of class characteristics associated with the working and upper classes, these identities served the Decadents in two ways – signalling their rebellion against the middle class while, at the same time, ironically enhancing their appeal to this class who were by turns fascinated and repelled by the spectacle of the alienated artist. While the middle-class fascination with the bohemian and dandy images of the artist resulted in a focus on these figures in popular fiction and the press and sometimes, though not usually, in increased sales for the works of Decadent writers, its disgust was registered through the stigmatization of the movement within the press.

Finally, I read against the grain of criticism that places poetry at the centre of British Decadence.[70] While not denying the centrality of poetry as a vehicle for Decadence, I prefer to draw attention to the large body of fiction that has been almost entirely neglected in critical studies,[71] not least because from the point of view of reception, it was the Decadence of fiction that caused the most consternation. While it is true that a great deal of attention has been paid to individual works such as Wilde's *Picture of Dorian Gray* and, to a lesser degree, Moore's *Confessions of a Young Man* there has yet to be a sustained study of the production, circulation, and reception of Decadent fiction, even while there has been such excellent scholarship on the publishers of this fiction.[72] One of the most significant implications this neglect of the fiction has had is to sustain the myth of Decadence as high art. To be sure, as poets, the Decadents were relatively free from the demands of the literary market-place. Yet, when they wrote fiction, as almost all of them did, their writing was mediated by various concerns, including different reading publics, differences between popular and 'serious' literature, the effect of popular culture on national and imperial culture, the debilitating or invigorating influence of writers such as J.-K. Huysmans and Emile Zola, and the simple need of writers to make a living, which often meant engaging with the commerce of publishing. These conditions of production and reception led to the creation of works that are far more implicated in the literary marketplace than the Decadent myth allows for. Constrained by these conditions, writers trod carefully in introducing high art Decadence to British fiction. Their fiction mediates in fascinating ways between the high and the popular, as it brings elements of Decadence to the romantic comedy, the fashionable society novel, the *fin-de-siècle* gothic in the style of Robert Louis Stevenson, and the detective story.

Fictions of British Decadence

By 'fictions of British Decadence', then, the title of this study alludes, quite simply, to its focus on narrative fiction. More broadly, however, the term 'fictions' highlights my methodological approach to the subject and the broader interest of this study in the great variety of representations of Decadence that have circulated from the *fin de siècle* on. Apart from the mythic aspects of Decadence that have applied very fixed notions to the movement, the term has otherwise been the site of an intense conflict over cultural meaning and value and has been defined in a variety of contradictory ways: as aristocratic, as working class, and as middle class; as high art and as popular art; as effeminate and as hyper-masculine and misogynistic; as cultured and as degenerate; as derivative and as innovative; as a moribund literature and as a literature of youth and renewal; as primitive and as over-civilized; as reactionary and as radical; as a continuation of Romanticism and as a revolt against Romanticism; as a feminist lesbian aesthetic and as a masculine misogynistic aesthetic; as introspective and as socially engaged; as fascist and as socialist, and so on.[73] Thus, while myths have fostered a scholarship that is too narrow in scope to provide a thorough and representative account of the movement, the multiplicity of meanings accorded to Decadence over the last hundred plus years has had the opposite effect. Far from reifying notions of Decadence, these contradictory meanings have rendered it highly intangible and seemingly undefinable.

This problem of meaning around Decadence derives, as numerous critics have argued, from the instability of the term itself. Because, as David Weir and Richard Gilman argue, the definition of Decadence is predicated on an opposition to 'arbitrarily defined norms', its meaning changes in relation to its context.[74] Decadence is thus an empty term, 'a word chosen to fill a space',[75] a word whose meaning is 'determined by the word to which it is opposed'.[76] As such, the naming of something as Decadent, Gilman insists, is 'a value judgment, a category of belief or opinion' rather than 'a fact'.[77] For Gilman, the instability of the term renders it meaningless and he wishes that the term could be dropped from the language altogether. For others, however, it is precisely the term's indeterminacy that makes it, in Charles Bernheimer's terms, 'important' and 'culturally productive'.[78] Liz Constable, Dennis Denisoff, and Matthew Potolsky agree, insisting that more can be gained by focusing on the *uses* to which Decadence is put than on its meaning.[79]

Taking a cue from this approach, this study examines the ideological and cultural uses to which the term Decadence was put in Britain, from its origins in 1884 as a literary and cultural practice, through the Wilde trials of 1895, and beyond into the Edwardian and Modernist periods. I examine the role played by writers, critics, journalists, and publishers in the construction of conflicting ideas about Decadence, as proponents of the movement sought to create a social and literary identity for themselves and as others in the field reacted to this particular social and literary type. These representations of Decadence, I argue, functioned strategically for Decadents, their proponents, and opponents in cultural debates about aesthetics, ethics, high culture, popular culture, and the function of art and the artist in society. Through these representations, a major conflict between the ideologies of high art and popular culture was being expressed, as Decadents and their opponents battled to assert their cultural authority in a field increasingly marked by hierarchical distinctions. I refer to these representations as 'fictions' in order to emphasize their constructedness. These representations did not, after all, stand for a literary, cultural, or social 'reality' because Decadence in Britain, as Gilman has argued, 'had no substantive meaning ... at this time, only a thin topical suggestiveness'.[80] It was precisely this suggestiveness that left the term open to deployment for a variety of polemical uses by writers engaged in the battle for cultural authority in a divisive literary field.

This study, then, approaches the emergence, development, and legacy of British Decadence as a dynamic process in which meaning was created in the context of a variety of cultural contests – between popular writers and the literary élite, between competing members of the élite, between writers and publishers, between critics and writers, between writers and readers, between one literary generation and another, and so on. The first two chapters concern the Decadents' positioning within the social and literary fields. Chapter 1 demystifies the class myths of Decadence, examining the rift between the professional and business middle class in the mid-Victorian period as an important context for the emergence of the Decadent bohemian and the Decadent dandy as social types. Turning from the social to the literary sphere, Chapter 2 describes the conditions of production in the increasingly commercialized literary field in the 1880s and 1890s and how Decadents and their opponents battled for cultural authority within it. Having established the contours of the *fin-de-siècle* literary field, I then go on, in the next four chapters, to trace the development of the discourses and counter-discourses, or 'fictions', of Decadence from 1884 until just after the Wilde trials. Chapter 3 considers the production and reception of Vernon Lee's *Miss Brown* (1884), George Moore's *Confessions of a Young Man* (1888) and *Mike Fletcher* (1889) in the context of debates over Aestheticism and Naturalism and argues that Decadence and its counter-discourse owed their development to these debates. Beginning with a consideration of the reception of Oscar Wilde's *Picture of Dorian Gray*, Chapter 4 describes the development of a popularized counter-Decadent discourse in the press and in fiction by women writers, notably Marie Corelli's *Wormwood* (1890) and Sarah Grand's *Beth Book* (1897). Turning to the proponents of Decadence, Chapter 5 examines how the conditions of literary production and reception in *fin-de-siècle* Britain forced them to mediate between the high and the popular and explores the tensions inherent in this project in a consideration of Robert Hichens's 'Collaborators' (1893), Ernest Dowson and Arthur Moore's *Comedy of Masks* (1893) and John Davidson's *North Wall* (1886). In its treatment of Arthur Machen's *Great God Pan and the Inmost Light* (1894) and M. P. Shiel's *Prince Zaleski* (1895), Chapter 6 continues to examine the fiction of British Decadents as a mediation between the high and the popular. In this case, however, attention is paid to how the establishment of the *Yellow Book* and the Bodley Head Keynotes series, of which these two books were a part, had a crucial impact on the development and reception of literary Decadence. Finally, the last two chapters re-evaluate the legacy of Decadence from the aftermath of the Wilde trial. Chapter 7 describes the impact of the trial on the *fin-de-siècle* literary field and how perceptions of Decadence played a role in shaping Edwardian and Modernist literature. In this context, Chapter 8 considers the 'afterlife of the Decadents'. In so doing it revisits the myth of the 'tragic generation', providing detailed accounts of the post-1895 careers and reputations of Dowson, Davidson, Machen, and Shiel as they sought to reinvent themselves as writers and to find a life after Decadence.

1
The Mystified Class Origins of Decadence

> Nothing, not even conventional virtue, is so provincial as conventional vice; and the desire to 'bewilder the middle classes' is itself middle-class.
>
> Arthur Symons, *The Symbolist Movement in Literature* (1899)[1]

As I have suggested in the Introduction, there are two prevailing class myths about the Decadent: the Decadent as aristocratic dandy and the bohemian Decadent. The first of these two myths owes its origin to the Regency dandy. The history of dandyism has been well covered by Ellen Moers who argues that in Britain 'the weakening of Victorian values and vitality, the strengthening of Continental influences, and the revival of Regency attitudes' during the *fin de siècle* were conducive to the emergence of the New Dandyism.[2] The Francophilic Prince of Wales and his elegantly dressed, gambling, smoking, and club-going social set brought a certain glamour to the aristocracy that had been lacking since the days of King George the fourth.[3] For those bored with the industriousness, earnestness, and utilitarianism of the Victorian middle class, this newly invigorated aristocracy was a spectacle, one worthy of emulation. The Decadents, in particular, glamorized the aristocracy seeing in it 'a breeding ground for art and charming people'.[4] 'Among such people', Yeats observed 'there lingered, if not a creative art, surely a true abundance of artistic material'.[5] At one extreme, then, the Decadents aspired to this life, celebrating and fashioning themselves after the elegant, witty, sophisticated, graceful, cultivated, and rakish aristocratic dandy. Oscar Wilde's Dorian Gray and J.-K. Huysmans's Des Esseintes are fictional examples of this type, while Max Beerbohm and Count Eric Stenbock serve as real-life examples, though Beerbohm was not a true aristocrat.

The second myth – the Decadent as bohemian – places them at the opposite social extreme, starving in a garret, living a reckless and carefree life among social outcasts and wretches, and, in extreme instances, battling addictions to drugs or drink. This myth draws its symbolic force more from the French than the British bohemian artistic and literary tradition. Thus, we are more likely to associate this kind of bohemianism with the representations of café and music hall life in the art of Toulouse-Lautrec and Edgar Degas and in the real lives of Toulouse-Lautrec, Paul Verlaine, and others. British Decadents such as George Moore, Arthur Symons, Oscar Wilde, and Ernest Dowson were aware of these figures and knew French bohemia quite well through their travels. When in France, many British Decadents circulated among the literary and artistic avant-garde and aspired to develop a similar bohemian culture in Britain.

But like most myths of British Decadence these divergent ways of iconizing the writers of this period remain remarkably misleading. Far less familiar than the aristocratic and bohemian stereotypes of the Decadent is the image invoked by Symons – the middle-class or bourgeois Decadent. This image is less familiar because the basis of Decadence – its central feature, more important even than stylistics according to Regenia Gagnier – is precisely its rejection of middle-class life.[6] And yet Symons's depiction of the Decadent as middle-class is closest to the true class origins of the Decadent. In reality, most of the British writers associated with Decadence came from the middle class and it was here that Decadence as a rejection of middle-class life originated. By fashioning their self-image as aristocrats and bohemians who held bourgeois society in contempt, British Decadents mystified their class origins. Ironically, this project, as Symons notes, only exposed them as the middle-class subjects that they were. He ought to have known. He was a middle-class Decadent himself.

This chapter examines the real class background of the Decadents and explores the development of the more exotic and extravagant class identities assumed by them and celebrated in their writing. My contention is that the images of the Decadent as aristocratic dandy and as bohemian emerged as a product of the tensions between the professional and business fractions of the middle class from the mid-nineteenth century on, as the middle class as a whole gained hegemonic power and as the professional fraction expanded rapidly. Whereas the professional middle class, intellectuals among them in particular, were trying to create the conditions of an ideal culture, the business middle class developed an increasingly commercial culture. These differing aims resulted in a rift between the cultural and economic leaders of the British Empire. This rift – a rift endlessly reproduced in the artistic productions of Decadents – created the cultural conditions for the emergence of Decadence and of what I call the 'Decadent sensibility'. The 'Decadent sensibility' represented a reaction to the rift by a fraction of the middle class in revolt against its origins, and helped to form an alternative identity that drew on both aristocratic and working-class cultural values. In order to understand how middle-class identity was internally divided we need to look at a number of developments in its formation during the decades that preceded the *fin de siècle*.

Professionals vs capitalists in the mid-Victorian period

It is extremely well known that the Reform Acts of 1832 and 1867 paved the way for the ascendancy of the Victorian middle class over the aristocracy in terms of social and economic power. This middle class was, however, a 'riven' class, and the Victorian period is notable not only for its cross-class conflicts but also, as social historian Harold Perkin has demonstrated, for the struggle for dominance within the middle class between professionals and those involved with business.[7] Both these fractions had benefited from the Industrial Revolution, which increased the power of the business middle class and led to an expansion of the professional middle class. New professions proliferated throughout the nineteenth century. Though the professions initially constituted the clergy, law, medicine, and the intellectual realm (that is, men of letters, scientists, university teachers, and artists), eventually surgeons, accountants, bankers, engineers, pharmacists, architects, librarians, and others became identified as professionals. Between 1880 and 1914 as many as 39 new professional associations were added to the existing 27.[8] The increased power of both fractions of the middle class instilled in each a desire to shape the values and ideals of Victorian society.

As social historians have long recognized, the power of professionals lay not in the ownership of material resources, but in specialized knowledge. Opposing the capitalist values of the business class, professionals felt they served a higher purpose within Victorian society. This purpose, as expressed in an 1857 guide to professional careers, was to 'head ... the great English middle class, maintain its tone of independence, keep up to the mark its standard of morality, and direct its intelligence'.[9] As Perkin explains, professionals saw themselves as critics of and mentors to society and sought to mould it according to an anti-industrial social ideal.[10] This ideal was based on the idea of public service, which professionals aimed to establish as 'a national and cultural, not a class ideal'.[11] In their efforts to promote this ideal, professionals drew on the existing ideals of the landed class and the business middle class and subtly transformed them to suit their own ideals. Thus, professionals borrowed from the aristocratic ideal of the English gentleman and the business middle class ideal of the gospel of work to create a new concept of the gentleman. This transformation of the idea of the gentleman was initiated largely through the reformation of public schools and universities in the early Victorian period. This professional ideal had a temporary influence on the succeeding generation of Victorian 'gentlemen', but ultimately the incompatibilities between professional and entrepreneurial ideals became apparent. Eventually, the gentleman, as defined by the professional class, stood in direct opposition to the middle-class entrepreneur, whose image had initially been incorporated into their concept of the gentleman. The new 'professional gentleman' was defined now 'by his "fine and governing qualities" [Matthew

Arnold's phrase], his cultured education, intellectual interests, and qualities of character, which rose above mere money making, while the work permissible to him was narrowed down to professional or public service to society, the state, or the empire, to the exclusion of "money-grabbing" industry and trade'.[12]

Within the professional middle class, those who felt the greatest discontent with the values of the business class were intellectuals. In this attitude, mid-Victorian intellectuals such as Matthew Arnold and John Ruskin served as the progenitors to the Aesthetes and Decadents. Indeed, Ruskin and Arnold's failure, from a professional viewpoint, to exert a civilizing influence on the business middle class would strongly shape the social attitudes of this younger and more cynical generation of intellectuals and artists. Unlike their successors, however, Arnold and Ruskin had hopes for transforming the middle class and believed that the arts might serve as a powerful cultural force in disseminating professional ideals. For Arnold, 'Culture', which he defined as 'getting to know ... the best which has been thought and said in the world' had the potential to transform British society at all social levels, from what he called the 'barbarian' upper classes, to the 'philistine' middle classes, to the working-class 'populace'.[13] Arnold asserted that the role of cultural leaders was 'not to make what each raw person may like the rule by which he fashions himself; but to draw ever nearer to a sense of what is indeed beautiful, graceful, and becoming, and to get the raw person to like that'.[14] And yet, despite his reform attempts in a number of professional roles – as inspector of schools, man of letters, professor, and cultural critic – Arnold was at heart sceptical about the ability of the business middle class to achieve the social ideals he professed.

More optimistic, at least initially, and more far-reaching than Arnold in his democratic ideals was Ruskin, who believed in the ethical and moral import of art and sought to explicate the relation of a nation's art to its social and moral values. Like Arnold, however, he too came to be disillusioned. Late in his career, surveying the results of his efforts to transform Victorian social values, he despaired at what he viewed as a misappropriation of his ideals by the middle class. To his mind, the middle class had ignored the social message of his work and had taken up his ideas in a superficial manner. In the case of *Stones of Venice*, for example, the public had overlooked the main focus – the 'relation of the art of Venice to her moral temper ... and that of the life of the workman to his work'.[15] Instead, as Linda Dowling argues, 'the minutiae of Venetian Gothic ornament had become a new gospel, pored over, misunderstood, misapplied, and, worst of all, given material embodiment in the greasy, striated monstrosities of [what Ruskin called] the "streaky bacon style" '.[16] Dismayed by the material mis-embodiments of his aesthetic and social message, Ruskin called them 'accursed Frankenstein monsters of, *in*directly, my own making'.[17] It was his misfortune that he was unable to control the way his work was taken up by audiences who turned 'Ruskin into "Ruskin," ... a cultural institution, an anthologized "master," whose critical authority could be invoked when necessary but conveniently ignored, or distorted, or elided, when not'.[18]

As the case of Ruskin makes clear, the increasing rift between professionals and the business middle class was due less to the inability of the middle class to absorb professional values than it was to its adaptation of these ideals to a capitalist value system. In the end, the business middle class was just as capable of transforming professional ideals to suit its ends as the professional class had been at appropriating the values of the business and landed classes in the creation of a professional ideology. Though the ideals of professionals did, as they had wished, come to have a significant social influence during the latter part of the Victorian era, from their point of view this influence too frequently manifested itself in superficial material forms – in fads in the realms of architecture, furnishing, home decoration, and dress – with no corresponding spiritual, social, or intellectual enlightenment. Such superficial manifestations of the projects of intellectuals such as Arnold and Ruskin were inevitable under the dominant entrepreneurial middle-class ideology that equated progress with material wealth and that relied on consumption and display as a means of demonstrating social importance. From the point of view of professional intellectuals, the middle class had debased and commodified art, the very thing that was meant to be the cultural, social, and moral salvation of Victorian society.

At least part of the reason for the failure of Arnold's and Ruskin's attempts to enlighten the Victorian public can be attributed to another 'Frankenstein monster' of mid-Victorian professional intellectuals – Aestheticism – an artistic, literary, and cultural movement that originated in the 1850s, reached its peak in the 1870s and 1880s, and shaded over into the Decadence of the 1890s.[19] Broadly speaking, Aestheticism valorized the beautiful in art over moral, social, religious, and political considerations and asserted the independence of art from the gross materialism of Victorian England. On the one hand, Aestheticism, as a stringent critique of capitalist culture, was a professional discourse par excellence and played a vital role, as Jonathan Freedman argues, in the development of professional culture. Aestheticism, he claims, was 'not just ... a means towards establishing "the culture of professionalism"; aestheticism helped to create the profession of culture making itself. It helped create a new caste of professionals who designated themselves as experts in cultural knowledge, and who defined their own role as that of instructing others in the lineaments of that knowledge'.[20] The 'new caste of professionals' created by Aestheticism included art experts, makers and vendors of fine books, furniture, wallpaper, and domestic goods, interior decorators, and a new brand of professionalized artist. On the other hand, however, as the nature of some of these new vocations suggest, Aestheticism, despite its status as a professional discourse, was highly implicated in the materialist culture it claimed to oppose. Consequently, Aestheticism, even though it developed from the projects of men like Ruskin and Arnold, became yet another 'Frankenstein monster'. Ironically, many of Aestheticism's central tenets fit all too well into the ideology of consumer culture as these tenets were exploited by the commercial press, the advertising industry, and by the manufacturers and vendors of 'aesthetic' commodities. What men like Arnold and Ruskin did not anticipate as they attempted to cultivate the classes and masses through social criticism was, as Freedman argues, 'the spectacular ability of an advanced consumer society to transform criticisms of that society into objects of consumption'.[21]

Aestheticism was appealing to a prosperous but culturally naive middle class because, unlike the vague Arnoldian definition of 'Culture', it provided tangible symbols of cultural competency. As Dianne Sachko Macleod notes, 'Aestheticism's well-crafted and expensive-looking objects served as easily identifiable markers for the socially mobile'.[22] In justifying what might otherwise have seemed a vulgar display of wealth, the middle class drew upon the ideals of the professional intellectuals: 'The ownership of luxury goods' Macleod argues, was 'not a self-indulgence as long as one's intellectual development was maintained' and '[middle-class] patrons of the aesthetic movement were encouraged to display their wealth in personalized shrines to beauty as tangible evidence of transcendent elevation of thought'.[23] The aestheticization of everyday life in home decoration, dress, and the consumption and display of art, then, served a number of functions for the middle class and the display of wealth, if not the least important, was certainly the most mystified.

The zeal with which Aestheticism's ideals were taken up and transformed by middle-class consumer culture affronted professional intellectuals. In the face of the vulgarization of their ideals, intellectuals became increasingly sceptical about their ability to impose professional values on the middle class. By the 1880s, some Aesthetes began distancing themselves from the bourgeois middle class that had distorted their ideals. Oscar Wilde and James McNeill Whistler, for example, adopted aristocratic stances and represented themselves as beings marked by refinements and tastes lacking in the middle class. At the same time, they used the discourse of Aestheticism 'to construct [themselves] as alienated, isolated, [and] oppressed'.[24] Thus, while Aesthetes maintained their professional role as instructors in the realm of cultural knowledge, roles that had been previously filled by those such as Ruskin and Arnold, their development of a deliberately antagonistic stance towards the middle class indicated their scepticism regarding the ability of the middle class to take up this knowledge in any meaningful way. This antagonism towards the middle class would be developed by the Decadents, who even more explicitly sought 'to bewilder the middle classes'.[25]

The emergence of the Decadent sensibility

Given the antagonism that developed between the professional and business middle class fractions in the mid-Victorian period, Symons's assertion that the Decadents' 'desire to bewilder the middle classes is itself middle class' should now seem less paradoxical.[26] The Decadents were virtually all born in the years between the mid-1850s and the early 1870s into middle-class families. They grew up as the rift between the business and professional class was becoming increasingly pronounced, and came of age at the height of the commercialized appropriation of Aestheticism by a bourgeois middle class. They were characterized, in Pierre Bourdieu's terms, by a shared 'habitus' – their feelings, tastes, and intuitions shaped by the similar social, material, and historical conditions in which they found themselves.[27]

By and large, the Decadents were from professional backgrounds within the middle class.[28] Oscar Wilde's father, for example, was a highly distinguished eye surgeon. By far the most prominent profession associated with the fathers of Decadents, however, was that of clergyman. Arthur Machen, John Davidson, Arthur Symons, and Robert Hichens were all sons of clergymen and all attended private schools (referred to as 'public' schools in Britain) where they received an education fit for those destined to enter the ranks of professional society. Many other Decadents, if not from the professional fraction, were from middle-class families that internalized professional values and had professional aspirations for their sons. Richard Le Gallienne, M. P. Shiel, Max Beerbohm, and Ernest Dowson, for example, came from the ranks of the business middle class, but their fathers were neither capitalists nor industrialists. Le Gallienne's father, though a brewery manager, wanted his son to join the ranks of the emerging professional class and sent him, therefore, to Liverpool College, a school that provided 'a passable, but not too expensive, imitation of a public school education'.[29] This education prepared Le Gallienne for a future in accounting, a profession his father was eager for him to pursue. Shiel's father, who was also involved in trade, had similar professional ambitions for his son. Though Shiel grew up in Montserrat and not Britain, he is included among the Decadents influenced by the rift between the professional and business middle-class fractions because of the parallels between his upbringing and those of his peers. Shiel's father, a ship-owner, store-keeper, and trader, prepared his son for a future in the Colonial Office by sending him to one of the best schools in the islands. The cases of Beerbohm and Dowson were somewhat different from those of Le Gallienne and Shiel, though their backgrounds, too, were acceptable within a professional ideological framework. Their families, though involved in trade and industry, were gentrified and their fathers well-educated, qualities that ensured them acceptability among professionals.

While many of the Decadents were educated in the kind of private schools that produced professional men, many also did not continue their education beyond this level. Shiel, Machen, Le Gallienne, and Symons did not attend university, while Davidson and Dowson did not complete their university studies. This lack of university education was not unusual within the professional class, however, for with the exception of clergymen, most professions were entered through apprenticeship. Indeed, many of the Decadents (including those with non-professional backgrounds) ended up pursuing the 'professional' callings they were trained for (such as law, medicine, teaching, accounting, and architecture) before turning to arts and letters, including Machen, Shiel, Davidson, Le Gallienne, Dowson, and Beardsley.

In addition to similar educational backgrounds, the Decadents, despite the disparity in their vertical positioning within the middle class, were in similar economic positions. At a time when £400–£500 represented a solid middle-class family income, many of the Decadents were well provided for. Machen and Hichens, for example, stood to earn £400–£500 per year from family inheritances. Hichens, however, never saw the £500 per year that his father had promised would be his due. His family lived an extravagant life and, as he noted, his father 'was too kind to those who came to him for money'.[30] Machen, on the other hand, did receive his inheritance. Had he invested it, he would have had a small yearly income for about 30 years and, after that, a very small income of about £60. Machen chose instead to live off it while he could. Thus, for a period of 11 years he received between £400 and £500 per year, an amount he described as enough for two people to live 'very sufficiently' on.[31] Though George Moore was part of the landed gentry rather than the middle class, he also had an income of about £500 a year in the 1880s (other income from the estate went to his mother and towards upkeep of the estate), though there was a period during which rents were not being paid and he depended on his writing for income.

As aspiring professionals and/or sons of professionals from families that often encouraged cultural and intellectual interests, the Decadents grew up with a sense of social superiority. Shiel's father, for example, was so convinced of his family's superiority within the Montserrat community that he had his son crowned king of Redonda, an island off the coast of Montserrat. So too, the predominance of cultural 'otherness' among Decadents such as Machen (Welsh), Symons (Welsh), Davidson (Scottish), Shiel (Irish / West Indian), Beerbohm (half Lithuanian), and Wilde (Irish) influenced their sense of difference, of distinction within British Victorian society.

Coming of age in the 1880s, informed by their sense of distinction, and witness to what was perceived by many among the intellectual class to be a misappropriation of professional ideals by the business middle class, the Decadents furthered the project of Aesthetes such as Wilde and Whistler who had already begun to distance themselves from the middle class. Decadents exhibited even more animosity toward the middle class than had their predecessors and their art reflects this disdain in a more powerful way than Aestheticism does. In Decadence, moral conceptions of art gave way to immoral ones and the cult of beauty was replaced by the cult of the beauty of ugliness and sin. Decadents interested themselves in the artificial, unnatural, morbid, perverse, and neurotic. In distinguishing themselves from the bourgeois middle class, the Decadents insisted on doing so in a more provocative manner than had the Aesthetes.

Whereas the Aesthetes were professionals in the sense that, as Freedman argues, they 'designated themselves as experts in cultural knowledge, and ... defined their own role as that of instructing others in the lineaments of that knowledge',[32] the Decadents, though equally endowed with cultural knowledge, were reluctant to perform their role as instructors. Instead of using a professional discourse to *instruct*, the Decadents used it to *alienate*. Most Aesthetes did not aggressively set out to attack the middle-class reader. Walter Pater, for example, had imagined himself addressing a community of like-minded readers, those he characterized as the 'select few, those "men of finer thread" who have formed and maintain the literary ideal',[33] and, though he worried about possible misinterpretations of his work, he did not deliberately set out to exclude others. The Decadents did. They imagined themselves speaking to a community of like-minded readers while at the same time provoking their ignorant and unsympathetic bourgeois reader whom Baudelaire characterized as the '*hypocrite lecteur*' (hypocrite reader) in the opening poem of the volume *Les Fleurs du mal* (The Flowers of Evil), a poem that seeks to implicate so-called upstanding citizens in the sins and vices of the poet whom they outwardly condemn.[34] The Decadents had little desire, or so it seemed, to translate their 'cultural knowledge' into the social and economic rewards that were the right of the professional because it would bring them into a relation of dependency with the bourgeois middle class they despised. They refused to serve. This refusal to serve constituted a significant element of the 'Decadent sensibility'.

Though in large part this abandonment of the professional service function was a gesture of defiance aimed at the business middle class, it also alienated the Decadents from their own professional roots. This division was, I would argue, a deliberately created one. To the Decadents, professionalism was subsumed in bourgeois capitalist ideology. The Decadents were not the only ones who held this view. Stephen Arata, for example, argues that Robert Louis Stevenson 'saw professionalism as inseparable from the middle classes' and aligned it with prostitution.[35] Like Stevenson, the Decadents cultivated a studied dilettantism in opposition to professionalism. The *Oxford English Dictionary* defines the dilettante as 'a lover of the fine arts; one who *toys with* a subject or studies it *without seriousness*'(emphasis added).[36] Dilettantism was an important concept in the emerging 'Decadent sensibility' insofar as it signalled a resistance to both professional and capitalist ideologies. At the same time, it represented knowledge-for-knowledge's sake to the Decadents, a non-productive economy akin to art-for-art's sake that is at once anti-capitalist and anti-professional. While dilettantes are knowledgeable, they do not put this knowledge to *productive* use: they 'toy with' the arts and do not cultivate knowledge for the purpose of making money. Decadents frequently employed this discourse of the dilettante. In his memoirs, for example, Machen writes of 'cultivat[ing] literature' and describes 'making books' as 'his chosen sport', a sport 'divorced from all commercial considerations'.[37]

Dilettantism also represented for the Decadents a form of rebellion against the kind of traditional education that, from their point of view, produced middle-class subjects. In *Confessions of a Young Man*, for example, a novel that provided a model for the self-education of the Decadent artist, Moore decries traditional education as 'fatal to anyone with a spark of artistic feeling', declaring that it 'destroys individuality'.[38] Decadents sought instead to educate themselves in a manner that would emphasize their individuality, their distinction from the middle class. For Moore, who described himself as a 'student ... of ball rooms, bar rooms, streets, and alcoves',[39] life provided this education, preferably a fast and raucous life. For others, including Machen and Shiel, alternative education took the form of studies in esoteric subjects and arcana such as the occult or ancient books and manuscripts. This dilettantish idea of education would come to be criticized by opponents of Decadence in the 1890s as 'cheap self-culture'.[40] For Decadents, however, the concept of dilettantism helped them to construct themselves outside the cycle of production.

Along with Decadence, dilettantism was a key term in Paul Bourget's *Essais de psychologie contemporaine*, a book that had a profound influence on the British Decadents. In 1889, in one of the first discussions of French Decadence in the British press, Havelock Ellis outlined Bourget's concept of dilettantism, noting that, in the nineteenth century, dilettantism has come to be 'identified ... with ... defects of frivolity and superficiality'.[41] Dilettantism was particularly suspect in Victorian Britain, a culture that valued industry and utility. Bourget and the British Decadents, however, tried to recuperate a positive connotation for dilettantism. Bourget countered the notion of dilettantism as frivolous with a positive view, describing it as 'a disposition of the mind, at once very intelligent and very emotional, which inclines us in turn towards the various forms of life, and leads us to lend ourselves to all these forms without giving ourselves to any'.[42] For the Decadents, this notion of experience without commitment to one particular idea or belief was central. It was a view that they derived not only from Bourget but also from Walter Pater whose espousal of art-for-art's sake aesthetic principles in the *Renaissance* (1873) had a profound effect on the Decadents. Like Bourget, Pater extolled the virtues of dilettantism, exhorting his readers 'to be forever curiously testing new opinions and courting new impressions, never acquiescing in a facile orthodoxy'.[43]

For the Decadents, dilettantism had strong associations with the aristocratic tradition and with the figure of the dandy. The Decadent, in his dilettantish cultivation of knowledge, was, according to Moore, a 'snob', a term popularized by William Makepeace Thackeray in his 1846–47 series in *Punch, The Snobs of England* (subsequently published in book form as *The Book of Snobs*). Thackeray used the term to describe aspirants to a superior social class who aped the manners and customs of their betters.[44] Moore idealized snobs, precisely for their abandonment of bourgeois class values.

The snob, he declared, was 'the ark that floats triumphant over the democratic wave'.[45] Unwilling to serve the capitalist middle class, the Decadents rejected their professional origins, aligning themselves instead with the aristocracy and aristocratic culture. In many respects, the appropriation of aspects of aristocratic culture by the Decadents was an attempt to hold on to a culture in decline – an aristocratic 'residual culture', in Raymond Williams's terms – that was being replaced in the nineteenth century by an 'emergent' middle-class capitalist culture.[46] One of the main causes of the decline of aristocratic culture, one that certainly rallied the anti-bourgeois Decadents in its defence, was an embourgeoisement within society that took two forms. On the one hand, the newly wealthy middle class was increasingly able to 'penetrate ... the magic circle of the aristocracy' through ennoblement and marriage.[47] On the other hand, aristocrats were becoming involved in the world of trade, a venture in which, as François Bédarida argues, they ran 'the risk of contaminating [their] patrician spirit by contact with the bourgeois mentality'.[48] Some Victorians, Bédarida claims, 'were repelled by the sight of the aristocratic spirit dabbling in commercialism'.[49] The Decadents certainly felt this way, yet they too strove to enter 'the magic circle of aristocracy' by adopting values they associated with the aristocratic dandy: dilettantism, an aristocratic hauteur, and the leisurely attitude and extravagant dress associated with the privileged aristocrat. At the same time, they cultivated more negative traits associated with the aristocracy: indolence, dissipation, and waste, qualities that stood in direct opposition to the bourgeois industry, thrift, utilitarianism, and respectability central to the Victorian middle-class ethos.

If aristocratic values were central to the 'Decadent sensibility', so too were values associated with the working class, values that also enabled the Decadents to resist middle-class hegemony. The period in which the Decadents came of age and began to formulate their anti-bourgeois ethos also marked a period of increased working-class radicalism and revolt. Both the Decadents and the working class were fighting the same enemy, though clearly the stakes for the working class were much higher. The cultural and aesthetic basis of the Decadent rebellion paled in comparison with the social injustices that the working class was protesting against. Nevertheless, from the Decadents' view, a shared enemy was reason enough to find themselves in sympathy with the working class – up to a point. This allegiance was certainly more vexed than the Decadents' cultivation of aristocratic culture. Their sympathy with the working class rarely extended to this class's struggle against social injustice. The image of the working-class masses was as repellent to the Decadents as it was to the middle class for whom 'the mass', as E. Spencer Wellhofer notes, 'presented three clear and eminent dangers: anarchy, mediocrity, and tyranny'.[50] Mediocrity was the worst of the three dangers to the Decadents who viewed democracy and universal education as instrumental in the mediocratization of British culture.

Though repelled by the vision of the working class as mass, the Decadents idealized those aspects of working-class culture that they identified as anti-bourgeois, most notably the music hall. British music halls originated in Victorian Britain as places of entertainment catering primarily to the working class and featured ballets, operettas, pantomimes, and vaudeville acts. Eventually the music halls gained wider appeal. By the 1890s, the middle- and upper-classes had halls that offered a representation of working-class culture suited to their tastes.[51] Despite the cross-class appeal of the music halls, the Decadents associated them with hedonism, ribaldry, and sensuality, values they ascribed to the working class and which stood in direct revolt against middle-class respectability. These values were, in fact, almost identical to those attributed to the Decadents' aristocratic role models at the other end of the social scale. A number of Decadents glorified the music hall in their work, including George Moore, Arthur Symons, John Davidson, Max Beerbohm, Theodore Wratislaw, Selwyn Image, and many others.[52] In *Confessions of a Young Man*, Moore offers a characteristically Decadent view of the music hall: 'The music-hall is a protest against Sardou[53] and the immense drawing-room sets, rich hangings, velvet sofas, etc. ... The music-hall is a protest against the villa, the circulating library, the club, and for all this the "'all" is inexpressibly dear to me.'[54] As Dowling explains, the Decadents' glorification of the music hall was strategic: 'To claim that music-hall performances represented serious art was to make one's position as a cultist and aesthete less marginal; for not only did the aesthete thus expand the sphere of art, and so the area of his special authority, but he more firmly secured ... the power of deciding what in fact constituted art'.[55] Thus, though the music hall had wide class appeal, the Decadents represented their understanding of it as special and this appreciation distinguished them from the masses and the middle class who were flocking to the hall in increasing numbers in this period.

In mystifying their professional middle-class backgrounds through an appropriation of so-called aristocratic and working-class values, then, the Decadents strove to construct a social identity for themselves, an identity that crystallized in the figure of the Decadent as bohemian. As Jerrold Seigel, Marilyn Brown, Elizabeth Wilson, Joanna Richardson, and other scholars of bohemianism have documented, the concept of artistic bohemianism, as we understand it today, arose in the mid-nineteenth century as the response of artists to the commercialization of art that brought them into greater dependence on the middle class.[56] This middle class, as I have already argued in this chapter, was regarded as incapable of appreciating true art and was increasingly resented by some artists who, as Wilson argues, 'became the opponent[s] of every aspect of bourgeois society, and acted out a wholesale critique of the social, political, and moral values of modernity'.[57] By this definition, the anti-bourgeois British Decadents were, by their very nature, bohemians. And yet, strangely, little attention has been paid to the British

Decadents in critical examinations of bohemianism. Wilson discusses bohemianism in relation to Byron, the Pre-Raphaelites, and the Fitzrovians, but, with the exception of Wilde, neglects the Decadents, while Seigel, Brown, and Joanna Richardson focus entirely on bohemianism as a French phenomenon. Richardson goes so far as to argue that in Britain 'there was no sense of a Bohemian movement …[and] no bohemian colony'.[58] This belief was even echoed by some British Decadents. Arthur Symons lamented the fact that there was no London equivalent to Parisian bohemian life when he complained that the Rhymers' Club 'was a desperate and ineffectual attempt to get into key with the Latin Quarter [an area of Paris strongly associated with bohemianism]'.[59]

In their presumption of an archetypal Bohemia, such arguments resemble those of critics who claim there is no British Decadence: if the model is not replicated exactly, it must not exist. We must, however, account for a culturally specific notion of Bohemia in the British context just as we must do for Decadence. Certainly, the lived experience, recorded in memoirs, of many in the Victorian period attests to the existence of Bohemia in Britain.[60] Indeed, the *Oxford English Dictionary* credits Thackeray, the British writer responsible for popularizing the term 'snob' as it is understood today, with introducing the term 'bohemian' as referring to one, especially an artist, writer, or actor who leads an unconventional life, in his 1848 novel *Vanity Fair*.[61] Scholars that have written on bohemianism in Britain do, however, note the distinctions between its French and British manifestations. Julie Codell, for example, demonstrates that the bohemianism of the early to mid-Victorian period was identified with harmless and carefree youth and with a bourgeois gentlemanly existence.[62] These were the sociable 'clubby Bohemians', in Codell's terms, who contrasted sharply with, and indeed distinguished themselves from, what they regarded as the undomesticated, vagabond, anti-bourgeois, and potentially subversive French types.[63] This notion of a jolly, carefree Bohemia persisted into the *fin de siècle* and was rendered hugely popular with the 1894 success of George Du Maurier's *Trilby*, a novel about British art students living a bohemian lifestyle in Paris.

Certainly, given both the Francophilia and the anti-bourgeois sentiments of the British Decadents, this earlier Victorian model of bohemianism was uncongenial and it is only natural that they began to look to France for a darker and more rebellious notion of artistic identity. And yet, because the Decadents had experienced what they thought of as the 'real' Bohemia in their travels in France, many of them regarded London as a poor substitute. But though different from both its earlier Victorian and its French counterparts, Bohemia did indeed exist in 1890s Britain in both geographical and ideological terms. Though London may not have had the café culture that Paris did, nor areas like Montmartre and the Latin Quarter, its Bohemia resided elsewhere: in Soho where artists, writers, journalists, actors, music-hall performers, and foreign immigrants mingled in the restaurants and coffee-houses; Bloomsbury, home to many young artists and writers and to the Slade school of Fine Art and the British Museum with its Reading Room, a popular workplace for aspiring writers; Chelsea, an area with a long-standing association with artists and writers including the Pre-Raphaelites, Algernon Swinburne, James McNeill Whistler, and Oscar Wilde; the area around Fleet Street (the newspaper publishing centre of London) where Arthur Symons and Yeats lived and which had many pubs and taverns, one of which was the Cheshire Cheese where the Rhymers' Club had their meetings; and St. John's Wood, an area associated with political and sexual radicalism known as 'the fastest neighbourhood in London'.[64] In addition to these neighbourhoods, London's bohemians of the 1890s also congregated in more upscale areas, at the Café Royal in Regent Street, for example, where French food, wine, and absinthe could be had, and at the West End music halls frequented by the upper classes and artists.

Despite Symons's protestations to the contrary, then, there were a number of areas in London congenial to the unconventional lifestyles of artists and writers. And certainly, London's cityscape and night life held substantial interest for the Decadents who paid tribute to its sordid beauty and mysteriousness.[65] Indeed, the Rhymers', as Gardiner argues, 'were the first to elaborate fully the daily compass and rhythms of the artist's urban existence, describing a cycle of moods and attitudes through which later modernist imaginations were repeatedly to pass'.[66] There was a 'cult of London', according to Le Gallienne, that glorified everyone from 'costers to courtesans'.[67] This cult included Symons, whose rhapsodizing over London in poems and prose belies his insistence, quoted previously, that it had no Bohemia: 'London was for a long time my supreme sensation, and to roam in the streets, especially after the lamps were lighted, my chief pleasure. I had no motive in it, merely the desire to get out of doors, and to be among people, lights, to get out of myself'.[68]

At the very least, then, Bohemia existed as a state of mind for the British Decadents. In particular, it helped to structure their resistance to the middle class by aligning them with the working class and London's underworld. At the same time, however, it also linked them to the upper classes at the other end of the social scale. Wilson insists that this cross-class bohemianism was specific to Britain. 'Oscar Wilde's version of the bohemian', she writes, 'had the peculiarly English aspect of connections with raffish elements of the aristocracy and upper class' while at the same time 'touch[ing on] Marx's underworld through the working-class male prostitutes with whom he consorted'.[69] Pierre Bourdieu, however, sees it as more symptomatic of bohemia in general, which he characterizes as 'near to the "people," with whom it often shares its misery, [but] separated from them by the art of living that ... is situated nearer to the aristocracy or the grande bourgeoisie than to the orderly petite-bourgeoisie'.[70] So, too, does David Weir who describes the bohemian as 'always at the lower end of the socioeconomic scale, either in reality or imagination', while 'imagin[ing] himself a cultural aristocrat'.[71] This class ambiguity is evoked in George Moore's discussion of his experience of bohemianism in *Confessions of a Young Man* which conjures up images of poverty, debt, music hall actresses, and prostitutes in the midst of the fashionable London district of Mayfair:

> I found in Curzon Street another 'Nouvelles Athènes', a Bohemianism of titles that went back to the Conquest, a Bohemianism of the ten sovereigns always jingling in the trousers pocket, of scrupulous cleanliness, of hansom cabs, of ladies' pet names; of triumphant champagne, of debts, gaslights, supper-parties, morning light, coaching: a fabulous Bohemianism; a Bohemianism of eternal hardupishness and eternal squandering of money, money that rose at no discoverable well-head and flowed into a sea of boudoirs and restaurants, a sort of whirlpool of sovereigns in which we were caught, and sent eddying through music halls, bright shoulders, tresses of hair, and slang: and I joined in the admirable game of Bohemianism that was played around Piccadilly Circus, with Curzon Street for a magnificent rallying point.[72]

Despite its apparent status as at once an aristocratic and working-class space opposed to middle-class culture and values, however, Bohemia is ultimately a middle-class construct, just as Symons claimed Decadence was. Not only are most bohemians middle class, but the concept of bohemianism itself, as Wilson, Seigel, and Brown have argued, is a bourgeois myth that seeks to resolve certain contradictions brought about by the processes of Western industrialization – contradictions about the role of art in an age of commerce and about the need of modern bourgeois individuals for both order and self-expression.[73] The bohemianism constructed by the British Decadents in the 1890s enabled them to deny their middle-class back-grounds and to indulge in both the high life and the low life while avoiding the stifling conservative middle (-class) way. It was a bourgeois space that imagined itself and was represented by Moore and others as a classless space of equality where aristocrats rub shoulders with paupers, where artists live like kings when they have money and like wretches when they do not, and where the middle class, though in reality everywhere, is made invisible. In constructing their own notion of bohemianism, the Decadents aligned themselves with a romanticized image of working-class life, while at the same time imagining themselves 'cultural aristocrat[s]', an act which only exposed the fact that they were, 'at base, thoroughly bourgeois'.[74]

For all the sincerity with which the Decadents rebelled against the capitalist Victorian middle class and with which they sought to distinguish themselves from the professionals who served this class, ultimately this rebellion served to confirm their middle-class status. Bohemia, like Decadence, was a middle-class construct that enabled rebellious members of this class to mystify their origins by creating new social and class identities for themselves. The Decadent sensibility, then, despite its apparent valorization of aristocratic and working-class ideals, was a sensibility that could only have emerged from the middle class in the same way that the concept of Bohemia did. Most aristocrats and members of the working class would not have characterized themselves as the middle-class Decadents did. The Decadents appropriated idealized and largely imagined values of both the aristocracy and the working class, values that were fast disappearing as a national culture based largely on middle-class ideals was being formed.

If the Decadents' cultivation of bohemianism only served to confirm their middle-class status, then other aspects of the rebellious 'Decadent sensibility' also implicated them more thoroughly in social and class structures that they were trying to escape from. Thus, though the Decadents cultivated a dilettantism that exalted the new, the perverse, the exotic, and the arcane in an effort to remove themselves from the cycle of capitalist and commercial production, their aristocratic dilettantism might also be read simply as an advanced form of what they sought to evade. As Rita Felski observes, Decadents participate in the 'cult of novelty which propels the logic of capitalist consumerism. ... Thus the [Decadents'] attempt to create a uniquely individual style reveals his inevitable reliance upon the very categories of evaluation against which he ostensibly pits himself. Similarly, while he affects a disdain for modern industrial and technological processes, these same processes form the taken-for-granted preconditions of his own pursuit of distinction and refined pleasures'.[75] One might also argue that the affected dilettantism of the Decadent, rather than being anti-professional, as they claimed, is yet another form of professionalism. Freedman and Arata have made this argument with respect to Henry James and Robert Louis Stevenson. For Freedman, James's 'urbane sophisticat[ion]' was calculated and was simply an 'idealizing' and 'mystified' professionalism.[76] Similarly, for Arata, Stevenson's 'hauteur regarding the reading public, as well as his commitment to the values of craft, of style, of culture and taste' can be read as 'a way of asserting one's own more authentic professionalism'.[77]

Can one read the Decadents' dilettantism in these terms? It is certainly true that in asserting their dilettantism the Decadents rejected their duty as professionals. That is, while they possessed the 'special knowledge and skills' of the professional, as dilettantes they did not, ostensibly, 'attempt to translate [this] order of scarce resources ... into another – social and economic rewards'.[78] This intention, argues Magali Sarfatti Larson, is a key element of professionalism, one that, I would argue, distinguishes the professional from the dilettante. And yet, the disavowal of social and economic rewards, as Bourdieu has shown, is an act that, in many historical cultural fields, promises precisely those rewards it seems to reject.[79] The British *fin-de-siècle* literary field was just such a field. In this period, as Freedman notes, the 'critique of commodification' was itself being commodified and 'the role of the "alienated artist" could (and did) achieve a considerable degree of financial success and social status in the very world whose utilitarian and moralistic ethos those writers and artists claimed to rebel against'.[80] The alienated artist's popularity among a middle class that enjoyed being the object of the artist's scorn complicates my earlier reading of the '*hypocrite lecteur*' trope. Though ostensibly used to signal the contempt of Decadents for the middle class, this trope also reveals a dependency on this audience. After all, the act of addressing the middle-class reader indicates the necessity of that reader for the Decadents who wanted to know that their attacks had been received. More important, though contemptuous of the middle class, they relied on this audience as a paying one. Thus, at the very moment that Decadents attempted a definitive break with the middle class, they apparently revealed both their dependency on and complicity with this class.

It is not my intention to undermine the sincerity of the Decadents in their rebellion against a society that they regarded as corrupt. Within the social sphere, I would argue, the 'fictions' of the Decadent were largely sustainable. The Decadents were quite successful at constructing an alternative social identity for themselves and of inhabiting their alternative social space. Furthermore, others recognized both this identity and social space as distinct. In terms of their work within the literary field and their careers, however, the hypocrisy of the Decadent sensibility becomes more visible. The Decadents, quite simply, were not aristocrats. Nor, in the end, did the romance of poverty hold much appeal. They could not afford to exist as dilettantes outside the cycle of production even if they wanted to. In entering the literary profession the Decadents became producers subject to the conditions of the marketplace. Though, as Gardiner notes, 'English decadents may have dreamed like dandies ... [they] had often to work like hacks, their works inscribed with material poverty and the fantastic banquets only the hungry can conjure up. The economy of the English decadence was a subsistence one of leisure longed for but business attended to, of literature ambiguously both a privileged occupation and a badly paid job.'[81] The careers of the Decadents and the products of their labour that I will discuss in subsequent chapters also embody these contradictions, contradictions which were a part of the emerging 'Decadent sensibility' as Decadents sought to construct an alternative social identity in response to the tensions within the middle class.

2
Decadent Positionings: Decadence and the Literary Field

I believe ... there is ... abundant evidence in favour of the view that the greater number of [Decadent books] are not the outcome of any spontaneous impulse whatsoever ... but of a deliberate intention to win notoriety and its cash accompaniment by an appeal to the sensual instincts of the baser or vulgarer portion of the reading public.
James Ashcroft Noble, 'The Fiction of Sexuality' (1895)[1]

thy heart was too full of too pure an ideal, too far removed from all possible contagion with the base crowd ... Never before was there so sudden a flux and conflux of artistic desire, such aspiration in the soul of man, such rage of passion, such fainting fever, such cerebral erethism. ... thy holy example didst save us [Symbolists and Decadents] from all base commercialism, from all hateful prostitution; thou wert ever our high priest.
George Moore, *Confessions of a Young Man* (1888)[2]

Like Arthur Symons's insistence on the inherently bourgeois nature of the Decadent project, James Ashcroft Noble's accusation – that Decadents were far from economically disinterested – goes against the grain of traditional representations of these writers. The more familiar view is that represented in Moore's idealized image of the 'high priest' – the disinterested martyr to art. It is this representation, not Noble's, that has prevailed in literary histories of Decadence. My intention in this chapter is not to privilege one of these interpretations over the other, but rather to understand the relationship between them, to examine how these 'fictions' came to be constructed, and how the material conditions of the British *fin-de-siècle* literary field made it possible for such diametrically opposed images of the Decadent to circulate simultaneously. What is the relationship between the Decadent and the writer motivated by cash who caters to the mass reading public or, in other words, the popular writer? Between Decadent fiction and popular commercial fiction? And how do stereotypes of the popular writer figure in struggles for power among the literary élite? Finally, how might these relationships force us to rethink the 'fiction' of Decadence as élite art that has become part of our common understanding of the literary movement?

Broadly, this chapter re-examines the idealistic high art representation of the Decadent by considering how Decadents were perceived and represented by others in the literary field. In particular, I examine the role that ethics, aesthetics, and economics played in the battle for cultural authority between Decadents and their opponents and how this battle led to the construction of the competing images of the Decadent artist. I also consider how the commercialization of literature and the conditions of publishing shaped the form Decadence would take in Britain in this period. To this end, I explore the Decadents' interest in literary role models who mediated between high art and the popular, namely George Meredith and Robert Louis Stevenson. Finally, I examine the role of *fin-de-siècle* publishers in determining the form Decadence would take in the British literary context.

The battle for cultural authority in the *fin-de-siècle* literary field

The positions and manoeuvrings of writers within the *fin-de-siècle* literary field were conditioned by a number of social and technological developments that contributed to a transformation of the field. Just as the Decadents were in the process of constructing a social identity in opposition to the dominant middle-class ideology, the literary field that they were entering was becoming, like Victorian culture more generally, increasingly commercialized. Developments in printing technology, the repeal of duties on advertising, stamps, and paper, an increase in the disposable income of middle-class families, and social reforms, such as the Education Acts of the 1870s and 1880s, created the conditions for a massive expansion of the periodical press, an increase in the amount of cheap fiction published, and a larger reading public.[3] These changes created opportunities for writers, opening up new venues for publishing and resulting in more jobs in journalism, a profession that had long had a symbiotic relationship with literature. In addition, the proliferation of newspapers and periodicals led to a demand for the writers of short stories and novels in serialized form.

These developments opened up the literary field significantly, though opportunities were more favourable to those who aspired to popular success and who were keen to address the new mass readership. To the Decadents, these new writing opportunities represented the antithesis of what they stood for, opposed as they were to anything produced for consumption by the masses. To the dilettante Decadents, literature, in the context of these developments, was reduced to a mere trade. It was hard to 'cultivate literature' in the way that Arthur Machen wanted to do when one was engaged in journalism of 'the more or less literary kind' – that is, writing 'turnovers' and stories for newspapers and periodicals.[4] Far from being a refuge from the embourgeoisement of Victorian society, the late-Victorian literary field seemed, from the point of view of the Decadents, merely to reproduce the situation of the social field. In its crass commercialism, the literary field was unwelcoming to the newly constructed social identity of the Decadents and the highbrow culture they endorsed.

If the commercialism of the literary field ran counter to the Decadent sensibility, so too did the increasing tendency towards the professionaliza-tion of authorship. One of the major developments in this respect was the establishment of the Society of Authors in 1883 by Walter Besant, a society that sought to protect authors' rights in the newly expanded and commer-cialized field of literature. To the self-proclaimed dilettante Decadents, Besant's professionalizing aims – which emphasized literary 'property' and the commercial aspects of literary production – were inextricably linked with the ideology of bourgeois capitalism. While the Society claimed to respect the differences between the literary and commercial value of a work and aimed to help both popular authors and writers devoted to literature as art, Besant's critics were unable to see beyond the 'vulgar and greedy' tradesmanlike nature of his schemes.[5] Moreover, as Peter Keating argues, the Society tended to favour writers that Besant felt were 'the real victims of commercialization', chief among whom were the 'anonymous providers of entertainment or instruction for hundreds of thousands of readers of cheaply produced novels ... religious in tone or romantic'.[6] To the Decadents, these writers were more likely to be regarded as conspirators in the commercialization of literature rather than victims of it.

The spectre of a mass readership and the wealth of cheap popular reading matter that catered to it was a nightmarish vision for many within the period. While the Decadents and other intellectuals doubted the ability of this readership to appreciate high art, others were more concerned about the moral effects of fiction on these readers. Though Victorians had always been concerned with the moral effects of literature this concern was now enhanced, as fiction became more accessible both to the working classes and to middle-class women and young people.[7] At the same time, reading increas-ingly became a private pursuit and, consequently, the policing of reading was more difficult. Within this context, there was strong resistance to the desire on the part of the literary élite to move towards a greater degree of realism in English fiction, resulting in novels that treated the more complex aspects of life for a mature and educated audience.

These aspects of the *fin-de-siècle* literary field – the expansion of the press, the increase in the production of cheap literature, the growth of the reading public, the professionalization of authorship, and concerns about the morality of fiction – resulted in what seemed to many writers, the Decadents among them, to be a complete degradation of literary culture. The reaction of

Decadents and others among the élite against this degradation led to what Andreas Huyssen calls 'the Great Divide'[8] – the élite discourse of art employed by both Noble and Moore in the quotations heading this chapter that seeks to distinguish 'high' art from 'low' or mass forms of entertainment. This divide had ramifications in both social and literary terms. On the one hand, it effected the kind of class division described in the previous chapter, whereby Decadents, breaking from their own class, defined their 'superior' culture in opposition to an 'inferior' bourgeois middle-class culture. On the other hand, it pitted writer against writer in what Nigel Cross has described as a 'schism ... in the bourgeois literary world' between middlebrow and highbrow literature.[9] This schism, Cross argues, was virtually non-existent before the 1880s when the

> distinction between the popular and the profound had been almost unknown. ... Serious literature, brimming with moral and social issues, had made no apology for its popularity. No one suggested that Dickens's *Oliver Twist*, Tennyson's *In Memoriam*, and George Eliot's *Middlemarch* were not literature because they contained ideas which found a wide and receptive audience. But in the 1880s changes in the price and distribution of books allowed readers to exercise a much more direct choice in their reading matter.[10]

This schism would define the terms upon which the struggle for cultural authority within the field would be based. In the context of a field that seemed increasingly dominated by middle-class consumer culture, it became more important than ever to distinguish between kinds of writer, particularly for those among the élite who sought to distance themselves from those who catered to the tastes of the middle classes and the masses.

In the context of this 'divide' or 'schism' between high art and mass culture, the literary field was characterized, on the one hand, by an élite and, on the other, by producers of mass culture.[11] The élite was composed of producers of high art that claimed aesthetic superiority for their work, disavowed economic interest, rejected the notion that art should serve moral and didactic ends, and understood success in terms of acceptance by literary connoisseurs and respected critics rather than by a mass audience. Moore's comments on the martyr-artist exhibit a number of these qualities from his aesthetic idealization of art to his disdain for 'base commercialism' and the 'base crowd'. Others who endorsed such ideals in this period include Oscar Wilde, Arthur Symons, Henry James, and Walter Pater.

In opposition to this élite stood producers of mass culture or popular writers who were associated with quite different aesthetic, ethical, and economic values. For popular writers of this period, extra-literary criteria often determined value. Economic principles generally prevailed, success depended on sales and size of audience, and works were designed to please the largest audience possible. Often popular writers in this period endorsed the moral or didactic function of literature. To those among the élite, these writers were the equivalent of the capitalist middle-class bourgeoisie that they despised, and indeed, popular writers often shared the social, cultural, moral, and political values of the dominant middle class which constituted their primary audience. Arnold Bennett stands as a model for the most mercenary of popular writers of the late-Victorian period, notably in his insistence that his aims were 'strictly commercial' and that 'fiction' was a thing to be 'sold and bought just like any other fancy goods'.[12] Others in this category include best-selling writer Marie Corelli, who celebrated her popular success and insisted on the morally edifying nature of her work, and Walter Besant, who judged success in monetary terms and took an enthusiastic interest in the mass reading public.

In their espousal of art-for-art's-sake principles, in their disavowal of economic interest, and in their disdain for the popular audience, the Decadents were clearly situated within the realm of the literary élite. How then, could Noble characterize them as writers interested in popular and commercial success? To answer this question, we must consider the field in its dynamic nature. Writers are constantly responding to changing cultural, social, and historical contexts and to the movements of others within the field. The field is always, as Bourdieu argues 'the site of struggles in which what is at stake is the power to impose the dominant definition of the writer and therefore to delimit the population of those entitled to take part in the struggle to define the writer'.[13] Aesthetics, economics, and ethics figured centrally in defining the writer in this period, but positions were not always as clear-cut as broad characterizations of the élite and popular realms of the field suggest. Artistic values and ideals were brought into play in complicated ways in the struggle to assert the dominant definition of writer in the *fin-de-siècle* field. Neither élite nor popular writers always wholly conformed to the dominating principles that defined their positions within the field.

Popular writers, for example, did not always characterize themselves as financially motivated in the way Bennett did. Many internalized the hierarchical principles of the élite and regarded themselves as artists. Marie Corelli, for example, was a popular writer who, like those among the élite, valorized high art and claimed economic disinterestedness. She differed from the élite, however, in her belief that aesthetic superiority was determined by size of audience as well as in her belief that aesthetic effects went hand in hand with didactic and moralistic intentions. This blend of élitist and popular views on aesthetics, economics, and ethics come together in her comments on the mass reading public in an 1895 article in the *Idler*:

> No author of old time ever had such a magnificent audience as now – an audience moved by all sorts of embryo heroisms, emotions, progressive ideas and fine perceptions, and ready for anything that will help them

think a little higher, or lift them up out of the merely sordid ways of life wherein they find themselves frequently exhausted, disheartened, or despairing. It is a privilege to work for such a public; and when it is pleased, satisfied, comforted, or moved in any way of nobleness, however slight, by what one has done, the reward is great though it is not discovered in a mere 'cash question' or in newspaper notoriety.[14]

Although there is no mistaking the missionary zeal which marks Corelli as decidedly 'bourgeois' in her thinking, her invocation of élite artistic values ('progressive ideas', 'fine perceptions', economic disinterestedness) indicates her understanding of what constitutes high art within élite circles and her desire to position herself among this group. This desire, however, does not prevent her from putting her own spin on the high literary aesthetic she invokes. Clearly, as the passage suggests, she has a different understanding than the Decadents of what might constitute 'progressive ideas' and 'fine perceptions' for, in addition to her decidedly non-Decadent zeal for fiction with a purpose, she also credits the masses with the ability to recognize and appreciate high art. In *The Silver Domino* (1892), for example, Corelli insisted that Universal education had developed the literary tastes of the 'masses' and that these tastes were now superior to those of the 'cultured'.[15] Thus, at the same time that she seemingly accepts the principles of high art as defined by the élite, she also brings them within her own framework, thereby asserting her view of the dominant definition of writer.

Corelli was notorious for her attacks against the Decadents whom she referred to disparagingly as 'new poets', 'little poets', and the 'exclusive set' of the 'Ishbosheth' (meaning 'man of shame').[16] Like Noble, she bolstered her claim to artistic superiority by undermining the high artistic claims of the Decadents and linking their work with popular sensationalistic writing. In *The Sorrows of Satan* (1895), for example, Prince Rimânez tells an aspiring author that a book with 'a judicious mixture of Zola, Huysmans, and Baudelaire ... would be sure of a success in these days of new Sodom and Gomorrah'.[17] In the novel, Corelli contrasts what she presents as the superior aesthetic and moral values of the woman novelist in the story, Mavis Clare, with those of the 'pernicious' Decadent writers favoured by Sybil, the protagonist's wife. Similar tactics were employed by other writers, particularly women writers, who represented Decadents not as the intellectual geniuses of a literary avant-garde but as inadequate, shallow, and superficial men, who were frequently contrasted with positively represented female artists. Through these representations, women writers such as Corelli, Lee, and Grand rejected the dominant principles of the literary field in an effort to redefine the qualities that endow a writer with symbolic capital.

It is no coincidence that women were such strong opponents of Decadence. The aesthetic, ethical, and economic discourses that dominated the literary field at this time were highly gendered. Women writers, even those among the élite, tended to be uneasy with the art-for-art's-sake principles endorsed by male Aesthetes and Decadents. Many women writers believed literature ought to serve an ethical function – whether moralistic or simply didactic. These beliefs went against the grain of the Decadent sensibility, though Decadents were certainly not alone in their condemnation of women writers. As Lyn Pykett has demonstrated, the view that women novelists 'compromis[ed] both the novel's claim as a serious art form and its possibilities for aesthetic development' was widely held by male writers within the *fin-de-siècle* field.[18] To the Decadents and others among the male-dominated élite, women writers' crimes against art were two-fold: they degraded art by writing commercial fiction for money and by approaching literature with the missionary zeal of the social reformer or moralist rather than as an aesthetic purist. The male élite also generally felt that women writers and their populist forms of fiction dominated the literary field. Women writers did not share this feeling, however. Though women writers may, in some cases, have been endowed with more economic capital than some of their male contemporaries, they nevertheless strongly desired the symbolic capital that was largely the property of the male-dominated élite. Corelli, for example, struggled to gain symbolic capital throughout her career, particularly early on when she sought recognition from the literary élite that she otherwise claimed to despise. Corelli always had high artistic aspirations for her novels and consistently believed that she could write a book that was at once commercially and artistically successful, one that would grant her economic and symbolic capital.

The ambivalence displayed towards the Decadents by popular writers such as Corelli was also felt by many of those who occupied positions alongside the Decadents among the élite. Thus, even writers who endorsed the same literary values battled against each other for dominance within the élite. Noble's comments about the Decadents, with whom he shared many artistic values, exemplify this particular struggle and indicate how those among the élite strategically manipulated the terms of the debate in the battle for dominance. His comments on the Decadents at once establish him as one of the élite, while undermining their claims to high art by suggesting that the Decadents are, in reality, nothing more than popular writers. Other critics and men of letters shared Noble's views regarding the Decadents. W. E. Henley decried the Decadents as 'myriad poetasters who inflate their own value by shrieking that only two hundred and fifty copies of their works may be distributed among the clamouring public? The artifice is old and tiresome. ... They are here to-day, because their bookseller, who has influence with a morning paper, and understands the profitable planting of garbage, chooses to sell them'.[19] T. P. Gill expressed a similar disdain for the Decadent coterie that centred around publisher John Lane, worrying about its influence on New Woman writer, George Egerton: 'I wish you were not going to the d---- – Odd Volumes Coroboree [*sic*]. They are a third-rate crowd. ... don't make yourself one of that horrible world of penny-a-liners and guinea-a-versers and city shopkeepers. ... I am anxious about the effect of this matter upon your *work* – your *art'*.[20]

The field, then, was not simply structured around a division between the popular and the élite. The élite itself was divided in a manner akin to the division between Decadents and professional intellectuals within the social sphere. For both popular writers and élite opponents of Decadence, the exposure of the Decadent project as a 'sham' served to assert their own superiority within the literary field. And yet, even if opponents of Decadence were justified in their accusations that Decadents were motivated not by high artistic principles but rather by profit, they too benefited from the so-called popular appeal of Decadence. How else are we to account for the way in which Decadence was so widely taken up by popular writers and the mainstream press and marketed to the masses? Popular novels featuring Decadents abounded in the period and the pages of middlebrow periodicals were filled with parodies of Decadence. *Punch*, for example, ran series through 1894 entitled 'Our Decadents' and 'Our Female Decadents' and frequently parodied Oscar Wilde, Max Beerbohm, Aubrey Beardsley and others. Neither were the financial advantages of discussions of Decadence lost on editors such as J. A. Spender of the *Westminster Gazette*, whose rage against Decadent and New Woman fiction in early 1895 stirred up controversy, prompting a large increase in the paper's circulation.[21] For his part, W. E. Henley sought to increase the circulation of his periodical, the *National Observer*, by serializing G. S. Street's parody of the Decadent dandy, *The Autobiography of a Boy*.[22]

The appropriation of Decadence by popular writers, the press, and counter-Decadents among the élite indicates the continuing fascination with the alienated artist figure that had begun during the Romantic period and had most recently exhibited itself in the aesthetic craze of the 1880s. That the Decadents merited attention in popular media consumed by the middle-class public certainly seems to validate the claims that the Decadents were in reality savvy publicity seekers and, in addition, compromises their ability to represent themselves as disinterested. Or does it? Can we attribute the popular appeal of the Decadents to their own efforts and just how popular was this appeal anyway? In reality, this popularity probably did more for the popularized representations of the Decadent artist than it did for the work of the Decadents themselves. One only has to compare sales figures for Corelli's novels *Wormwood* and the *Sorrows of Satan* – both of which exploit the interest in the Decadent artist figure – with those of any work by the Decadents to realize the relativity of the term 'popular' in this context. Where Corelli's books sold in the tens and hundreds of thousands, a good sale for a Decadent work was a couple of thousand. Sales for Bodley Head productions, a firm associated with Decadence were small in comparison. Among its biggest sellers, for example, were the first issue of the *Yellow Book* and George Egerton's *Keynotes*, both of which sold around 6000 copies in a short time.[23] The most famous Decadent work of this period, Oscar Wilde's *The Picture of Dorian Gray*, sold surprisingly few copies – less than a thousand in five years, though these poor sales do not necessarily reflect a sparse readership as the story sold very well in its initial magazine format.[24] Still, the Decadents were perceived to be more popular than they really were partly because of all the press attention they received and partly because they figured so prominently in popular fiction and the press. But these popular representations were likely as close to Decadence as most of the British reading public ever got.

Despite the apparently fictional nature of the Decadents' popularity, a popularity that benefited popular writers and the press more than it did them, the Decadents were not immune to the lures of writing for money. They represented their engagement in this type of work, however, in strikingly different terms than their opponents did. Whereas opponents of Decadence claimed that Decadent writers concealed their money-grubbing with false pretensions to high art, Decadents distinguished between their art and their hack writing. John Davidson, Arthur Symons, and Lionel Johnson complained about having to 'pot-boil' by doing reviewing work and other kinds of prose writing because it detracted from their purist aims. Symons, for example, distinguished between his poetry, which he considered his 'life's work', and the prose writing that he was 'obliged to do – for money'.[25] Even Johnson, who, with 'private means', was far from poor, complained, 'I do not recommend literature from the pecuniary side. ... At present, I have given up the idea of it, and must stick to pot-boiling in the reviews.'[26] The Decadents made a virtue of necessity and, rather than letting their hackwork serve to undermine their artistic credibility, they used it to further their image as artistic martyrs.

Though some Decadents really did depend on hackwork to earn their living, the fact that even those who had little need to pot-boil, such as Johnson, adopted this attitude attests to the importance of the notion of artistic martyrdom to the Decadents' self-representation. Clearly, for those who had reasonable yearly incomes, the martyr-artist pose was a way of mystifying work that, if not truly necessary for survival, was essential to establishing contacts and associations in the field in order to further their careers. After all, with the exception of Davidson, who was a ghost-writer for a popular novelist, the hackwork described by Decadents was mainly reviewing. This was hardly the kind of writing that threatened to undermine one's artistic credibility. Rather, it was work that stood to enhance the Decadent's legitimacy and authority within the field by asserting his power to consecrate and give value to literary works.

But were the Decadents really as opposed to popularity and commercial success as their views of hackwork seem to suggest? Some, such as Richard Le Gallienne, were less conflicted about the seemingly contradictory positions of the artist as purist and the artist as money-maker. Le Gallienne happily occupied a number of contradictory positions within the field. He was a columnist for the *Star* – one of the leading papers of the 'new journalism' that catered to the masses; a member of the Rhymers' Club – an élite coterie of poets including W. B. Yeats, Ernest Dowson, and Arthur Symons; and a writer of both Decadent and anti-Decadent poems. Le Gallienne took an opportunistic view of his 'hacking', using his position as a journalist for a popular newspaper to promote Decadent 'minor poets'. Others such as Ernest Dowson, Arthur Machen, M. P. Shiel, and John Davidson wrote fiction that was highly indebted to popular genres – the society novel, the romantic comedy, the Stevensonian gothic romance, and the detective story – works that will be considered in subsequent chapters.

Generally speaking, these works have been accounted for in literary history by accepting at face value the claims of Decadents regarding hackwork. Consequently, they are largely ignored. The poems of Dowson and Davidson – work regarded as having literary merit and having been approached as such by the two writers – are given ample consideration in histories of Decadence where their novels are virtually ignored. Dowson has come to represent the quintessential Decadent martyr-artist, one who, as Yeats declared, 'made it a matter of conscience to turn from any kind of money-making that prevented good writing'.[27] This statement obscures Dowson's very real involvement with and interest in the kind of writing for money he undertook in his novel-writing. Yeats's economically disinterested Dowson is very different from the Dowson who, in his excitement regarding his novel-writing collaborations with Arthur Moore, writes with as much enthusiasm as irony of 'inherit[ing] the Kingdom of Mudie!'[28]

In a like manner, Machen and Shiel are largely absent from histories of Decadence because their work goes against the grain of the image of Decadence as an avant-garde precursor to Modernism. Though their work is seemingly too popular to be accounted for in Decadent literary history, Machen and Shiel were perceived as Decadent in their day. Far from ignoring them then, we need to examine more thoroughly the Decadent stance on the 'popular'. In truth, though the Decadents made great claims for their artistic martyrdom, their aesthetic idealism, their economic disinterestedness, and their hatred of the masses, none was averse to the rewards popularity might bring – provided it could be achieved without sacrificing artistic integrity. Like Corelli, many Decadents were interested in producing work that was artistically, critically, and commercially successful. As such, they, too, sought to mediate between the claims of high art and the claims of the marketplace.

'Other' Decadent role models: George Meredith and Robert Louis Stevenson

Before discussing the attempts by Decadents to produce fiction that was both artistically and commercially successful, I want to draw attention to some of their role models in this endeavour, models that complicate the traditional literary history of Decadence. In this history, writers such as Algernon Swinburne, Walter Pater, D. G. Rossetti, Charles Baudelaire, Arthur Rimbaud, J.-K. Huysmans, Paul Verlaine, and Guy de Maupassant figure as key influences on the development of British Decadence. And indeed, these writers were frequently invoked by British Decadents for whom they represented a commitment to high literary ideals. The literary tastes of British Decadents, however, were often far more eclectic than they have been made out to be. Studies that position Decadence as a precursor to Modernism within the literary canon tend to ignore or marginalize these eclectic interests, interests not easily accommodated into a master narrative of literary inheritance. I wish to talk here about the Decadents' admiration of George Meredith and Robert Louis Stevenson, an admiration that complicates traditional understandings of British Decadence.

Though seemingly strange bedfellows for the Decadents, Meredith and Stevenson figure consistently among their influences. Of the two, Meredith had less of a visible influence on Decadent fiction, though the Decadents admired him and some even characterized his writing as Decadent. Dowson, for example, praised his lack of sentiment, his cleverness, and described him as 'hard and cold as a piece of crystal',[29] while Davidson thought Meredith 'the foremost man of letters in England'[30] and sent him copies of his poetic efforts. Like Davidson, Shiel revered Meredith as a great 'stylist'.[31] And though Machen would, in the 1920s, express distaste for Meredith's 'obscure affectations, convolutions, [and] complexities of ... diction', he admitted that in the 1890s he had 'venerated Meredith ... by rumour'[32] for these Decadent qualities: 'I had heard of both [Meredith and Pater] that they were very great and subtle doctors of literature, who demanded high & subtle qualities in those who read them. Of course I knew that I must possess such qualities, & was quite sure that I should appreciate the two masters'.[33] Machen's admission of 'veneration by rumour' attests to the power Meredith's name had among the Decadent aspirants to the literary élite and also to the importance they placed on cultivating a refined literary taste in the establishment of a credible artistic identity. In an essay written in 1897 for the *Fortnightly Review*, Arthur Symons noted Decadent qualities in Meredith's writing, a writing notable for its 'learned corruption of language by which style ceases to be organic, and becomes, in the pursuit of some new expressiveness or beauty, deliberately abnormal'.[34]

Despite the Decadents' admiration of his style, Meredith's importance as a role model for the Decadents was more symbolic than practical. To the Decadents, Meredith was a writer who had been uncompromising in his dedication to literature and who had ultimately been rewarded for this dedication. For these writers, Meredith's career reconciled the seemingly irreconcilable demands of high art with the demands of the marketplace. Having struggled since the mid-century as a poet and novelist, Meredith only achieved real fame in the mid-1880s with the publication of the highly successful *Diana of the Crossways* (1885) and his collected works. He therefore stood as an example of the disinterested artist whose talent is eventually recognized, who is rewarded with fame and money, and who demonstrates that artistic integrity, fame, and financial rewards are not necessarily irreconcilable. In him, Decadents saw a comrade-in-arms against bourgeois taste and morality for, like them, Meredith was one who had, as George Allen Cate argues, suffered at the hands of 'Victorian middle-class blindness and injustice'.[35] Symons was 'fired by Meredith's "delightful" and "exhilarating" hatred of philistinism'.[36] Similarly, Le Gallienne in a letter to publisher John Lane, expressed his disgust at Meredith's belated popularity among the philistine middle class, referring disparagingly to 'the British public's long insensitive disregard of Mr. Meredith finding voice and endeavouring to justify itself, graceless and unrepentant'.[37]

Like Meredith, Robert Louis Stevenson appealed both to the broader British public and to the Decadents and others among literary élite. Though Stevenson's *Dr Jekyll and Mr Hyde* develops a number of *fin-de-siècle* themes that would be taken up in Decadent fiction, he was foremost a writer of adventure-romance, a genre regarded as the antithesis of French realism and Decadence. In fact, critics such as Andrew Lang who contributed to the romance/realism debates of the 1880s, argued that romance would re-invigorate, indeed re-masculinize, British fiction and viewed it as 'an antidote to the feminizing – and thus morbid – effects of the virus of French realism'.[38] Despite the endorsement given to romance by critics such as Lang, however, romance was also associated with mass-produced fiction of questionable literary merit. James A. Noble, for example, who condemned the Decadents as money-grubbing, identified Stevenson's *Dr Jekyll and Mr Hyde* as mass-produced fiction in his review of the book: '[*Dr Jekyll*] is simply a paper-covered shilling story, belonging, so far as external appearance goes, to a class of literature familiarity with which has bred in the minds of most readers a certain measure of contempt.'[39] He goes on, however, to qualify this statement, drawing attention to Stevenson's unique status within the *fin-de-siècle* literary field: 'In spite of the paper cover and the popular price, Mr. Stevenson's story distances so unmistakably its three-volume and one-volume competitors that its only fitting place is the place of honour.'[40]

Though Stevenson was a producer of popular shilling shockers and boy's adventure stories, his gifts as a literary artist enabled him, as Noble's remarks suggest, to transcend the limits of the popular genres he wrote in. Noble acknowledged Stevenson's dual status as popular writer and artist, a status Noble was unwilling to confer upon the Decadents, whose work he believed only to be money-grubbing. Noble's view of Stevenson was held widely among the élite, even by Decadents. Dowson, Symons, Machen, Davidson, and Yeats were attracted to Stevenson's 'Paterian attention to the intricacies of style' rather than to the 'blood-and-thunder celebrations of male adventure'[41] that critics such as Lang believed would help re-invigorate the English novel, yet they acknowledged Stevenson's broad appeal. On the occasion of Stevenson's death, Symons paid tribute to his popular and avant-garde appeal: 'He was a fastidious craftsman, caring, we might almost say, pre-eminently, for style; yet he was popular. He was most widely known as the writer of boys' books of adventure; yet he was the favourite reading of those who care only for the most literary aspects of literature.'[42]

Stevenson appealed to the Decadents because he shunned conventional middle-class life and enjoyed a Bohemian lifestyle. Also, like them, he was compelled to write for money and was ashamed of it. Like Dowson, who complained of having to write for the 'many headed Beast',[43] Stevenson was ashamed of the work he 'rattled off ... for coins',[44] and, in a letter to friend Edmund Gosse, he decried 'the bestiality of the beast whom we feed'.[45] The Decadents sympathized with Stevenson's need to pander to the public and admired the fact that he could do so while still producing works of literary merit. In 1889, Dowson expressed his wish that Stevenson, a family friend, might offer advice concerning *Dr Ludovicus*, a 'trashy novel' he was collabo-rating on with Moore.[46] Similarly, Machen acknowledged 'a vast respect ... for the fantastic *Arabian Nights* manner of [Stevenson] to those curious researches in the byways of London',[47] while Shiel declared him 'the most underrated English writer'.[48]

Stevenson's ability to transcend the limits of the popular genres in which he wrote was an inspiration to writers who had high artistic ideals and yet depended on writing for their living. In this respect, he was a more realistic role model for the Decadents than Meredith. While many Decadents liked to imagine themselves as uncompromising artists who would, like Meredith, be rewarded late in life, the exigencies of everyday living, their desire for more immediate gratification and for the freedom that popular success would give them in terms of future writing projects, made Stevenson's career easier to emulate. For the Decadents who did imitate him, he served as a model for how popular genres might be made the vehicles for the produc-tion of works of literary merit and/or for promoting the alternative and oppositional cultures ascribed to by the Decadents.

Paving the way for Decadence: publishers of Decadence

The Decadents' interest in identifying role models who mediated success-fully between the claims of high art and the demands of the marketplace was prompted, to some extent, by the conditions of publishing in the *fin-de-siècle* literary field. Unable to finance their own publications, Decadents were answerable to publishers who were in turn answerable to the public. In many respects, publishers were the true mediators of Decadence in that they determined what would be published on the basis of a double sense of responsibility, to the public and to commerce on the one hand, and to the writer and art on the other. Aesthetic, ethical, and economic factors registered not only in the minds of writers, then, but also in the minds of publishers who played an important role in shaping the production of Decadence within the British context. Decadent writers imagined that their work could be both commercially and artistically successful in large part because they wanted it published, and publishers generally require that their books make a profit or, at the very least, that they do not lose money.

The Decadents, as I have argued, were anxious about the commercialization of literature in the wake of social and technological developments. These changes resulted in what Josephine Guy and Ian Small call the 'bubble economy' in publishing, which created a more innovative and enterprising publishing industry.[49] Generally, the publishing houses that had dominated the fiction market since the mid-century were traditional, conservative, family-run businesses such as Bentley's, which issued novels in three volumes, the standard format through most of the nineteenth century. Because of the exorbitant price of the three-volume novel (more than even a middle-class family could afford), Britain was a book-borrowing rather than a book-buying nation. For the most part, publishers sold books directly to circulating libraries. The literary market under this system was, therefore, far less competitive than that which would develop from the 1880s on. Though conservative houses that specialized in the publication of three-volume novels continued to dominate through the 1880s, a considerable number of enterprising new firms arose at this time, many of which undertook to market their books directly to a reading population that had tripled in the years between 1850 and 1880 and that was continuing to grow.[50] Walter Scott (established 1882), Dent (established 1888), and Hutchinson (established 1887), for example, specialized in the publication of cheap books: reprints of novels and works out of copyright, editions of the classics, series of science and of great prose writing, and so on.

Not all of these newly established firms specialized in cheap fiction, however, and, in reality, despite the Decadents' fears that they would be shut out of the literary market, the 'bubble economy' in publishing benefited all writers, not just those seeking commercial success. Some firms, for example, recognized the potential profit in catering to the rising middle class's desire for cultural capital and also even to the smaller niche market of intellectuals, literary connoisseurs, and book collectors. The most significant publishers of this type to emerge in terms of the production of Decadent fiction were the Bodley Head (established by Elkin Mathews and John Lane in 1887, run by John Lane from the summer of 1894 on)[51] and Heinemann (established 1890). Both firms combined an interest in the art of fine bookmaking, as practised by less commercial firms such as the Vale Press, with shrewd business practices. Both were also innovators in the push to break the power of the circulating libraries on the fiction market, a power that ensured the dominance of the three-volume novel. Heinemann, for example, was among the first to publish six-shilling single-volume fiction[52] and, though cosmopolitan in his own tastes, was less fastidious than Lane in the popular fiction he published. He catered both to a mainstream middle-class audience through his publication of popular best-selling novels and to a more select intellectual audience in his publication of foreign literature, plays by living playwrights, and general scientific and art books. Heinemann and the Bodley Head would become popular with up-and-coming writers eager to establish themselves, not only because they published the latest in modern European literary trends in an attractive format, but also because they welcomed new and unknown authors.

These firms, however, did not, as it seems, immediately come to the attention of the Decadents. Dowson, who had considerable knowledge of publishers of popular fiction from trying to place his and collaborator Arthur Moore's shilling shockers, was unsure of whom to approach with his more artistic productions, such as his Jamesian *Madame de Viole*, which he was working on in 1888. He told friend Charles Sayle, 'no one will publish it. ... it is too *risqué* for the majority and not sufficiently so for Viziteli [*sic*]. However I do not much care. I am afraid my constitutional inaction is distressingly apparant [*sic*] even in fiction and three volumes of nothing but analyses where nobody does anything and everybody analyses everybody else will appal the most original publisher.'[53] Dowson also complained to Sayle about the difficulty faced by an unknown writer in getting published, let alone read: 'I am quite sure that if [*Madame de Viole*] ever sees the light of print it will have to be some years hence & at my own expense. ... Do you know of any publishing firm who are moderately likely to *read* a novel submitted to them by an unknown hand?'[54] In 1889, when Dowson expressed these doubts, his pessimism was well founded. Of the firms that would eventually publish his work, only the Bodley Head was yet in existence and, at this period, its focus was on poetry and *belles-lettres*. Of Dowson's other publishers, Methuen would be established later that year, Heinemann in 1890, and Leonard Smithers in 1894.

As Dowson's experience makes clear, the crop of new publishing firms that emerged in 1889 and 1890 could not have come at a better time from the point of view of emerging writers experimenting in new forms of fiction. Within a year of Dowson's complaints about the lack of suitable publishers, two of the four firms that would publish him and other Decadents were established. For those whose works tended towards the Decadent, the Bodley Head was particularly welcome, especially under Lane's influence, because it 'deliberately went after unknowns and rebels, authors who could not count on any publisher to be interested in their work or who had manuscripts that had already been rejected on the grounds of risqué or unpopular subject matter'.[55] These new publishing houses, however, did not immediately strike emerging writers as ideal locations for the publication of innovative fiction. It took time for the reputations of these firms to develop. Machen, for example, approached neither Heinemann nor the Bodley Head in 1891 when seeking a publisher for *The Great God Pan*. Similarly, Dowson did not turn to Heinemann until 1893 when he submitted the manuscript for *A Comedy of Masks*. New writers often looked first to established firms, Blackwood's in the case of Machen, Bentley's in the case of Dowson and Moore, both of which rejected the manuscripts of these young authors. By 1893, however, the Bodley Head and Heinemann had come to be regarded by young writers as, what Pierre Bourdieu has called, 'natural sites' for the publication of modern and pioneering writing.[56] In 1894, for example, Robert Hichens was advised to submit *The Green Carnation*, his topical satire of Aestheticism and Decadence, to Heinemann by a friend who had heard that the publisher was interested in short works by unknown writers.[57] On the same principle, George Egerton was advised to approach Heinemann or Lane with her manuscript for *Keynotes*.[58]

While Heinemann and Lane may have been more progressive and pioneering in their publishing than traditional firms or those that catered to the masses, they were not immune to market forces. Though both were appreciators of *belles-lettres* and modern European literature each, in their own way, catered to the commercial literary marketplace. Thus, while Heinemann was no 'lover of popular fiction', he 'sometimes pandered to his public ... giv[ing] it ... a mixture of [what he called] "bawdry and religion" '.[59] Notably, he published best-selling authors like Hall Caine, Ouida, Rudyard Kipling, and Flora Annie Steel. Strategically, Heinemann's publication of best-sellers was wise. From the profits these works generated he subsidized highbrow publications which, though less economically profitable, commanded him the cultural capital that would establish his reputation as a publisher with discriminating tastes.

Lane, on the other hand, whose market was smaller and more select than Heinemann's, employed more complicated and manipulative strategies in his pandering. Trading on the vogue for limited editions, he 'presented aesthetic value in terms of material rarity'.[60] Bodley Head books were of value because they were not best-sellers nor were they tainted by commercialism. And yet, this very marketing strategy was designed to make best-sellers, albeit not to the level of a work by Corelli or Hall Caine. As Stetz points out, the Bodley Head was a forerunner of modern advertising techniques in that its marketing strategy sold not only books, but a lifestyle and a means of self-identification as well. The firm's success, she argues, lay 'in convincing buyers that consumption was the chief, if not the only, way of making a positive public statement about oneself – about one's own values, education, and ideals'.[61] Even in the 1890s, the speciousness of such a strategy did not go unnoticed. Cynics recognized the calculation and commercial interests that the firm's practices sought to mystify. The Decadents who were associated with John Lane bore the brunt of the criticism resulting from his marketing strategies in the form of accusations of commercial interestedness levelled at them by Noble and others. Of course, they profited by these strategies also, as critics were quick to point out. A parody in *Granta* magazine of the *Yellow Book* prospectus joked that the 'yellow' in the title referred to 'the complexion of the poet and ... the gold which inspires him'.[62] 'A Legend of Vigo Street', a satirical poem published in the *Realm*, made a similar accusation: 'There's a street that men call Vigo, / Whither scribblers such as I go; / With a badly written story / On the grab for gold and glory'.[63] If the Decadents were bothered by such attentions, Lane was not. Indeed, another of his innovative marketing strategies was to use negative reviews as advertisements for his publications. These reviews appealed at once to Lane's élite readership who tended to value what was rejected by a mainstream press, but also to a more general middle-class audience interested in the racy and risqué matter that the negative reviews promised.

These examples of Lane's marketing strategies undermine his status as a promoter of high art. As Stetz has commented, 'The Bodley's commitment to the avant-garde was less a loving embrace than a marriage of convenience'.[64] Lane, it seems, was primarily interested in what would make a popular success. He was, however, a good mediator and, for some time, was able to balance the claims of the literary marketplace with the aims of his stable of idealistic writers. Lane's Keynotes series, a series consisting of 19 volumes of short stories and 14 novels, is a good indicator of the way he capitalized on popular trends while providing a venue for modern and avant-garde writing. Thus, although the works in the series are notable for their innovation in literary technique and style,[65] they are also indebted, in various ways, to popular forms of literature. The publication of George Egerton's *Keynotes* (1893), for example, followed close on the heels of and profited from the massive success of Sarah Grand's *The Heavenly Twins* (1893), a 'New Woman' novel that sold 20,000 copies and went into six editions in its first year.[66] The Bodley Head continued to publish the most controversial of the popular 'New Woman' novels including Grant Allen's *The Woman Who Did* (1895), which had an even greater success than *Keynotes*. The series also responded to other popular trends. M. P. Shiel's *Prince Zaleski* (1895), a collection of Holmesian detective stories, filled a gap that had been left when Arthur Conan Doyle killed off Holmes in December 1893. At the same time, Arthur Machen's *Great God Pan* (1894) and *The Three Impostors* (1895) borrowed from the style and themes of Robert Louis Stevenson's *New Arabian Nights* and *Dr Jekyll and Mr Hyde*. Neither was Lane averse to participating in the popular counter-Decadent movement. He published George Street's *Autobiography of a Boy* (1894), a story that exploited the popular representation of the Decadent as pompous young member of the upper class, as well as Owen Seaman's *Battle of the Bays* (1896), reprints of Seaman's *Punch* parodies of Bodley Head poets.

If commercial considerations played a considerable role in determining what even the most pioneering of British publishers would publish in the 1880s and

1890s, moral considerations were also paramount. Though conditions were changing, Mrs Grundyism exerted a powerful influence over the literary market, determining the subject matter and style of treatment in fiction. For many writers, readers, publishers, and intellectuals, the dominance of Mrs Grundyism put Britain well behind other nations in the development of modern fiction. At a time when continental European and Russian writers were exploring the limits of naturalistic representation, the British novel's reticence seemed hopelessly outdated. 'Life is now treated in fiction by every race but our own with singular candour', lamented Edmund Gosse,[67] who, as editor of Heinemann's International Library series of foreign literature, had to exercise caution in choosing works for the series. To the chagrin of British writers keen to test the limits of fiction, Gosse's caution was standard in the industry at this time. Publishers were all too aware of the fate of Henry Vizetelly, who had been jailed in 1889 for issuing what the court determined to be 'obscene' works by Zola and other contemporary French authors. Those such as Heinemann and Lane, who were also publishing translations of French and continental writers and their British imitators, had to be especially careful. Heinemann was generally more cautious than Lane. Though his International Library series included controversial European fiction, Gosse, the series editor, assuaged potentially morally censorious readers with a promise that the books would be 'amusing' and 'wholesome', expunged of anything which might 'give offence'.[68] Heinemann also rejected books on the grounds of immorality, as he did in the case of Strindberg whom he believed was 'the most pernicious and detestable writer that ever lived'.[69] Finally, he did not pursue, as Lane did, 'the most advanced and modern of the younger men'.[70]

Though the Bodley Head under Lane's command built its reputation upon publishing that which other publishers deemed immoral or controversial, Lane shrewdly gauged the public's limits of acceptability. By 1894, when Lane was fully engaged in the publication of controversial modern genres including New Woman fiction, Decadent poetry, Naturalistic and Decadent fiction, the climate, though still hostile, was more tolerant of new developments in fiction than it had been in the late 1880s when Vizetelly was jailed for publishing 'obscene' works. In any case, Lane did not base his list solely on controversial writers. As Margaret Stetz argues, 'For every so-called "advanced" novel in the firm's lists, there was a fussily conservative work ... or a bland and neutral one'.[71] As I have argued above, Lane's commitment to modern literary trends was conditional. Public notoriety and moral condemnation was fine so long as it contributed to sales but not when it threatened to put him out of business, as it did when the Wilde scandal broke, a controversy that led him to radically restructure his business.

In many respects, then, the conditions of publishing determined the course that Decadence would take within the British literary context. Both Heinemann and Lane ran commercial publishing houses to a greater or lesser degree, and though they established good reputations among rebellious young writers who despised the middle-class readership, they also colluded with this readership. This collusion often meant treating what writers regarded as art with a view to marketability and profitability and it also set limits on the extent to which Decadence and other emerging Modernist literary forms could develop. Stetz, for example, has argued concerning Lane that 'Despite the wish of many Bodley Head authors … to overturn the social order, [he] understood the commercial wisdom of appealing to that order.'[72] This savvy marketing of Decadence influenced the perception many had of them as money-grubbing writers of trashy fiction. Many Decadents, as we shall see, were at odds with such practices and regarded Lane and others within the Bodley Head group with some ambivalence. At the same time, Lane's aggressive marketing practices, which made the Bodley Head and 'Decadence' synonymous in the public mind, left many writers with a label they were uncomfortable with, though they were grateful for the opportunities that Lane provided at a time when few publishers would take on their writing.

Clearly, as this chapter argues, there was more to the Decadents than the idealized image of themselves they tried to project. In looking beyond their self-proclaimed identities to the ways in which they were understood by others within the literary field and to how the conditions of the field circumscribed their activities, a different image of the Decadent emerges. The competing 'fictions' of the Decadent – the Decadent as proponent of high art and the Decadent as producer of fiction for the masses – were the result of a complex dialectical relationship between the popular and high art in this period and of the battle for cultural authority between Decadents and their opponents. The examination of these competing representations of the Decadent in context forces us to look at the literary field in a different way, to understand it as a battleground in which various positions on aesthetics, ethics, and economics function strategically in constructing particular artistic identities for polemical purposes. So too, it forces us to see that Decadence as high art and Decadence as popular are not always strictly oppositional. In ideal terms, the Decadent and the popular writer are located at opposite poles of the literary field. In real terms, however, they meet somewhere in between as writers' interactions, literary allegiances, influences, and associations determine their positioning within the field, forcing mediations as writers struggle to assert their cultural authority. The next four chapters take up the battle between Decadents and their opponents in the literary field as it spills over into the fiction of the period, a fiction remarkable for its interest in Decadence and the Decadent writer.

3
The Birth of the Decadent in Fiction, 1884–89

I turn now from the 'fictions of Decadence' as they operated in the social and literary field to the 'fictions of Decadence' in the literature of the period. Although the literary field is always a site of struggle in which writers battle for the power to impose the dominant definition of writer, the *fin-de-siècle* field was particularly divisive. This claim is borne out by the numerous representations of writers in the fiction of this period, fiction that seeks to define the writer in aesthetic, ethical, and economic terms. Writers figured centrally, for example, in Marie Corelli's *Wormwood* (1890) and *The Sorrows of Satan* (1895), George Gissing's *New Grub Street* (1891), Arnold Bennett's *A Man from the North* (1898), George Moore's *Confessions of a Young Man* (1888), *Mike Fletcher* (1889), and *Vain Fortune* (1891), George Paston's *A Writer of Books* (1898), Leonard Merrick's *Cynthia* (1896), Ernest Dowson's and Arthur Moore's *Adrian Rome* (1899), Richard Le Gallienne's *Book-Bills of Narcissus* (1891) and *Young Lives* (1899), John Davidson's *The North Wall* (1885) (republished as *A Practical Novelist* [1891]), Mary Cholmondeley's *Red Pottage* (1899), James Payn's *A Modern Dick Whittington* (1892), J. M. Barrie's *When a Man's Single* (1888), Vernon Lee's *Miss Brown* (1884), Morley Roberts's *In Low Relief* (1890) and *Immortal Youth* (1902), David Christie Murray's *A Rising Star* (1894), Walter Besant's *All in a Garden Fair* (1883), Cyril Arthur Edward Ranger Gull's *The Hypocrite* (1898), Sarah Grand's *Beth Book* (1897), Henry Murray's *A Man of Genius* (1895), Henry James's stories about writers, and a host of other works.

Peter Keating attributes this interest in the writer to a number of factors: the influence of French novels about writers including Balzac's *Illusions perdues* and Flaubert's *L'Education sentimentale*; the 'cult of Aestheticism', which pitted the artist against society, resulting in an introspective art; and, the expanding literary market, which generated excitement about the profession.[1] Margaret Stetz offers another reason, arguing that this interest was manufactured through the aggressive marketing of authorship in interviews, photographs, and biographies.[2] I would add that the interest in the writer figure, at least on the part of writers themselves, also attests to the anxiety caused by the changing conditions of production. Fictions about the writer could be used to embody arguments in the form of narrative, literalizing issues that were being discussed in the literary debates of the period. They could also be used to simplify the complex situation of the literary field. Thus, whereas the position of real writers in the field was often contradictory – as in the case of the Decadents whose self-professed élite status might be said to be compromised by their hack writing – fictions of the writer could obscure the real conditions of production by focusing on idealized representations of the uncompromising artist. Through these fictions, writers offered competing models of authorial identity for the benefit of their readership, a readership significantly larger than that of the literary periodicals, which served as more formal venues for literary debates. Fiction, then, became an important site for the battle over cultural authority, through which writers involved readers and critics in the process of legitimization of particular models of artistic identity.

Among the most popular artist types in this fiction was the Decadent, who was used in particular ways by writers in the struggle to assert a dominant definition of writer among many competing models. Over the next four chapters, I examine the role played by this fiction in the development of 'fictions' of Decadence from 1884 to just after the Wilde trials, looking also at the critical reception of these works and related literary debates. In their representations of Decadence, these fictions engaged in contemporary artistic debates about the purview of fiction, the function of the artist, gendered conceptions of artistic genius, and the qualities defining high and popular art.

Aestheticism, Naturalism, and the emergence of Decadence

From the point of view of writers exploring alternative models of artistic identity in the 1880s, Decadence came to represent a more effective counter-discourse to the popular fiction that they believed dominated the literary field than either Aestheticism or Naturalism. Aestheticism had been extremely controversial in the 1860s and 1870s, notably in the case of Swinburne's *Poems and Ballads* (1866), Robert Buchanan's 1871 attack on the 'fleshly school of poetry', and Pater's 1873 conclusion to *The Renaissance*. In this period, Aestheticism invoked hostility for its 'false feeling', 'morbid affectation', and 'spurious devotion to whatever is foreign, eccentric, archaic, or grotesque'.[3] By the 1880s, however, Aestheticism had been co-opted and commercialized by the middle class and was now more often the target of ridicule, as in Frank Burnand's *The Colonel* (1881), Gilbert and Sullivan's *Patience* (1881), and George Du Maurier's sketches for *Punch*. Even Oscar Wilde, Aestheticism's most high-profile proponent, abandoned the movement after coming under the influence of French Decadents in Paris in 1883. Soon his idealistic Aestheticism shaded over into the darker Aestheticism of Decadence and, rather than promoting the cult of beauty, he interested himself in the artificial, the perverse, and the exotic. In keeping with his new interests, Wilde abandoned his flamboyant Aesthetic dress for the dignified apparel of the Decadent dandy. Wilde's conversion to Decadence was a sure sign of Aestheticism's declining influence.

With Aestheticism on the decline, Naturalism became the new controversial movement. Though Naturalism had been a subject of debate in Britain since the 1870s, the debate intensified from 1884 onwards as translations of Emile Zola and other French Naturalists became available in Britain for the first time. These translations expanded the circulation of these writers in Britain beyond intellectuals to the larger public, causing anxieties about the pernicious influence of such literature on women, young persons, and the working class. Opponents of Naturalism included both popular writers and those among the élite.[4] They complained that though Naturalism professed to give a true and objective view of life, it gave an unbalanced view, focusing with unnecessary attention on the sordid and mean. They also objected to the high status the school held among writers who were attempting to bring elements of Naturalism to the English novel. Naturalism's opponents sought to undermine the movement's high art status by arguing, as Noble would about the Decadents, that Naturalists were motivated by monetary interests. Lang, for example, was cynical about Zola's scientific-based definition of art and the artist, insisting that 'M. Zola and his peers like to write on scandalous topics, because scandal brings notoriety and money'.[5]

Even the more avant-garde among the élite were dissatisfied with Naturalism, despite the fact that, in its exposure of middle-class hypocrisy and vice, it clearly affronted their opponents within and without the literary field. Unlike other opponents of Naturalism, however, these critics' objections were based on aesthetic rather than moral grounds. Wilde, for example, found Zola to be an ethical writer but a poor artist:

> his work is entirely wrong from beginning to end, and wrong not on the grounds of morals, but on the ground of art. From any ethical standpoint it is just what it should be. The author is perfectly truthful and describes things exactly as they happen. What more can any moralist desire? We have no sympathy with the moral indignation of our time against M. Zola. ... But from the standpoint of art, what can be said in favour of the author of *L'Assommoir, Nana*, and *Pot-Bouille*? Nothing. ... [M. Zola's characters] have their dreary vices and their drearier virtues. The record of their lives is absolutely without interest. Who cares what happens to them? In literature we require distinction, charm, beauty and imaginative power. We don't want to be harrowed and disgusted with an account of the doings of the lower orders.[6]

George Moore, a one-time proponent of Zola, who had once believed that 'if the [Naturalists] should catch favour in England the English tongue may be saved from dissolution',[7] also came to share Wilde's opinion, declaring that Zola had 'no style'.[8] Moore's fiction of the 1880s was largely an attempt to improve on Zola's method – a method he in many respects admired – by experimenting with the stylistic techniques of Walter Pater and J.-K. Huysmans. In so doing, Moore sought to develop an aestheticized Naturalism, the kind of writing that would eventually come to be labelled Decadent.

The Decadent Aesthete, aestheticized Naturalism, and Vernon Lee's *Miss Brown*

Popular writers, critics, and some among the literary élite responded swiftly to the development of Decadence, which seemed, to them, to embody the worst elements of Aestheticism and Naturalism. One of the earliest acknowledgements of the emerging Decadent type is Vernon Lee's *Miss Brown* (1884). As the product of a female writer with a relatively high status in the literary field of the day, the novel participates in the battle for cultural authority within this field. Lee, born Violet Paget (1856–1935), counted among her friends some of the period's most prominent writers and artists, including Henry James, Walter Pater, John Sargent, Oscar Wilde, and William Morris. Sensitive to the prejudice against women writers in the field at this time, Lee adopted her male pseudonym at the age of 21 because, she explained to a friend, 'I am sure no one reads a woman's writing on art, history, or aesthetics with anything but mitigated [*sic*] contempt'.[9] Male pseudonym in place, Lee successfully navigated within a predominantly male sector of the literary field as a kind of female Walter Pater, publishing critical studies on aesthetics, essays on medieval and Renaissance culture, historical sketches, and a historical novel.

In the context of these highbrow productions, *Miss Brown*, a topical three-volume novel satirizing Aestheticism, was clearly a departure from her usual work. As a woman writer successfully established among the élite, it is curious that Lee should decide to write a popular novel. Indeed, she had, three years earlier, dismissed a publisher's suggestion that she write such a novel with the response, 'even had I time, I should shrink from writing what would certainly be vastly inferior to my other work'.[10] More surprising, perhaps, than Lee's foray into novel-writing was her choice of subject matter. In writing a satirical *roman à clef* about the literary and artistic circle in which she circulated Lee was, in effect, biting the hand that fed her. In addition, her virulent critique of Aestheticism as a corrupt school, though prescient in its anticipation of Decadence, is, in other respects, dated. One reviewer, for example, wondered 'whether so much talent is not wasted in assailing a worn-out creed'.[11] But, while it is true that *Miss Brown* is an attack on Aestheticism, a movement that was indeed on the wane by 1884, the reviewer fails to note the degree to which the novel is also a critique of the newer creed of Naturalism. Indeed, the novel demonstrates the ways in which the interests of Naturalism and Aestheticism were coalescing in the period, resulting in the darker brand of Aestheticism that would become Decadence.

The novel represents an attempt to offer a corrective to the French Naturalist method, a method that, in some respects, Lee admires as an effective counter to the bland English novel. That Lee's intention was to offer a critique of Aestheticism through the medium of a modified Naturalism is suggested by her essay, 'A Dialogue on Novels', written just after she completed *Miss Brown*. In this essay, Baldwin, a mouthpiece for Lee's views, attacks the French Naturalist novel for its 'shamelessness' and the English novel for its 'timidity'.[12] In arguing for freedom of subject matter and for the necessity of 'counterbalanc[ing]' the 'presentation of remarkable evil' with the 'presentation of remarkable good', Baldwin endorses fiction that draws on the best elements of the French and the English novel.[13] Counterbalancing good with bad in the presentation of evil, *Miss Brown* was Lee's attempt to produce the 'wholesome' novel described by Baldwin – a novel that 'would maintain our power of taking exception, of protesting, of hating' the vices portrayed in it.[14]

Like many among the élite who took up the writer as a subject for fiction, Lee was responding to the failure of Aestheticism to account for the role of the artist in the changing social and literary field. Her sense of the problem, however, differed from that of many of her peers. While Lee was certainly no Mrs Grundy, she did deplore the lack of ethical responsibility on the part of many among the élite. Furthermore, as a woman among this élite, she resisted the objectification of women that she regarded as an inherent part of the Aesthetic and emerging Decadent creed. In *Miss Brown*, Lee uses the figure of the Decadent writer, Walter Hamlin, to critique both the misogyny of the emerging school and its lack of ethical responsibility. She contrasts this Decadent Aestheticism with the ethical Aestheticism of the female protagonist, Anne Brown, an Aestheticism that, borrowing from Naturalism, tells the truth about life but does so, not in a demoralizing manner, but in a way that inspires hope and encourages change. In so doing, Lee undermines the cultural authority of the Decadent artist, endorsing instead the legitimacy of the socially engaged and ethically responsible writer. Ultimately, then, Lee promoted what was seen by many of her élite male peers as a feminized middle-class form of Aestheticism and she did so in the very medium they most associated with the middle-class female readership they deplored – the three-volume topical novel.

In her portrayal of Hamlin, Lee acknowledges the importance of social factors in fostering the Decadent sensibility – the growing power of the business middle class and the rise of professionalism. Hamlin's exposure to and reliance on bourgeois middle-class society breeds in him a desire to retreat from the world into an aesthetic utopia: 'The world is getting uglier and uglier outside us; we must, out of the materials bequeathed us by our former generations, and with the help of our fancy, build for ourselves a little world within the world, a world of beauty, where we may live with our friends and keep alive whatever small sense of beauty and nobility still remains to us.'[15] Specifically, Hamlin's Decadent misanthropy is a product of his disgust with the commodification of Aestheticism by an affluent bourgeois middle-class. Under this class's patronage, Aestheticism, he feels, has become a 'clique-and-shop shoddy aestheticism'.[16] He is appalled at the notion of 'professional' poetry and art because it puts artists at the service of the middle class and turns out art as if out of an 'aesthetic factory'.[17] And though he insists on his difference from 'professional artists' – 'those pen-and-pencil driving men of genius, those reviewer-poets and clerk-poets, those once-a-week-studio-receiving painters',[18] he is also dependent on middle-class patronage: 'That's the misfortune of London, that a lot of vulgar creatures, merely because they buy our pictures and give dinners, have come and invaded our set, showing us, like so many wild beasts, to the fashionable world.'[19] Increasingly disdainful of fashionable middle-class life, Hamlin, like his real-life counterparts, attempts to distance himself from it. His writing of Decadent poetry, poetry that Anne describes as 'horrible' in 'subject and tone', signifies his rebellion against middle-class values.[20] In addition, his increasingly Decadent lifestyle, involving drinking, drug-taking, and sexual licentiousness, also signals his break from both the middle class and from the conservative 'old-fashioned, long-established aesthetes' who cater to this class.[21] Hamlin's rebellion against the middle-class Aesthetic circle and his turn towards Decadence is further marked by his relationship with the aristocratic Madame Elaguine. Through her, Hamlin begins to associate with a 'more mystical and Bohemian' crowd.[22] Hamlin's deliberately provocative poetry and his bohemian and aristocratic Decadent lifestyle serve for him as markers of distinction that legitimate his cultural authority as an artist in ways that anticipate similar modes of legitimization adopted by 1890s Decadents.

If Lee is prescient about the emergence of Decadence from Aestheticism in *Miss Brown*, she also anticipates the objections of later women writers including Sarah Grand and Marie Corelli, whose counter-Decadent works are discussed in the next chapter, as well as those of writers such as George Egerton and Ada Leverson, whose relationship to Decadence was complicated by their involvement with the Decadent male literary élite. Lee, along with some of these women writers, was attracted to the tenets of Aestheticism even as she tried to correct its more problematic aspects. Many of these women did not object so much to the subject matter taken up in Aestheticism and Decadence. After all, they, too, were seeking ways to modernize the rather prudish English novel. What they did object to in Aestheticism and Decadence was the priority given to form over matter and the divorce of the aesthetic from social concerns. In *Miss Brown*, for example, Lee exposes the blindness of the Aesthete and the Decadent to the commodifying nature of their own aesthetic, particularly in relation to women. Thus, Hamlin gazes upon Anne acquisitively when he first meets her in what Margaret Stetz has described as 'a form of masculine connoisseurship dependent on silent and passive female spectacles'.[23] Hamlin sees only the surface of Anne Brown, objectifying her in a manner akin to Pater's famous account of the Mona Lisa or to that of a pre-Raphaelite 'stunner'. To him, she is 'a beautiful and sombre idol of the heathen', a 'strange type, neither Latin nor Greek, but with something of Jewish and something of Ethiopian', like one of the 'mournful and sullen heads of Michaelangelo'.[24]

In critiquing Hamlin's act of masculine connoisseurship, Lee's narrative continually juxtaposes moments of fantasy with reality. In the moment described above, Hamlin is brought down from his exotic reverie by Anne's declaration that she is English.[25] Though Anne is actually half Italian and half Scottish, her insistence on her Englishness more effectively explodes Hamlin's fantasy. Knowledge of Anne's Englishness 'spoils the effect' for Hamlin, as does any information about her 'intellectual' or 'moral' qualities.[26] Ultimately, Hamlin decides to invest in her, a decision that the narrator equates with the commodification of Anne: 'He had determined on educating, wooing, and marrying a woman like what Anne Brown seemed to be, as a man might determine to buy a house in a particular fishing or hunting district.'[27] In his objectification of Anne, Hamlin misses that which is far more valuable than her beautiful form – her rich inner life or what the narrator calls her 'life-poem'.[28] In juxtaposing Hamlin's objectification of Anne with the narrator's insistence that her beauty lies within, Lee participates, Stetz argues, in a feminist aesthetic project in which women writers attempted 'to rescue the worship of beauty ... from its association with the exploitation of women as nothing more than beautiful "occasions" for masculine discovery, theorizing, and reverie'.[29]

In another critique of Hamlin's Decadent Aestheticism, the narrative again juxtaposes 'the real' with the Aesthete's fantasy, providing contrasting ideas of the beautiful. This time the critique is socialist and humanist rather than feminist. When Anne tells Hamlin about his tenants' cramped quarters and the degradation and sin that living in such conditions leads them to, Hamlin, in typically Decadent fashion, sees the situation as one fascinating for the subject of a beautiful poem. Anne's suggestion that he might better the tenants' lives by setting up a factory to give them work and 'ideas of decent living' horrifies him with its practical realism.[30] In his mind, a factory would 'befoul all that pure and exquisite country with smoke and machine refuse'.[31] Anne's feminist and socialist Aestheticism, insists on the connection between the aesthetic, the beautiful, and the social. In this respect, Anne's views align her with the 'missionary Aesthetes' of the real-life Kyrle Society, which followed the ideals of William Morris. Indeed, Anne admires Morris and Ruskin, whose 'generosity of aspiration' suggests to her that Aestheticism is not incompatible with humanitarian impulses.[32]

In representing the rift in the Aesthetic school between a humanitarian and a degenerate Aestheticism, Lee, as I have said, anticipates the emergence of Decadence. Though neither Lee nor others within the literary field had yet employed the term 'Decadent' to describe this manifestation of Aestheticism, many critics noted that Aestheticism was in a process of transformation. In discussions of this new form of Aestheticism, critics borrowed from the critical discourse against Naturalism. Harry Quilter, for example, described it as the dead carcase' [sic] of the 'pure', 'original', and 'healthy' Pre-Raphaelitism and as a 'morbid and sickly' school, terms that would soon come to signify Decadence.[33] Similarly, Cosmo Monkhouse distinguished between the new and old Aestheticism, contrasting those 'who have deemed it glory to indulge in nasty dreams, and to be credited with thoughts and actions of which they should be ashamed' with those for whom 'art and poetry ... has been food instead of poison'.[34] Though at this point, both types of artist are associated with Aestheticism, clearly Quilter and Monkhouse intend to differentiate those they perceive as artistically and culturally legitimate from those they regard as illegitimate. Similarly, in valorizing Anne's feminized missionary Aestheticism over Hamlin's increasingly anti-social and immoral Decadent Aestheticism, Lee grants cultural and artistic legitimacy to those of the Aesthetic school who bring the aesthetic and the moral into meaningful relation.

The negative reception of *Miss Brown* reveals the cost Lee paid in terms of her own struggle for cultural legitimacy in her critique of a Decadent Aestheticism. While few doubted the existence of the Decadent type of Aesthete she described, many took offence at the manner in which she framed her critique. For those familiar with Lee's highbrow work, *Miss Brown* represented a case of literary slumming, undermining her claims to cultural authority. Henry James, for example, imagined that Lee's critique of Aestheticism would be something like his own in *The Portrait of a Lady* (1881) and he eagerly awaited what he believed would be a 'very radical and aesthetic' novel.[35] Later, he was disappointed to find it 'very bad, *strangely* inferior to her other writing' and 'without form as art'.[36] And, whereas Lee's other work put her on a par with the much-respected Walter Pater, *Miss Brown*, in Monkhouse's opinion, reduced her to the level of the popular female novelist: 'Whatever made you write about such beastly people, do you want to rival Ouida?'[37] George Moore shared this view, including *Miss Brown* in an unpublished version of 'Literature at Nurse' as an example of the deplorable fiction endorsed by circulating libraries and favoured by middle-class women readers.[38]

For many of her peers, Lee's work failed as art because it betrayed the high artistic principles that would accord it status as a masterpiece. James believed that the novel lacked the 'delicacy or fineness' to make it an effective satire.[39] At the same time, it failed as a realist novel because, as he told Lee, '*life* is less criminal, less obnoxious, less objectionable, less crude, more *bon enfant*, more mixed and casual, and even in its most offensive manifestations, more *pardonable*, than the unholy circle with which you have surrounded your heroine'.[40] In the same letter, he also objected to Lee's over-emphasis on moral issues and her lack of attention to form. Lee had 'appealed', he said,

> too much to ... the intelligence, the moral sense and experience of the reader; and too little to 2 or 3 others – the plastic, visual, formal – perhaps you have been too much in a moral passion. That has put certain exaggerations, overstatements, *grossissements*, insistences wanting in tact, into your head. Cool first – write afterwards. Morality is hot – but art is icy. ... Write another novel. ... Be, in it, more piously plastic, more devoted to *composition* – and less moral.[41]

James's discomfort with the 'moral passion' of the novel, his insistence on the 'iciness' of art, and his prioritization of formal elements over 'moral' ones, are representative of the dominant aesthetic views of the élite in this period and the high Modernist aesthetic more generally. The writer with whom Lee had been disparagingly compared by Monkhouse – popular novelist and favourite of the circulating library, Ouida – did not share these views, however. She loved *Miss Brown* and found it realistic: 'I think the character of the hero quite possible. ... The *Athenaeum* seems to live in such a circle of common-place goody-goodies that every character such as one meets in the big world seems impossible.'[42] And, though 'The book [gave her] the impression of having been written at a galop [*sic*]', she believed that 'this [was] better than weeding and pruning till all flavour is gone'.[43]

The discrepancy between the views of Ouida and James over realism and form shows not only how ideas about literary value differed depending on one's status as popular or élite writer, but also how gender figured in this determination. James's claim that Lee's writing was too 'hot' and 'morally passionate', was a charge frequently made against women writers in this period as the male-dominated élite sought to exclude women's writing from the domain of high art. By insisting on the priority of formal elements and disciplined writing and on the inappropriateness of moral concerns, male writers denied cultural legitimacy to women writers, many of whom had less education and formal training than men and were more interested in the novel as a vehicle for social reform and moral edification.

For James, as we have seen, the most significant aspect of Lee's failure to create a truly artistic work lay in her moralistic stance. From the point of view of the élite, Lee's over-zealous 'moral passion' marked her novel as fodder for the circulating library. The conflicting views of James and Lee over the place of morality and didacticism in art was part of a broader literary debate in the period and formed one of the central oppositions in the competing claims of writers for cultural authority. In this debate, endorsers of the moral and ethical responsibilities of fiction tended to occupy positions within the realm of the popular and/or to be women writers, whereas those who advocated art-for-art's-sake principles were generally men within the literary élite. Lee's advocacy of moral and ethical literature is complicated, however. She cannot so easily be accused of the kind of Mrs Grundyism that purists like James associated with writers who believed that fiction should have a conscious moral purpose. Lee, as I have argued, sought to mediate between two extreme positions in her attempt to write a modern realistic novel – between the overly frank French novel and the too reticent English novel. In the end, after experiencing much negative feedback, Lee was convinced that she had failed, a failure she reflected on in 'A Dialogue on Novels'. The mediation she had attempted was impossible, impossible because, as her mouthpiece Baldwin says in what amounts to a summary of the criticism against *Miss Brown*, such a novel would only be 'laughed at as stuff for schoolgirls by my French and Italian friends, and howled down as unfit for family-reading by my own country people'.[44] James's disdain for Lee's 'moral passion' was equivalent to the reactions of Baldwin's Italian and French friends, while the reaction of Monkhouse, who called the novel 'very nasty',[45] and the *Spectator*, which found it 'repulsive',[46] accorded with Baldwin's anticipation of the views of the English. Achieving the balance between representing vice and writing with a moral intention would continue to be a difficult task for writers attempting to extend the purview of British fiction in the 1880s and 1890s. Sometimes, as in the case of Lee, writers genuinely believed in the moral function of literature. In other cases, however, writers compromised, obeying the moral dictates of the British Matron, Mrs Grundy, and the circulating libraries in order to get their work in print, struggling all the while to push the limits of representation in fiction.

George Moore's ur-texts of Decadence: *Confessions of a Young Man* and *Mike Fletcher*

George Moore, who regarded Lee's *Miss Brown* as typical fodder for the circulating libraries, presented a very different view of the Decadent type in *Confessions of a Young Man* (1888), in which he attempted to bring French influence to bear on the British novel. Moore holds an important place in the cultural history of British Decadence – one might even call him the father of British Decadence – though his role in this history is often overlooked.[47] Moore himself sought to write himself out of this history by excluding some of the products of his Decadent years from his collected works compiled in the 1920s and by revising and reframing *Confessions* and other works throughout his career in what amounted to a highly mediated version of his literary activities in the 1880s.

Moore, however, was steeped in French Decadence, more so than many of his contemporaries, including Wilde, who has hitherto been credited with bringing Decadence to England. As Susan Dick notes in her introduction to

Confessions, Moore was particularly attracted to the Decadent aspects of nineteenth-century French literature – 'the paganism and aestheticism of Gautier, the decadence and cynicism of Baudelaire, the elitism of the symbolists, the precision and concreteness of Parnassian verse, and the uninhibited subject matter enjoyed by the Impressionists and naturalists'.[48] Furthermore, he was acquainted with a wide range of French Decadents, including Théophile Gautier, Charles Baudelaire, Théodore de Banville, François Coppée, Catulle Mendès, Paul Verlaine, Stéphane Mallarmé, Philippe-Auguste Villiers de l'Isle Adam, Arthur Rimbaud, Gustave Kahn, and J.-K. Huysmans. Moore was the first to introduce French Decadence to the English reading public in an 1884 review of J.-K. Huysmans's *A Rebours* and in an article entitled 'Les Decadents' in the *Court and Society Review* in 1887. At the same time, he published two volumes of Decadent poetry – *Flowers of Passion* (1878) and *Pagan Poems* (1881) – and a number of what he called 'aesthetic novels',[49] including the 'purely Decadent'[50] *Mike Fletcher* (1889). Finally, Moore's *Confessions of a Young Man* was highly influential in the development of the Decadent type in literature and served for his younger contemporaries as 'an index to many of the major artistic movements in France and England in the late nineteenth century'.[51] Indeed, Gleeson White of the *Artist and Journal of Home Culture*, a magazine which did much to promote Decadence, said of *Confessions*, 'if there was ever a volume worthy of study by an artist it is this'.[52] And clearly, Decadents of the younger generation did study it. Symons described Moore's novels of the 1880s – *Mike Fletcher, Confessions of a Young Man*, and *A Mere Accident* – as 'entertaining, realistic, and Decadent; and certainly founded on modern French fiction'.[53] Le Gallienne declared his 'youthful enthusiasm' for Moore, while Hichens called Moore 'one of the greatest writers of the time'.[54] Machen, too, enjoyed Moore's Decadent fiction of the 1880s.[55] Symons, Le Gallienne, Machen, and Hichens were precisely the kind of young men being hailed by the protagonist in the closing pages of *Confessions*, a section which, despite the satiric tone of much of the novel, is sincere in its appeal to the younger generation to 'be young as I was' and to 'love youth as I did'.[56]

Moore struggled as a writer in the 1880s. He had difficulty finding publishers for his work and, once published, he sometimes had trouble getting it circulated. The subject matter of his early novels and his association with the notorious Vizetelly, the publisher jailed for issuing Zola translations, were regarded with distaste by the circulating libraries, which banned two of his pre-*Confessions* novels. For the publication of *Confessions*, Moore turned to a progressive publisher, Swan Sonnenschein, who did not rely on the circulating-library market, so that he might 'escape the total censorship' of the libraries.[57] Despite the firm's publication of the controversial writings of Karl Marx, George Bernard Shaw, and Edward Carpenter, Swan Sonnenschein was a respectable house, specializing in scholarly works of philosophy and social science and publishing little fiction. But while William Swan

Sonnenschein was, as Moore biographer Adrian Frazier notes, a 'man of wide culture, who especially liked to publish works of philosophy and advanced socialism', his partners, Hubert Wigram – a High Churchman – and Walter Sichel – a Tory who would later apply for the post of stage censor – were far more conservative.[58] Consequently, Moore was subject to some degree of censorship by the firm with Wigram insisting on the omission of obscenities from the novel. Sichel considered the novel acceptable enough, with some censoring, to be serialized in the firm's 'family' magazine, *Time*, where it ran from July to November 1887. When the novel came out in book form, however, it shocked and offended many. Booksellers responded adversely to Moore's name according to Sonnenschein's travellers – 'Wouldn't have his book in my establishment, for any consideration' – and Sonnenschein anticipated that the circulating libraries would ban the novel.[59]

Moore's representation of the emerging Decadent type in *Confessions* contrasts sharply with Lee's. Whereas Lee's representation functioned as a critique of certain negative tendencies in the development of Aestheticism, *Confessions* celebrates the emergence of a defiant oppositional culture. Perhaps most significantly, where Lee operates in the low cultural sphere of the three-volume popular novel with its generic conventions, Moore rejects this format. Instead, he experiments with form and genre, writing a one-volume novel that is part *künstlerroman*, part confessional novel in an effort to assert his literary and cultural authority. The *künstlerroman* originated in the Romantic period, a period which idealized the artist and man of genius. It was a form well-suited, then, to those among the *fin-de-siècle* literary élite who wanted to assert their authority in the face of a society whose commercial ethos signalled, to their minds, a disrespect for the arts. Like Rousseau's Romantic-era *Confessions*, Moore's novel serves ultimately as a self-vindication and valorizes the writer-protagonist's individualism and rebelliousness. Moore, however, denied Rousseau's influence in the 1917 preface, preferring to view the novel as a refiguring of Augustine's *Confessions*.[60] Rather than Augustine's 'god-tortured soul', however, Moore offered his readers an account of an 'art-tortured soul',[61] a focus that emphasized the sacred nature of art to the Aesthetes and Decadents.

Based on Moore's experiences in Paris in the 1870s and influenced by J.-K. Huysmans's *A Rebours* (1884), the novel traces the development of Edward Dayne (who becomes 'George Moore' from the second edition on)[62] from his childhood in Ireland through his artistic apprenticeship in Paris to his beginnings as a literary man in London. In form, the novel is a loosely constructed narrative consisting of impressions, opinions, passions, enthusiasms, art and literary criticism, poems, and invective social commentary – what David Weir calls 'a complete record of Decadent tastes [and of the] sensibility of a young man living in a period of literary ferment and experimentation'.[63] In Dayne, Moore establishes the key elements of the Decadent artist that would be exploited by the writers in the 1890s. His 'young man',

Madeleine Cazamian argues, was a prototype for characterizations of the Decadent in Wilde's *Dorian Gray*, Le Gallienne's *Book-Bills of Narcissus*, Machen's *Hill of Dreams*, Hichens's *Green Carnation*, and G. S. Street's *Autobiography of a Boy*.[64]

Moore's narrative is the story of the 'soul' of this type of artist and begins with the words 'My soul'.[65] What follows is a very personal, even intimate, laying bare of Dayne's soul to his readers. Ironically, however, Dayne's exposure of his authentic self seems only to undermine the notion that there is such a thing. Dayne is changeable and contradictory, his enthusiasms of one moment are distasteful to him the next as in his interests in Shelley and Zola. This very 'natural' representation of the vagaries of human character has the effect of a pose. In *Confessions*, there is no authentic self beyond the moment and, therefore, no seamless and consistent narrative. Instead the narrative shifts and digresses, with abrupt changes in tone and style – from discursive narration to evocative and moody description to aggressive rantings. Personal narrative is juxtaposed with literary and artistic criticism, social commentary, and lengthy quotations from the works of French authors. Moore even experiments with interior monologue in *Confessions*, a form he learned from reading Edouard Dujardin, and which he felt was an effective medium for representing the 'daily life of the soul'.[66] In these respects, the narrative structure reflects the restless energy of the Decadent who is, in Pater's terms, continually 'testing new opinions and courting new impressions'[67] in their efforts to rid themselves of ennui. The narrative, then, is structured differently than traditional plot-driven novels. As a narrative of 'the soul' of an artist, the story is propelled forward not so much by action as by what Dayne calls 'echo-auguries', that lead to his discovery of influential writers, writers whose effects on him are then analysed in detail. Long descriptive passages that seem to exist for their own sake are typical of Decadent texts and constitute one of the ways that Decadence breaks down or disrupts traditional narrative form.[68] In this case, however, these long descriptive passages about Dayne's reading actually propel the narrative in that they launch him into the next phase of his life. At the same time, Dayne's reading functions as a way of reading character in a novel with little dialogue or character interaction.

As a character, Dayne represents the values and ideals of the Decadent type that emerged from the rift between the professional intellectuals and the business middle class as artists began to search for alternatives to the Aestheticism that had been appropriated by the middle class. Dayne covers the full spectrum of attitudes held by those who rebelled against the middle class in the social sphere and against popular writers in the literary field. He decries universal education, the mediocrity of the new reading public, the detrimental effect of women readers on the state of English literature, the commercialization of literature, and the capitulation of British writers to the literary marketplace and to the tastes of bourgeois readers. He discredits modern-day journalism and valorizes forms of art and literature that were regarded in England as noxious and corrupting. He has an 'appetite for the strange, abnormal and unhealthy in art',[69] displays exotic and outré tastes in interior decoration, rails against middle-class respectability,[70] and idealizes martyr-artists.[71] In addition, he adopts the deliberately provocative stance of the Decadent artist in addressing the *'hypocrite lecteur'*.[72] To his other audience, however, the audience idealized by Decadents as the 'select few', represented in the final pages of *Confessions* as the 'young men' to whom Dayne, now in his mid-thirties, is yielding his place, he proposes an alternative form of education, a Paterian ideal of self-culture and self-education.[73]

Dayne is unlike his real-life counterparts, however, insofar as he is an idealized fictional reflection of them, one who is not subject to the economic realities of the literary market. He is independently wealthy and therefore, as he tells the reader, 'it was not incumbent upon me to live by my pen'.[74] He can afford to take risks in his literary pursuits, whereas his real-life counterparts often had to make compromises, involving themselves in the commercial literary marketplace. Even Moore, despite his control of the family estate, was in this situation, relying for a living on the sales of his works in the 1880s. Moore's insistence on Dayne's (and consequently his own) financial independence was strategic, as Dick notes, serving to emphasize 'the purity of his interest in literature'.[75] Such fictional constructions of the audacious, risk-taking writer helped to perpetuate the image of the defiant artist unanswerable to bourgeois middle-class culture by concealing the economic realities that made Decadent writers more dependent on this class than they cared to admit. Fictional representations of the uncompromising writer were instrumental in establishing the cultural superiority of the artist figure vis-à-vis the middle class and of the literary superiority of this type over other writers who either catered to the middle class or who were inferior artists.

Despite the importance of *Confessions* in establishing a prototype for fictional representations of the Decadent, most critics have tended to gloss over its relationship to Decadence and little attention has been paid to the effect of Moore's work in its immediate social context. Holbrook Jackson and Richard Cave disavow the novel's Decadent status, arguing that Moore merely 'played at Decadence' and that he intended *Confessions* to be a satire.[76] It is true that Moore himself called the book a satire in a letter to Edouard Dujardin in which he complained that the French translation made the protagonist 'deadly serious' where 'In English I have my tongue in my cheek.'[77] But Moore cannot help but maintain an ironic distance from his protagonist, who represents his younger, foolish self. Overall, however, the novel is hardly an out-and-out satire of the type that Dayne represents. The strongest criticisms are directed against middle-class Victorian society and, in these views, the reader is meant to sympathize with Dayne, while recognizing that he represents these views in an audacious and provocative manner. Cave, however, insists that Moore is 'far removed from shocking us' and that while Dayne may be 'pretentious and naughty ... his exaggerations do not disturb us, they move us merely to laughter'.[78] Yet this reaction is surely that of a modern-day reader, one well-versed in the stereotype that Moore describes. This type would not become stereotypical until well after Moore wrote his novel. If *Confessions* was meant to be a satire, it could not be a very effective one since the type of artist Dayne represents was only just emerging and, for satire to work, the type has to be a widely recognizable one.

At the same time, however, it can be argued that the novel, and indeed Decadence more broadly, problematizes models of satire that characterize it as a conservative mode or genre. Decadent writers such as Moore and Wilde demonstrate that satire, even self-satire, could function well as a radical counter-discourse. In the context of an earnest and hard-working bourgeois culture, the most successful revenge against the dominant middle-class's insistence on earnestness and industry was, as Wilde most famously demonstrated, to characterize oneself as not taking oneself seriously – *especially* in matters where seriousness should be paramount, as when Moore declares that one great work of art is worth the deaths of millions.[79] This statement is at once an instance of Moore with 'his tongue in his cheek' and a deliberate provocation to Victorian moral values.

However Moore himself understood his novel, it was certainly not its satire that garnered attention in its immediate social and historical context. Few, apart from Walter Pater, remarked on the novel's satiric elements and, as Robert Langenfeld argues, it is important to note that Pater called it 'satiric' and not a satire, a significant distinction.[80] Far from seeing *Confessions* as a work that censured folly and vice, Pater was greatly disturbed by what he called the 'morally ... questionable shape' of the novel.[81] Like Pater, reviewers of the novel found other elements more important than its satiric qualities. In fact, most took the novel and Dayne very seriously. Even as it was being serialized in *Time, Confessions* received attention for its innovativeness. *Vanity Fair*, for example, attributed to Moore the 'invent[ion]' of 'a new style' which was at once 'personal', 'attractive', and 'provoking' and described the novel as a 'brilliant piece of rottenness'.[82] The reviewer for the *Hawk*, a magazine that Adrian Frazier identifies as being targeted towards 'youthful, caddish, hyper-male' types,[83] praised the uniqueness of Moore's style.[84] This reviewer further claimed that the book contained 'the hardest, most audacious, most rigid thinking that our generation has seen' and described Moore as a writer unparalleled in English prose.[85] *Confessions* appealed not only to the manly, caddish readership of the *Hawk*, however. It also received praise in a journal with a vastly different audience from that of the *Hawk* – the *Artist and Journal of Home Culture*. This magazine appealed both to artists, particularly Aesthetes and Decadents, but also, as Laurel Brake has argued, to a community of 'gay' readers who functioned as an 'important backup to its dominant address to ... "artist" readers'.[86] Gleeson White, a reviewer for the *Artist*, extolled the novel as a work of 'Modern

Art', that 'swept away' the 'neatly balanced theories and painfully built-up formulas of knowledge' of Victorianism, replacing them with 'a new standard of excellence ... with its rules couched in a tongue strangely unfamiliar'.[87]

White's reference to Moore's expression of ideas in 'a tongue strangely unfamiliar' echoes many of the reviewers' feelings about the novel and, more particularly, about Dayne. To them, Dayne represented a new type of artist with new ideals and values, very unlike the familiar figure of the Aesthete. Far from viewing these ideas as satirical, reviewers found them fresh and exciting. In their descriptions of Dayne, they are clearly searching for words to describe this apparently new type. When the novel was published, the terms 'Decadent' and 'Decadence' had not yet come into common usage and were still used to refer to the work of specific French writers. It is clear, however, from the reviews and from the ensuing controversy that a term for this new breed of writer was becoming necessary. The term 'Aesthete' was clearly not adequate and was not used at all by reviewers. The critic for the *Athenaeum*, for example, wrote a scathing review in which he characterized Dayne broadly as 'a disagreeable young man, of bad education and vicious habits, with a passion for literary garbage'.[88] William Sharp attempted a more precise definition, describing Dayne as 'a young man of the "pure Pagan" kind' and as a ' "sensualist," not in its derogatory, but in its actual sense',[89] descriptions that recall Pater's *Renaissance* with its recurring discussion of pagan impulses in the human spirit and the hedonistic doctrine of its 'Conclusion'. *Vanity Fair* also came nearer the mark, describing Dayne as 'a morbid fellow'.[90] At the height of the Decadent controversy in the 1890s, the term 'morbid' would become synonymous with Decadence.

Already, in the negative reviews of the novel, the beginnings of what would come to constitute a counter-discourse to Decadence are emerging. This counter-discourse was instrumental in undermining the cultural authority of Decadents and was an integral part of counter-Decadent constructions of them. Such constructions upheld the status quo both socially and in literary terms and attacked the Decadent type on these terms. Hence, the *Athenaeum* critic's view that the self-education represented in the novel is simply 'bad education' and that the protagonist's supposedly refined literary tastes are, in fact, 'garbage'. The most stringent attack on Moore and, more particularly, on the artist type he represented, however, was launched by Robert Buchanan a year later in 1889. Buchanan's attack appeared in the *Universal Review*, a periodical edited by Harry Quilter.[91] Buchanan and Quilter were both strident opponents of art-for-art's-sake tendencies in art and literature. Quilter penned diatribes against Aestheticism and Decadence in 1880 and 1895 respectively, even using the same title for both articles, an indication of his belief in the connection between the two movements. For his part, Buchanan had achieved notoriety for a longstanding battle with Swinburne and Rossetti, whom he dubbed 'the fleshly school of poetry'.

In Moore, and other proponents of realism, the belligerent Buchanan found a new target for his energies. His article against this trend, 'The Modern Young Man as Critic', appeared just after *Confessions* went into its second edition, an edition notable for Moore's changing of the name of his protagonist from Dayne to Moore. In the article, Buchanan categorizes the various types of 'Modern Young Man'. In addition to Moore, who is cast as 'the Bank-Holiday Young Man', Buchanan attacks Henry James (the 'superfine young man'), Paul Bourget (the 'detrimental young man'), Guy de Maupassant (the 'olfactory young man'), and William Archer (the 'young man in a cheap literary suit'). Though these men differed in many respects in their approach to modernizing literature and drama and not all were strictly 'Decadent', Buchanan noted in them the defining features that would come to characterize the Decadent, notably pessimism, cynicism, and an interest in Realism and '*Art pour Art*'.[92]

Buchanan's description of Moore as the 'Bank-Holiday Young Man' and as ''Arry', 'the Cockney Bohemian of the Latin Quarter' may seem strange given Moore's real class position as member of the upper class.[93] The description, however, speaks powerfully to the way in which, in its day, Decadence appeared to disturb class distinctions. 'Arry was a familiar music hall figure, a favoured haunt of Decadents. The music hall itself also disturbed class boundaries, even though it was becoming a more mainstream institution in this period. For the Decadents, the music hall was a place where the aristocratic and working-class culture they appropriated in their self-fashioning came together. Real and would-be aristocrats mingled in the hall, the would-bes counting among them both Decadents and working-class dandies or toffs. As Peter Bailey explains, '[The music hall] was a perfect setting for the aspirant swell, the young clerk from the latchkey class, decked out in all the apparatus of the toff, graduating from the protective cluster of his own kind at the side bar to the public glory of a seat at the singer's table with a personal spittoon, glass-bottomed tankard and welcoming nod from the chairman.'[94] This is the figure with whom Buchanan associates Moore. It is easy to see how this conflation might be made given the Decadents' propensity for extravagant dress and the shared interests of Decadents and working-class dandies in the music hall, sporting, drinking, and love-making, interests Buchanan characterizes as 'pipes and beer', 'indecency, horseplay, the jolly Bank Holiday and all its concomitant delights'.[95] In associating Moore with the working-class dandy, Buchanan undermines the Decadent ideal of self-culture, claiming that far from being a cultivated intellectual, Moore is merely a 'confused, ill-balanced' person.[96]

Buchanan's association of Moore with working-class culture would be taken up by future opponents of Decadence as would the medical and gendered discourses he employs in the article. These discourses characterized a number of attacks against literature in the 1880s and 1890s including those against Zolaism, Ibsenism, and pernicious literature, but they would be most finely honed in the attacks on Decadence in the 1890s. In anticipation of the discourse of degeneration that would be used against the Decadents, Buchanan claims that the 'modern young man' lacks 'moral health' and, in hereditary terms, he represents the 'gradual process of deterioration' of a literary genealogy that has resulted in 'an exhausted breed'.[97] He even goes so far as to draw an analogy between these writers and Jack the Ripper in terms of their adherence to the creed of pessimism and their treatment of women, whether literal or literary.[98]

Buchanan's critique of the 'modern young man' in gendered terms centres on this relationship to women. For Buchanan, the 'modern young man's' brutal treatment of women is a sign of his lack of 'virility' or 'manly vigour'.[99] Though charges of 'unmanliness' or 'effeminacy' have often been read as a calling into question of the sexual orientation of Decadents, Alan Sinfield, in an examination of changing notions of effeminacy in modern culture, has convincingly argued that we must be careful about how we interpret such charges, noting that, before the Wilde trial, effeminacy connoted excessive sexual attachment to women, aristocratic idleness, emotionality, or general debauchery.[100] To understand how radically some notions of manliness have changed, consider that what for Buchanan is 'unmanly' in Moore is what we might now think of as 'macho' behaviour or, what Adrian Frazier calls Moore's 'hyper-male' style, the 'ugly masculinity of the caddish club'.[101] Buchanan explains his view of manliness in response to an editorial on his article that appeared in the *Daily Telegraph*:

> One of my strongest contentions against the Modern Young Man as Critic ... is that, thanks to him ... Chivalry is fast becoming forgotten; that the old faith in the purity of womanhood, which once made men heroic, is being fast exchanged for an utter disbelief in all feminine ideals whatsoever. ... the Pessimist of To-day ... pollutes the tabernacle of woman's soul. He frankly despises, and persistently depreciates, what was once a temple where all strong men, all men who were sons, husbands, or fathers, might meet and pray.[102]

Buchanan's complex sense of unmanliness hinges on a man's relation to a woman. To be unmanly is to fall away from one's traditional chivalric role towards women, to be weak where a strong man would uphold his duty. It is this sense of unmanliness that Buchanan charges the otherwise 'hyper-male' and 'caddish' Moore with and not unmanliness with implications of same-sex desire, a notion of unmanliness that would come to be associated with Decadence after the Wilde trials.

Despite Buchanan's claim that the public was growing weary of the 'modern young man' who, he claimed, was 'fast becoming a public bore',[103] the type of Decadent young artist that Moore introduced would reappear in many different guises through the 1890s. Moore himself returned to the type in

Mike Fletcher (1889). This novel not only represents the Decadent artist but is also an early example of a British Decadent novel. Unsurprisingly, Moore had difficulty getting the novel published. Though Swan Sonnenschein considered it for serialization in *Time* as well as for publication in book form, it was rejected after the Vizetelly trial in May 1889, a trial which demonstrated the power that the National Vigilance Association had in preventing what it regarded as 'obscene' works from circulating. Reacting to the scandal, Sonnenschein advised Moore, 'burn your new [manuscript]. If you intend to write for the public in the future, you will never repent it.'[104] Moore eventually found a publisher for *Mike Fletcher* in Ward and Downey, a firm that specialized 'mainly in "Irish humour" and romantic Irish fiction', but which was always eager to help struggling Irish artists.[105]

The novel centres on Fletcher, a writer and journalist who works for the *Pilgrim*,[106] a magazine that, in Moore's characterization, upholds the anti-bourgeois values of the Decadent: 'Consider[ing] as worthless all that the world held in estimation, and ... laud[ing] as best all that the world had agreed to discard', the *Pilgrim* promoted the genius of obscure Latin writers and Renaissance painters, the divinity of the bar-room and the music-hall, 'the genius of courtesans', and 'the folly of education'.[107] Fletcher's Schopenhauerian Decadent literary productions include a poem about Adam and Eve at the end of the world – in which Adam, refusing to bring forth another race of doomed men into the world, resists the temptations of Eve – and a projected play about John the Baptist and Jesus featuring Salomé.[108] This novel, however, unlike *Confessions*, focuses less on the trials and tribulations of the Decadent in the face of a commercialized literary sphere than it does on the Decadent as a doomed modern social type. The novel traces Fletcher's attempts to cure himself of *ennui*, which include womanizing, socializing with caddish aristocrats and members of the upper class, retiring to the country, gambling, taking up social work, and running away, Rimbaud-like, to join a tribe of Bedouins in the desert. When these efforts fail to bring a sense of purpose to his life, Fletcher kills himself.

Where *Confessions* was a defiant declaration of the emergence of a new type of writer, this writer was, in a sense, one without a characteristic art beyond his own self-valorizing manifesto. *Mike Fletcher*, by contrast, is an attempt to envisage what kind of novel this new Decadent writer might produce. In *Mike Fletcher*, then, Moore uses the figure of the Decadent not so much to voice the beliefs, values, and ideals of a new breed of artist, but rather as the subject matter of a new breed of fiction that he believed would re-invigorate the British novel. Moore's belief that the Decadent or 'modern young man' novel would be crucial in the development of the British novel is attested to by his earlier treatment of the subject in *A Mere Accident* (1887), a novel about a des Esseintes-like young man, John Norton (who also appears in *Mike Fletcher*), who is torn between a sensually aesthetic and ascetic nature. For Moore, the subject of the Decadent young man greatly expanded the purview of fiction in the way of Naturalism beyond the confines of standard British novels that he felt catered to British matrons and young ladies. At the same time, this genre, in exploiting the artistic sensitivity of the protagonist, allowed for the development of an 'artistic' and 'aesthetic' novel, something he felt that Zola and his followers had not been able to achieve.

Mike Fletcher, then, marks Moore's attempts to combine elements of Zolaesque Naturalism with the luxurious Decadent style of Huysmans and the Aestheticism of Pater. In his early novels, Moore had been attempting to develop a 'new method' that would not be 'a warming up out of Dickens and Thackeray.'[109] While he was convinced that the method he was developing would 'certainly be adopted by other writers', he feared that he would not be recognized for his achievements.[110] Moore was right on both counts. First, his method was adopted by other writers and the subject of the Decadent's search for ever rarer sensations in an attempt to cure *ennui* became a quintessential *fin-de-siècle* theme. Second, it would be Oscar Wilde, not Moore, who would be recognized for introducing Decadence to the British novel in *The Picture of Dorian Gray* (1890).

Moore's initial belief in his novel's greatness was crushed by its negative reception. Though it had a small commercial success, critics, including his friends, were hard on it. An exception was the *Artist and Journal of Home Culture*, a journal which, as I have argued, was a main venue for the promotion of both Decadence and Moore. The reviewer thought that *Mike Fletcher* was Moore's best work and decried the unfair treatment he had received at the hands of a hypocritically moral public.[111] Moore, however, focused only on the negative reviews, disavowing the book that he had thought had so much promise. With the failure of *Mike Fletcher*, he began to rethink his literary identity. He now regarded himself as a 'man of talent' rather than a 'man of genius',[112] and felt he should choose his subjects accordingly. 'Genius' was necessary, he felt, in a writer who wished to tackle the abnormal in art. As a writer with only a 'dash of genius', Moore had committed the sin of the 'man of talent' who attempts to treat the abnormal but 'slips into sterile eccentricity, which is the dreariest form of commonplace'.[113] As such, Moore abandoned his attempts to combine Naturalism with the Decadent and abnormal style and subject matter of Huysmans and the Aestheticism of Pater. He told friend Clara Lanza, 'All experimentation is now over and henceforth I shall only sow seeds in the garden that is suitable to my talent.'[114] Moore was so ashamed of *Mike Fletcher* that it was, as Hone notes, 'the only one of his novels which he never wished to revise, and the only one of his books, not excluding the [Decadent] poems, of which in his old age he preferred never to speak'.[115] The novel was never reissued. In later years, Moore would gloss over much of his Decadent period, giving 'the impression that *Esther Waters* was the immediate successor of *Confessions* and *A Drama in Muslin*'.[116] With Moore's experimentation with Decadence at an end, it would be left to others to take up the 'abnormal' and 'eccentric' subject matter of the Decadent novel. So thoroughly did he reinvent himself that the significance of his role in the creation of the Decadent novel is, as I have said, largely forgotten.

The introduction of the Decadent type in Lee's *Miss Brown* and Moore's *Confessions* was part of an overall project to advance the English novel, though Lee and Moore differed in their view of what constituted this advancement. For Lee, the Decadent functioned as a negative type in her efforts to mediate between the too overt frankness of the French novel and the too timid reticence of the English novel. For Moore, however, Decadence represented a happy medium between the overly journalistic Naturalism of Zola and the Paterian Aestheticism that he admired. Certainly Lee and Moore were not the only artists involved in trying to pave the way for the advancement of the English novel in this period, a project challenged by the power of the circulating libraries and the National Vigilance Association as well as by the increasing commercialization of literature. The Decadent that figured so strongly for these writers in their attempts to modernize the novel would continue to serve an important function in the battle to assert the dominant definition of writer and the dominant mode of fiction in the *fin de siècle*.

4
Writing Against Decadence, 1890–97

Moore's prediction that the 'new method' he had employed in writing *Mike Fletcher* would be taken up by other writers and that he would not receive recognition for its development was realized within a year with the publication of Oscar Wilde's *Picture of Dorian Gray* in *Lippincott's Monthly Magazine* (1890). While *Mike Fletcher* received little attention, *Dorian Gray* created a controversy that gave a name and a face to Decadence for a broader public not attuned to the intellectual, philosophical, and artistic weight it was being given by those writers who were considering how Decadence might be used to expand the purview of British fiction. Wilde's story garnered more attention than Moore's novel due to its popular form. Where Moore's book had appeared under the imprint of a small publishing house, Wilde's was cheaper and more accessible and his Decadence was embodied in a more popular and feminized form. Thus, in addition to borrowing from high artistic sources such as Huysmans and Pater, Wilde also drew on the society novels of the Ouida type and on supernatural melodrama.[1] Moore's novel, by contrast, was the highly masculinized Decadence of the coarse and brutally virile kind that, while deplored by many critics, did not rouse as much ire as the effeminacy that critics saw in Wilde's story. Consequently, though *Mike Fletcher* was, as Adrian Frazier has described, a virtual 'ABC of Decadence',[2] it was *Dorian Gray*, with its combination of the effeminacy of Aestheticism and brutality of Naturalism that would become recognized as the Bible of British Decadence in the popular imagination.

Wilde's story was certainly not more Decadent than Moore's. Both were studies of Decadent ennui-ridden souls, whose attempts to cure their ennui lead them to vice and, ultimately, suicide. *Dorian Gray*, however, did have a moral, at least for those who cared to see it, as did Christian and mystical journals such as the *Christian Leader* and *Light*. *Mike Fletcher*, by contrast, was a graphic and cynical Schopenhaurean vision of the modern young man. In a period, however, when there was a strong concern about the corrupting influence of fiction on the masses, on women, and on young persons, *Dorian Gray* would cause more consternation than *Mike Fletcher* simply because it circulated more widely and presented itself in a more popular and accessible form.

In the reception of *Dorian Gray*, a discourse directed specifically against Decadence, rather than against an unnamed combination of Aestheticism and Naturalism, begins to emerge. This counter-discourse preceded the efforts of many writers to bring Decadence to British fiction. That a counter-discourse to Decadence existed almost before Decadence itself did in Britain is a testament to the powerful models of resistance already in place from earlier attacks on Aestheticism and Naturalism. The counter-Decadent discourse that emerged in the early 1890s derived largely from these earlier models, which were refined and perfected as they were used against a new pernicious literature.[3] The combination of the morally censorious attitude towards Bohemian artists among the middle-class readership and a salacious interest in their lives ensured that sensationalized negative representations of Decadence would have a powerful sway, taking hold of the popular imagination to become the dominant view. Because of the centrality of these counter-Decadent representations in public perceptions of Decadence, I take them up before discussing the development of Decadence by the Decadents themselves. This chapter looks at the development of a counter-Decadent discourse and of 'fictions' of Decadence in the critical reception of Wilde's *Dorian Gray* and in two novels by women writers – Marie Corelli's *Wormwood* and Sarah Grand's *Beth Book*.

'Delighting in dirtiness and confessing its delight': the reception of *The Picture of Dorian Gray*

A confluence of factors contributed to making Wilde's *Picture of Dorian Gray* the first widely recognized work of British Decadent fiction. In addition to the availability of well-rehearsed discourses against pernicious literature that applied equally well to an emerging Decadence, crusaders against so-called pernicious literary schools were galvanized by the October 1889 conviction of publisher Henry Vizetelly for issuing 'obscene' novels by Zola, Flaubert, Bourget, and Maupassant. The renewed sense of confidence among moral crusaders, the existence of a 'yellow' press eager to sensationalize any topic, and the seriousness with which French Decadence was being taken by some among the élite were important factors in the demonization of Decadence that began in earnest with the reception of *Dorian Gray*, a book that critic Samuel Henry Jeyes accused of 'delight[ing] in dirtiness and 'confess[ing] its delight'.[4]

Dorian Gray created a sensation on its first appearance, boosting the circulation of *Lippincott's* and prompting, by Wilde's account, over two hundred reviews[5] – an unprecedented number for a story in a monthly magazine. The most vociferous reviews appeared in journals associated with strident anti-Aesthetes – the *St. James's Gazette* and the *Scots Observer*. Samuel Henry Jeyes, the reviewer for the *St. James's Gazette*, 'had no indulgence', editor Sidney Low claimed, for *fin-de-siècle* fads and he 'waged strenuous warfare against … Yellow-Bookism, Water-Paterism [*sic*], aestheticism' and other 'isms' of the period'.[6] The *Scots Observer*, meanwhile, was led by William Ernest Henley, an important figure among the literary élite, who, like Wilde, had a number of young disciples. Though Henley and the Decadents shared purist artistic principles, and though he and Wilde were friendly for a brief period, Henley, as Peter McDonald has argued, despised those among the élite whom he suspected were commercially interested self-promoters.[7] Both of these periodicals exploited Wilde's controversial story to the full. The *St. James's Gazette* even publicly advertised its negative review, placarding the town with posters that read, 'Mr Oscar Wilde's Latest Advertisement: A Bad Case'.[8] The *Scots Observer*, meanwhile, persisted in its attack on Wilde for nearly two months, publishing a series of letters from correspondents, including Wilde, on the subject of art and morality. The vociferousness of the debate enhanced *Lippincott's* sales and the magazine continued to promote the story after it appeared, publishing two essays on *Dorian Gray* in September by Julian Hawthorne and Anne Wharton and re-issuing the story in special volumes of the magazine's best material of the year.[9]

Though critical attacks on *Dorian Gray* would begin to develop a distinctively counter-Decadent discourse, they continued also to borrow from the discourses against Aestheticism and Naturalism. While the charges of unmanliness and effeminacy, so common in attacks against Aestheticism, are not surprising to find in the criticism of *Dorian Gray*, the employment of an anti-Naturalist discourse requires examination. Where Moore had explicitly combined Aestheticism and Naturalism in his 1880s works, Wilde's *Dorian Gray* was clearly indebted to Aestheticism and the gothic romance rather than to the realist mode of Zola and his followers. Wilde cleverly foregrounds stylistics, only hinting at the frank brutality of Naturalist subject matter that formed the 'unsaid' in the story – the unnamed sins of Dorian Gray. It was to this 'unsaid' that reviewers who characterized the novel as a work of Naturalist realism responded. Certainly, with Vizetelly's conviction fresh in the minds of the public, an anti-Naturalist discourse was more effective in damning a work of literature than the discourse against the largely outmoded Aestheticism. The critical attacks on *Dorian Gray* borrowed from the attacks on Zola and Naturalism leading up to Vizetelly's prosecution. During this time, Zola's writings were described variously as 'dirt and horror', inartistic garbage', 'deadly poison', 'noxious and licentious', and 'fit [only] for swine'.[10] Critics of *Dorian Gray* invoked similar terms, calling the story 'ordure', 'garbage', 'poisonous', and describing the act of reading it as 'grubbing in muck heaps'.[11] In both cases, the reading of such works was linked directly with the commission of sin or crime. Samuel Smith, MP, for example, declared 'that it would be impossible for any young man who had not learned the Divine secret of self-control to have read [two pages of Zola] without committing some form of outward sin within twenty-four hours', while the *Daily Chronicle* insisted that *Dorian Gray* 'will taint every young mind that comes into contact with it'.[12] Smith further hinted that young women who read Zola novels turned to prostitution,[13] a connection between reading and 'sexual depravity' that was also made in the case of *Dorian Gray* by the reviewer for the *Scots Observer* who, alluding to the Cleveland Street homosexual scandal, called Wilde's book one for 'perverted telegraph boys'.[14] Jeyes, of the *St. James's Gazette*, even invoked the spectre of the National Vigilance Association, which had been instrumental in bringing Vizetelly to trial, wondering 'Whether ... the Vigilance Society will think it worth while to prosecute Mr Oscar Wilde or Messrs. Ward, Lock & Co. [the British publisher of *Lippincott's*]'.[15] At a moment in time when the status of Naturalism was so low, the association of Wilde's work with this literature, whether justified or not, functioned strategically for critics attempting to undermine his claims to high artistry.

Critics undermined the work's high artistry in other ways too. Jeyes, for example, compared Wilde's writing with that of Ouida: 'The grammar is better than Ouida's; the erudition equal'.[16] As the controversy ensued, with Wilde insisting on the aesthetic superiority of his work in letters to the editors of these journals, his opponents discredited him further. On the one hand, they aligned Wilde more fully with women writers, characterizing his bitterness in dealing with his critics as the behaviour of 'one in petticoats' and of 'a young lady who has published her first novel'.[17] On the other hand, critics also consistently rated *Dorian Gray* inferior to those works it drew inspiration from: 'Gautier could have made it romantic, entrancing, beautiful';[18] 'Mr. Stevenson could have made it convincing, humorous, pathetic';[19] 'Nathaniel Hawthorne ... would have made [it] striking and satisfying';[20] it lacked 'Gautier's power';[21] where Zola is an 'artist', 'Wilde is not', and so on.[22]

One of the most distinctive features of the attacks on *Dorian Gray* that differed from reviews of Moore's work is the employment of the term 'Decadent' to describe the story. While critics had thus far been without a term to describe literature that embodied characteristics of Aestheticism and of Naturalism, increasing attention to French Decadence by the British literary élite brought the term into broader circulation. Where Moore's critics had resorted to terms such as 'pagan', 'sensualist', and 'morbid' to describe his blending of Aestheticism and Naturalism, Wilde's critics identified his combination of a Naturalist interest in 'leprous[ness]' and 'garbage'[23] with the 'sensuous and hyperdecorative manner' of Aestheticism[24] as 'Decadent'.[25] With a more insidious literary influence to attack, critiques against Decadence developed beyond those against Aestheticism and Naturalism. Criticism became more personal in nature and, increasingly, the moral character of the writer was brought into question. The attack on the artist's moral character represents an important development in the discourse against 'pernicious' forms of art and distinguishes attacks on

Decadence from those against Naturalism and Aestheticism. Though many regarded Zola's Naturalist works as immoral, he himself was not impugned in the attacks on Naturalism in the way that came to be characteristic in attacks on Decadence. And, while *ad hominem* attacks had characterized the discourse against Aestheticism, especially during the 'fleshly school of poetry' controversy, this form of attack gained added authority when enhanced by the popular pseudo-scientific discourse of Césare Lombroso and others that emerged in the late 1880s. This discourse pathologized the 'man of genius' (the title of one of Lombroso's books), in particular the man of artistic genius, and figured the artist's works as both signs and symptoms of his insanity. This argument served as the basis of Max Nordau's notorious book *Degeneration* (1893), published in an English translation at the time of Wilde's trials. Though disparaged by many critics, his book was influential, substantiating the increasingly popular view that writers and artists of many of the nineteenth-century literary and artistic schools were degenerates.

Though the attacks on Wilde in 1890 were nowhere near as personal as they would become in 1895, the tenor of some of the criticism indicates that he already had enemies within the literary community who may have heard rumours about him. The *Scots Observer*'s invocation of the Cleveland Street homosexual scandal of 1889–90, for example, and its insistence that Wilde stop writing for 'outlawed noblemen and perverted telegraph boys'[26] link Wilde with sexual degenerates and suggest that the unnamed sins of *Dorian Gray* are homosexual in nature. Neither this interpretation of the novel nor indeed this knowledge of Wilde's sexuality were widespread at this time, however, even though, as Regenia Gagnier and Joseph Bristow have argued, the novel addressed both a homosexual and mainstream audience[27] and 'develop[ed]' and 'advertis[ed] available cultural models of homosexuality'.[28] While some, such as Henley and his followers and Wilde's homosexual audience, may have read the novel in the terms that would be put forth in Queensberry's plea of justification in 1895 – as an intentional effort to 'describe the relations, intimacies, and passions of certain persons'[29] – most readers did not. It is only after the trials that, as Sinfield argues, *Dorian Gray* becomes 'deafeningly queer', making it impossible not to understand the story in these terms.[30] In the first half of the 1890s, however, Wilde's homosexuality was largely unknown, even among his friends. Frank Harris and W. B. Yeats, for example, did not believe the charges against Wilde even after the trials had begun.[31] Thus, although hints of the association between homosexuality and Decadence are in evidence before Wilde's trials, 'same-sex passion', as Sinfield argues, was 'only a minor and indeterminate element' of 'the debate over Decadence'.[32] Wilde may have used Decadence to promote a 'gay' discourse but most other writers of British Decadent fiction did not.[33]

The construction of a vicious, threatening, and ridiculing counter-discourse to Decadence as seen in the reception of *Dorian Gray* slowed the emergence of Decadent fiction by Decadents and coloured the way it was received. As

I have demonstrated, the critique of Decadence as constructed by the male-dominated critical élite undermined the cultural authority of the Decadents by aligning their fiction with low or pernicious literature – from the trashy Naturalism of Zola and his school to the commercialized, popularized, and feminized Aestheticism of Ouida. At the same time, these critics sought increasingly to link the life and moral character of the writer with the fiction he wrote. Due to its sensationalized nature, this counter-Decadent discourse popularized the Decadent and nourished a popular fiction centred on the figure of the Decadent artist and his corrupt and bohemian lifestyle. This trend troubled Jeyes who deplored the 'Puritan prurience' of the public's attraction to works that, while claiming to be moral critiques of pernicious-ness, indulged in the gory details of 'disgusting' subject matter.[34] Such works were as bad in his mind as Wilde's more 'frank Paganism'.[35] Treatments of the sordid, corrupt, bohemian lifestyles of a negatively stereotyped Decadent abounded in popular fiction of the period, forming a significant sub-genre of the large body of fiction that focused on the figure of the writer. Like Aestheticism before it, then, Decadence was taken up, albeit in a modified fashion, in popular middle-class literary culture.

Many of these popular novels merely capitalized on the prurient interest in the bohemian lifestyle of the Decadent. Works like Morley Roberts's *In Low Relief: A Bohemian Transcript* (1890), for example, do little beyond rehashing what were, even in 1890, rather tired stereotypes of the Decadent. Roberts was one of the best paid novelists and short story writers of the 1890s who wrote a number of successful but now forgotten stories about artists and writers.[36] The protagonist of *In Low Relief*, John Torrington, is a starving writer of high artistic principles with a hatred of the bourgeoisie. Little attention is paid to Torrington's art in the novel. Instead it is his life that draws attention for its Decadence, a life that has been 'a Walpurgis night, a dance of death, a maniacal, demoniacal rout, of all the virtues and all the vices, who have fought for conquest and precedence in the kingdom of my soul'.[37] As a popular novel, *In Low Relief* goes into very little detail con-cerning Torrington's Decadence. Primarily, the novel uses the Decadent artist as a doomed romantic figure whose attempts to find love with an artist's model fail because of her love for a successful, commercial artist. Roberts was one of many writers of the period, including the more famous George Du Maurier of *Trilby* fame, who exploited Decadent and bohemian lifestyles in a largely sanitized fiction catering to a popular audience.

Women writing against Decadence

In addition to the novels of the Roberts and Du Maurier type that cashed in on the vogue for fiction about Decadent and bohemian artists, there were many writers who used the figure of the Decadent more strategically as part of the battle for cultural authority within the literary field. Chief among these were women writers whose view of Decadence was more polemical than that of writers such as Roberts and Du Maurier but that also differed from the counter-Decadent view of conservative male critics. Women writers, for example, did not sense that the cultural authority of Decadents was challenged within the élite. On the contrary, from their point of view Decadents seemed to hold an unrivalled position as respected artists. Women writers felt that their interests in art with a purpose – whether social, moral, or didactic – were not taken seriously in a field dominated by art-for-art's-sake principles. So too, while male critics insisted on the effeminacy of Decadence and on its status as a low, popular genre associated with women, women writers regarded it as a hyper-male artistic discourse that excluded women. Denigrated on the one hand by male Decadents who associated them with popular and didactic fiction, and on the other by counter-Decadents who aligned them with Decadents, women writers faced a double dilemma when treating Decadence. Though anxious to distinguish their art from that of the Decadents with which it was associated as either morbid, degenerate, and neurotic or as silly, sensationalistic, and trashy,[38] women writers were largely denied access to male-dominated critical venues where they might defend themselves and represent their own views on art. Few had the critical clout that Vernon Lee did, a woman writer who circulated among the literary élite though, even she, as we have seen, suffered abuse at the hands of her male peers.

Many women writers, then, voiced their criticism in acceptably 'feminine' venues such as fiction, a genre with low hierarchical status within the literary field, particularly when taken up by women who, it was thought, 'compromised the novel's claims as a serious art form and its possibilities for aesthetic development'.[39] Fighting against these prejudices, women writers embodied their arguments against the male domination of the literary field in their fiction, often attempting, as Lee had, to bring the ethical and the aesthetic into relation. Decadence served women writers in a number of ways in these fictions. In many respects, the Decadent, an immediately identifiable and widely denigrated type, functioned as a scapegoat in this fiction, standing in for the whole male literary élite. There were also, however, other motives behind the representation of the Decadent by women writers. For writers such as Marie Corelli, who desired the cultural authority the Decadents seemed to hold among the male élite, the appropriation of and engagement with Decadence functioned, in part, as an attempt to accrue the symbolic capital associated with this high art form, while at the same time asserting her own moralized version of a high art aesthetic. For other women writers, such as Sarah Grand, who were associated with the Decadents even while they objected strongly to the Decadent aesthetic, the Decadent was a necessary figure in a fiction that sought to distinguish between the projects of the New Woman writer and the Decadent.

Marie Corelli's *Wormwood*: a counter-Decadent discourse?

One of the first and most significant engagements with Decadence by a woman writer after Vernon Lee's *Miss Brown* was Marie Corelli's *Wormwood: A Drama of Paris* (1890), published just months after Wilde's *Dorian Gray*. Corelli's subject, like Lee's, is the degeneration of a Decadent writer. Like many popular fictional representations of the Decadent artist at this time, Corelli focuses on the lifestyle of the Decadent – in this case his absinthe addiction and his moral corruption – rather than on his literary endeavours. The novel was a popular success. The first three-volume edition of *Wormwood* of 1500 copies sold out in ten days[40] and the novel was in its seventh edition by the time of Wilde's trials. It continued to sell well after this point, reaching its twenty-third edition in 1924, the year of Corelli's death. Annette Federico argues that '*Wormwood* ... is an excellent example of middle-class curiosity about and appropriations of Decadence'.[41] Certainly, for Corelli's many readers, this sensationalized image of Decadence would colour their understanding of the Decadent fiction that emerged in the following years.

Though recognized primarily as a novelistic tract against the dangers of absinthe, the novel is also an attack against the French Naturalist school and its English imitators.[42] With the novel, Corelli intended to expose 'the absinthe trail which lies all over France and makes French literature obscene and French art repulsive'.[43] Published, however, just as ideas about Decadence were beginning to circulate more widely among the public, the novel also participates in the developing counter-Decadent discourse, particularly since the protagonist, Gaston Beauvais, bears all the signs of the stereotype Decadent – from his degenerate lifestyle and morbid interests to his promise to provide a glimpse of 'loathsome worms and unsightly poisonous growths' as he lays himself on the 'modern dissecting table'.[44] Corelli's representation of the Decadent Beauvais is in keeping with the development of the medicalized Lombrosian discourse against Decadence in that his art (that is, the narrative) is a direct result of his degenerate lifestyle – both sign and symptom of his Decadence. On a larger scale, *Wormwood* also functions as an allegory of the degeneration of France itself with Beauvais figuring as modern French Everyman. The depravity of French literature, after all, as Corelli states in her introduction to the novel, is a direct result of the depravity of the French people.[45] In the British context, the fate of France stands as a lesson at a time when controversies about the influence of French writers on British literature were in full swing.

In many ways, the novel reflects Corelli's ambivalent feelings about the literary field of her day and her awkward positioning within it as a popular woman writer aspiring to the élite. Like those among the élite, Corelli, as I have argued earlier, valorized high art and claimed to be economically disinterested. Unlike these writers, however, she disparaged the critical élite, believing instead in the power of the masses to recognize high art. For Corelli, popularity with the masses assured her status as an 'Artist' as surely as did her unpopularity with the literary élite, a point she made repeatedly in novels, essays, and interviews. In *The Sorrows of Satan*, for example, a bookseller says of the idealized female artist figure in the novel (widely recognized as a portrait of Corelli herself), 'Miss Clare is too popular to need reviews. Besides, a large number of the critics, the "log-rollers" especially, are mad against her for her success, and the public know it.'[46] Though Corelli was criticized for these defensive personal diatribes against critics and other writers, which often sat awkwardly within her fiction, as a popular woman writer largely disparaged by critics, fiction served as her main voice. In her mind, the male literary establishment was corrupt. Publishers' readers and critics, she argued, were bitter writers themselves, jealous and unwilling to promote good writing. Publishers were unscrupulous cheaters of authors and critics were either 'log-rollers' who promoted their friends and slashed every-one else or corrupt reviewers whose praise could be bought. Overall, it was a system that 'foster[ed] mediocrities and suppresse[d] originality'.[47] What Corelli most resented was that male writers among the élite so often served also as critics and her strongest ire is directed against writer-critics among the Decadents, those she characterized as a 'group of low sensualists, who haunt Fleet Street bars and restaurants, and who out of that sodden daily and nightly experience get a few temporary jobs on the press and "pose" as a cult and censorship of art'.[48] Corelli's point was, of course, not unfounded, as there were many such writer-critics among the Decadents, including Arthur Symons, John Davidson, and Richard Le Gallienne (who even called himself 'Logroller' in a weekly column for the *Star*). Nonetheless, she invests Decadent writer-critics with more symbolic capital than they actually held given that they too suffered abuse at the hands of critics.

Corelli's outrage at the inequities of the literary field seems out of proportion given her own spectacular success, but it speaks to the importance she invested in the symbolic capital that critical acclaim and peer recognition represented. Though she accused the male-dominated establishment of hypocrisy in declaring 'the public an "ass" while ... desiring ... the said "ass's" applause and approval',[49] she, likewise, declared the élite an 'ass' while seeking its approval. She often courted the élite, sending a copy of *Wormwood*, for example, to Symons, one of the Decadent writer-critics she claimed to despise. Furthermore, at one point in her career, Corelli entered into negotiations with John Lane, a publisher associated with the Decadents. In a letter to Lane, acknowledging that she has heard she is his 'favourite aversion', Corelli assures him of her artistic integrity, adopting the econom-ically disinterested discourse of the élite: 'If I am an "aversion" of yours, still you must try to remember that I have quite other aims in view than those of [making] money or fame – such that in my work I care nothing for myself at all – as to whether I am praised or blamed, bricked or crowned.'[50]

The contradictions that governed Corelli's manoeuvrings within the field and her ambivalence about the literary establishment come into play in *Wormwood*, a novel that is characterized by competing discourses of Decadence and counter-Decadence: that of the Decadent absinthe-addicted narrator and that of Corelli, a novelist with moralistic intentions. These two discourses operate uneasily within a text that, while attacking Decadence seems, at the same time, to have many of its qualities. Corelli feared that readers might mistake the novel for a work of Decadence and took a number of precautions to ensure they would not, notably in the introductory note, epigraph, and dedication. In the introductory note, Corelli condemns the French nation for its 'morbidness ... open atheism, heartlessness, flippancy ... flagrant immorality' and 'taste for vice and indecent vulgarity' in art.[51] She also reminds her readers that authors are not to be confused with their characters, assuring them that she has 'nothing whatsoever to do with the wretched "Gaston Beauvais" beyond the portraiture of him in his own lurid colours.'[52] Corelli's judgemental view is emphasized by the epigraph, a quotation from the book of Revelation that sets an apocalyptic tone: 'And the name of the star is called WORMWOOD: and the third part of the waters became *wormwood*; and many men died of the waters, because they were made bitter.'[53] As if her moralistic intentions were still not clear, Corelli follows the epigraph with a dedication to 'les absintheurs de Paris, ces fanfarons du vice qui sont la honte et le désespoir de leur patrie'.[54] The novel is also interspersed throughout with moralistic rants against the French nation, its literature and against absinthe. These rants are clearly designed to promote Corelli's moralistic agenda – her desire, as she told Bentley, to '*rouse* some few to think of the deterioration they are bringing on themselves and their children'.[55] And yet these rants, coming as they do from the absinthe-addicted atheistic Decadent narrator, often strain the credibility of a story that Corelli intended to be 'realistic'.[56]

Corelli's moralistic discourse and her sensationalism mark her as a producer of low art for the masses. And yet, this discourse sits uneasily within a text that is, as Annette Federico has pointed out, 'packaged as the very flower of Decadence' – from its physical appearance (green with a serpent on the cover and with a red ribbon like those found on absinthe bottles) to its 'dependen[ce] on Decadent tropes'.[57] Like the novels of the literary élite that were charged with Decadence, *Wormwood* is a study in morbid psychology. Beauvais promises, as writer of his story, to provide a Decadent realist narrative that will 'strip his soul naked' in his account of 'the history of his life and thought'.[58] Though the rhetoric of 'laying the soul bare' is similar to Moore's in *Confessions of a Young Man*, the results are decidedly different. Where Moore provides the thought and the structure of the Decadent sensibility, Corelli gives us the lifestyle of the Decadent as imagined by a prurient middle-class readership. Hers is a novel to feed what Jeyes described in his review of *Dorian Gray* as the British public's 'Puritan prurience.'[59] Still, the novel is ambivalent in its relationship to Decadence for, even while denouncing the Decadent, Corelli evokes the 'seductive powers' of absinthe.[60] At the same time, the absinthe-fired reveries of Beauvais in the narrative exploit the stylistic extravagance and imagery associated with Decadence, as in this description of a *femme fatale*: 'and out on that yellow-glittering water rests one solitary gondola, black as a floating hearse, yet holding light! She, that fair siren in white robes, with bosom bare to the amorous moon-rays – she with her wicked, laughing eyes and jewel-wreathed tresses – is she not a beautiful wanton enough for at least an hour's joy?'[61]

If Corelli's attempts at a Decadent stylization render her so-called critique of Decadence ambiguous, so too does her praise of French Decadent poet Charles Cros – absinthe addict and friend to Arthur Rimbaud – who is quoted extensively in the novel and whom she eulogizes in a footnote as 'a perished genius', 'young and ... full of promise', who was 'never encouraged or recognized in his lifetime'.[62] Given that she quotes from Cros's, 'Lendemain', a poem about absinthe, she must have suspected he was an absinthe addict. Federico reads Corelli's reverential attitude towards the absinthe-addicted Cros as a sign of her 'susceptibil[ity] to the myth of the perished genius'.[63] I would add that it signals her desire to accrue cultural capital within a literary élite for whom the recognition and promotion of obscure and neglected artists function as a sign of one's authority. Corelli's seemingly contradictory impulses in the novel – her moralistic intentions on the one hand and her Decadence on the other – indicate her desire to appeal both to the public and to the literary élite. While the sensationalistic and moralistic aspects of the novel aimed to please her popular readership, her employment of Decadent tropes and her praise of obscure French Decadent verse may be seen as an attempt to curry favour with the Francophilic élite, such as Arthur Symons to whom she sent a copy of the book. Indeed, she acknowledged such an impulse when she first conceived of writing a realist work, writing Bentley that her novel 'may suit *even* them [admirers of Naturalism and Decadence] though ... it will not be *their* realism'.[64]

As might be expected, middlebrow periodicals – those that pruriently engaged in Corelli's examination of Decadence while applauding her moralistic treatment of the subject – praised *Wormwood*, taking it as a realistic representation of the Decadent type. The *Graphic*, an illustrated periodical that catered to the middle class, admired Corelli's 'courage' in treating her subject from the point of view of the Decadent and found her 'frantic' style 'appropriate to the homicidal maniac whom she has made his own biographer'.[65] Similarly, *Literary World*, an American middlebrow periodical that circulated in Britain also, applauded Corelli's exposure of the dangers of absinthe and her attack on 'its more widespread and subtle secondary phase – the corruption and debasement of literature and art'.[66] Her engagement with Decadence was convincing to this reviewer who compared her work with that of the French Decadents, noting, however, that Corelli employs this type of art to a 'worthy end'.[67] Equally convinced was the reviewer for the ladies' society magazine, *Kensington Society*, whose language echoes Corelli's own pseudo-Decadent style: 'Corelli's eloquently vigorous language flows through the ... present thrilling work in lava torrents of bitter passion and pitiless revenge. The reader is whirled about like a leaflet amidst lurid flashes and wild gusts of maddened invective, almost blinded by the efforts he or she makes to realise the tempest which rages through the man possessed of the "liquid fire" '.[68] For these middlebrow periodicals, Corelli had provided all the sin, sensation, and luridness her audience associated with Decadence, while tempering it with the compensatory moral.

If Corelli's successful reception in middlebrow periodicals is not surprising, the praise of highbrow periodicals for *Wormwood* is. The novel received fairly positive reviews in the *Athenaeum*, the most influential of literary reviews, and the *Academy*, a periodical that, under the influence of Andrew Lang, George Saintsbury, and Edmund Gosse, was characterized by its 'systematic intention to raise the general "trashy" and "coarse" level of the English novel ... to that of the French'.[69] Both journals praised the novel's realism. The *Athenaeum* called it a 'grim, realistic drama',[70] while the *Academy* described it as a 'psychological study',[71] a genre associated with highbrow writers such as Henry James and Paul Bourget. What made these critics regard as realistic what others among the critical élite mocked mercilessly as 'wildly inconsistent' and suitable only for 'railway bookstalls'?[72] The praise of *Wormwood* by the two foremost literary journals attests, I believe, to the strong resistance to the emerging Decadence, even within the literary élite.[73] Though the *Academy* published the work of and had on its staff members of the young literary élite, such as Arthur Symons, there was still a representative body of the older, more conservative élite whose 'supercilious' anti-Philistinism was of a different order from the more 'vigorous radicalism' of the young literary élite.[74] Thus, while Saintsbury, Gosse, and Lang promoted French literature, it was the French literature of an earlier generation. All were, in varying degrees, hostile to Naturalism and to the emerging Decadence. 'Be vicious and have done with it', urged Saintsbury, who objected to the focus on the grimness of life in the French novel and thought it in a 'less healthy condition' than the English.[75] For his part, Gosse objected to the French novel's unrelenting interest in 'amatory intrigue'.[76] Though we do not know how these critics viewed Corelli's novel which, though it has a moral, is nonetheless an exploration of the vicious side of life, Corelli's counter-Decadence may have represented a welcome corrective to the French literary trends that they feared were becoming an all too pervasive influence on British writers. To proponents of Decadence such as Arthur Symons and Havelock Ellis, whose views will be discussed in the next chapter, such moralizing had no place in a literature which, in Havelock Ellis's view, was in need of 'treating the facts of life with the ... frankness and boldness characteristic of the French novel'.[77]

The counter-Decadence that emerged in 1890 was, then, quite widespread, finding its way into popular periodicals, fiction and, even into élite literary venues. At the same time, it made strange bedfellows out of popular novelists such as Corelli and highbrow critics like Lang, Gosse, and Saintsbury. Though these critics did not, for the most part, engage in the kind of mudslinging that characterized more popular counter-Decadent representations, together the artistic condemnation of Decadence as a literary practice by some among the élite and the character assassination of Decadent artists by popular writers combined to form a strikingly negative image of the movement. These negative representations of Decadence were dominant in the period, more so than the views of proponents of Decadence who wanted to modernize the British novel. As Decadence emerged as the new form of literary perniciousness in the 1890s it was used as a catch-all term for anything progressive, shocking, or new, leading Hubert Crackanthorpe to declare, 'Decadence, Decadence: you are all Decadent nowadays. Ibsen, Degas, and the New English Art Club; Zola, Oscar Wilde, and the Second Mrs Tanqueray. Mr Richard Le Gallienne is hoist with his own petard; even the British playwright has not escaped the taint'.[78]

The Beth Book and the 'Grand' stand against Decadence

In 1894, when Crackanthorpe wrote the essay in which these comments on Decadence appeared, being Decadent had acquired a kind *enfant terrible* cachet. Not everyone who was called Decadent, however, appreciated the label. The resistance to the term was particularly strong among New Woman writers, especially in the aftermath of the Wilde trials, which had significant repercussions for those associated with literary Decadence. It was in this context, during the summer of 1895, that Sarah Grand began writing *The Beth Book* (1897), in which she sought to differentiate the New Woman and the Decadent. These figures, as Linda Dowling argues, were strongly linked in the popular imagination in the 1890s:

> To most late Victorians the Decadent was new and the New Woman Decadent. The origins, tendencies, even the appearance of the New Woman and the Decadent – as portrayed in the popular press and in periodicals – confirmed their ... unhealthily near relationship. Both inspired reactions ranging from hilarity to disgust and outrage, and both raised as well profound fears for the future of sex, class, and race. To [the late Victorians]... the figures of the New Woman and the Decadent, like the artists who created them and the works in which they appeared, seemed to be dangerous avatars of the 'New,' and were widely felt to oppose not each other but the values considered essential to the survival of established culture.[79]

In the context of the Wilde trials, trials which were as much about the perniciousness of modern literary trends as they were about Wilde's sexual practices, the association between the New Woman and the Decadent became more firmly entrenched. During the trials, New Women were described as 'creatures of Oscar Wilde's'.[80] New Woman writers were also held accountable for what critic Thomas Bradfield described as 'a stage of Decadence' in the history of English fiction.[81] Some even considered New Woman novels more dangerous than the works of male Decadents because they were more popular. Sarah Grand's *Heavenly Twins*, for example, sold 20,000 copies and went into six editions in its first year,[82] a remarkable sale for an expensive three-volume novel. As the most prominent New Woman writer, Grand was often singled out as the originator of this whole school of fiction.[83] New Woman novels were castigated along with those of the Decadents in a rash of articles that appeared in the first half of 1895 and were deplored for their free treatment of the relations between the sexes and for their interest in the morbid and abnormal. Given the strong backlash against New Woman novelists and Decadents in the first half of 1895, a backlash that only increased after the Wilde trials, it is not surprising that Grand should wish to distinguish the New Woman from the Decadent male artist.

Like Corelli, Grand was one of the more vocal female critics of Decadence in the period. However, though both were popular writers, they differed widely in their social and political views and in their ideas about the function of art. Corelli, who equated the New Woman with Decadents, would have been appalled to be compared with Grand. Whereas Corelli favoured a litera-ture of spiritual and moral uplift, what she called an 'elevating and purifying' fiction,[84] Grand believed that art could serve more practically in solving social problems. Grand herself was no fan of Corelli. Commenting to F. H. Fisher, editor of the *Literary World*, on Corelli's aggressive self-promotion, she remarked: 'Marie Corelli seems to be an amusing little person! I never met her, and can't read her works, but hear of her continually in some new pose. I wonder if this last one of injured author will answer. But even if it does, I am not likely to imitate her.'[85] If she did not imitate Corelli's adoption of the pose of 'injured author' in the press, Grand was certainly as vocal in her condemnation of French literature and the Aesthetes and Decadents – for whom she uses the catch-all term 'stylists'. Subtitled 'Being a Study of the Life of Elizabeth Caldwell Maclure, A Woman of Genius', *The Beth Book* was one of many novels about women writers in this period. These novels were part of the larger trend of novels about writers which, as I have suggested, attests to a particularly competitive field in which writers battled for cultural authority in the wake of substantial changes in the conditions of produc-tion. As Teresa Mangum argues, however, Grand's novel stands out from similar works in its explicit condemnation of 'a literary establishment that made success difficult for a woman writer, particularly one interested in woman's rights'.[86]

Adopting the *küntslerroman* form, as Moore had in *Confessions*, and using this form in a similarly defiant manner, Grand charts the development and formation of the 'woman of genius'. But where for Moore the Decadent artist is formed in his rejection of bourgeois life and in his engagement with alternative cultures, for Grand, whose novel demonstrates women's lack of social freedom and access to formal education, genius is figured in natural terms. To this end, Beth's genius, Mangum argues, is represented as 'intuitive, instinctive, and mystical' and Grand makes a virtue of Beth's lack of schooling by resorting to Romantic conceptions of genius.[87] Mangum makes much of Grand's strategic invocation of the term 'genius', noting that Grand plays on its classical, Romantic, and spiritual connotations.[88] Mangum does not, however, consider the negative connotations that circulated around the term 'genius' in the 1890s as a result of Césare Lombroso's *Man of Genius* (1888; English trans. 1891), a psychological study that linked genius and criminality. Lombroso's work influenced a number of subsequent studies in this field including Havelock Ellis's, *The Criminal* (1890); J. F. Nisbet's *The Insanity of Genius* (1891); Francis Galton's *Hereditary Genius* (1892); and Max Nordau's highly popular *Degeneration* (1893; English trans. 1895). These works, as I have suggested earlier, played a significant role in the pathologization and criminalization of the Decadent. Grand was surely also thinking of these works – notably Lombroso's *Man of Genius* – when she applied the term 'woman of genius' to Beth in a narrative that contests the connection between genius and criminality. Grand, however, challenges this connection only insofar as it concerns her protagonist. As far as male artists, Decadents in particular, are concerned, Grand's narrative endorses this link. Grand's project, after all, is to distinguish between New Women and Decadents, a project which necessitates de-pathologizing the New Woman, while sustaining the 'fiction' of the Decadent as degenerate. Ultimately, she wants to insist that the 'woman of genius', or New Woman, differs significantly from the 'man of genius', or Decadent.

Like Corelli, Grand employs the discourse of degeneration to excoriate French Decadent literature, using Dr Galbraith as her mouthpiece: 'If France is to be judged by the tendency of its literature and art at present, one would suppose it to be dominated and doomed to destruction by a gang of lascivious authors and artists who are sapping the manhood of the country and degrading the womanhood by idealising self-indulgence and mean intrigue.'[89] Though Beth does read this literature as part of her mentorship, it is made clear that she derives none of her ideas about art from it. For Beth, it serves purely as a negative model. Characterizing Decadents as 'vain, hollow, cynical, and dyspeptic' men whose writing appeals to the head but not the heart, Beth forges her own artistic identity in opposition to these writers and their English imitators, the 'stylists', represented in the novel by Alfred Cayley Pounce.[90]

Pounce embodies the artistic principles of the Decadent artist. He is anti-bourgeois in his sentiments and scorns the novel with a purpose, a genre he associates with 'lady' novelists.[91] He is an imitator of French Decadent literature and a proponent of high literary style. While these qualities are valorized by Moore in *Confessions*, in Grand's novel these same qualities take on a negative connotation in contrast to the ethical feminist aesthetic of Beth. From Beth's point of view, Pounce 'idealise[s] mean intrigues' and 'delight[s] in foul matter if the manner of its presentation [is] an admirable specimen of style'.[92] Pounce is further represented as a philanderer whose physical appearance bears all the signs of his moral degeneration: 'an ignoble life had written [lines] prematurely on his face, and his attitude emphasized the attenuation of his body. He looked a poor, peevish, neurotic specimen.'[93] Endorsing the view taken by Wilde's critics, Corelli, and other counter-Decadents, Grand links Decadent artistic principles with a Decadent lifestyle, a view based on the works of Lombroso, Nordau and others. Drawing on these theories, Beth's friend, Ideala (a character who appears in three of Grand's novels) points to the fate of Wilde and some of the French Decadents: 'The works of art for art's sake, and style for style's sake, end on the shelf much respected, while their authors end in the asylum, the prison, and the premature grave.'[94]

Though denigrated in the novel, Decadent artistic principles are recognized as a dominant force in the literary field, so dominant that Beth herself is at first influenced by 'intellectual ingenuities and Art and Style':[95] 'From the time she began to think of the style and diction of prose as something to be separately acquired, the spontaneous flow of her thoughts was checked and hampered, and she expended herself in fashioning her tools, as it were, instead of using her tools to fashion her work.'[96] Beth, the narrator argues, ignores her 'natural faculty', believing that 'the more trouble she gave herself the better must be the result'.[97] Beth's fault at this point, the narrative suggests, is her unquestioning acceptance of the aesthetic dictates of the Decadent school.

The falseness of the Decadent style is fully revealed through the juxtaposition of Beth and Pounce. By the time Beth meets Pounce, she has moved beyond her fixation on style to develop a manner free of the falseness, artificiality, and imitativeness associated with the Decadent stylists:

> Foreign phrases she discarded, and she never attempted to produce an eccentric effect by galvinising obsolete words, rightly discarded for lack of vitality, into a ghastly semblance of life. Her own language, strong and pure, she found a sufficient instrument for her purpose. When the true impulse to write came, her fine ideas about style only hampered her, so she cast them aside, as habitual affectations are cast aside and natural emotions naturally expressed, in moments of deep feeling; and from that

time forward she displayed, what had doubtless been coming to her by practice all along, a method and a manner of her own.[98]

Beth has discovered that matter is paramount and 'if the matter is there in the mind it will out, and the manner will form itself in the effort to produce it'.[99] This view contrasts sharply with that of Pounce who is completely under the spell of fine style. Pounce is shocked at the speed with which Beth writes in comparison with his Flaubertian approach: 'Why it takes *me* a week to write five hundred words',[100] he tells Beth. 'But then, of course, my work is highly concentrated' he adds, warning her against writing so quickly, 'You can only produce poor thin stuff in that way.'[101] 'Poor thin stuff' it may be, but, as Beth's friend Ideala points out, it is this type of writing that will be read and loved. Beth associates her non-Flaubertian approach to literature with Thackeray, a 'Titan' who, despite his often 'slipshod style', could not have 'been a scrap more vital, nor he himself the greater',[102] had he suffered with Flaubertian angst over the intricacies of style. Offering an account of her awakening to the false ideals of the stylists, Ideala distinguishes between their work, work that is 'respected' but not read, and Beth's, which will have an influence on people's lives for years to come.[103]

> Then one day a ... friend of mine took me into a public library; and we spent a long time among the books, looking especially at the ones that had been greatly read, and at the queer marks in them, the emphatic strokes of approval, the notes of admiration, the ohs! of enthusiasm, the ahs! of agreement. At the end of one volume some one had written: 'This book has done me good.' It was all very touching to me, very human, very instructive. I never quite realised before what books might be to people, how they might help them, comfort them, brighten the time for them, and fill them with brave and happy thoughts. But we came at last in our wanderings to one neat shelf of beautiful books, and I began to look at them. There were no marks in them, no signs of wear and tear. The shelf was evidently not popular, yet it contained the books that had been recommended to me as best worth reading by my stylist friends. 'There is style for you!' said my friend. 'Style lasts, you see. Style is engraved upon stone. All the other books about us wear out and perish, but here are your stylists still, as fresh as the day they were bought.' 'Because nobody reads them!' I exclaimed.[104]

Unlike the vociferous critics of Wilde's *Dorian Gray* who associated Decadence with sensational writing aimed at a popular audience, Grand endorses an alternate 'fiction' of Decadence in this passage, one which, though meant to undermine Decadence, corresponds with the Decadents' self-representation as martyrs to art. Decadents would not be surprised that their books were not thumbed over by appreciative readers in the public library, nor indeed, given their professed disdain for the reading public, would they wish their works to be taken up in this way. Admiration by this reading public would only suggest that their writing was inferior trash with no claims to artistic worth.

For Grand, however, as for Corelli, popularity with the public was a sign of genuine talent and was worth more than critical success in a corrupted literary field. Like Corelli, Grand questions the value of success among those such as Pounce – 'clever young men' who, 'having written some little things of no consequence', take it upon themselves 'to give [their] opinion, with appalling assurance, of the works of other people, which are of consequence'.[105] At one point, Beth even determines to write only for women, an aim that Dr Galbraith regards as naive in its generalization of the male readership.[106] Grand is also, however, as ambivalent as Corelli about success among the élite. In *The Beth Book*, Beth is granted success in this domain. Her success is particularly striking because the book she eventually writes is not a novel, but a work of social theory – a genre associated with male intellectuals. Even Pounce, who had already written a scurrilous review based on what he thought Beth would write, publishes a 'highly eulogistic article' on her book before discovering the author's identity.[107]

While Mangum argues that this section of the book 'provides a dose of feminist humor as well as female victory',[108] surely it is a hollow victory. First, Pounce's eulogistic reception of Beth's book is improbable given their very different social views. Second, if anything, the novel is ultimately pessimistic about the place of women writers in the literary field, particularly women writers of fiction. Though Beth believes that the novel can be made a vehicle for social protest and that novel-reading need not be a vice, she does not, in the end, write a novel. And, though it is significant that Beth achieves success as a writer of social theory, a genre associated with male intellectuals, does Beth's turn to non-fiction suggest that deep down Grand accepts that aesthetics and ethics are irreconcilable in fiction? Furthermore, though Beth achieves success among the male-dominated élite, she abandons this world for the political platform, further suggesting that women's concerns are better addressed outside the literary field. Lyn Pykett reads Beth's turn from writing to speaking as an inability 'to break free of the discourse of the proper feminine. Within this discourse it proves impossible to write the woman writer. The portrait of the artist as a young woman is replaced by the portrait of the mature woman as public speaker'.[109] The novel also attests to the difficulty women writers had in gaining cultural authority and in creating a literary discourse capable of mediating between ethics and aesthetics in contrast to the dominant artistic discourses of the male establishment. Women lost in two ways in this establishment. Decadents and other proponents of art-for-art's sake scorned moralistic and didactic fiction, while more conservative members of the male-dominated literary élite viewed women writers' frank treatment of social issues as Decadent and immoral rather than as progressive and moral.

The reception of *The Beth Book* illustrates this contradictory status of New Woman writing as well as Grand's failure to establish the superiority of New Woman writers over the Decadents they were associated with. Grand's feminist ethical aesthetic was disparaged in a number of venues, from highbrow periodicals such as the *Spectator*, the *Athenaeum*, the *Saturday Review*, and the *Academy*, to middlebrow periodicals such as the *Bookman*. Grand's novel was even denigrated in a feminist periodical, the pro-suffragist *Woman's Signal*, which said of *The Beth Book*, 'from the moment purpose enters in, the art is destroyed'.[110] 'Frank Danby', the male pseudonym of Julia Frankau, a critic for the *Saturday Review*, made a similar complaint:

> apparently she *must* preach her wonderful doctrine of the equality of the sexes, she *must* jumble up medical and moral questions in one inharmonious whole, she *must* ruin her own works of art and deface them, with iconoclastic fervour, by all refuse of the controversies that raged twenty years ago around the dead C[ontagious] D[iseases] Acts. It is a strange and hideous obsession. It is such a simple, elementary obvious truth that any absolutely fine work of art produced by a woman does more toward the convincing of a sceptic world of the equality of the sexes than whole volumes of hysteric shriekings about the imaginary wrongs they suffer at the hands of the sanitarians.[111]

The critic for the *Bookman* and Frank Harris of the *Saturday Review* even suggested that Grand might benefit by reading some of the stylists she rails against in the novel including Balzac, Flaubert, and Maupassant.[112] These suggestions incensed Grand who, responding to Harris's review in particular, wrote to F. H. Fisher of the *Literary World*,

> Mr. Frank Harris can have no sense of humour otherwise would he, in the same paragraph in which he professes that I have outraged his sense of delicacy, have recommended me to study, among others, Guy de Maupassant, author of *Bel Ami, Une Vie, La Maison Tellier* and other volumes innumerable, with the most indecent passages in them, and all distinguished by immorality unrelieved by a single aspiration towards something more elevating. I should think after a course of Maupassant a student would not know what decency was.[113]

While Grand, who believed in literature with a social purpose, cared little what critics thought of her artistry, she was sensitive when it came to discussions of Decadence, particularly since her intention in writing *The Beth Book* had been to denounce precisely the kind of fiction Harris told her she ought to emulate. She must, therefore have been even more troubled by the charges of Decadence levelled against her than she was by the remarks of Harris. The *Academy*, for example, called Grand's book inartistic and nasty: 'to play with nasty subjects, to treat a few vile types as normal products, is not art'.[114] Harshest of all was the above-cited Julia Frankau, writing as Frank Danby in the *Saturday Review*. Frankau begins her review with a lengthy anecdote about an inmate at an 'Asylum for Idiots'. Drawing on the discourse linking insanity and degeneracy with artistic genius as propounded in the works of Lombroso and others, she describes the inmate's degenerate physical appearance, his 'unkempt hair' his 'restless' hands, and 'his wandering eyes' that 'conveyed an impression of deep-rooted and abiding melancholy'.[115] She then goes on to characterize the inmate's artistic 'genius'. His art, though 'marvellous',[116] is characterized by 'lurid'[117] images, 'lewd suggestion[s]',[118] 'abominations',[119] and 'revolting details'.[120] Finally, Frankau reveals her purpose in relating this anecdote, saying 'in some vague way, Sarah Grand has reminded me again of this unfortunate'.[121] In other words, Frankau charges Grand with the lewdness, bad taste, and indecency that many claimed characterized the works of Decadents such as Aubrey Beardsley, whose perverse sense of humour in his art recalls the art of Frankau's inmate.

As an attempt to distinguish between the interests of the New Woman and those of the Decadents and as a formulation of an ethical feminist aesthetic that challenges the male high artistic literary discourse, *The Beth Book*, then, failed in the eyes of many. And, while Corelli had somewhat more success in her engagement with Decadence in *Wormwood*, a book that earned her praise in élite literary journals, increasingly through the 1890s, her diatribes on art turned the establishment against her and made her an object of ridicule. Even where they were in agreement with the counter-Decadents of the male élite, women writers who took on the subject of Decadence in their work were either branded Decadent, as Grand was, or derided for a lack of cultural and artistic sophistication, as Corelli was by some reviewers. In large part, the male-dominated critical élite that shaped a counter-Decadent discourse in the press – a more powerful and respected venue than popular fiction – denied women the authority to engage in literary debates and denigrated the counter-Decadent discourse produced by these women in fiction. The attacks on Grand by even women within the field, women such as Frankau and the feminist reviewer of the *Woman's Signal*, testify powerfully to the dominance of male artistic discourses. Ultimately, women writers faced great difficulty in bringing the ethical and the aesthetic into relation, whether they circulated in the realm of the élite, as Vernon Lee did, or whether they were popular writers such as Corelli and Grand. Still, their views of Decadence, if derided by the literary community, were integral in shaping ideas about Decadence for the broader public which was more likely to come into contact with the counter-Decadent discourse in fiction by women than in élite periodicals dominated be men.

Between the female-dominated fictional counter-Decadent discourse and the male-dominated critical counter-Decadent discourse, the Decadents would find it hard to make a case for themselves either with the public or in the literary field itself. Where women engaging in Decadence would find themselves struggling to create a high art aesthetic that addressed their ethical concerns, the Decadents would juggle aesthetics and economics as they attempted to bring an élite aesthetic into a field that was increasingly subject to the demands of an expanding popular readership and was not really that open to expanding the purview of fiction. The Decadents' engagements in this process, as I shall demonstrate in the following two chapters, would be as fraught as those of women writers who were trying to accommodate ethics to aesthetics.

5
Decadent Fiction Before the Keynotes Series

In the late 1880s and early 1890s as attacks were launched against Decadence in novels and in the periodical press, a case for literary Decadence was being made by proponents of the movement, mostly through the limited venues of little magazines such as the *Century Guild Hobby Horse, Pioneer*, and the *Artist and Journal of Home Culture*.[1] Where critics of Decadence focused on its more sensationalistic aspects, proponents articulated intellectual theories that represented Decadence as a high artistic genre. These proponents included Havelock Ellis and Arthur Symons, who wrote influential essays on Decadence, Ellis for the progressive journal *Pioneer* (1889), and Symons for the more mainstream *Harper's New Monthly Magazine* (1893). Ellis and Symons became acquainted with French Decadence while visiting France together. In their articles, both focused on Decadence as a perspective or style of writing. In turn, they downplayed, though did not deny, the often risqué subject matter of Decadent literature. In describing Decadence, Ellis borrowed from French writer Paul Bourget's definition: 'The style of Decadence is one in which the unity of the book is decomposed to give place to the independence of the page, in which the page is decomposed to give place to the independence of the phrase, and the phrase to give place to the independence of the word.'[2] In a similar vein, Symons described Decadence as 'an intense self-consciousness, a restless curiosity in research, an over-subtilizing refinement upon refinement'.[3] Both insisted that Decadence was an appropriate literary form for what Ellis described as 'a society which has reached the limits of expansion and maturity', and both defended its psychological realism.[4] 'It reflects all the moods, all the manners', wrote Symons, 'of a sophisticated society; its very artificiality is a way of being true to nature: simplicity, sanity, proportion – the classic qualities – how much do we possess them in our life, our surroundings, that we should look to find them in our literature.'[5]

For Ellis in particular, Decadence represented a potentially reinvigorating force for the English novel, a genre that he argued was 'feebly struggling after a new literary ideal'.[6] His endorsement of Decadence contributed to an ongoing discussion about the state of the English novel and its future, a subject central to the realism/romance debate, the candour in English fiction debate, and the controversies over pernicious literature and Naturalism. Given the resistance towards foreign influence exhibited in these debates, Ellis thought it unlikely that there could be 'any successful union of the French and English novel' through the introduction of a Decadent aesthetic.[7] He would have been less hopeful had he known that Moore had just given up his experimentation with Decadence for, in the article, Ellis singles him out as one of the few writers 'possessed of artistic earnestness and consistency' whose novels best exemplified the influence of French Decadence.[8] The situation was no better when Symons wrote his article on Decadence in 1893. By this time, Moore's artistic self-transformation was well under way and his contribution to the development of Decadence was neglected by Symons who cited Walter Pater as the only example of a writer of English Decadent prose.

Ellis's pessimism regarding the union of the French and English novel and Symons's identification of Pater as the only English prose writer of Decadence indicate the difficulty faced by the pro-Decadent élite in developing the more avant-garde notions of Decadence. Pater was successful because, with an independent income, he was less affected by the forces that had constrained Moore. So too, while Pater's *Marius the Epicurean* and *Imaginary Portraits* might be considered Decadent in terms of their luxurious and affected style, they hardly challenge the limits of representation in ways that evoke shock. Most Decadents did not share Pater's independence from the field, however, and most wanted to go further than him in pushing the limits of representation. Many aspiring writers in Britain were sympathetic to and desirous of implementing the Decadent aesthetic as described by Ellis and Symons. These writers were faced, however, as Ellis himself acknowledged, with strong resistance: 'English novelists who have been touched by the French influence', he wrote, 'constantly offend by their crude and vulgar extravagance'.[9] This offence was felt even when writers were cautious in their mediation between English and French novelistic traditions as both Lee's and Wilde's experiences indicate. The kind of overhauling of the British novel through Decadence that Ellis called for was impossible given the historical, social, and cultural conditions of *fin-de-siècle* Britain. These conditions, which were different from those in France that nurtured the form of Decadence idealized by Ellis and Symons, shaped the culturally specific form that Decadence would take in the British context. But though Decadence may not have exhibited itself in British literature at this time in the way that Ellis desired, many writers were nevertheless 'struggling' to introduce Ellis's 'new literary ideal' of Decadence to the British public, unwelcome though it might be.

Throughout this book, I have emphasized the forces constraining those interested in bringing Decadence to British literature. I have outlined the conflicting positions of the Decadents whose desire for fame and money compromised their status as high literary disinterested artists. I have also described the manner in which the conditions of literary production influenced the form that Decadence would take in the British literary context. Moreover, I have considered how these factors – the desire on the part of Decadents for fame and money and the conditions of literary production – led Decadents to look to popular contemporary British literary models, quite apart from their French literary models, in order to imagine how to reconcile high artistic ideals with the demands of the literary marketplace. Finally, in the preceding chapter, I have described the way in which popular counter-Decadent representations were a powerful force within the British context. These counter-Decadent representations overshadowed the more serious discussions of Decadence by writers such as Ellis and Symons that I have just described. I am now in a position to consider the productions of those writers committed to Decadence and how literary, social, and cultural conditions shaped a Decadence that differed from the 'literary ideal' outlined by Ellis and Symons.

Even with this contextualization in mind it might still seem strange to insist that writers looked to popular fictional genres to promote Decadence. Strange, because Decadence has traditionally been understood as avant-garde or as commercially disinterested high art. At the same time, a cynic might wonder how the Decadents' exploitation of the popular is any different from the popular novelist's appropriation of Decadent themes. The difference, it is true, is not always easy to see. For certainly, despite their pose of disinterestedness, Decadents were, as I have argued, trying to make money with their art. Overall, however, the difference between popular exploitations of Decadence and Decadent exploitations of the popular centres on the writer's relationship to Decadence. Whereas popular writers are critical of Decadence, Decadent writers who employ popular genres attempt, often in subtle ways, to promote Decadent artistic principles as well as their anti-bourgeois cultural values. The mediation by Decadents between the artistic and the popular was more far-reaching than the 'fiction' of the Decadent as martyr to art has suggested. Decadents understood their mediation between the high and the popular, as we shall see, in two main ways. Some, such as Robert Hichens and Ernest Dowson and Arthur Moore, regarded their work as a 'collaboration' between high and low, while those less comfortable with what they perceived to be literary slumming, like John Davidson, felt compromised, a view that resulted in fiction that highlights the tensions between high and popular art as 'interference'.

Robert Hichens's 'The Collaborators': a model for Decadent literary production

> In collaboration, no man can be a law unto himself. ... We are both ambitious devils. We are both poor. We are both determined to try a

book. Have we more chance of succeeding if we try it together? I believe so. You have the imagination, the grip, the stern power to evolve the story, to make it seem inevitable, to force it step by step on its way. I can lighten that way. I can plant a few flowers ... on the roadside. And I can, and, what is more, will, check you when you wish to make the story impossibly horrible or fantastic to the verge of the insane. ... This book, if we write it, has got to be a good book, and yet a book that will bring grist to the mill.

Robert Hichens, 'The Collaborators' (1893)[10]

Robert Hichens's story, 'The Collaborators', was first published in *Pall Mall Magazine* in 1893 and was later anthologized in *The Folly of Eustace* (1896), a collection of his short stories. The story makes a similar argument to the one made by Vernon Lee in 'A Dialogue on Novels' but, whereas Lee framed her discussion around the necessity of mediating between the artistically superior French novel and the reticent English novel, Hichens argues for a mediation between high art and the popular. In its depiction of the problems faced by both popular writers aspiring to artistry and by Decadent writers in getting their risqué work published, 'The Collaborators' encapsulates many of the issues I have been concerned with so far and proposes a solution to the problems of literary production in the increasingly commercialized *fin-de-siècle* literary field. In addition, the story provides a framework for understanding how some Decadents conceived of the relationship between high and popular art in their own literary productions.

Though largely forgotten today, Hichens was a writer who mediated very successfully between the élite and the popular realms of the *fin-de-siècle* literary field. Thus, while Hichens may have had less financial and popular success than Marie Corelli, he achieved more critical acclaim and circulated with relative ease among the élite. Though primarily associated with popular fiction, Hichens is regarded in current literary criticism as an 'Artist' within the popular sphere, something of a rich man's Marie Corelli. Richard Bleiler, for example, finds Hichens better at 'provid[ing] vivid and minute descriptions of exotic locales' and more 'capable of treating soberly subject matter that in [Corelli's] hands would be sensationalized or vulgarized'.[11] Even in the 1890s, the names of Corelli and Hichens were often paired in criticism, with Corelli always designated the less talented of the two. Significantly, however, critics also frequently paired Hichens's name with Decadent French writers respected by those among the British literary élite. A reviewer of his 1897 novel, *Flames* (a Decadent mystical story of soul possession), for example, praised his 'Bourget-like felicity' in creating evocative descriptions and compared his depictions of city life with those of Maupassant, Huysmans, and Zola.[12] Such compliments were rarely bestowed on Corelli who was more often criticized for factual errors and stylistic excesses.

In its account of the collaboration between a popular and a Decadent writer, 'The Collaborators' attests to and serves as a justification for Hichens's unique position within the literary field as one who circulated freely between the élite and popular realms. The 'collaborators' of the title are popular writer Henley and the Decadent Trenchard. Henley is 'full of common-sense' and endowed with 'a keen sense of humour', qualities he employs in his writing for *Punch, Fun*, and a 'lively society paper'.[13] Trenchard, by contrast, is an 'excitable', 'intense', and 'intelligent' writer of weighty fiction and articles.[14] Trenchard bears all the hallmarks of the popularized Decadent whose bohemian exploits receive more attention than his literary endeavours. He has an 'irregular life', is fascinated with 'horrors', has an 'immense sense of evil and tragedy and sorrow', and is a morphine addict.[15] The story provides all the titillation of the popular representations of the Decadent that appealed to a middle class fascinated by sensationalized and bohemian aspects of the Decadent's life, for although the story focuses on the collaborative writing project of the two men, the subject of the project (unbeknownst to Henley) is Trenchard's life: the story of a man's obsessive and adulterous relationship with a morphine addict who drags him down until he, too, becomes an addict. The relationship culminates in a tragic murder-suicide perpetrated by Trenchard and written into the story by him just before he proceeds with the act.

But while the story caters to a popular audience in its sensationalized representation of Trenchard's Decadence, it also presents an interesting account of the plight of writers in the *fin-de-siècle* literary field – both of popular writers who aspired to artistry and of Decadents who wanted recognition and money and, more importantly, to be published. The story suggests that a 'collaboration' between the two kinds of writers is the solution to the problem of literary production in the *fin-de-siècle* field. Together, Trenchard and Henley can produce a novel that is at once artistic, popular, and profitable. Trenchard, with his 'imagination ... grip and stern power',[16] will supply the artistic elements while Henley, with his instinctive knowledge of 'what was likely to take and what would be caviare to the general' and his ability to 'tincture a book with a popular element [without] spoil[ing] it' will ensure the book's popular success.[17] Henley will also serve as Trenchard's censor, 'check[ing]' him when he 'wish[es] to make the story impossibly horrible or fantastic to the verge of the insane'.[18] The end product of their efforts will be a book that is 'powerful, but never morbid; tragic ... but not without hope',[19] the kind of book that Lee envisioned when she wrote *Miss Brown*. They will not 'pander ... to the popular taste', but rather 'hit the taste of the day'.[20] In effect, they will write a novel that appeals to all possible audiences from intellectuals and critics to the masses – all without sacrificing artistic integrity or profit.

Idealizing both the imaginative power of the Decadent and the common sense of the popular writer, Hichens imagines the literary product of the mediation between high and low in positive terms as a 'collaboration' rather than as a compromise. As such, the story confirms his own cultural authority as a writer who regarded himself both as an 'artist' of imaginative power and as one who knew what would appeal to the popular taste. In its representation of the merits of collaboration, Hichens's story serves as a validation of writers like himself who were successful at mediating between high and popular art, a success indicated in their appeal to both an élite and popular readership.

A real-life collaboration: Ernest Dowson and Arthur Moore's *Comedy of Masks*

A real-life example of the kind of collaboration imagined by Hichens occurred in the partnership of Ernest Dowson and Arthur Moore,[21] a relationship in which Dowson served as Trenchard to Moore's Henley. While Dowson supplied much of the imaginative inspiration in their collaborations, he relied on Moore to decide whether his schemes were 'practicable' or 'too risqué'.[22] In *A Comedy of Masks*, they bring Decadent high art elements to the popular genre of the three-volume society romance. Peopling the novel with the stock characters of romantic fiction whom Dowson identified as 'the self-sacrificing lover', 'the weak good looking, backboneless, egotistical, shallow successful lover', and the 'charming girl' or 'jeune fille of a million vaudevilles, loved of the British public', Dowson and Moore aimed to produce 'pommade' for 'the many headed Beast'.[23] They conceived of the novel as a 'Besant and Rice pudding' or as a romantic realist novel in the manner of popular writer W. E. Norris.[24] Another likely influence, though unacknowledged by Dowson, was Ouida, whose aesthetic novels, as Talia Schaffer has compellingly argued, were an important influence on male Aesthetes and Decadents who 'masculinized Ouida's aestheticism'.[25] Though Dowson and Moore's female characters are not nearly as engaging as Ouida's, the novel features an older *mondaine* figure whose taste for Watteau, lap dogs, and luxurious home decoration along with her epigrammatic wit recall Ouida's heroines. Dowson and Moore's first choice of publisher was Bentley, an established firm with an impressive list of popular novelists including W. E. Norris, Ouida, Rhoda Broughton, and Marie Corelli. Bentley rejected the novel, however, and it was eventually published by Heinemann. The novel was fairly successful for one of its type by unknown writers. The first three-volume edition of five hundred copies quickly sold out and a second one-volume edition of one thousand copies was printed.

The novel centres on a tragic love triangle between Philip Rainham, 'the self-sacrificing lover' plagued with consumption, Dick Lightmark, popular artist and villainous 'shallow successful lover', and Eve Sylvester, the 'charming girl' of typical romantic fiction. Added to the mix are the witty society matron of fashionable novels, the deceived maiden of romantic fiction, and the newly popularized figure of the Decadent artist. Dowson and Moore clearly knew the formula of such fiction well and many reviewers commented on the novel's indistinguishability from the generic popular novel of the time. 'The story has nothing to recommend it; it is the same old thing told, without spirit, in the same old way', remarked one reviewer.[26] Others criticized the formulaic and predictable characterizations: 'The authors ... have not gone out of their way in search of fresh types or combinations of character';[27] 'Dick Lightmark ... is perhaps a little too like the ordinary villain of fiction'.[28] One reviewer said that Dowson and Moore's novel had 'a strong spiritual affinity' with Beatrice Harraden's *Ships that Pass in the Night*, a bestselling popular romantic tragedy of that year that focused on a doomed love affair between two invalids.[29] Meanwhile, the *National Observer* called it a piece of 'ephemeral writing' and characterized it as a book full of *clichés*.[30] But while Dowson's and Moore's novel was widely acknowledged as the 'pommade' that they had set out to offer the 'many headed Beast',[31] some critics regarded it as modern and original. The *Pall Mall Gazette*, for example, praised it as a distinctly 'modern' book: 'Every character is a product of our nervous, "weary," aesthetic, half-callous, and half-restless age, and they are delicately and vividly drawn.'[32] Emerging as it did before the tide of 'Decadent' and 'sex' fiction that would create such controversy in 1894 and 1895, the novel was praised for qualities that would later stand for the worst excesses of Decadent modern fiction (the depiction of 'nervous', 'weary', and 'aesthetic' types, for example).

The novel, then, occupied at one and the same time two seemingly contradictory categories and was, at least by critical standards, more successful at mediating between high and low art than Wilde's widely disparaged *Dorian Gray* had been. *A Comedy of Masks* was both high and popular art, combining the psychological analysis of the modern Jamesian novel with the epigrammatic wit of the society or drawing-room novel of popular female novelists. As the *Daily Chronicle* reviewer noted, the novel's principal storyline had a 'breadth' and 'solidity' that made it quite unlike 'the vagueness of modern impressionism, and the pettiness of modern realism'.[33] And yet, the reviewer continued, in its 'treatment of subsidiary characters, and of the general background of which they form a part' modern impressionist and realist techniques contributed to 'the delicate emphasis of significant detail; the reticent allusiveness of presentation; the unobtrusive lowness of general tone, giving value and effect to some sudden touch of warmer, brighter colour, which are among the notes of the latest school of contemporary art'.[34] For this reviewer, who was generally critical of modern artistic trends, the novel succeeded precisely because the Impressionist, realist, and Decadent elements were made subservient to the more important task of telling a good story. In other words, it was the perfect collaboration of high art and the popular: it was artistic but it also had a plot, something the modern realist novel often lacked according to critics such as Andrew Lang for whom such novels were characterized by their 'unrelenting exclusion of exciting events and engaging narrative'.[35]

This contradictory reception of the novel as both derivative popular trash and innovative modern art appears less strange if we recall Dowson's position within the field and the conditions governing *fin-de-siècle* literary production. Though setting out to write a popular novel in order to establish himself and to garner a sufficient income to live solely by his pen, Dowson was nonetheless influenced by those writers admired by the élite – writers such as Emile Zola, Henry James, George Meredith, Paul Bourget, Guy de Maupassant, and Gustave Flaubert. Like Havelock Ellis and Arthur Symons, Dowson believed that these writers accurately reflected a modern sophisticated society, a sentiment he expressed in a note written in his copy of Olive Schreiner's *Story of an African Farm*: 'The time for romance, for novels written in the stage method is gone. In a worldly decaying civilization, in an age of nostalgia like the present – what is the meaning of Mr Rider Haggard? He is an anachronism. It is to books like *Madame Bovary* and de Maupassant's *Une Vie* ...[that] one must go to find the true significance of the XIXth century.'[36]

Despite his desire, however, to write 'a study of morbid anatomy in the vein of Paul Bourget',[37] he was all too aware, as his letters indicate, of the conditions of literary production that presented obstacles to this endeavour. Acknowledging the prudishness that governed literary publishing, he wondered, for example, if his idea for a '[Bourget-like novel] would ever go down' and believed 'it would require delicate treatment'.[38] Dowson admitted capitulating to public taste with respect to the literary quality of *A Comedy of Masks*: 'It is not particularly good or particularly original. ... It will be pommade I am afraid, this novel – but it is that is it not which the many headed Beast demands? ... [The story is] melo[dramatic] of course & rather violent but the sort of stuff which takes in this country'.[39] And yet, as much as he was guided to produce such 'pommade' by a desire for fame and economic freedom, Dowson could not entirely stifle his 'artistic' side, which yearned to be part of the literary élite. As he worked on the novel, Dowson gradually came to believe, like Henley and Trenchard in Hichens's story, that the high and the popular were not necessarily irreconcilable. Shortly after beginning the novel, he wrote Moore, 'I am more taken with the novel than I was at first I must say. And I think conceivably we may work it out in a less pommadish spirit than I feared.'[40] Within a few months, he was declaring it 'a superior production'.[41] Dowson's interest was stimulated by certain artistic elements that he conceived for the novel, reflecting his interest in Decadence and in the analytic novels of James and of French writers. These artistic elements were 'shaded in', as Dowson said, to the 'melo' (meaning melodramatic) plot that was designed to please the 'many headed Beast'.[42]

Dowson's use of the phrase 'shaded in' provides another metaphor for the relationship between Decadent high art and the popular. For Dowson, 'to shade in' meant adding artistic elements to an otherwise conventional genre. To this end, he and Moore incorporated minor characters and episodes into the novel to give it a Decadent flavour or, what the *Daily*

Chronicle referred to as, its '*unobtrusive* lowness of general tone' (emphasis added).[43] Dowson's term 'shading in' also, however, suggests other ways in which Decadent or high art elements relate to the popular genre it imposes itself on. Synonyms for the verb 'shade' include 'eclipse', 'obfuscate', 'overshadow', 'blacken', and 'change by imperceptible degrees into something else'.[44] These synonyms hint at the potential distortion effected by Decadence on its host genre. That Dowson and Moore did not, according to the *Daily Chronicle* reviewer, let the 'lowness of general tone' dominate the story is a testament to the writers' abilities to reconcile the apparently competing discourses of the popular and the Decadent in their 'collaborative' effort.

This collaboration ensured that the Decadent or modern elements would form but a minor part of the novel. These elements are indeed, as the *Daily Chronicle* noted, subservient to the more conventional elements of the main story. Impressionistic Decadence colours many of the descriptive passages of the novel, creating a sombre *fin-de-siècle* tone. It is also apparent in the episodes that feature Brodonowski's, a restaurant frequented by artists, modelled on Soho establishments patronized by Dowson and other Decadents. The main character, Philip Rainham, is an ennui-ridden soul, similar, in certain respects, to George Moore's Mike Fletcher, a type that would come to embody the Decadent as described at the height of the notoriety of Decadent fiction in 1895. Dowson and Moore, however, did not go as far as George Moore in developing their protagonist's Decadence, though in 1889 Dowson expressed a desire to write about a Fletcher-like character: 'a man *two-sided*, i.e. by temperament etc, humanus, pleasure loving, keenly sensible to artistic impressions, & to the outward & visible beauty of life – & ... at the same time morbidly conscious of the inherent grossness & futility of it all', whose pessimism 'ma[kes] him either a suicide, a madman, or simply a will-less, disgustful drunken debauchee'.[45] Though Rainham has some of the characteristics of the world-weary Decadent, Dowson and Moore embody the most Decadent elements in a secondary character, Oswyn, an absinthe-drinking painter whom Lightmark describes as 'a virulent fanatic, whose art is the most monstrous thing imaginable'.[46] As originally conceived by Dowson, Oswyn was the stereotypical debauched Decadent artist of popular fiction: 'violent and rather venomous', a 'disreputable artistic *genius*, refusing to adapt himself in any way either in art or life to convention: He might eventually die of excessive absinthe drinking & general disgust at the bêtise of a public which boycotts his oeuvre & buys [Lightmark's] pretty little ineptiae.'[47] This stereotype was precisely that invoked by Corelli in her portrayal of two absinthe-addicted artists in *Wormwood*, Beauvais, the protagonist, who is dying as a result of his absinthe drinking, and Gessonex, his absinthe-addicted painter friend who, disgusted with the bourgeois Parisian art scene, kills himself.[48]

If Dowson and Moore take the Decadent stereotype as a starting point, however, they purposefully move beyond this conventional representation to a reconsideration of the type. So, though Oswyn has an 'uncouth' and 'savage' appearance[49]and rants about the bourgeoisie and the artists who cater to them, the reader is made to see, through the perceptions of Rainham, that Oswyn is endowed with 'nobility', 'singleness', and 'virtue'.[50] Oswyn even becomes the hero of the novel, taking on the responsibility of fathering Lightmark's rejected love-child, thereby proving he has strong ethical and moral principles despite his less-than-conventional lifestyle. Dowson and Moore further undermine the stereotype of the Decadent by re-envisioning his fate. Oswyn does not, therefore, 'die of excessive absinthe drinking & general disgust at the bêtise of a public'[51] as Dowson first planned and as Corelli's stereotypical Decadent artist does. Instead, ironically, Oswyn lives to enjoy commercial artistic success. His work is displayed in the gallery of a prominent dealer and his paintings sell to the society people that he has so much contempt for. Most importantly, however, Oswyn achieves this success without having to compromise his artistic principles.

In rewarding the artist who is uncompromising in his artistic principles, *A Comedy of Masks* upholds the alternative cultural values of the artist who opposes bourgeois culture. Of this culture, Dowson had had little experience. His upbringing had been bohemian in nature. Living off the profits of a family-owned dry dock in Limehouse, Dowson and his parents spent much time travelling abroad and his father educated him. This bohemian existence eventually came to an end, however, when their dry dock business was hit hard by the shift of the shipbuilding and repairing industry from the Thames to the Clyde and the Tyne. This drying up of the family income coupled with the ongoing illnesses of his consumptive parents gave Dowson a keen sense of privation. These factors may have prompted his decision to leave Oxford and to help his father run the dock while pursuing a literary career in his spare time.

Dowson's position as a once carefree bohemian now forced to earn a living shaped his worldview and coloured the representations of artistic life in *A Comedy of Masks*. Thus, although the novel demonstrates sympathy towards the ideals of the uncompromising artist, it also illustrates ambivalence towards this figure. Oswyn's rant against the '*Pompiers, fumistes*, makers of respectable *pommade* ...[with] their thread-paper morality, and their sordid conception of art – a prettiness that would sell'[52] – is greeted by Rainham with impatience, despite his sense of the finer qualities of the artist: 'Rainham had heard it all before; it was full of spleen and rancour, unnecessarily violent, and, conceivably, unjust.'[53] Written by Dowson, who was responsible for the bohemian episodes, this section employs free indirect discourse, a narrative technique central to the psychological novels of the period, to mediate between the extreme positions of the martyr-artist and the commercial sell-out, represented in the novel in the characters of Oswyn and Lightmark. The result of this mediation is a view sympathetic neither to Lightmark or Oswyn, but rather to the authors of the novel, Dowson and

Moore, whose mediation between the high and the popular is endorsed, the narrative reveals, by the sympathetic and intelligent non-artist protagonist Rainham.

Oswyn's invocation of the term 'pommade' in this section is particularly striking given how it recurs in Dowson's letters to Moore during their collaboration on the novel. In these letters, Dowson admits to being one of those 'makers of *pommade*' so loathed by his character Oswyn. At times during the making of this 'pommade', Dowson was disgusted with himself as when he wrote Moore: 'the evil that is done in perverting and warping one's intellectual vision by vicious & trashy novels, such as "Dr Ludovicus" [an earlier collaboration] is simply incalculable. For Heaven's sake let us assert our reason & soothe our consciences by writing an antidote – a novel without any love-making in it at all – or with only love making à la Zola.'[54] As he developed enthusiasm for his excursion into the popular, however, Dowson believed he might produce 'less pommadish' work.[55] Rainham's common-sense reaction to Oswyn's outburst – his sense that Oswyn, as the mediating narrator tells us, is '*conceivably* unjust' (emphasis added) in his views concerning 'the makers of respectable *pommade*'[56] – represents the views of writers such as Dowson who had to come to terms with compromises they made on behalf of the literary marketplace. And although the following sentences of this passage evoke sympathy for the ranting Oswyn, as Rainham acknowledges his 'nobility', 'virtue', and 'genius', there is also a subtle plea for the victims of Oswyn's rancour – those towards whom Oswyn might be being '*unnecessarily* violent, and *conceivably*, unjust'[57] (emphasis added); in other words, artists such as Dowson who appreciated high art as much as Oswyn were not complete commercial sell-outs like Lightmark, but compromised out of a need for money or a desire to establish an artistic reputation.

Just as Rainham's tempered view of Oswyn undercuts the artist's heroic status, so too does the ending, which rewrites the stereotypical fate of the absinthe-addicted, bourgeois-hating, and uncompromising artist. On the one hand, this ending exalts the uncompromising artist figure by demonstrating that his bohemian values are, in fact, more moral than those of a hypocritical bourgeoisie. On the other hand, by granting Oswyn success in his lifetime rather than the more conventional death by absinthe and posthumous fame as Corelli had done for the absinthe-addicted Gessonex in *Wormwood*, Dowson and Moore exact an ironic revenge on him. After all, they are among those 'respectable makers of *pommade*' whom he has 'conceivably' wronged in his censure.[58] Although Oswyn does not sell out in order to obtain fame, his popularity among those he despises forces him to regard his art as a commodity in much the same way as artists such as Dowson, who may have preferred to produce high art but were compelled, out of the desire for fame and/or money, to compromise by producing 'pommade'.

Once again – this time by demonstrating the discomfort of Oswyn as he struggles against but eventually accommodates himself to his success among the bourgeois middle class – the novel indirectly appeals for sympathy for artists like Dowson who mediated between the claims of the marketplace and the claims of high art. *A Comedy of Masks* was the product of just such a mediation as its origins in the minds of its makers and its ambiguous reception as both a conventional and ultra-'modern' novel in the press amply demonstrate. But whereas Oswyn might characterize Dowson's and Moore's mediations as a selling out or a compromising of their art, the writers themselves preferred to view their work as what I have been calling a 'collaboration' between popular and high art in the production of a novel that managed to achieve, in the words of Robert Sherard, both 'a commercial *and* artistic success' (emphasis added).[59]

Collaboration or interference?
John Davidson's *North Wall*

Where Decadence, under Dowson and Moore, was adapted successfully to the popular society romance, it was less well suited to the romantic comedy to which it was brought by John Davidson in *The North Wall* (1885; reissued in 1891 under the title *A Practical Novelist*). In this novel, Davidson brought two of the most seemingly incompatible art forms together to reflect on ideas about the art of novel-writing. As in Dowson and Moore's novel, *The North Wall*'s popular form ironizes the Decadent aesthetic ideology that it seemingly endorses. But whereas Dowson and Moore reconcile the Decadent and popular discourses by indirectly sanctioning the artist who compromises with the public taste in a work conceived as a 'collaboration', for Davidson the Decadent and popular are always in a state of tension. David Weir has called this tension that exists between Decadence and the genres in which it operates 'interference', specifically 'an interference of ideas and literary tendencies':[60] 'the epithet *decadent*', he argues 'comes to be applied to certain novels for their "failure" to adhere to the aesthetic dictates of realism or to the conventions of some established genre (such as the historical novel, the naturalistic novel, the portrait novel, and so on)'.[61] This aspect of Decadence is instrumental in understanding the uneasy relationship between high and popular art in Davidson's Decadent comic romance, in which collaboration results in an interference of ideas.

In outward appearance *The North Wall* (1885) appears to be a cheap popular novel. Its price, one shilling, aligns it with 'shilling shockers', mass-produced sensational fiction that had an even lower status within the literary field than the three-volume novel. At the same time, the novel is framed by nine pages preceding and following the text which contain ads for waterproof cloaks, opticians, travel guides, nerve tonics, clothiers, tricycles, corn plasters, and sponges. Titled, 'The North Wall Advertiser', the advertising section commodifies the novel, implicating it in the consumer-driven literary marketplace.

The opening of the novel, however, challenges its seemingly commercial status, as the protagonist, Maxwell Lee, a struggling author, announces his avant-garde intention of inventing a new artistic form because, to his mind, 'the novel is played out'.[62] Lee, who holds the high art ideals of the Decadents, refuses to compromise his art for profit: he has 'composed dramas and philosophical romances which no publisher, nor editor could be got to read' and has most recently 'refused scornfully the task of writing "an ordinary vulgar, sentimental and sensational story" ' for a 'country weekly'.[63] At the same time, Lee adopts the Decadent view of Naturalism, complaining that it is 'not art', but rather a 'mere copying, a bare pho-tographing of life'.[64] Lee proposes instead to create art in life: 'I am going to create a novel. Practical joking is the new novel in its infancy. ... the centuries of written fiction must culminate in an age of acted fiction. ... Novel-writing is effete; novel creation is about to begin. We shall cause a novel to take place in the world. We shall construct a plot; we shall select a hero; we shall enter his life, and produce the series of events before determined on.'[65] As his 'novel creation' involves living subjects, the project is, necessarily, a collabo-rative one. Indeed, he asks Briscoe, his brother, to 'collaborate' with him in his act of 'novel creation', a request that leads Briscoe to 'bag a hero' for Lee, Henry Chartres, a millionaire who just happens to be a dead ringer for Lee.[66] Lee's project also, of course, involves the collaboration of the Chartres family who are the subjects of his novel-creation. In the end, however, the project is far from collaborative. Lee balks at his brother's ideas, while the Chartres family are, necessarily, unwitting participants. Lee is, rather, an interfering force in the life of the Chartres family in his efforts to create his masterpiece.

As might be expected, 'life' in the novel bears little resemblance to real life. The world Lee enters is the familiar world of romantic comedy with its star-crossed lovers and foundling plots. Though Lee does indeed create a new genre of art by interfering in the lives of others in his act of 'novel-creation', he actually does little to alter the conventional tropes of the novel: he simply transposes them to a new medium. For example, in a chapter entitled 'A "Heavy" Father', Lee's interfering actions mark him as the conventional 'heavy', a type found in melodramatic romances. In addition, his ideas and actions are continually mediated through the discourse of popular romance. Thus, in his confrontation with Franklynne, the star-crossed lover whom he has prevented from eloping with his so-called daughter, Lee outlines a number of conventional novelistic fates for the young man:

> I don't know exactly what course you should follow. It would be very striking, certainly, if you were to go off and drown yourself at once; but I don't think that you'll do that. For myself I would prefer that you shouldn't. I like you too well, and hope that you will continue to play a part in our story. Perhaps you might take to drink. That's a good idea. Go in for dissi-pation: there's nothing like it for the cure of romance. Unworldly diseases

need worldly remedies. And yet that's too common, especially with lady novelists.[67]

Effectively, then, Lee is trapped within the discourse of the 'ordinary vulgar, sentimental, and sensational story' that he otherwise scorns to produce,[68] the only difference being that he has created it in life rather than committing it to paper. Given the ultimately conventional nature of his work, Lee is understandably dissatisfied with what he calls the 'inartistic' result of his experiment,[69] one that replicates the traditional ending of the comic romance plot in which the star-crossed lovers are united.

As if to compensate for this failure to 'interfere' with or disrupt the conventional tropes of the romantic comedy, Lee makes one more attempt in the final chapter, a chapter that provides a frame for the action that has preceded it. Entitled 'Prefatory', the final chapter introduces the reader to 'the author' who has taken it upon himself to write up Lee's adventures since Lee himself has abandoned novel-writing for novel-creation.[70] The chapter is post-modern in its staging of a confrontation between the so-called author and his character, a character who is also an author, and it sits strangely in a narrative that, until this point, has been transparent insofar as the narrative voice is very unobtrusive. In the chapter, Lee approaches 'the author' with a request to 'set down' in its pages 'a variety of matters which some will be glad to carry with them on their way through the book'.[71] These matters, including conventionalized descriptions of the hero and heroine, Lee tells 'the author', are of no interest to the 'imaginative reader',[72] but are expected by readers of conventional popular novels whom he calls variously – the 'proximately experienced reader', the 'unimaginative and thoughtless reader', and the 'fatuous reader'.[73] Included among these conventional readers are businessmen, members of the learned professions, shopkeepers, politicians, matrons, mothers, and unmarried young women.[74] Ultimately, all of the middle class is implicated in Lee's pages-long invective: 'I say, whatever flower of that huge, gaudy, ill-flavoured nosegay of a holiday-making many-headed middle-class monster you may be, this chapter is for you'.[75] Indebted to Baudelaire's address to the '*hypocrite lecteur*' in *Les Fleurs du mal* and recalling Dowson's comments on the 'many-headed Beast', Lee's attack is part of the counter-discourse developed by writers aspiring to high art status in a literary field which seemed increasingly to reduce art to the level of the commodity. At a more general level, Lee's invective also, of course, points to the Decadent's construction of himself outside of his own middle- and professional middle-class origins.

But if Davidson's novel represents an attack on popular literature and its readers, it also satirizes the pretensions of the Aesthetes and Decadents by exploring the *reductio ad absurdum* of the desire to live life as art. Davidson's exploration of life's imitation of art precedes Wilde's more famous consideration of it in 'The Decay of Lying' by four years, as do Lee's

Wildean quips – 'Success is the only failure',[76] 'Ideals cease to be when realized',[77] and 'There is nothing more absurd than reality.'[78] In addition, Lee's status as a comic figure within the novel weakens the seriousness of his position as a Decadent proponent of high art. His apparent 'Decadence' is undermined by his inability to escape the discourse of popular fiction in his 'novel-creation'. Even his *'hypocrite lecteur'* invective cannot salvage his credibility, for it, too, is undermined by 'the author's' deflating comment to Lee – 'not one of the individuals you have addressed ... will read this book'.[79] In addition to mocking both Lee's pretensions to high art and his belief that the novel might reach the broad public he rails against, this comment asserts the artistic superiority of 'the author' at Lee's expense, reminding readers that, despite its appearance and pricing, this is a book, not for Lee's bourgeois addressees, but rather for the few 'imaginative readers' that 'the author' implies are the readers of his book about Lee's adventures. Where Lee's interference is unsuccessful, 'the author' implies that his book, though appearing in the guise of a popular fiction, is really a book targeted towards a sophisticated audience.

Like Dowson's passage critiquing Oswyn's anti-bourgeois sentiments, this chapter is a highly self-conscious reflection on the difficulty of creating art in the commercial marketplace. Ultimately, however, as many critics of Davidson's work argue, it is difficult to determine the object of Davidson's satire. How does Davidson understand the relationship between high and popular art and how does Decadence come into the equation? In many respects, *The North Wall* attests to Davidson's own highly ambiguous feelings about his position within the literary field. We have seen, in Dowson's case, how the compromises he made for the literary market necessitated a distancing of himself from the extreme position within the field occupied by the fictional Oswyn. This distancing resulted in an affirmation of the artist who engages with the marketplace in a reasonable if cautious manner. But where Dowson's and Moore's reaction to the conflicting demands of art and the marketplace resulted in a 'collaborative' novel that reconciled these demands, Davidson's reaction to these contradictory pulls led to a work that emphasized the tensions of his position as a writer, his feeling that the financial needs that involved him in hack writing 'interfered' with his high artistic aims.

As a writer, Davidson's attitudes reflected those of the Aesthetes and Decadents who rejected middle-class values and insisted on the autonomy of art. Like other Decadents, Davidson believed that true art, as he wrote Edmund Gosse in 1900, 'will appeal genuinely only to half a hundred people in a generation'.[80] Furthermore, as he wrote John Lane that same year, he desperately wanted to pursue literature as 'an art and not as a livelihood'.[81] At the same time, his reaction against his father's stern Scottish evangelicalism also made him suspicious of anything that bred in its followers a fervent devotion, hence his scepticism of the Aesthetes' and Decadents' worshipping of the 'religion of art'. This scepticism, already evident in his 1885 novel, *The North Wall*, became more apparent in the 1890s. Though associated with the Rhymers' Club, which counted among its members a number of Decadent poets, Davidson was ambivalent about the group. He 'refused', said fellow Rhymer Ernest Rhys, 'to become an out-and-out member, saying he did not care to be ranked as one of a coterie'.[82] In addition, as a married man with children, Davidson was more dependent on and consequently more bitter about hack writing than other Decadents. His family ties made it less possible for him to occupy what Pierre Bourdieu has called the 'most adventurous' positions within the field – the 'exposed outposts of the avant-garde'[83] that Davidson and his Decadent peers aspired to.

Davidson, then, felt like an outsider. Neither a popular writer nor one who was at ease among the élite, he displayed contempt for both poles of the field, hence the difficulty in determining the object of his satire. Ultimately and ironically, Davidson's ambivalence towards Decadence was coloured by his dawning belief in its inextricable link to the popular and its sham status as high art, a feeling that was brought on by his association with publisher John Lane. At first, the Bodley Head was a godsend to Davidson who was tired of reviewing and 'devilling' for other writers. The Bodley Head was known to make poetry pay and, in 1893, when control of the company lay more firmly in the hands of Elkin Mathews, Davidson was pleased to be publishing with the firm. By 1894, however, as Lane came to dominate and the firm became more commercial, Davidson grew disenchanted with the Bodley Head circle which he characterized as composed of 'those new women who wear their sex on their sleeves ... and ... those new men who are sexless – very pleasant abominations of the time'.[84] His experience with what he regarded as a sham literary avant-garde coloured his view of his early work, particularly his novels which, like the Decadent productions of John Lane's Keynotes series that will be discussed in the next chapter, mediate between the claims of high art and the marketplace in ways that Davidson would come to regret.

Davidson's evident disgust with the Bodley Head and the *Yellow Book* as sites of fashionable bourgeois rather than genuine literary avant-gardism corroborates recent criticism by Laurel Brake and Margaret Stetz that has explored the strategies employed by Lane in selling high art to the middle class.[85] Given Lane's commercial approach to the publishing of the 'beautiful book', it is hardly surprising that Decadence took the form it did – a mediation between the high and the popular. As the examples of Dowson and Moore and of Davidson indicate, however, Decadence had taken this form before Lane made the Bodley Head the main venue for Decadent fiction. The high-profile nature of this enterprise simply served to formalize this process of mediation. As R. D. Brown argues, 'without Lane's publishing ventures, the movement known as Decadence would not have taken the form it did'.[86] Though Brown does not examine Lane's shaping of Decadence in terms of a mediation between the high artistic and the popular, it is clear that this approach informed Lane's understanding of his publications. It makes sense then to turn now to these publications in order to see how the 'collaboration' between the high and the popular manifested itself in works that emerged from the most famous venue of British Decadent fiction – the Bodley Head's Keynote series.

6
'Keynotes' of Decadence, 1894–95

Whereas the introduction of Decadence to popular genres had provoked no critical outrage in the cases of John Davidson's *North Wall* or Ernest Dowson and Arthur Moore's *Comedy of Masks*, this same combination elicited virulent attacks by early 1895. Something had happened between the publication of Dowson and Moore's novel at the end of 1893 and the beginning of 1895 to prompt the emergence of an aggressive counter-Decadent discourse. That something was the launching of the Keynotes series and the *Yellow Book*, both issued from the Bodley Head in 1894. Though, as I have suggested throughout this study, Decadence had been explored in the 1880s and early 1890s in a wide variety of fiction and periodicals, it was through the efforts of publisher Lane that Decadence found its most visible 'public forum'.[1] While neither the books in the Keynotes series nor the *Yellow Book* ever achieved sales figures nearing those of large commercial publishers and popular periodicals, the notoriety surrounding them garnered them much attention in the popular press. In 1894 and 1895, *Punch*, for example, satirized Bodley Head books, the *Yellow Book*, and the New Woman and Decadent writers associated with them, ensuring that, even had one not read these publications, one knew what they were like. Soon, Decadence superseded other literary controversies in the public's attention and the Bodley Head and the *Yellow Book* became synonymous with this literary movement.

The increasing antagonism towards Decadence in 1895, then, was largely prompted by the establishment of a publishing enterprise that seemed wholly designed to promote Decadence. With the launching of the *Yellow Book* and the Keynotes series, Decadence seemed no longer to be a matter of an isolated text here and there: rather, it seemed to be an industry of its own. In addition, the perceived popularity of Bodley Head publications seemed, to opponents of Decadence, to promise a host of imitators in what would amount to a large-scale degradation of literature. It was precisely this perceived popularity that distressed critics of Decadence. If Bodley Head publications had been seen as catering to an intellectual élite there would have been far less consternation. But, as in the case of Vizetelly's translations of French Naturalists, Decadence seemed to many critics to be catering to a popular audience, an impression no doubt strengthened by the Decadents' engagement with popular forms.

Defining the keynotes of Decadence: Perfecting the counter-Decadent discourse

Critics reacted swiftly to the success of the Bodley Head's Keynotes series and its magazine, the *Yellow Book*, making a concerted effort to bring down Decadence by undermining its status as high art. In the first six months of 1895, the counter-Decadent discourse was developed in a flurry of articles denouncing the literary movement. The charges laid against Decadence in these articles run counter to many of the received notions of Decadence as they have come down to us in literary history. For whereas in literary history, Decadence has been described variously as avant-garde, élitist, anti-democratic, aristocratic, misogynistic, and as a high art form radically opposed to the popular, contemporary opponents of Decadence characterized it as a popular art form, appealing to women and the masses, with socialistic and even anarchistic tendencies. In part, these characterizations were strategic, determined by a desire on the part of opponents of Decadence to undermine what they saw as a dangerous literary tendency. What better way to take down Decadence than to challenge its status as high art by linking it with women and the working classes and by exposing the Decadents as hypocrites? And yet, at the same time, the critics were, in some ways, correct in their estimation. After all, much Decadent fiction did indeed combine popular and high art and this disturbed critics at a time when issues of access were of paramount concern in literary debates. For critics of Decadence, the mediation between high art and the popular practised by the Decadents was not only hypocritical, it was also dangerous. For these critics, the blurring of the boundaries between popular and high art threatened to blur important social distinctions as well.

This association of Decadence with popular art, as we have seen, charac-terized the counter-Decadent discourse from early on. By 1895, the views that the Decadents were motivated by cash to produce sensational works aimed at the masses and that Decadent fiction was massively popular were critical commonplaces.[2] James A. Noble, as we have seen, characterized the Decadents in this way, as did Hugh E. M. Stutfield, who worried about the '*enormous* sale of hysterical and disgusting books' (emphasis added).[3] Others noted 'the market value which attaches to an outrage on good taste' and insisted that the treatment 'of the vicious, or impure side of life ... in a superlative degree of naseousness ... act[s] as a bold advertisement to the book, so that money may be made out of it'.[4]

Far from being considered avant-garde, then, Decadent fiction was seen as fodder for the masses as well as more particular readerships within the mass.

Women, for example, were characterized as the main consumers of popular fiction throughout the literary debates of the 1880s and 1890s. Despite the antipathy with which Decadents viewed women readers, whom they blamed for everything from the low standards of journalism to the pervasiveness of second-rate fiction,[5] counter-Decadents identified women as the primary consumers of Decadent fiction. Women writers also figure in this criticism as producers of 'low, loathsome, and vulgar' Decadent fiction,[6] despite women writers' almost unanimous distaste for Decadence. At the same time, while there is no evidence that Decadent fiction was consumed to any considerable degree by the working classes, counter-Decadents feared its influence on them. Thus, despite the anti-democratic nature of much Decadent fiction, critics aligned it with socialist and communist radicalism. Stutfield, for example, insisted that 'Both [the aesthetic sensualist and the communist] have a common hatred of and contempt for whatever is established or held sacred by the majority, and both have a common parentage in exaggerated emotionalism.'[7]

The furore over Decadence might not have been as fierce if the Decadents' claim to be writing for the select few had been taken at face value. Decadence was a source of anxiety because it seemed, from the point of view of its critics, to be widely accessible to women, the masses, and the young. This perception was fed, I would argue, by the ambiguous status of the Decadent text which, to use just a few of the descriptors applied to this work then and now, embodied 'modern', 'avant-garde', 'advanced', 'artistic', 'progressive', 'morbid', and 'abnormal' ideas in a *popular* form or genre. Zola, after all, lost his status as a pernicious influence after the imprisonment of Vizetelly, when cheap editions of his novels were prevented from circulating. The unexpurgated Lutetian Society Zola translations of 1894–95 raised no anxieties, even in the midst of a renewed attack on perniciousness, because their high price put them beyond the reach of the general public who might be corrupted by them. Zola was even received warmly on his 1893 visit to London and ultimately sought refuge in England during the Dreyfus affair (1898–99). As with the controversy over Naturalism, the reaction against Decadence centred on the issue of access, a central issue as Lyn Pykett has argued, in the literary debates of the 1880s and 1890s.[8]

The ambiguousness of Decadent texts explains the emphasis on hypocrisy in the counter-Decadent discourse. In this discourse, the terms 'affectation', 'eccentric', 'pose', '*poseur*', and 'artificial' were employed to denounce Decadents and their works. These words carried particular resonance in the midst of the Wilde trials. Wilde, after all, was accused by Queensbury of 'posing' as a sodomite and Wilde consistently endorsed artificiality and posing. In 'Phrases and Philosophies for the Use of the Young', for example, Wilde extols these qualities in epigrammatic form: 'The first duty in life is to be as artificial as possible. What the second duty is no one has yet discovered'; 'In all unimportant matters, style, not sincerity, is the essential. In all important matters, style, not sincerity, is the essential.'[9] In a pre-postmodern context and with the Wilde trials as a backdrop, affectation and posing became cardinal sins to be avoided by the serious *litterateur*. And though most Decadents took themselves more seriously than Wilde, who engaged in a playful manner with posing and masks, critics tarred them with the same feather. As Noble insisted, the best way to put an end to Decadence was 'to make it ridiculous'.[10]

Making Decadence ridiculous by exposing its hypocrisies was precisely what the *National Observer* had in mind in its bitter denunciation of Decadence in February 1895. Despite the 1894 departure of William Ernest Henley, avowed hater of Decadence, the journal was still a hotbed for anti-Decadent sentiment:

> And what are these who now howl and whine and write their sickly stuff about *décadence*, and pretend to gird at *décadence*, hoping all the while to gain the glory of being classed themselves among the *décadents*, whom, with their puling whimper, they pretend to decry? ... Such creatures are the most despicable excrescences that can grow upon literature. They have not the daring for immorality, and they hug themselves upon being above or beneath morality. ... They make their miserable attempts at a vile and cowardly prurience and might blush to find themselves known for what they are, had they an ordinary honest blush left among them.[11]

The writer's French spelling of Decadence indicates his view that the literature is not native to Britain and that British writers are mere imitators and *poseurs*. The confusing image of the Decadents he puts forth – they pretend to despise '*décadence*' but want to be classed as '*décadents*'; they are not immoral though they should be ashamed at themselves if they could feel shame, and so on – says much about the complex positioning of these writers within the literary field. Decadence was fashionable but only within certain limits. Fashionable too, with an emerging interest in lives of writers and a press willing to report on these lives, were writers. Cultivating an artistic persona, then, something that Wilde was a master at, was an important part of establishing artistic legitimacy. For those among the élite anxious to distinguish themselves from the commercial writer and the 'professional', the dilettante, bohemian, and Decadent were popular models. The fad for anti-bourgeois bohemian artists put writers in a bind, a bind that is unsympathetically described by the *National Observer*. Decadents mediated cautiously between the high literary and the popular, the moral and the immoral, both in the production of their work and in the construction of their identities. From their point of view, this caution was necessary to advance British fiction in a hostile climate. To their enemies, however, this mediation smacked of hypocrisy.

Arthur Machen's *Great God Pan* and Decadent pan(ic)

Given the importance of the Bodley Head in bringing Decadence to the attention of the public, it is not surprising that the *Yellow Book* and the books of the

Keynotes series figure so prominently in the critical attacks on Decadence in 1895. In its vitriolic attack, for example, the *National Observer* invoked the *Yellow Book* and a book it described as a 'work of fiction lately published, the proper place for which would be a jar of spirits in a strictly scientific museum'.[12] This unnamed work was undoubtedly Arthur Machen's *The Great God Pan and the Inmost Light*, which featured prominently in the debates on Decadence at this time and was described in similar terms in other articles and reviews. Though Machen completed *The Great God Pan* in 1891, he was unable to find a publisher until 1894. Before Lane took it on, it had been rejected by Blackwood's, which 'shr[unk] from its central idea', and by *Belgravia* Magazine, which had initially commissioned 'The Inmost Light'.[13] Number five in the Keynotes series, it was one of the series' most successful titles, going into a second edition in February 1895 and sparking numerous parodies including Arthur Compton-Rickett's 'A Yellow Creeper' and Arthur Sykes's 'The Great Pan-Demon: An Unspeakable Story'.

The book consists of two Faustian over-reacher tales which owe much to Robert Louis Stevenson's *fin-de-siècle* gothic fiction, particularly his *Dr Jekyll and Mr Hyde* with its interests in science, the unknowable, and degeneration theory. In the first, 'The Great God Pan', Dr Raymond performs a brain operation on a young woman in the hopes of 'seeing the god Pan' or 'lifting the veil' to see the world beyond.[14] The operation renders the woman a 'hopeless idiot' but she gives birth to a child,[15] the offspring of Pan – a she-devil who leads men to their deaths by exposing them to unnamed horrors. The second story, 'The Inmost Light', also concerns a doctor whose experimental operation on his wife results in the creation of a species of she-devil.

Like *A Comedy of Masks* and *The North Wall*, *The Great God Pan* bears all the signs of its writer's attempt to establish himself in the literary field through a mediation between the popular and the 'artistic'. Though Machen insisted on his arch-purist principles in his 1923 biography, stating that his writing had always been 'entirely divorced from all commercial considerations' and the he 'wrote purely to please [him]self',[16] much of his 1890s work belies these statements. His belated self-representation as an uncompromising writer might well have been coloured by his perceived failure to make his mark in literature, a failure attested to by his claim that he made only £635 from 18 books over a period of 42 years.[17] By the contradictory logic of the field of cultural production, his claim to economic failure functions as a form of symbolic capital where failure to achieve popular success ensures that one's work is true art and emphasizes one's artistic martyrdom.[18] While Machen may well have become more uncompromising as his career progressed, his position in the 1890s resembled that of so many of young writers aspiring to the élite who found it necessary to engage in money-making work.

Machen came to London from Wales in the 1880s intending to be a journalist. Unable to make a start in journalism, he tutored children, wrote poetry in the manner of Swinburne, translated esoteric works, read voraciously, and worked for booksellers and publishers on the fringes of the literary field. During this period, Machen had two of his own works published – *The Anatomy of Tobacco* and the Rabelaisian *Chronicle of Clemendy*, both of which he at least partially financed. Though he was a published author by 1890, Machen's books, written in an antiquarian style and dealing with esoteric interests, were hardly destined to make him an important figure in the literary field nor did they earn him much money. As Mark Valentine indicates, not even the popularity of medievalism among late-Victorians attracted readers to the *Chronicle of Clemendy*, for Machen's medievalism was earthy and bawdy, not the fashionable drawing-room medievalism popularized by Aestheticism.[19]

By 1890 Machen realized that he would not succeed in the literary world with such esoteric work and determined to pursue a more commercial literary path. He abandoned his antiquarian style and began, as William Gekle notes, to 'write in the modern manner'.[20] From this point on, his stories began appearing in periodicals such as the *Globe* and the *St. James's Gazette*. In addition, Machen began cultivating relationships with those among the élite, Wilde in particular, to whom he sent a copy of his translation of Béroalde de Verville. Ever the iconoclast, though, Machen also delighted in shocking the élite. He was convinced, for example, that his admission to *Yellow Book* editor Henry Harland that he admired the popular *Memoirs of Sherlock Holmes* was the reason he was never asked to contribute to the periodical.[21] Like other Decadents, Machen developed himself as a more commercial writer by adapting his avant-garde and esoteric interests to a popular medium. Despite his claims, then, that commercial considerations never entered his mind, Machen's *Great God Pan* bears all the signs of the compromises characteristic of the writer mediating between the claims of art and the claims of the marketplace in a product that represents a 'collaboration' between high and popular art.

The Great God Pan's claims to 'high art' lie in its treatment of the arcane and its concern with elements of literary style. Certainly in its physical appearance *The Great God Pan* resembled books of a high literary and belletristic character. Design, after all, was an important feature of Bodley Head publications and each of the first 21 volumes of the Keynotes series had a cover, title page, and key monogram of the author's initials designed by Aubrey Beardsley. At least one reviewer remarked on *The Great God Pan*'s 'striking covers, the beautiful title-page especially, the fine paper, and the handsome type', which he felt 'point[ed] to the perfection of taste in the art of book production'.[22] The book's beautiful appearance, according to this reviewer, was in keeping with the 'artistic' tale[23] contained in it. In all respects, the book presented a 'highbrow' image and appealed to the younger élite. Richard Le Gallienne extolled the work and George Egerton, though she disliked its theme and content, thought that 'for its writing alone the *Great God Pan* was undeniably worth publishing'.[24]

The book's high art status also lay, as I have said, in its representation of the 'modern young man', the Decadent type that Moore had introduced in *Confessions of a Young Man* and *Mike Fletcher* and that Wilde had popularized in *The Picture of Dorian Gray*. Like Moore's 'young man' and the dilettantes that people *Dorian Gray*, Machen's protagonists are examples of the Decadent social type that emerged as a result of the rift between the professional and business middle class and many of them are also aspiring *litterateurs*. They are idealized images, however, as none of them make the artistic compromises that their real-life counterparts did. Dyson, for example, who figures in 'The Inmost Light' and in later Machen stories, is endowed with 'a good classical education and a positive distaste for business'.[25] Like many of his real-life Decadent counterparts, Dyson lacks a university education due to his father's precarious finances and, like them, he is largely self-educated, declaring, as Moore did in *Confessions*, that Piccadilly has been his university.[26] Dyson's dilettantish existence as a literary man who writes purely for his own pleasure is supported by an inheritance. His high literary endeavours are 'a profound mystery'[27] to his lowbrow friends – friends such as Salisbury who reads novels that treat 'sport and love in a manner that suggested the collaboration of a stud-groom and a ladies' college'.[28] These friends, whose reading tastes incline towards the cheap and popular, cannot understand why they never see Dyson's works among 'the railway bookstalls'.[29] Clarke, of 'The Great God Pan', though not a literary man, prides himself on his 'literary ability' but prefers instead the 'reading, compiling, and arranging and rearranging' of his studies into esoteric and 'morbid' subjects.[30]

In privileging the esoteric, Machen's dilettantes valorize the anti-bourgeois and anti-professional values of the Decadents who aimed to escape their class origins. Like real-life Decadents, his characters distinguish their dilettantism from middle-class professionalism and all have interests in alternative cultures and forms of knowledge. Dr Black, of 'The Inmost Light', resents having to pursue 'professional studies' because it means the sacrifice of his interests in 'curious and obscure branches of knowledge'.[31] Austin, of 'The Great God Pan', has an 'intimate knowledge of London life, both in its tenebrous and luminous phases',[32] while Dyson of 'The Inmost Light' is an expert on London's criminal underworld, a world unknown to the mainstream press which only reports on 'commonplace and brutal murders'.[33]

Even their homes represent their oppositional cultural interests. In contrast with his lowbrow friend Salisbury's bourgeois home with its 'green rep ... oleographs, [and] ... gilt framed mirror',[34] Dyson's abode reflects 'all the colours of the East' with its 'strangely worked curtains', its 'oak armoire' with 'jars and plates of old French china', and its 'black and white etchings not to be found in the Haymarket or in Bond Street', which 'stood out against the splendour of a Japanese paper'.[35] Austin, of 'The Great God Pan', has equally exotic tastes. His rooms are 'furnished richly, yet oddly, where every chair and bookcase and table, every rug and jar and ornament seemed to be a thing apart, preserving each its own individuality'.[36] Of course, the 'individuality' of Austin's and Dyson's furniture in contrast with the bourgeois decor of Salisbury's rooms is symbolic of the individuality of its owners, whose cultivation of eccentric tastes is part of an attempt to distinguish themselves from bourgeois consumer culture. And yet, ironically, as Rita Felski argues, this form of dilettantism – 'the search for ever more arcane objects not yet trivialized by mass reproduction' – merely 'echoes the same cult of novelty which propels the logic of capitalist consumerism'.[37] Ultimately, the Decadent's 'attempt to create a uniquely individual style reveals his inevitable reliance upon the very categories of evaluation against which he ostensibly pits himself'.[38] The same might be said of Machen's book, a book that, in appearance, attests to its distinction from cheap popular fiction and yet which relies on its trappings.

Though *The Great God Pan* was deemed artistic by Machen's peers and by some reviewers, most equated it, at some level, with cheap popular fiction. As in the more general criticisms of Decadence that I have described, critics reacted against the collaboration of popular and highbrow elements in the work. From an artistic viewpoint, for example, the popular elements lowered the status of the work as art. Thus, a reviewer for the *Guardian* exhorted Machen to 'make a choice between the art of fiction and penny-a-lining'[39] instead of producing a hybrid work that was unsatisfactory in both artistic and popular terms. Another reviewer made a similar complaint, arguing that the hybrid nature of Machen's work would prove unsatisfactory to all readers: to the less educated, the book would prove 'mystifying' in its treatment of the occult, while 'intellectual readers' would think it was simply 'poking fun ... about the unseen'.[40] The *Cork Examiner* was harsher, insisting that Machen had no right to consider himself an 'artist': 'In our judgement, this is what children call "a frightened story", and as an artistic piece of fiction, it calls for no serious consideration.'[41] In their zeal for literary homogeneity, these critics were insisting on distinctions between kinds of literary works, with these kinds being determined according to readership. Books like Machen's, and indeed those of other Decadents, threatened to erase these distinctions by promiscuously mixing elements of high and low. These critics were offended at being catered to by a book that also addressed lowbrow or juvenile tastes.

Moral critics, by contrast, feared the effects on a general readership of mature content best reserved for educated readers. Thus, while the *Cork Examiner* found Machen's book childish, other reviews insisted that this was no book for 'imaginative young people' or 'the proverbial girl of fifteen', let alone children.[42] Less worried about the 'artistry' or lack thereof in the work, these critics were concerned about access. Their insistence that the book was not for young people was necessary because, as a romance in the Stevensonian vein, it certainly appeared to be the kind of fiction directed at such readers. For these critics, the treatment of advanced subject matter in a popular form represented a disturbing disruption of genre conventions that constituted in their minds a Decadent text. *The Great God Pan* combined elements of romance and realism – the 'high imaginative faculty' characteristic of romance, with the chirurgical interests of realist fiction.[43] The result of this combination was, as one critic argued, 'an imaginative art eaten into by the canker of morbidity and reeking with the air of decay and death'.[44] For these reviewers, Machen's mediation between high and low was not a successful collaboration of the artistic and the popular. Rather, it produced a popular fiction rotting, infected, and diseased from its contact with so-called high art.

The book, then, failed to provide the compensatory allegory of the Stevensonian gothic romance. Thus, where Stevenson's 'gruesome studies in dehumanisation' in *Dr Jekyll and Mr Hyde* were 'justified', according to one critic, Machen's were not.[45] Unlike Stevenson's allegorical tales of terror, Machen's book was 'So strangely terrible and unclean ... that its perusal leaves an evil odor on the air of the mind, and we are unable to discover any counterbalance in the way of lesson or deduction'.[46] Other reviewers also thought an allegory was necessary to redeem the otherwise nasty subject matter of the story.[47] By not providing an allegory, Machen broke the rules of the genre, producing a book that was 'disgust[ing]',[48] 'unwholesome',[49] 'morbid',[50] 'repulsive',[51] and 'evil'.[52] Moreover, it was 'unmanly',[53] exactly what the masculinized romance celebrated by Stevenson, Haggard, and Lang was intended not to be.

Machen's mixture of romance and realism or, what was called, 'The mingling of old mythology with *fin de siècle* Piccadilly',[54] resulted in a story J. A. Spender considered 'most truly Decadent',[55] but what we now consider nothing more than a horror story. Machen himself considered his work 'realist' in a symbolic sense in that, like Dr Raymond in *The Great God Pan*, he wanted to reveal the 'reality' beyond material existence in his work.[56] Susan Navarette has examined how the *fin-de-siècle* horror tale responded to nineteenth-century scientific theories by embodying the cultural anxieties these theories produced. These texts were realist, she says, in that writers of these tales developed 'structural, stylistic, and thematic systems' in order 'to record and to reenact in narrative form what they understood to be the entropic, devolutionary, and degenerate forces prevailing within the natural world'.[57] For opponents of Decadence, however, these texts were also, in Nordau's terms, 'psycho-physiologically accurate', exposing the 'psychological and physiological stigmata of their makers'.[58] That writers of Decadent litera- ture were morbid, neurotic, hysterical, and degenerate was a critical common- place of the counter-Decadent discourse. The *Literary News* said of *The Great God Pan*, for example, that it was 'too morbid to be the production of a healthy mind',[59] and this is just one example among many of the tendency to equate the often morbid subject matter of Decadent fiction with its authors.

Like Navarette, Linda Dowling regards Decadence as intellectually engaged with late Victorian scientific theories, though Dowling focuses specifically on language. Decadence, she argues 'emerged from a linguistic crisis, a crisis in Victorian attitudes towards language brought about by the new comparative philology earlier imported from the continent'.[60] Both Navarette and Dowling argue that Decadence reflects this crisis in stylistic terms and both see disruption, hesitancy, and what Dowling calls the 'unutterability topos' as central features of Decadent stylistics.[61] For Navarette, these stylistic effects *'embody*, rather than merely emphasize themes of madness, alienation, and decay',[62] while for Dowling they represent attempts at linguistic renewal in a time of cultural crisis.[63] Ultimately, for Dowling, Decadence in Britain existed primarily as a series of stylistic effects. The 'displacement of cultural ideals and cultural anxiety onto language', she argues, 'explains why we also glimpse in the background of Victorian Decadence no lurid tales of sin and sensation and forbidden experience but a range of stylistic effects, of quiet disruptions and insistent subversions'.[64]

But the absence of lurid tales of sin and sensation and the abundance of stylistic disruptions, hesitancies, and silences was also, more practically, a function of the conditions of production that governed the British literary field of the 1890s. Quite simply, the force of moral pressure was too strong within late-Victorian culture to allow for the production of lurid tales of sin and sensation on a par with French literature. As I have suggested earlier, publishers and, consequently, authors proceeded with caution in an environment in which the wrath of the circulating libraries and of organizations like the National Vigilance Association had serious consequences. In this context, gaps, silences, and hesitancies stood in for what could not be written about. These self-censoring techniques are likely what Henley of 'The Collaborators' imposed when Trenchard tried to 'make the story impossibly horrible or fantastic'[65] and what Moore, by Dowson's account, brought to their collaboration.[66]

Some writers, such as Wilde, turned what were, in a sense, stylistic imperatives imposed by a morally vigilant society from an evil necessity into an artistic strategy. If Wilde was influenced in his writing of *Dorian Gray* by the literary marketplace, he was not, as one of the literary élite, going to admit it to his detractors. Where his detractors read evil and corruption in Wilde's silences, gaps, and indeterminacies, he turned the tables on them. Writing to Henley, the editor of the *Scots Observer*, in response to the journal's scathing review of the story, he said,

> It was necessary ... for the dramatic development of this story to surround Dorian Gray with an atmosphere of moral corruption. ... To keep this atmosphere vague and indeterminate and wonderful was the aim of the artist who wrote the story. I claim ... that he has succeeded. Each man

sees his own sins in Dorian Gray. What Dorian Gray's sins are no one knows. He who finds them has brought them.[67]

Wilde's defence of his vagueness and indeterminacy, then, has the added bonus of exposing the prurience of his detractors. He used this artistic defence of his stylistic indeterminacy as the basis of the epigrams forming the preface of the book version of *Dorian Gray*. Many of these epigrams emphasize the role of the reader as the maker of meaning in the text, most notably, 'Those who find ugly meanings in beautiful things are corrupt without being charming' and 'It is the spectator, and not life, that art really mirrors.'[68]

Despite Wilde's clever artistic defence, there were, of course, practical reasons governing the vague and indeterminate nature of his style, not least of which was the fact that the story was originally written for a family magazine. This style, however, did not save Wilde from charges of Decadence and indecency. It did, however, provide a model for writers of Decadent fiction following him. Vagueness and indeterminacy were important features of Decadence, then, not only in their capacity for embodying cultural anxieties of the period, as Dowling and Navarette have ably demonstrated, but also as part of a strategic effort to publish 'advanced' material in a hostile climate. These stylistic features provided a means of mediating between the claims of high art and the claims of the marketplace. One could defend them artistically, as Wilde had done, while at the same time finding yet another means of attacking the bourgeois *hypocrite lecteur*. Additionally, these indeterminate and disjointed narratives with their silences and gaps represented a distinctively modern artistic style that symbolized the Decadents' break with conventional Victorian narrative form. Finally, this narrative indeterminacy around *risqué* subject matter was a piece of marketing ingenuity. In seeming to acquiesce to the reticent public, the silences and gaps within Decadent texts rendered them publishable and saved writers and publishers from prosecution. But also, since there was as much prurience as reticence among the general reading public, this indeterminate style was titillating to the reader.

Though contemporary reviews more often linked *The Great God Pan* to the tales of Stevenson, Wilde also influenced Machen. Machen first met Wilde in the summer of 1890, after he had just read *Dorian Gray*. Their meeting coincided with Machen's determination to produce more popular work and it was during this summer that he began working on his own vague and indeterminate tale, *The Great God Pan*. Like Wilde, Machen put vagueness and indeterminacy, stylistic features in part imposed by the moral scruples of the British public, to an artistic end. But if Wilde intended his vagueness and indeterminacy to expose the hypocrisies of his reading public, Machen teased his readership with omissions and gaps, checking himself, and failing to deliver just when the narrative seems about to offer up salacious details.

The Great God Pan is full of gaps, silences, and omissions and readers are continually made aware that they know less than the dilettante Decadents in the story. At one point, for example, Clarke takes up a volume from his collection of research into 'morbid subjects'.[69] These notes describe the interaction of Helen V. with Rachel M. who consort with Pan in the woods. When Clarke reaches the point in the account in which Rachel is about to reveal what happened in the woods, he suddenly closes the book, denying the reader access to the terrible secrets of the god Pan. Clarke's impulse to shut the book at the most terrible point in the narrative leads him to recall that when he first heard the story he had insisted that his friend stop at the very same instant. Despite his plea, however, his friend, the narrative tells us, 'had told his story to the end'.[70] Within the space of two pages, the reader has twice been titillated and twice denied access to knowledge that only the characters in the story have. A similar incident occurs when Austin flings down a manuscript after seeing just 'a word and a phrase' of the account of a witness to Helen V.'s 'nameless infamies', a witness who has been driven insane by what he has read.[71]

These documents that threaten to destroy those that read them just as the incidents they recount have destroyed those who have written them symbolize the 'Decadent' work Machen's story might have been had he not employed reticence in the telling of it. The gaps and silences make an otherwise unpublishable story publishable, just as Henley's 'checks' in Hichens's story make his collaboration with the Decadent Trenchard acceptable. As it stands, Machen's work is, therefore, unlike the manuscripts detailing the 'most morbid subjects'[72] that circulate among the Decadent dilettantes in his story. So too, it is unlike the arcane occult and erotic works that he dealt with while working in the bookselling and publishing underground. Machen's gaps enable the story to be circulated beyond the few dilettante readers who constituted the ideal readership of Decadents. In deciding to write for a more popular readership, Machen abandoned his earlier style, a style of interest only to the dilettantes who served as customers of the publishers and booksellers he had previously worked for. The gaps turned his previously unmarketable esoteric knowledge into a marketable commodity, while still advertising his esotericism to like-minded souls among the literary avant-garde.

Machen's mediation between the high and the popular, however, failed to result in a book that appealed to both a general and a sophisticated readership. Despite his vagueness, the book was still too explicit for some who deplored the book's 'unclean ... suggestions'[73] and the 'glimpses' it provided of things that were 'singularly repulsive'.[74] For others, the vagueness made the book quite simply 'absurd'.[75] It was an 'impossible subject' for treatment in popular form according to one reviewer,[76] a sentiment shared by another who, on the one hand, 'congratulate[d]' Machen on 'having failed in the courage to make plain the mysterious horrors' of a tale meant for popular readership while, on the other, criticized the 'inchoate and confused' story such reticence produced.[77] For other, less faint-hearted reviewers, Machen had, however, not been courageous enough. His lack of courage undermined the potential 'art' of the work: 'His art' declared the *Observer*, 'has been hampered by the limitations imposed upon it through his having to leave his ingenious horror "indescribable" and "unutterable" from first to last ... the general effect ... is, we fear, hardly so creepy as it would have been if it had dared to be intelligible'.[78] Similarly, *Woman* criticized the writer's belief that 'the art of writing is the art of leaving out', declaring that the art of writing was *also* 'the art of leaving in'.[79] In focusing on his failure to produce 'art', these reviewers neglect to consider what was at stake for Machen in being more explicit about his horrors than he had been. The reviewer for the *Observer*, who implied that Machen lacked the *daring* to be intelligible, refers to 'limitations imposed' upon the writer, but suggests that these were self-imposed.[80] But Machen's 'having to leave his ingenious horror "indescribable" and "unutterable" ', was, if self-imposed, nevertheless based on a practical understanding of the conditions of production and reception in *fin-de-siècle* Britain. These conditions determined that the production of Decadence was highly circumscribed and that, even if reticence was employed, Decadent fiction was likely to be received with outrage by moral watchdogs such as Spender for whom, 'incoherent' though it might be, Machen's *Great God Pan* was a 'most truly Decadent ... nightmare of sex'.[81]

Transcending genre: high/low collaboration in M. P. Shiel's *Prince Zaleski*

Though certainly not the 'nightmare of sex' that Machen's tales were, M. P. Shiel's collection of stories, *Prince Zaleski* (1895), number seven in the Keynotes series, was also part of the controversy over Decadence in 1895. Like the Decadent fiction discussed in this and the previous chapter, Shiel's *Zaleski* is a collaboration of high and low, bringing an elevated style and archaisms to one of the most popular genres of the 1890s – the detective story, a genre brought into prominence by the spectacular success of Arthur Conan Doyle's Holmes stories which appeared in the *Strand* magazine. Shiel no doubt recognized the profitability of creating a similar detective hero after Doyle killed off Holmes in December 1893. Indeed, Shiel himself had published stories in the *Strand* at the height of Holmes's popularity.

Like his Decadent counterparts, Shiel eventually turned away from his professional roots. Coming to Britain from Montserrat in 1885, he had intended to secure a position in the Colonial Office. Instead, he did some teaching while reading for his BA and may have begun studying medicine as well, before turning to a literary career in about 1889. Again, like other Decadents, Shiel initially resigned himself to the necessity of hackwork. His first publication was a prize story for the cheap mass periodical *Rare Bits* in December 1889. He also served as assistant to the editor of a weekly paper in addition to his contributions to the *Strand* and other magazines. Finally, in early 1894, Shiel offered *Prince Zaleski* to John Lane.

Prince Zaleski consists of three stories, cases brought by 'Shiel', the narrator, to Zaleski, an exiled Russian prince living in a former abbey in Monmouthshire. Like Doyle's Holmes, Zaleski suffers from *ennui*, is anti-bourgeois, has exotic tastes and arcane knowledge, and indulges in drug-taking (cannabis in Zaleski's case). Zaleski, however, is even further removed from society and contemporary culture than Holmes, living the life of a hermit, reading no newspapers, and donning himself in Asiatic dress. His surroundings, too, are more extravagantly appointed than Holmes's. He reposes behind a door 'tapestried with ... python's skin' in the 'semi-darkness of the very faint greenish lustre [which] radiate[s] from an open censerlike *lampas* of fretted gold in the centre of the domed encausted roof. ... The hangings [are] of wine-coloured velvet, heavy, gold-fringed and embroidered at Nurshedebad'.[82] He is surrounded by curios, among them a palaeolithic implement, a Chinese 'wise man', a Gnostic gem, a Graeco-Etruscan amphora, Flemish sepulchral brasses, runic tablets, miniature paintings, a winged bull, Tamil scriptures on lacquered leaves of the talipot, medieval reliquaries, Brahmin gods, and an open sarcophagus containing the mummy of an ancient Memphian, and so on.[83] In degree, then, Shiel's detective exceeds Doyle's in Decadence.

The three stories, however, are the familiar fodder of the detective genre. The first, 'The Race of Orven', concerns the murder of a wealthy patriarch of an aristocratic but no longer wealthy English family. The second, 'The Stone of the Edmundsbury Monks', treats the murder of Sir Jocelin Saul, orientalist and descendent of a great English family, also in decline. Finally, 'The S. S.' centres on a mysterious rash of murders and/or suicides throughout Europe that are in some way connected. As in many *fin-de-siècle* examples of this genre, the theme of degeneration figures largely, from the sterile family lines of the Orvens and the Sauls, to the hereditary insanity among the Orvens, to the widespread degeneration of European nations that prompts the mass killings in the final story. In some respects, then, Shiel's tales are no more Decadent than Doyle's, with little to distinguish them from commercial fiction. The incorporation of Decadent elements into this type of fiction was not unprecedented. Doyle, for example, had incorporated Decadence unproblematically into the genre. Context and style, however, counted for much in defining Decadence in this period. Popular novels that featured Decadence such as Corelli's *Wormwood* were generally not mistaken for Decadent. Her style and moralizing militated against this charge as did the novel's publication venue – Bentley's was not a publisher of Decadence. Similarly, though Holmes was sometimes suspiciously Decadent, the stories aroused no controversy. Doyle's style bore little trace of an affinity with art-for-art's-sake principles. Besides which, his stories appeared in the respectable pages of the *Strand*. As a product of the Bodley Head, Shiel's *Zaleski*, by contrast, was Decadent by association. As one reviewer put it, 'As is the *Yellow Book* to the *Strand Magazine*, so is *Prince Zaleski* to Sherlock Holmes'.[84]

This reviewer might also have remarked, 'As is the *Yellow Book* to the *Strand Magazine*, so is Shiel to Doyle'. That Shiel offered his stories to John Lane rather than to the *Strand*, for which he had already written, is telling and suggests a degree of strategic calculation. Though eager to profit from a popular literary trend, he also had high artistic aspirations and the Bodley Head was at once a centre for writers aspiring to the élite and a firm that was able to sell and draw attention to their works. Shiel's stories give every indication of his intention to outdo his more popular rival in the genre. At every turn, Shiel sought to better Doyle, to produce a collaboration between the popular and the high artistic that would transcend the limits of the genre. Zaleski's exaggerated Decadence described above is a case in point. So too are Shiel's digressive intellectual diatribes and his indulgence in Decadent stylistics – his preciosity of style, his exoticism, archaisms, and use of foreign words – what reviewers referred to as his 'tropical luxuriance', 'inflated language and ... [the] extravagance of his descriptions'.[85] These elements contrasted Shiel's stories sharply with Doyle's, which were noted in contemporary reviews for their 'directness and pith' and 'free[dom] from padding'.[86] Some critics believed that Shiel had outdone Doyle. The *Times* reviewer, for example, regarded *Zaleski* as a decided advance within the genre, finding Shiel's detective a 'more gifted personage – the *dilettante* Œdipus' – than was to be found in standard detective fiction.[87] Never one for modesty, Shiel himself believed that his poetic style made *Prince Zaleski* transcend the base and, to his mind, inartistic, Holmes story and he hated being compared to Doyle for whom he had a snobbish contempt: 'Why do you insist on comparing me with Conan Doyle?' he asked his sister, 'Conan Doyle does not pretend to be a poet. I do.'[88]

If Shiel disliked being compared with Doyle, he invited comparisons with Edgar Allan Poe, to whose work he was even more greatly indebted. The opening lines of the story, for example, evoke Poe's hermit-like characters and eerie, otherworldly settings:

> Never without grief and pain could I remember the fate of Prince Zaleski – victim of a too importunate, too unfortunate Love, which the fulgor of the throne itself could not abash; exile perforce from his native land, and voluntary exile from the rest of men! Having renounced the world, over which, lurid and inscrutable as a falling star, he had passed, the world quickly ceased to wonder at him. ...
>
> I reached the gloomy abode of my friend as the sun set. It was a vast palace of the older world standing lonely in the mist of woodland, and approached by a sombre avenue of poplars and cypresses, through which the sunlight hardly pierced.[89]

Shiel called Poe's Dupin '*the* detective and father of detectives' and declared 'Zaleski' his 'legitimate son', while Holmes, he argued, was Dupin's 'bastard son'.[90] The comparison with Poe is apt, not least because Poe, like Meredith and Stevenson, was a writer whose popularity bridged the 'great divide' between an élite and popular readership in *fin-de-siècle* Britain. Poe was 'a great literary artist, as well as a clever constructor of plots', remarked one reviewer of *Prince Zaleski* who regarded Shiel as a 'true disciple' of the American writer.[91] The existence of distinct readerships for Poe in *fin-de-siècle* Britain is attested to by the variety of publication venues for his work. While his élite readership, the Decadents among them, was catered to by publishers such as Leonard Smithers and Chatto and Windus (who published the 'choice works' of Poe with an introduction by Baudelaire), the masses were supplied by publishers of cheap fiction such as Walter Scott, Newnes, and Ward Lock. Shiel's desire to be compared with Poe is in keeping with the Decadents' interest in finding literary models who mediated successfully between the claims of high art and the demands of the literary marketplace and who transcended the limits of genre, writers who were great stylists but who were also able to attract the larger reading public by constructing engaging plots.

Though comparisons with Poe were numerous in the reviews of the book, Shiel was not able to span the 'great divide' between reading publics as well as Poe did. For the most part, his work was seen as 'high art' for 'the select few who can appreciate delicate work, and who are not bored by a touch of metaphysics'.[92] '[*Prince Zaleski* is] a very superior article altogether', declared *Vanity Fair*, 'and intended for the delight of a very superior class of readers'.[93] Shiel's artistry overwhelmed the plot, his 'over-elaboration' and 'superabundance of detail' were 'not quite simple and direct enough' for the average reader in a genre in which the 'most successful' stories 'attain their end by an almost bald clearness of plot'.[94] His stories were, quite simply, too obscure for some, such as the *Guardian* reviewer who declared, 'We do not pretend to have entirely understood any one of them'.[95]

Though the *Guardian* reviewer may have claimed not to understand Shiel's stories, he knew he did not like them or the ideas contained in them. The *Guardian* was a 'High Church' weekly, a family and literary review,[96] not likely to endorse the cultural values of the Aesthetes and Decadents. Zaleski, like the protagonists of Moore's and Machen's works, is a *dilettante* with exotic tastes in the obscure and arcane, counter-knowledges to the utilitarian and practical knowledge endorsed by the Victorian middle class. Zaleski solves all cases through his unorthodox knowledge of the histories of aristocratic European families, European countries, philology, and Oriental, ancient Greek, and Roman literature, culture, and history. Zaleski is 'a consummate *cognoscente* – a profound amateur'.[97] His specialist knowledge is not used in the way professionals use it – in the service of the public or in the pursuit of social and economic rewards.[98] Though through his interventions the innocent are rewarded and the guilty punished, Zaleski takes on cases only insofar as they challenge him. He has no particular philanthropic interests. His knowledge is for knowledge's sake and he eschews ethical and moral imperatives in the same way that Decadents and Aesthetes did in their valorization of art-for-art's-sake principles. Zaleski's knowledge is precisely the kind pursued by the sons of professionals who became Decadents and who sought an aristocratic form of self-culture in opposition to the utilitarian education of the bourgeois middle class. This was the 'self-culture' so openly disparaged by conservative critics of Aestheticism and Decadence since the 1880s when Moore was attacked for his valorization of this form of education in *Confessions*. Like Moore before him, Shiel was ridiculed for his promotion of esoteric knowledge. The *Times* critic, for example, took exception to Shiel's pretensions to intellectual superiority by noting that he was 'perhaps more widely than exactly' read and by pointing to his error in identifying Sophocles as an 'epic poet'.[99]

While Shiel's valorization of self-culture left him open to mockery, his ideas about degeneration were most offensive to the reviewer for the 'High Church' *Guardian* reviewer. The reviewer responds to Shiel's representation of degeneration in the stories by drawing on the then-popular theories of Nordau and Lombroso. Shiel's representation of degeneration in *Prince Zaleski* is significant because ultimately he aligns the Decadent Zaleski with regeneration and cultural salvation, locating degeneration and Decadence in British society. Explaining his view of cultural development to the narrator 'Shiel', Zaleski says,

> By the term [culture] I mean not so much attainment in general, as *mood* in particular. Whether or when such mood may become universal may be to you a matter of doubt. As for me, I often think that when the era of civilisation begins ... when the races of the world cease to be credulous, ovine mobs and become critical, human nations, then will be the ushering in of the ten thousand years of a *clairvoyant* culture. But nowhere, and at no time during the very few hundreds of years that man has occupied the earth, has there been one single sign of its presence. In individuals, yes ... but in humanity never. ... The reason, I fancy, is not so much that man is a hopeless fool, as that Time ... has, as we know, only just begun.[100]

In the process of this discourse, Zaleski counters the popular belief that culture is degenerating. He insists, rather, that it is already degenerate or, more properly, primitive and that it is moving towards regeneration, though it is continually threatened by degenerating forces such as 'Medical Science'. Zaleski condemns 'Medical Science' on eugenic principles, arguing that it is a means by which we 'conserve our worst'.[101] At the same time, he insists that what society regards as 'progress' is really 'Decadence, fatty degeneration'.[102] Locating Decadence in what he calls the 'thoughtless humanism' that is traditionally regarded as progress,[103] Zaleski challenges readers' perceptions that he is Decadent. Rather, both he and his friend 'Shiel' are exceptional individuals, indications that society may be able to develop beyond the 'ovine mob' culture that currently exists. They are proof, he insists, that

> It *is* possible, by taking thought, to add one cubit – or say a hand, or a dactyl – to your stature; you *may* develop powers slightly – very slightly, but distinctly, both in kind and degree – in advance of those of the mass who live in or about the same cycle of time in which you live. But it is only when the powers to which I refer are shared by the mass – when what, for want of another term, I call the age of the Cultured Mood has at length arrived – that their exercise will become easy and familiar to the individual; and who shall say what presciences, prisms, *séances*, what introspective craft, Genie apocalypses, shall not *then* become possible to the few who stand spiritually in the van of men.[104]

Zaleski's and 'Shiel's' distinction from the mass of humanity is far from a gift however, as Zaleski is quick to explain. Instead, it is a 'handicap', a martyr-dom almost, for 'To attain anything, [the distinctive individual] must need screw the head up into the atmosphere of the future, while feet and hands drip dark ichors of despair from the crucifying cross of the crude present – *a horrid strain'*.[105]

Offended by Shiel's redefinition of the terms 'Decadent', 'degenerate', 'civilisation', 'progress', and 'culture', and also at his suggestion that figures like Zaleski represent regenerative rather than degenerative forces, the reviewer for the *Guardian* mocks Zaleski's claims about the coming of a clair-voyant culture in an attempt to restore the more familiar senses of these terms. The reviewer counters what he sees as a spurious argument by citing the authority of Nordau, whose widely popular *Degeneration* had gone into five editions in the four months between its first publication in Britain and the appearance of the *Guardian* review of *Prince Zaleski* in June 1895. Writing less than a month after Wilde's conviction, the reviewer's comments suggest his larger concern with condemning not just the book but the author as well as part of the insidious Decadent movement: 'Prince Zaleski might very well have been written to justify all that Max Nordau tells us about "higher degenerates". The Prince clearly belongs to that class and judging by the style and the ideas, we think the author must also be of it.'[106] The reviewer uses Nordau to undermine Zaleski's credibility as regenerative man, quoting a portion of the text that represents the detective in familiar degenerate terms. The passage depicts Zaleski in deep thought during which time his 'small, keen features distorted themselves into an expression of what … can only [be] describe[d] as an abnormal *inquisitiveness* – an inquisitiveness most impatient, arrogant, in its intensity. His pupils, contracted each to a dot, became the central *puncta* of two rings of fiery light; his little sharp teeth seemed to gnash ... till, by a species of mesmeric dominancy', he untangled the problem that had been set before him.[107] Certainly this passage, with its focus on the abnormal physiognomy of Zaleski, seems to reinforce the idea the he is the primitive degenerate the reviewer claims he is. Shiel, however, had argued that Zaleski was only 'slightly' in advance of the ovine mob. The reviewer does not engage with Shiel's more complex argument about degeneration, an argument that other reviewers had found 'original and ... interesting' and 'convincingly and ably put forth'.[108] Nor does he take up the more general charge that society itself is degenerate. Instead, he counters with Nordau's popular, though by no means universally credited, concept of the degenerate genius and resorts to what would become an increasingly familiar reaction of counter-Decadents in the aftermath of the Wilde trial – a celebration of philistinism, ordinariness, and mediocrity: 'If this is a true prophecy of the general mood of culture in the far future' he mockingly declares, 'how thankful we all ought to be that our lot has been cast in the ages of ovine stupidity!'[109]

The Decadent fiction of Dowson and Arthur Moore, Davidson, Machen, and Shiel did not fulfill the promise Decadence seemed to represent to its 1880s proponents, George Moore and Havelock Ellis, who thought it would advance the British novel. By the late 1880s George Moore had abandoned his Decadent aesthetic and Ellis had little hope that Decadence would be welcomed by a reticent British culture. Where Moore had aggressively undertaken to transform British fiction in the 1880s, his younger followers proceeded more cautiously adopting a 'collaborative' model by mediating between the claims of high art and the claims of the marketplace. This collaboration between high and popular art, though not the perfect solution for those with high literary ideals, enabled these writers to get published. At the same time, as I have argued, it gave them a wider venue for the promotion of alternative social and cultural values. Certainly Dowson, but other Decadents also, imagined that, as they established themselves more firmly within the literary field, they would be freer to produce the kind of art they wanted to. These hopes would be challenged in the wake of the Wilde trial, however, a trial that gave counter-Decadents the ammunition they needed to put an end to Decadent trends in fiction and to celebrate, in the words of the *Guardian* reviewer of *Prince Zaleski*, their 'ovine stupidity'.[110] To counter-Decadents, this so-called stupidity represented a refreshingly wholesome contrast to a literary school that would finally be exposed as utterly vitiated with the downfall of Oscar Wilde – the high priest of Decadence.

7
Decadence in the Shadow of the Wilde Trials and Beyond

The swan song of Decadence: Arthur Machen's *Hill of Dreams*

In the autumn of 1895, despite the hostile climate for Decadence in the wake of the Wilde trials, Arthur Machen began work on *The Hill of Dreams* (written 1895–97; published 1907). He was determined to write an artistic novel, one that would not be governed by the demands of the marketplace. In this respect, he produced a novel that accorded with Symons's 1893 characterization of high art Decadence as the 'morbid subtlety of analysis ... and curiosity of form', and as 'a disembodied voice, and yet the voice of a human soul'.[1] These elements made the novel unpublishable when it was written, though Machen did try to place it. His failure in this regard supports what I have argued throughout and what Havelock Ellis sensed in 1889: Britain was simply not receptive to Decadence in the terms in which so many of the writers I have been discussing wanted to pursue it as a literary form.

In its status as a high art Decadent novel, *The Hill of Dreams* bears comparison with Moore's *Confessions*. Both are *küntslerromans*. But, where Moore heralded the emergence of the brash and rebellious Decadent in *Confessions* – what Robert Buchanan called the 'modern young man' – Machen, writing in the aftermath of Wilde's trials and imprisonment, charts the demise of the Decadent in a novel that Wesley Sweetser has called 'a monument and an epitaph for the aesthetic-decadent period'.[2] Though vastly different in style and tone, Moore's and Machen's novels have similarities. Both writers, for example, are more interested in analysis than incident and both describe their works as narratives of the 'soul': Moore called his the story of an 'art-tortured' soul,[3] while Machen labelled his a 'Robinson Crusoe of the soul'.[4] Both novels explore the inner workings of the minds of the protagonists, articulating the tastes, attitudes, values, and ideals of the kind of artist that emerged from the rift between the professional intellectuals and the middle class in the mid-Victorian period. Lucian Taylor, Machen's protagonist, despises the bourgeois provincialism of his neighbours, has Decadent tastes in literature (François Villon, Thomas De Quincey, Edgar Allan Poe), is interested in the occult and the arcane, indulges in a form of worship involving self-flagellation, and becomes addicted to laudanum. Both novels end on a sombre note, though there is a distinct difference in the post-narrative outcomes they anticipate for their protagonists. Though Moore's novel leaves off with Dayne working on his novel at a desk in his grim lodgings, 'shiver[ing] ... haggard and overworn',[5] the reader is left with the impression that he will succeed. After all, we are reading the product of his efforts. For Machen's hero, on the other hand, there is no such hope. Like *Confessions*, *The Hill of Dreams* ends with a writer at a desk in his miserable lodgings. In this case, however, the writer is dead and the manuscript he has been working on is illegible.

For Linda Dowling, *The Hill of Dreams* is a 'parable' of what she calls 'antinomian Decadence'.[6] Ultimately, she argues, the novel is critical of Decadence in that it exposes 'the dead end of the cult of style'.[7] This analysis is certainly justified by the conclusion of the novel in which Lucian's body is discovered by a couple who have the following conversation:

> [Man] 'What's all those papers that he's got there?'
>
> [Woman] 'Didn't I tell you? It was crool to see him. He'd got it into 'is 'ead he could write a book; he's been at it for the last six months. Look 'ere.'
>
> She spread the neat pile of manuscript broadcast over the desk, and took a sheet at haphazard. It was all covered with illegible hopeless scribblings; only here and there it was possible to recognise a word.
>
> [Man] 'Why nobody could read it if they wanted to.'
>
> [Woman] 'It's like that. He thought it was beautiful. I used to 'ear him jabbering to himself about it, dreadful nonsense it was he used to talk'.[8]

As Dowling argues, the novel is critical of the Decadent sensibility because the Decadent celebrates a form of 'solipsism' the only possible outcome of which is 'a language so perfected in its private symbolism that it will no longer yield its meaning even to the select few, but only to the unique reader, [the Decadent] himself'.[9]

And yet, if the novel finally reveals the limitations of the Decadent sensibility, it also represents in a sympathetic manner the plight of the writer aspiring to artistry. After all, the ending of the novel is rather ambiguous. Lucian's manuscript may be the illegible scribblings of a drug-addled brain, but Machen's emphasis on the vulgarity and virtual illiteracy of the couple (through spelling anomalies and indications of a working-class dialect) also suggests they may not be able to recognize art when they see it. This analysis is strengthened by the mercenary interests that occupy them, for, after declaring Lucian's art gibberish, they proceed to discuss the woman's inheritance from Lucian and whether it might be compromised if they are suspected of being involved in his death. They may not understand art, but they certainly understand money. Art and pecuniary interests are juxtaposed here, as they are throughout the novel, as Lucian faces the familiar plight of the Decadent artist struggling to come to terms with an idealized vision of art and the debasing demands of the marketplace.

In this respect, the novel dramatizes the issues facing real-life Decadents as they positioned themselves in the literary field. Though initially Lucian holds strictly to the 'high art' assumptions that 'a painstaking artist in words [is] not respected by the respectable' and that 'books should not be written with the object of gaining the goodwill of the landed and commercial interests',[10] he comes to think – as did his real-life counterparts Dowson, Machen, Shiel, and Davidson – that it might be possible to mediate successfully between 'Art' and the marketplace:

> He was aware that if he chose to sit down now before the desk he could, in a manner, write easily enough – he could produce a tale which would be formally well constructed and certain of favourable reception. And it would not be the utterly commonplace, entirely hopeless favourite of the circulating library; it would stand in those ranks where the real thing is skilfully counterfeited, amongst the books which give the reader his orgy of emotions, and yet contrive to be superior, and 'art,' in his opinion.[11]

When such productions are greeted with the disrespect of the so-called respectable middle classes, however, as Lucian's book is by an 'influential daily paper' which asks of his novel, 'Where are the disinfectants?',[12] then one might well begin to despair of the task altogether. Lucian's illegible manuscript, in this respect, is more than simply a representation of the *reductio ad absurdum* of the Decadent project that Dowling argues for. It also stands as a testament to the utter impossibility of communication between the Decadent artist and the vulgar reading public – particularly in the context of the Wilde trials.

Both the death of Lucian – a death at least indirectly attributed to an environment hostile to the artist – and the unintelligibility of his manuscript are part of Machen's myth-making as he responds to the backlash against Decadence in the wake of the Wilde trials. In literary history, many Decadents, including John Davidson, Lionel Johnson, Hubert Crackanthorpe, Ernest Dowson, and Aubrey Beardsley have come to be figured in similar mythic terms, as martyrs to art who lived sordid, tragic, and miserable lives. But while an early and often tragic death might well be characteristic of many Decadents, it is a mistake to foreshorten the period between 1895 – a moment that had a profound impact on their literary careers – and their deaths and to represent this time as simply a clocking in of their remaining time on earth in misery and squalor. In reality, most Decadents stayed actively engaged in the literary field, in direct contrast to the myth of the isolated Decadent. For some, such as Machen and Shiel, who defied this myth by living until 1947, their involvement in the literary field continued well through the Edwardian and Modernist periods.

Taking as my aim the demystification of the so-called tragic generation, in this chapter and the next, I go beyond where histories of Decadence usually end. Decadence may have died in 1895 but the Decadents, unlike Lucian, did not. Instead, they adapted themselves to the transformations in the literary field that the Wilde trials occasioned, re-opening the lines of communication between themselves and an audience, however they had now come to understand that audience. This chapter examines the impact of the Wilde trials on the *fin-de-siècle* literary field and describes the status of Decadence in the Edwardian and Modernist literary fields, before going on, in the next chapter, to revisit the myth of the tragic generation through case studies of Dowson, Davidson, Machen, and Shiel that examine their engagements with and status in these post-1895 literary fields.

Decadence, Decadents and the literary field in the shadow of the Wilde trials

Machen's articulation of the breakdown in communication between the artist and the public in *The Hill of Dreams*, had, it is true, always been an integral part of Decadent artistic discourse. Implicit in the discourse was the idea that the artist and the public speak two different languages and that each is unintelligible to the other. The *hypocrite lecteur* trope invoked so frequently by Decadents attests to this communication problem as do Wilde's epigrams in the preface to *Dorian Gray*. In these epigrams, Wilde makes a distinction between the 'elect' who understand the artist's language and to whom 'beautiful things mean only Beauty', and the 'corrupt' who, in misunderstanding the artist, 'find ugly meanings in beautiful things'.[13] The Wilde trials only worsened relations between artist and public, relations that Machen was reflecting on in *The Hill of Dreams*, a book that also privileges the beauty of the artist's conceptions over the interpretations of a vulgar public. From the time of the trials on, however, the public would insist on having its own say in the matter of artistic versus ordinary discourse.

The trials began in March 1895 when Wilde brought an action for criminal libel against the Marquess of Queensberry who, objecting to the friendship between Wilde and his son, Lord Alfred Douglas, left a card at Wilde's club on which was written, 'To Oscar Wilde posing Somdomite [*sic*]'. The libel case broke down after Queensberry's lawyer, Edward Carson, established that his client's accusation against Wilde was justifiable. Wilde was promptly arrested and charged with committing acts of gross indecency. The first of the two trials on these charges resulted in a hung jury, while the second found him guilty. Wilde was sentenced to two years hard labour. Though Wilde was not charged with having written indecent or pernicious literature, *Dorian Gray* was used as evidence in the trials, an act that had serious implications for Decadent writers and for the immediate future of British fiction more broadly.

Opponents of Decadence regarded the Wilde trials as an opportunity to re-assert right reason, to expose the corrupting nature of Decadence by linking this literary practice with Wilde's unlawful sexual practices. The numerous calls in the press for an end to Decadence in fiction – a fiction that 'poison[ed] the springs of English life' in its promotion of everything from sex-mania to ego-mania to political anarchy[14] – had been mounting since the beginning of 1895 and reached a peak during the trials. The strategy for bringing about the demise of Decadence was to foreground the irreconcilable differences between artistic and ordinary discourse and consequently between artistic and ordinary culture. The point was to insist that the Decadent artistic discourse had perverted the meanings of things: what was beautiful to the artist was ugly to the ordinary individual and so on. Though these differences had always existed, it had been the artist and not the public who had hitherto persisted in drawing attention to the inability of the artist and the bourgeoisie to communicate. The middle-class public, by contrast, had, at least to some minds, shown far too much willingness to be dictated to by artists with respect to cultural matters, particularly since the 'Aesthetic' craze of the 1870s and 1880s. The Wilde scandal provided moralists with the opportunity to re-assert a bourgeois cultural hegemony and to take pride in rather than be ashamed of their philistinism.

The emphasis on the opposition between an artistic and ordinary discourse from the point of view of the 'ordinary' person featured prominently in the Wilde trials. During the libel trial, for example, Carson was unapologetic in his defence of the views of the 'ordinary individual' in contrast to the 'artistic' views of Wilde.[15] The 'ordinary individual', Carson insisted, might describe *Dorian Gray* as a 'perverted novel', to which Wilde responded, with typical Decadent disdain for 'ordinary' people, that such an interpretation was possible only among 'brutes', 'illiterates', and 'Philistines'.[16] Wilde's repeated assertions of the superiority of an artistic viewpoint nettled Carson, leading him to blurt out a defiant declaration of his ordinariness: 'I do not profess to be an artist and when I hear you give evidence, I am glad I am not.'[17]

The attack on the Decadent artistic discourse by the advocates of ordinary discourse extended beyond the courtroom to the press. The *Westminster Gazette* opened a feature article on the first trial with Carson's defiant rejection of artists.[18] A week later, *Punch*, a periodical noted for humorous parodies, printed a harsh invective against the Decadents' perverted notions of 'Art', 'Culture', 'Beauty', and 'Poetry'. The poem, entitled 'Concerning a Misused Term; viz., "Art" as recently applied to a certain form of Literature', laments the sway this artistic discourse has had over the nation and calls for a return of the right meanings of words as expounded by an old-fashioned Philistine:

Is this, then, 'Art' – ineffable conceit,
Plus worship of the Sadi-tainted phrase,
Of pseud-Hellenic Decadence, effete,
Unvirile, of debased Petronian ways?

Is *this* your 'Culture,' to asphyxiate
With upas-perfumes sons of English race,
With manhood-blighting cant-of-art to prate
The jargon of an epicene disgrace?

Shall worse than pornographic stain degrade
The name of 'Beauty', Heav'n-imparted dower?
Are *they* fit devotees who late displayed
The symbol of a vitriol-tainted flower?

And shall the sweet and kindly Muse be shamed
By unsexed 'Poetry' that defiles your page?
Has Art a mission that may not be named,
With 'scarlet sins' to enervate the age?

All honour to the rare and cleanly prints,
Which have not filled our homes from day to day
With garbage-epigrams and pois'nous hints
How aesthete hierophants fair Art betray!

If such be 'Artists,' then may Philistines
Arise, plain sturdy Britons as of yore,
And sweep them off and purge away the signs
That England e'er such noxious offspring bore![19]

A few weeks later, *Punch* again printed a poem that insisted that the British middle class had too long accepted Decadent artistic views. In the poem, entitled 'A Philistine Paean; Or, the Triumph of the Timid One', the speaker laments the domination 'high' artistic principles have had over him till he 'hadn't a taste that [he] dare call his own'.[20] Relieved that he need no longer pay tribute to false artistic ideals, the subject declares, 'I know I'm relieved from one horrible bore, – / I need not admire what I hate anymore.'[21] Both poems attest to an impasse between artists and the general public in their insistence on the need for a replacement of Decadent artistic values which are figured as noxious, foreign, effeminate, and pagan, with clean, Philistine, manly, and British values.

The insistence on the eradication of Decadence and its perverted interpretations in the press during the Wilde trials could take more threatening forms. Indeed, the press, insofar as it could, put the Decadents on trial alongside Wilde. On the day after the libel trial ended, for example, the *National Observer*, home to many counter-Decadents, called for 'another trial at the Old Bailey ... of the Decadents, of their hideous conceptions of the meaning of Art, [and] of their worse than Eleusinian mysteries'.[22] On the same day, the *Star* declared that while it was 'absurd to suggest that ... the "literature of the Decadence" or "fin de siècle-ism" will or can be arrested upon the warrant of a stipendiary magistrate', it nonetheless hoped that

Wilde's case would have an 'effect ... upon the precious "movement" which imagines that it is a part of literature'.[23] The *Westminster Gazette*, in whose pages J. A. Spender (as 'the Philistine') had conducted a campaign against Decadent and New Woman fiction in early 1895, also used the example of Wilde to condemn the Decadents more broadly. Commenting on the 'terrible risks involved in certain artistic and literary tendencies of the day' the writer hoped that the Wilde case would 'burn ... its lesson upon the literary and moral conscience of the present generation'.[24] In effect, then, though specific works of literature were not, as these articles pointed out, on trial, the rhetoric employed amounted to a kind of trial by press.

Certainly publishers felt threatened in such a climate. Many, as James G. Nelson explains, 'were not eager to harbor the Decadents or any of the young moderns ... [and were] fearful ... to publish anything in the way of literature and art which could be considered immoral'.[25] This caution was particularly true of John Lane, whose Bodley Head was regarded as the main venue for Decadent publications. If the spectre of imprisoned publisher Vizetelly and the furore over Naturalism had been forgotten by the public in the intensity of its latest anti-Decadent causerie, it loomed large for Lane who responded quickly to negative public opinion. Attempting to purge the firm of its Decadent associations, Lane withdrew Wilde's titles from his list and fired Aubrey Beardsley. He also published a collection of counter-Decadent verse by Owen Seaman, a writer of Decadent parodies for *Punch*, the *World*, and the *National Observer*. At the same time, he launched two new series, the 'Arcady Library of keepsake verse' and 'Lane's Library of light fiction', series decidedly different in tone than the controversial Keynotes series. Behind the scenes, Lane hired John Buchan, an avowed hater of Decadence, as reader for the firm and pressured those of his writers associated with Decadence to tone down their writing. Through the spring and summer of 1895, for example, Lane appealed to Machen to consider his 'literary reputation', urging him to alter certain ' "dangerous" and "risky" passages' in *The Three Impostors*, Machen's follow-up to *The Great God Pan*, which Lane had committed to publishing before the Wilde scandal began.[26] Lane also suggested omitting the titles of Machen's other works, which might be perceived as Decadent, from the title page.[27] When Machen refused, Lane threatened to 'put *The Three Impostors* in a corner'.[28] Lane treated George Egerton, New Woman writer and Keynotes series author, similarly and, like Machen, she remained defiant: 'You did not say you wished a "milk and water" book on entirely different lines to that which made the success of *Keynotes* when we made our autumn arrangements, and now on the eve of completing my book it comes as a back-hander. You gave me the impression on Friday of not caring to continue to publish for "George Egerton".'[29]

Lane's treatment of Machen and Egerton most certainly stemmed from a disinclination to continue publishing authors who were so strongly associated in the public mind with Decadence. Certainly, some of Lane's writers turned or were forced to look elsewhere, either immediately or within a few years after 1895. A publisher to whom they turned was Leonard Smithers, an exception to the general timidity of publishers at this time, who gave 'instant financial and emotional relief to the increasingly destitute and demoralized *avant-garde*'.[30] Smithers provided a publishing venue for Dowson, Beardsley, Yeats, Symons, Egerton, and even Wilde in the puritanical cultural milieu of the post-Wilde trials period. For Smithers, the backlash against Decadence among publishers represented a boon, enabling him to acquire talented writers for his newly established firm. He boldly declared that he would 'publish anything that the others are afraid to',[31] a boast that led to the publication of Symons's virtually unpublishable *London Nights* (1895).[32] In addition to publishing the pariahs of the literary field, Smithers established the *Savoy*, a rival to the *Yellow Book*. In effect, Smithers took over where the Bodley Head left off in the publication of so-called 'pernicious' literature, prompting Beardsley to joke that Smithers should call his firm the 'Sodley Bed'.[33] Smithers's willingness to publish what no other publisher would touch enabled those who fell under his wing to maintain their high artistic principles. With his support, writers associated with Decadence declared 'warfare', as Yeats said, 'on the British public at a time when we had all against us' and when '[we] delighted in enemies and in everything that had an heroic aire [*sic*]'.[34] But if Smithers proved one could publish Decadence without facing the dock, he did not prove that money could be made from it. His publications sold poorly, the *Savoy* folded after just one year, and he was bankrupt by 1900, at which time he resumed the more lucrative publishing of pornography and pirated works. Smithers died in 1907 and would take no part in promoting the writers associated with Decadence through the Edwardian and Modernist periods.

Like Smithers, Grant Richards also profited from the timorousness of John Lane following the Wilde trials. Establishing his firm in January 1897, Richards sought out and was approached by numerous former Bodley Head authors, including Machen, Shiel, Davidson, and Egerton. Richards, however, was not as daring as Smithers and, despite his interest in the Decadents, he exercised caution in his publishing activities. Inspired by the success of Lane and Heinemann, Richards established himself as a quality commercial publisher who catered to an educated, arty but somewhat conservative middle- to upper middle-class readership. Taking a cue from Heinemann, Richards published best-selling authors such as Eden Philpotts and Edgar Wallace in order to subsidize the unprofitable high art that interested him and for which he wished to establish a wider audience. Given Richards's desire to mediate between the claims of high art and the demands of the literary marketplace, it is not surprising that he gravitated towards writers such as Machen, Shiel, and Davidson, whose works were characterized by a combination of highbrow and popular elements that resulted in marketable high art.[35]

The rise of Richards and Smithers, publishers willing to take on the pariahs of the literary world in the wake of the Wilde scandal, meant that the situation was not as bleak for the Decadents as it might have seemed. Many writers were flippant about the situation, for it brought clearly to mind the most basic principle of their artistic ideology – namely, that the public was hostile to true art. Dowson, for example, joked with Smithers about translating Pierre Louÿs's controversial novel *Aphrodite*: 'I suppose it would mean joining Oscar in his gardening operations in Reading Gaol'.[36] Ella D'Arcy, a Bodley Head writer, joked with Lane in a similar manner during the trials: 'I'm inclined to give up Art and Literature altogether, (since they seem inseparable from Decadence), and go back to the comfortably prosaic circles of suburban grocers from which I so (foolishly) came'.[37] Machen also took a humorous view of his situation, at least until Lane began pressuring him to censor his work:

> I have just been reading Mr Quilter's very entertaining article ['The Gospel of Intensity']... and it seems to me, taking this and other literary events into consideration, that the present summer is likely to be somewhat unhealthy for *The Three Impostors*. There seems to me a rather severe attack of virtue abroad, and I should not be greatly surprised if a short act were to run through Parliament, bringing in the writing of literature as distinguished from twaddle as an offence within the purview of the Criminal Law Amendment Act.[38]

These instances of levity, however, masked serious consternation about the state of literature. For those who had hoped to raise British literature to the level of Continental European literature, the Wilde trial and the backlash against modernity in literature, now labelled 'Decadent', represented a setback. Whether or not writers thought of themselves as 'Decadent', they were forced to face the consequences of being labelled Decadent in considering their literary futures. Some believed that these consequences would be severe indeed. B. A. Crackanthorpe, mother of Bodley Head writer Hubert Crackanthorpe and a writer herself, spoke in dire terms about the fate of the Decadents in the aftermath of the Wilde trials, urging Lane to distance himself from those she called the 'living dead':

> of one thing I am *certain*. It is this – that if the YB [*Yellow Book*] is to prosper – to have the future which we all hope for it – true wisdom on the part of its owner lies in the avoiding – for some time to come – any con-tributors, men, or women, who belong markedly to the *avowedly* Decadent school who have moulded themselves + their writings on the writings of people who are now the living dead – and must remain so.[39]

Crackanthorpe's comments are ironic given that her own son's gritty realism had earned him an association with the Decadents, an association that would be confirmed by his mysterious death (a probable suicide) the following year at the age of 26. It remained to be seen whether any of those among the 'living dead' would be able to rise phoenix-like from the ashes of the hostile environment depicted by Crackanthorpe.

Decadence and the Edwardian and Modernist literary fields

The influence of the Wilde scandal and the concomitant backlash against literature considered 'advanced', 'modern', or 'artistic' on the subsequent development of literature cannot be stressed enough. Certainly, it had a profound effect on writers associated with Decadence, but it also affected writers not linked with Decadence. Thomas Hardy, for example, disgusted at the reception of *Jude the Obscure*, resolved, in 1895, to abandon fiction writing altogether, while H. G. Wells, whose 1890s output John Batchelor has characterized as Decadent and *fin de siècle*, began to produce socially engaged fiction in the new century.[40] Similarly, Arnold Bennett, who had set out to write an 'artistic' novel in 1895, decided, in 1898, to become a popular novelist.[41]

The post-1895 literary field was in a state of considerable flux as the Edwardian period approached. Though the precise origins of the Edwardian period have been debated,[42] there is no doubt that the period's literature was shaped in reaction to the literature of the *fin de siècle*. Scholars have broadly characterized Edwardian literature as rich in its range of subject matter but weak in formal innovation. Jefferson Hunter, for example, argues that the 'two most salient facts about Edwardian fiction' are its 'thematic adventurousness' and its 'formal conservatism'.[43] The novel was certainly the dominant literary form of the period. Edwardian and Georgian poetry, by contrast, stand low in the canon and its poets have been overshadowed by the 'Modernists' that followed. The 'sheer generic diversity' of the novel in this period was a result of the continuing expansion of the reading public which had begun in the late nineteenth century.[44] This reading public was catered to by an ever-expanding mass periodical and publishing industry dominated by men such as Alfred Harmsworth and Charles Pearson. The increasing awareness of the existence of niche readerships on the part of writers and publishers encouraged the development of what Hunter calls 'coterie fiction' – fiction characterized by 'highly conventional specialities addressed to an identifiable readership of enthusiasts' such as detective fiction, fantasy, horror, and the historical novel.[45] This awareness of the multiplicity of readerships encouraged writers to experiment with different genres in what amounted to what Kemp, Mitchell, and Trotter describe as the 'generic promiscuity' of many Edwardian writers.[46]

The tendency towards generic over stylistic innovation owed its origins, at least in part, to the association of formal experimentation with the Aesthetes and Decadents who were now out of favour. Though certainly writers such as Joseph Conrad and Ford Madox Ford experimented with style in the Edwardian period, there were risks involved in such a venture. Nordau's claims about the degeneracy of artists continued to hold sway in the popular imagination well into the Edwardian period and terms such as 'morbid', 'Decadent', and 'degenerate' – what William Greenslade has called the 'labelling system of the nineties' – still carried critical weight, reflecting negatively on the artist.[47] In general in this period, preciosity of style was a sign of Decadence and increasingly Edwardian literature was taken up with social issues. In this respect, Edwardian literature differed radically from the Aesthetic and Decadent fiction of the 1880s and 1890s, though it was certainly indebted to the socially conscious fiction that emerged in the *fin-de-siècle* period.

While writers such as Machen and Shiel had demonstrated a strong commitment to high artistic and Decadent stylistic principles in the 1890s, their work had also significantly engaged with popular genres. The generic diversity that characterized the Edwardian period had already begun to manifest itself in the 1890s and both Machen and Shiel had contributed significantly to genres that would flourish in the Edwardian period such as the detective story and the horror tale. But where they had tried to negotiate between the demands of art and the marketplace, the conditions of the new literary field seemed inimical to such mediations. How, as writers formerly aligned with Decadence and art-for-art's-sake, would Machen and Shiel respond to the backlash against preciosity of style that characterized the Edwardian literary field, a field strongly invested in fiction focused on contemporary social issues? Would they still try to mediate between the realms of high art and popular fiction or would they choose one at the exclusion of the other – high art over popular or vice versa?

With the advent of a 'Modernist' sensibility, a sensibility which defined itself in opposition to Edwardianism, writers who had been involved in the 1890s Decadent movement were confronted with yet another context within which to position themselves. Though new in some respects, many of the issues taken up by high Modernists were familiar to the former Decadents. The high Modernist disdain for the masses, its interest in subjectivity, in 'difficulty', and in the problems inherent in language as a form of expression had all been concerns of the 1890s Decadents. Robert Hichens and Arthur Machen, for example, had explored the subjectivity of morbid types in *An Imaginative Man* (1896) and *The Hill of Dreams*. Machen had also treated the inability of language to express certain states of mind in his horror fiction of the 1890s. And finally, the Decadents, though more willing perhaps than Modernists to cater to the popular audience that they disdained, also employed difficulty or obscurity as a means of rendering their work more challenging. Shiel's *Shapes in the Fire* (1896) is a case in point, with its linguistic playfulness and its obscure historical and cultural allusions. In a manner anticipating the British reception of T. S. Eliot's *Waste Land*,[48] critics of the 1890s remarked on Shiel's inaccessibility to the general reader: 'The volume will prove a curious intellectual exercise to certain circles, and will become suitable for general reading about the time when the British work-man takes to the Upanishads or the differential calculus for pastime. Mr Shiel is too clever by a thousand degrees for the sober, burden-bearing portions of the world.'[49] Even a critic for a more highbrow review, The *Academy*, complained of Shiel's 'extravagance of expression', 'liberal coinage of impossible and ugly words', and his 'ostentation of occult and intricate lore', pronouncing him 'incomprehensible ... at his best' and guilty of the 'sheerest impertinence ... at his worst'.[50]

Though the Modernists admittedly engaged with issues of subjectivity, language, and difficulty differently and, to some minds, in a more 'advanced' manner than *fin-de-siècle* writers, these writers shared similar interests which, in their zeal to fashion themselves as self-originating, the Modernists obscured. The Modernists were as invested in disavowing Victorianism as they were Edwardianism and this included *fin-de-siècle* Decadence. Wyndham Lewis, for example, scorned Roger Fry's 'greenery-yallery' tendencies,[51] an insult that linked Fry with outmoded *fin-de-siècle* Aestheticism and Decadence. Pound, though an admirer of 1890s Decadence in his youth, would denounce it in 'Hugh Selwyn Mauberley' (1919) and in his introduction to a collection of poems by Lionel Johnson in 1915.[52] His high Modernist disdain for the Decadents extended to those of his own gen-eration sympathetic to these older literary values, including J. C. Squire and Edward Marsh who continued to promote 1890s Decadence and spoke out against high Modernism.

Literary history has largely obscured the vast array of literary and intellectual activity during the war and post-war period in its privileging of specifically 'Modernist' productions and producers. The literary activities of Squire, Marsh, and others indicate that there was more going on in this period than simply high Modernism and that there was a strong interest in *fin-de-siècle* modernist forms such as Decadence. Decadence, however, though once 'modern', 'new', and 'avant-garde', had now become 'traditional', partly because of the Modernists' need to disavow their literary forbears, but also because of the desire on the part of anti-Modernists such as Squire and Marsh to oppose high Modernism. For example, in the first issue of the *London Mercury*, Squire attacked high Modernism as 'dirty living and muddled thinking' and as 'fungoid growths of feeble pretentious impostors',[53] charges that are strikingly similar to those levelled at the Decadents in the 1890s. This pro-Decadent, anti-Modernist aesthetic dominated periodicals such as the *Mercury*, carried over into the work of Ronald Firbank, E. F. Benson, P. G. Wodehouse, Noël Coward, Christopher Isherwood, Evelyn Waugh and others, and was endorsed by publishers of the period such as Grant Richards, who disliked high Modernism.[54] The re-emergence of interest in *fin-de-siècle* Decadence in the Modernist period also manifested itself in a host of memoirs and histories that appeared in the 1910s and 1920s: W.G. Blakie Murdoch's *Renaissance of the Nineties* (1910), Holbrook Jackson's *Eighteen Nineties* (1913), Robert Sherard's *The Real Oscar Wilde* (1911), and Bernard Muddiman's *Men of the Nineties* (1920) as well as memoirs by Richard Le Gallienne, Victor Plarr, Edgar Jepson, W. B. Yeats, Frank Harris, Lord Alfred Douglas, and many others. These publications catered to what Theodore Wratislaw, a minor poet of the 1890s, referred to in 1914 as a 'thriving interest in the products of the 1890s' when he offered up his own memoirs to Elkin Mathews.[55]

The nostalgia for the 1890s in this period was prompted by a number of things. During the years of the 'Great War' and after, the 1890s must have seemed a simpler and more romantic age, much in the same way as the Edwardian era, from the post-war perspective, seemed to have been one long country house party. It may also have been that artistic martyrdom seemed glamorous in contrast to the unglamorous reality of young men being killed in war. At the same time, the glamour of the bohemian artistic life was no doubt appealing at a time when fiction seemed more commercialized than ever. It certainly held this appeal for W. G. Blakie Murdoch who praised the Decadents for fighting 'Philistia' and had little faith that anything as 'precious as the renaissance of the nineties' would rise again.[56] Or, quite simply, this nostalgia may have been part of the larger reaction against the emerging high Modernist sensibility which denigrated the achievements of the writers of the 1890s.

The existence of this formidable oppositional presence in an age that has come to be so strongly characterized by the work and ideas of high Modernist writers casts new light on the anti-1890s sentiments of writers such as Ezra Pound who attacked Victor Plarr in the guise of 'M. Verog' for being 'out of step with the decade, / Detached from his contemporaries, / Neglected by the young' because of his interest in 1890s culture.[57] The institutionalization of Modernism has made these lines register differently from how they did when Pound wrote them. While Pound's now canonical status lends authority to his condemnation of this forgotten poet, at the time he wrote the poem, he was struggling to assert his cultural authority in a battle which was very much ongoing. The poem functions as a farewell to London, a place where he felt unappreciated within the literary field.[58] The anti-Modernists and the 1890s writers he writes against, writers who are largely forgotten now, were a formidable presence in a field where high Modernists found it necessary to set about creating their own venues for publication – the small presses and 'little magazines' of the period.

In a literary history that privileges 'high' Modernism, the Decadents and the pro-Decadent contemporaries of the high Modernists have come down to us as non-entities or losers in the battle for cultural authority. Yet, at the time of the battle, this outcome was not a given. If Pound and other high Modernists had a disdain for the Decadents and those of their own generation who revered them, the Decadents who continued to be active in the period of Modernism were equally disdainful of Modernists. In 1924, for example, Machen expressed his disdain for modern fiction in a letter to Munson Havens: 'When I do read a modern novel', he declared, 'I often make two reflections. Firstly: "How very clever"; secondly: "And yet this can never last." '[59] For his part, Shiel thought 1890s writers were 'wittier' than the moderns[60] and his preferences among living writers – G. B. Shaw, John Gawsworth, William Somerset Maugham and Margaret Kennedy – were far from Modernist.[61] The Decadents who were still actively engaged in the literary scene in the Modernist period were alienated by the 'new' modern. They prided themselves on their anti-intellectualism and distinguished themselves as dilettantes in opposition to the intellectual Modernists. The difference in the tenor of intellectualism might well be accounted for by the fact that while the Decadents were largely self-educated, high Modernists, particularly Americans such as Eliot and Pound, were often university educated. And while the Decadents' self-culture constituted a form of avant-garde intellectualism in its own day, by high-Modernist standards this self-culture was anti-intellectual. The antipathy of the Decadents, a former literary élite, for the Modernists indicates that the Modernist period was not simply about the new rejecting the old. Rather, it was a two-sided affair with the surviving 'old' capable of an equally critical condemnation of the 'new'. Both sides felt at times threatened, at times triumphant, in the context of a diverse and divisive literary field.[62]

The literary fields of the Edwardian and Modernist periods offered distinct challenges for Decadents who had been schooled in the *fin de siècle*. Though issues of readership, authorship, professionalism, ethics, aesthetics, high art, popular art, and economics were still central in establishing one's artistic identity, the changing contexts altered the way these issues were used in positioning writers within the field. In the immediate aftermath of the Wilde trials, the backlash against Decadence put pressure on writers, particularly Decadents, to abandon their artistic principles and to conform to the demand for a healthy national literature. This overt attempt to eradicate literary Decadence resulted in an Edwardian fiction characterized by generic rather than formal adventurousness, particularly given the ongoing association of preciosity of style with Decadence. Finally, though the Modernist period, which saw an aggressive promotion of high art principles by some writers, may have seemed a welcoming place for those writers who had espoused similar principles in the 1890s, the period presented other kinds of challenges for the Decadents who continued to be active in the literary field. Even though the Decadents shared with the Modernists certain basic artistic principles, the distinction between the old and the new and a traditional and a radical concept of high art marked the difference between the old 'new' art of Decadence and the new 'new' art of Modernism.

8
The Afterlife of the Decadents or, Life After Decadence

Arthur Machen's *Hill of Dreams* figures the death of the Decadent in both literal and figurative terms as a response to what he saw as a hostile climate for the artist. Though real-life Decadents have been romanticized in much the same way as Machen's tragic hero, the image of the Decadents as, in Holbrook Jackson's terms, 'burdened by the malady of the soul's unrest', 'restless and tragic figures thirst[ing] so much for life, and for the life of the hour, that they put the cup to their lips and drained it in one deep draught',[1] distorts a fuller picture of their careers. This chapter examines the post-1895 careers of four of the Decadents who have been central to this study, arguing for an alternative to the stereotypical 'tragic generation' interpretation of their lives. On the one hand, I take up those who cannot be accommodated within the tragic-generation model – Arthur Machen and M. P. Shiel. It is no coincidence that they are largely absent from histories of Decadence, which too often insist on a correspondence between Decadent literary practice and a Decadent lifestyle leading to a tragic end. On the other hand, I take up the so-called tragic-generation figures of Ernest Dowson and John Davidson, balancing the representation of them as doomed and isolated martyr-artists with one that accounts for their productive engagement with the literary field in the post-1895 moment. My examination of the continuing engagement of these Decadents with post-1895 literary fields focuses on the immediate and longer-term context. In the immediate aftermath of the Wilde trial, I am concerned with how they adapted to the backlash against Decadence. How did the position of these writers within the field alter and/or to what extent did they actively re-position themselves? Did they persist in promoting Decadence or did they alter their style to accord with the new literary conservatism? Were they forced to choose between art and the marketplace where heretofore they had demonstrated a willingness to mediate between the two? In the longer-term, I consider how Decadents adapted themselves to and/or were received in the Edwardian and Modernist literary fields. How did their concerns about readership, authorship, professionalism, aesthetics, high art, and popular art carry over into these newly configured literary fields and what new challenges did they face? In the case of writers who were dead in one (Davidson) or both (Dowson) of these periods, I consider their posthumous reputations and how, as 'Decadents', they functioned in the mythologization of the *fin de siècle*.

Ernest Dowson (1867–1900): The 'Dowson legend' as 'fiction of Decadence'

Of all *fin-de-siècle* writers, Ernest Dowson has come to best typify the stereotypical Decadent. This stereotype, argue Desmond Flower and Henry Maas, figures Decadents as 'idle, penurious, drunken, promiscuous, living with [their] head[s] in a cloud of artistic ambition but doing little towards its achievement, tempted towards drugs and perversion, often addicted to them, producing exquisitely fashioned small works, but doomed, after material failure, to an early death'.[2] This image bears little resemblance, however, to the Dowson we glimpse in his letters, as does Yeats's representation of Dowson as a poet who 'made it a matter of conscience to turn from every kind of money-making that prevented good writing'.[3] Dowson's letters, as I have argued, demonstrate his willingness to mediate between the claims of high art and the claims of the marketplace. In drawing attention to Dowson's commercial literary pursuits I do not mean to undermine his artistic integrity, but rather to demonstrate the complexity of the literary field and of writers' attempts to position themselves within it. My aim is not so much to redress so-called injustices done to him by what has been called the 'Dowson legend', but rather to suggest how this legend, myth, or 'fiction' came to be constructed in the aftermath of the Wilde trial and through the Edwardian and Modernist periods.

Though Dowson, as I have insisted, was not immune to the lures of fame and fortune, it is true that, as his career developed, his interest in writing shockers and achieving popular success waned. Even before the Wilde scandal broke, he was focusing on the less commercial prospects of poetry and experimental short stories. From 1892 to early 1895 Dowson contributed to two Rhymers' Club volumes, worked on a collection of short stories, and did translations of Zola and Louis Couperus. From mid-1895 on, however, Dowson's manoeuvrings within the literary field became more restricted. With the exception of *Adrian Rome*, another Dowson–Moore collaboration, which was published by Methuen, Dowson was now exclusively associated with Leonard Smithers. Dowson's allegiance to Smithers was more personal than it was strategic. Smithers had acted as his saviour during a dark period: Dowson's parents had died – his mother a suicide, his father a likely suicide – and he was ill and poor. Smithers gave him emotional support and provided him with a weekly salary of 30 shillings for translation work in addition to royalties he earned for his own work.[4] Smithers's generosity came at a time when Dowson was a pariah in the literary community.

Dowson's association with the publisher, however, had serious consequences for his status within the literary field. The translation work Smithers provided was hackwork, often wasted hackwork, as he did not always have the capital to publish it. In addition, his publications sold poorly and were subject to scurrilous reviews: 'Oftenest', as one of his authors recalled, 'there was not even a pretext of impartial judgement or of merely trying to understand. It was just welting and socks in the jaw.'[5] The hostility towards Smithers's publications within the literary world stemmed from his reputation as a purveyor of pornographic books. This reputation prompted even sympathetic members of the avant-garde to be wary of him. Max Beerbohm, for example, commented on the scape-goating of Smithers by the press[6] and Yeats, even while publishing with Smithers, described him as a 'scandalous person'.[7] Dowson's reputation, along with those of other Smithers authors, was affected by the publisher's low status within the field, a status that did nothing to recuperate the reputations of the writers who turned to him in the aftermath of the Wilde scandal.

Dowson, however, was not bothered about his reputation. He was one of a select few who showed public support for Wilde by attending the trial (others who attended included Robert Sherard and Max Beerbohm). At the same time, Dowson embraced his vilified status, commenting to Symons on the reception of his 1896 *Verses*, 'I foresee that I am to dispute the honour with you of being the most abused versifier in England, and am flattered at the position'.[8] While Dowson did not aggressively publicize his Decadent artistic persona in the way Wilde did, he did sanction the image of him put about by his literary friends. In particular, Dowson endorsed a lurid portrait written by Arthur Symons for the August 1896 issue of the *Savoy*, in which Symons discusses Dowson's 'dilapidated' appearance, his experimentations with hashish, and his love of drink, ending with an image of Dowson as a solipsistic Decadent:[9]

> So the wilder wanderings began, and a gradual slipping into deeper and steadier waters of oblivion. That curious love of the sordid, so common an affectation of the modern Decadent, and with him so expressively genuine, grew upon him, and dragged him into yet more sorry corners of a life which was never exactly 'gay' to him. And now, indifferent to most things, in the shipwrecked quietude of a sort of self-exile, he is living ... somewhere on a remote foreign sea-coast. ... [In his verse] I find ... all the fever and turmoil and the unattained dreams of a life which has itself had much of the swift, disastrous, and suicidal energy of genius.[10]

Though Dowson took exception to some details that presented 'too lurid' an account of him and asked Symons to make some revisions,[11] overall, he approved of the piece. To this extent, he was complicit in the construction of at least one instance of what I have been calling the 'fictions of Decadence'. R. K. R. Thornton argues similarly, declaring that 'Dowson [was] striving for a mythical status which Symons captures'.[12] Dowson knew he was not exactly the lonely exile Symons described. He was, on the contrary, actively engaged, even from far away, in the British literary scene. Symons's portrait appealed to Dowson on a symbolic level in that it captured what Machen and Moore had characterized as the 'soul' of the artist. Thus, Dowson concurred with Symons's description of his 'swift disastrous, and suicidal energy' and went further, comparing himself with Verlaine, a poet he claimed was 'destroyed' by this energy.[13]

Symons's portrait, revised and reissued in various forms over the following years, was largely responsible for creating what would be called the 'Dowson legend'. It formed the basis of his 1900 obituary of Dowson and the introduction to the Bodley Head collected edition of Dowson's poems. This collection was, ironically, Dowson's most successful work, going through an edition about every two years between 1905 and 1917, prefaced always by Symons's sensationalistic portrait. This portrait had particular currency from 1910 on, when the nostalgia for the *fin de siècle* was in full flower. Dowson, in large part thanks to Symons's account of him, was, along with Wilde, one of the most visible figures of the period, though others helped to reinforce the myth of the 'tragic generation' that was being formulated in these years: Francis Adams, a suicide at 31 in 1893; Hubert Crackanthorpe, a probable suicide, in 1896, aged 26; Aubrey Beardsley, dead at 26 of tuberculosis in 1898; Lionel Johnson, dead at 35 in 1902, reported to have fallen from a bar stool. John Davidson's suicide in 1909 and Symons's emotional breakdown and confinement in 1908 further strengthened the tragic stereotype of the Decadent such that, in 1910, W. G. Blaikie Murdoch insisted: 'It is nature's law that the artist should be unhappy, and should succumb to the philistine and the commercialist.'[14] Though Symons's lurid depiction was repeatedly refuted by Dowson's friends, their efforts did little to dispel the aura of martyrdom surrounding the poet. Perhaps Dowson would have refuted it too had he lived. That, at least, was the pattern of others associated with Decadence as they sought to establish themselves in the altered literary field of the twentieth century.

In 1896, however, Symons's image of the Decadent artist embodied in his description of Dowson accorded precisely with the idealized representations constructed in works ranging from Moore's *Confessions* to Machen's *Hill of Dreams*. This representation of the Decadent at odds with society gained added currency in the wake of the Wilde trials when, more than ever, these artists sensed an insuperable divide between themselves and the public. In this climate, it became more necessary than ever to assert a symbolic representation of the Decadent artist over the material reality. Far more glamorous and beneficial to the cause of art is the representation of Dowson as misunderstood poet and exile than as a writer actively engaged in the literary culture of his time, the Dowson we find in his letters. Dowson participated in this sensationalistic construction of himself and, strategically, it functioned well for him, securing him a posthumous reputation that he might not have achieved had a more mundane representation of his literary endeavours prevailed. Symons's portrait coupled with the early death of the poet at age 33 made Dowson a minor best-seller and popularized him as the posterboy of *fin-de-siècle* Decadence. Whereas in his lifetime Dowson's works had sold in the hundreds, his posthumous *Poems* sold thousands through the Edwardian and Modernist periods. Through his death and his mythologization as the quintessential Decadent, Dowson had garnered the kind of symbolic capital that translates itself into economic capital. He had also achieved the critical and popular acclaim he had desired early in his career. The irony is, of course, that he had to die in order to achieve this goal.

Though Dowson achieved some posthumous fame, he was regarded with ambivalence by the emerging élite of high Modernists. While much has been made of the debt of Modernist poets to the Decadents, this debt was acknowledged only once the Modernists achieved institutional and canonical status. Within the period itself, Modernists disavowed any connection to the Decadents. In 1924, for example, T. S. Eliot told Pound that the 'poets of the nineties' had had no influence on him because he had 'never read any of these people until it was too late for me to get anything out of them'.[15] In the period when Modernism was being established and its practitioners were vying for cultural authority, it was necessary to discredit the Decadents in order to promote Modernist originality and newness. Thus, in 1915, Pound criticized the Decadents for their 'muzziness', a quality that appealed 'to the fluffy, unsorted imagination of adolescence', and not to the 'more hardened passion and intellect of early middle-age'.[16] A. R. Orage took an even dimmer view of the Decadents, singling out Dowson for criticism in the Modernist organ the *New Age*. Orage disparaged those of his day who waxed nostalgic about the *fin de siècle* and equated 'genius with disaster and suicide'.[17] Such romanticized nostalgia, in his view, merely served as 'an incentive to the little artists to trade on their neurosis'.[18] And, whereas for Pound Decadence was linked with adolescent immaturity, for Orage it was 'infantil[e]'.[19] Dowson, he claimed, 'was not ripe, but ... rotten. He remained in the cradle sucking sensations long after he should have been out in the world creating sensations.'[20]

In the period of high Modernism, then, Modernists disavowed their debt to Dowson and other Decadents, establishing themselves as hard, neat, and mature in contrast to the muzzy, soft, adolescent, and even infantile Decadents. This disavowal is all the more understandable considering the esteem with which the Decadents were held by Georgian poets such as Rupert Brooke, whom Modernists were also anxious to establish themselves in opposition to. For high Modernists, Dowson's popularity within the period served as a mark against him and the steady flow of editions of

Dowson's poems between 1905 and 1917 initiated no response on their part to embrace this 1890s poet who would later be acknowledged as a forerunner of Modernism.

John Davidson (1857–1909): a Decadent *malgré lui*

As with Dowson, it was John Davidson's death that garnered him more publicity than he had ever had before. His disappearance and the eventual discovery of his suicide was widely covered in the press.[21] His situation at the time of the Wilde trials also paralleled Dowson's, for he, too, had already begun to devote himself more to the production of high art than of popular fiction. His association with the Decadents had always been tenuous at best. While Davidson shared their distaste for commercialism and philistinism and their interest in an impressionistic aesthetic and unorthodox subject matter, his suspicion of refinement and cosmopolitanism and his 'delight in all that seemed healthy, popular and bustling'[22] aligned him ideologically with counter-Decadents such as W. E. Henley and Rudyard Kipling. 'He persisted in the uneasy relationship' with the Decadents, however, as Townsend argues, 'partly from an ungovernable inclination to imitate and thereby capture the literary market, partly from an ingenuous notion that all rebels had the same aims as he'.[23]

Eventually, however, Davidson began to feel that his fellow rebels did not, in fact, have the same aims as himself. Where previously a belief in the aims of the Decadents justified his potentially profitable association with the group, Davidson now felt disenchanted with the Bodley Head set and tainted by his association with the Decadents. He envied Robert Bridges's 'unsullied ... singing robes', a poet and friend whom he admired as 'a master in the craft'.[24] Never very comfortable with mediating between the claims of high art and the claims of the marketplace, Davidson determined in early 1895 to 'unsully' his robes by dropping hack work altogether and focusing entirely on his poetry.[25] For Davidson novel-writing was hackwork. The novel was a genre which, as I have argued, lent itself most easily to the mediation between high and popular art and Davidson's novels – *The North Wall* (1885), *Baptist Lake* (1894), *Perfervid* (1890), and *Earl Lavender* (1895) – had demonstrated his willingness to attempt works that were both popular and artistic. Certainly his failure to achieve either popular or critical success figured in his abandonment of the genre. After 1896, Davidson ceased writing fiction altogether.

Though Davidson committed himself to the production of high art before the Wilde trials began, he was affected by Wilde's fate and viewed it as a tragedy for the literary community. In a letter written during the trials to friend William McCormick, an academic and man of letters, Davidson quotes from Edgar Allan Poe's 'Haunted Palace', a poem that describes the downfall of Porphyrogene, a king who rules over a beautiful kingdom in a golden age and in whose palace are 'Echoes whose sweet duty / Was but to sing, / In voices of surpassing beauty, / The wit and wisdom of their king.'[26] Likening Wilde to Porphyrogene, Davidson cites the last two stanzas, which describe the king's defeat at the hands of 'evil things' and the occupation of the Palace by 'a hideous throng'.[27] The poem serves as an apt allegory, not only for Wilde's fate, however, but for the position of the Decadents more broadly in the wake of the Wilde scandal when they felt, more than ever, vulnerable to the philistinism of the British public.

For Davidson, as for other Decadents, 1895 was a watershed year. The Wilde trial and the ensuing backlash against Decadence effectively freed him from a label and from a literary style with which he was never at ease, enabling him to pursue his own interests. He could not, however, afford to continue indefinitely on the high artistic course he had proposed for himself. Recognizing this fact, Davidson, who was always searching for the lesser among evils with respect to hackwork, substituted novel-writing with play-writing. For Davidson, who had published plays early in his career and 'regarded the drama as his true province',[28] play-writing represented a happy compromise between the claims of high art and the demands of the marketplace. An offer from Johnston Forbes-Robertson to adapt François Coppée's popular French play *Pour la couronne* in 1895 hastened his return to play-writing.

The years from 1895 to 1900, then, saw Davidson engaged in two primary pursuits. On the one hand, to satisfy his artistic ideals, he was 'exhausting his lyric impulse' in the production of two volumes of poetry;[29] on the other hand, he was play-writing, work that was meant to satisfy both his artistic ideals and his need to make money. In many respects, Davidson was well positioned to succeed in theatre because his interests matched the tastes of the time. In these years, blank verse romantic historical dramas were in vogue and were as, if not more, popular than the 'modern' plays of George Bernard Shaw, Henrik Ibsen, and Arthur Wing Pinero. These plays, Townsend argues, appealed to a middle-class desire for the restoration of a 'poetic, ennobling, and moral ... theater' and Davidson's love of blank verse and his tendency towards 'rhetoric and unrestrained emotionalism' suited him admirably to the task of writing such plays.[30] In Bourdieu's terms, Davidson's position at this time was one in which a homology existed between the expectations inscribed in his position as producer and his disposition,[31] a situation which explains his willingness to engage in what others among the literary élite might have regarded as a compromising of artistic principles.

Davidson's adaptation of *Pour la couronne* achieved a solid, if not spectacular, popular and critical success and he began to receive numerous offers of work. To Davidson's chagrin, however, the offers were for adaptations, not for the original plays he wanted to write. He continued to adapt plays and began writing his own in 1898, receiving commissions from prominent figures within the theatrical community, including Herbert Beerbohm Tree, Mrs Patrick Campbell, George Bernard Shaw, and George Alexander. Despite the support of the theatrical élite, his success did not last. Of all he wrote during this period, only four of his adaptations were produced and none of his original works. The apparent affinity between public taste and his own interests was superficial at best and Davidson failed once again to mediate successfully between his artistic ideals and the demands of the commercial theatrical marketplace. Though he had made concessions to public taste in his theatrical enterprises, his plays contained too much philosophizing for a mainstream audience. By 1900 his belief in his ability to write plays that were at once popular and artistic was diminishing. Davidson now began to regard his ventures in the commercial theatre as hackwork necessary to subsidize a new-found vehicle for his artistic expression – dramatic monologues in blank verse that he called *Testaments*.

Davidson published five *Testaments* in the early 1900s: *The Testament of a Vivisector* (1901), *The Testament of a Man Forbid* (1901), *The Testament of an Empire Builder* (1902), *The Testament of a Prime Minister* (1904), and *The Testament of John Davidson* (1908). The *Testaments* reveal the degree to which Davidson had rejected the Decadent and Aesthetic artistic credo that he had gone at least some way towards promoting in his *fin-de-siècle* work. While Davidson had never been a delicate stylist in the manner of Symons or Dowson, he had dabbled in the impressionistic verse popular among Decadents. In the *Testaments*, however, Davidson moved further towards developing what Townsend has called an 'intellectualized polyglot diction' and an 'anti-literary, synthetic language'.[32]

Davidson's development of a new aesthetic in the *Testaments* anticipates Modernist, particularly Poundian ideas. Like high Modernists, Davidson was not interested in pretty lulling poetry in a Decadent aesthetic manner. Rather, he wanted to jar the reader into awareness by juxtaposing scientific and intellectual language with colloquial speech much as Pound would go on to do. Davidson was also now fully guided by the decidedly non-Decadent belief that writers should be teachers and messengers for their age. He therefore gave full reign to his scientific materialist and imperialist totalitarian philosophies, ideas which had been kept in check in his plays. Where the Decadents had insisted on style over matter, for Davidson matter was now paramount, a quality that many critics insisted marred his poetry. This reaction was characteristic both of contemporary criticism and of later Modernist assessments of Davidson's *Testaments*. Virginia Woolf, for example, complained that Davidson was 'so burdened by all the facts which prove him right in his materialism that the poem breaks down beneath their weight; it becomes a lecture on biology and geology delivered by an irate and fanatical professor'.[33] Here, too, the analogy with Pound is apt, as Pound has also been regarded as one whose pedantry, didacticism, and social views often marred his poetic efforts.[34]

If Davidson's emphasis on matter and his disregard for 'poetic' language in his *Testaments* were un-Decadent, his stance towards his public remained characteristically Decadent. In *The Testament of a Vivisector*, for example, Davidson insisted the work would 'offend both the religious and the irreligious mind' and was suitable only for those 'who are not afraid to fathom what is subconscious in themselves and others'.[35] Similarly, he began *The Testament of an Empire Builder* with an autobiographical parable about an artist who comes into the marketplace 'to sing songs that had not been sung before' but is stoned by a public that wants only to hear his 'old songs'.[36] Only once he is dead does the public wish it had read his 'Testaments'.[37] This parable reflects Davidson's increasing bitterness towards an unreceptive public but also his frustration at being so strongly associated with his 'old songs'. Having embarked on what he regarded as uncompromising artistic work, he was ashamed of his old commercialistic work, which appealed, he said, to 'average minds' because 'there is just a little genius in [them]: [average minds] feel it, they can see it: it is only a rung or two above them on the ladder'.[38] Out of financial necessity Davidson gave in, in 1904, to Lane's desire to issue a volume of selected poems from the 1890s. By 1906, however, he was so averse to his old work that he was attempting to buy back the rights for it and was threatening legal action against those who published it. He repeatedly rejected Grant Richards's suggestions that he should re-publish his 1890s works, a stance that mystified Richards's reader, Filson Young, who insisted that these were 'the only books of [Davidson's] that have a chance of selling'.[39]

Though Davidson felt contempt for the public, abjured his early works, and displayed no willingness to cater to public taste, he still yearned for popular success. He believed that an audience for his work could be created and urged Richards to promote his work more aggressively and, despite his contempt for commercialistic society, he proved willing to involve his artistic work in its processes. Urging Richards to embark on a large-scale promotion of his play *The Theatrocrat* in 1905, Davidson described his work as a commodity, albeit a luxury one: 'Books are a luxury, and therefore they compete with everything for which money is paid, with cigars and soap, whisky and Cook's tours, fur coats and kisses.'[40] By seeking the kind of advertising normally reserved for popular writers, Davidson had discovered another way of trying to bridge the gap between highbrow and lowbrow culture. In the 1890s, Davidson had bridged this gap by making concessions to popular taste. Now, however, he refused to make such compromises, believing instead that his 'art' would come to be appreciated if put within the reach of the public through large-scale advertising. Davidson's attitude was once again baffling to Richards and Young. Where they advocated re-issuing Davidson's older work to enhance his popularity among a broader readership, they could not comprehend his desire for greater publicity for his contemporary work. To them, Davidson, in his current guise, was a coterie writer appealing to a small niche among the intelligentsia who needed no vulgar publicity to promote his new work. Advising Richards against advertising Davidson, Young wrote:

> I hope you will not be tempted into advertising Davidson's book, as in the first place Davidson's books are not the kind that can be advertised into success, nor do they need advertising. A bare announcement of them is enough to show those who are interested that they can be purchased. And if I were Davidson I would not want them advertised. I think it is much more dignified not to.[41]

Young's remarks indicate the degree to which ideas about positioning within the literary field were coloured by élitism. Though an argument against advertising Davidson could certainly be made by appealing to the poor sales of his works, Young couches the argument in terms of his positioning as a coterie writer with an audience unlikely to be swayed by vulgar advertisement. This status circumscribed Davidson's manoeuvrings within the literary field. Publicity-mongering, though effective for popular writers, was not 'dignified', according to Young, for those positioned as Davidson was.

Davidson ultimately failed in his efforts to achieve critical and popular success with what he called a 'new poetry ... a new cosmogony, a new habitation for the imagination of men'.[42] While his philosophy of poetry anticipated Pound's and though often regarded as 'the first of the moderns',[43] Davidson, like Dowson, fell victim to the high Modernists' disavowal of their literary predecessors. His attempts to 'make it new' in the first nine years of the twentieth century were disregarded by the Modernists who disliked the dogmatic nature of Davidson's twentieth-century work and would 'make it new' in a different manner. W. B. Yeats excluded Davidson from the *Oxford Book of Modern Verse 1892–1935*, while Virginia Woolf described the manner of his later works 'as of one dinning the Gospel into the heads of an indifferent public'.[44] T.S. Eliot was similarly scornful. Though Eliot would acknowledge Davidson's influence once he himself was an established canonical poet, early in his career, anxious to set himself in opposition to the old guard, he dismissed Davidson as 'a violent Scotch preacher with an occasional flash of exact vision'.[45] Once Eliot did acknowledge Davidson's influence, he expressed a marked preference for the 1890s verse. For Eliot, Davidson's blank verse was 'rather hard going' and the philosophy 'uncongenial'.[46] It was as a poet of the 1890s, then, and not as the Poundian proto-Modernist of his *Testaments* phase that Modernists ultimately acknowledged Davidson. Despite his attempts to forge a new and modern poetry that would wipe all memory of his hated 1890s work from the minds of the public, Davidson was unable to break away from the Decadent label. He was a Decadent in spite of himself. Davidson's suicide in 1909, following close upon the heels of Symons's 1908 breakdown, helped to confirm the stereotype image of the Decadent and his fate would become one of the 'fictions of Decadence' so popular in memoirs and histories of the *fin de siècle* from the 1910s on.

Arthur Machen (1863–1947): the difficult Decadent

Machen's writing of *The Hill of Dreams* – one of the most Decadent novels of the period – was a decidedly rebellious act at a time when the climate for Decadence was so hostile. But this action came not without a great deal of thought and certainly not without costs for Machen. Though he adopted a decidedly jocular tone in a letter to Lane written just days after Wilde's imprisonment in which he suggested postponing the publication of *The Three Impostors* because of an 'attack of virtue' on the part of the general public,[47] his tone belied real concerns about his literary future. Indeed, as he indicated to Lane a few weeks later, he *had* been giving a great deal of thought to his 'literary reputation' and 'the best course to take in the future'.[48] Machen's concerns about the consequences of the Wilde trials on his own career were magnified because of his own involvement in a court case concerning the racy *Memoirs of Casanova*, a book which he had translated and had a pecuniary interest in.[49] The hearing was set for 15 June 1895, a couple of weeks after Wilde's imprisonment. Though the case had nothing to do with the perniciousness of the Casanova memoirs (the publishers, Robson and Kerslake, were suing the printers, Nichols and Co. for making and selling extra copies of the book, thus spoiling the market for the publishers), Machen was concerned that the law would not protect such a book and was therefore seeking support from booksellers and men of letters, including Bernard Quaritch, Richard Garnett, and George Saintsbury, asking them to testify to the book's 'great literary and historic interest'.[50] In light of the recent Wilde trials, Machen feared discovery of his involvement with a book considered pornographic by many and he implored Lane not to 'mention *my partnership* in the Casanova affair. Nobody knows that I have any pecuniary interest in the matter + of course I don't desire anybody to know of it.'[51] The case appears to have been settled with no consequences for Machen's reputation and, by the end of June, he was no longer anxious about his literary future. Though he had previously shown himself willing to adopt a more commercial Stevensonian style in order to extend his audience beyond the select few connoisseurs interested in his medievalist and Rabelaisian works, he now declared himself unwilling to make concessions to public taste. 'I am not going to be "quiltered" in any manner whatsoever', Machen insisted in response to Lane's request to tone down *The Three Impostors*, declaring himself indifferent to Lane's threat to shelve the project.[52] Apparently, the events of the first half of 1895, both those that directly and indirectly involved him, steeled him in his resolve to remain true to his artistic ideals.

This determination altered Machen's position within the literary field. If previously he had mediated between the claims of high art and the demands of the marketplace, he was now exiling himself to the extreme reaches of the autonomous sector of the field where, as Bourdieu notes, 'the only audience aimed at is other producers'.[53] That Machen was conscious of this withdrawal is revealed in the attitude he took towards his manuscript for *The Hill of Dreams*. Presenting it to Grant Richards in 1897, Machen warned him that he would probably find it 'impossible' and expressed doubts that it would find a publisher.[54] Indeed it was rejected by at least four publishers that year including Richards, Lane, Methuen, and the Unicorn Press.[55] Even in 1902, Richards still feared that the book, if published, might 'land the publisher in the dock'.[56]

In his attempt to develop what he described as 'another manner, which would be more worthy of being called a style, an expression of individuality',[57] Machen followed the example of Lucian in *The Hill of Dreams*, writing in so solipsistic a style that the resulting work was, by the standards of the time, unable to perform its communicative function with the outside world. Even when the hitherto timid Richards published the novel in 1907,[58] it was met with abuse by critics whose rhetoric recalled the counter-Decadence of the 1890s. One reviewer referred to it as 'art ... fallen on unclean and fatal days',[59] while others commented on its unhealthiness[60] and its 'morbidity'.[61] Another described it as a 'morbid phase of English fiction in which sound, color, and scent are put to superfine use by neurotic young gentlemen who should be shut up or set at manual labor'.[62] If this discourse characterized the novel's reception in 1907, a full 12 years after the Wilde trials, it is hardly surprising that Machen could not find a publisher in 1897 when he first completed the manuscript.

In developing his new manner, Machen focused on perfecting his style. In this respect, he seemed firmly committed to Decadent principles at a time when stylistic preciosity was frowned upon. Actually, however, he was working towards a mystical re-figuring of Decadence that he would later explain in *Hieroglyphics* (1902). This project was similar to that of Arthur Symons and W. B. Yeats who were developing the Symbolist aesthetic outlined in Symons's *Symbolist Movement in Literature* (1899).[63] Symons, for example, characterizes Symbolism as 'a literature in which the visible world is no longer a reality, and the unseen world no longer a dream'.[64] Machen's description of what he calls 'fine literature' is similar, but whereas for Symons the key word is 'symbolism', for him it is 'ecstasy', though like Symons's symbolism, it seeks to impart a 'sense' of and a 'desire' for the 'unknown'.[65] So too, Machen's fine literature represents a 'withdrawal from common life and the common consciousness'.[66] This aesthetic helped Symons to fashion a post-1890s identity for himself and also influenced Yeats's and T. S. Eliot's Modernism. For Machen, however, the aesthetic seemed – at least from the point of view of contemporary critics, who called his theory 'false, unwholesome, and effeminate'[67] – to entrench him more firmly in the Decadent 1890s. Through the Edwardian and Modernist periods, Machen would be repeatedly castigated for the 'watery Paterian mysticism' and 'unrelieved preciosity' of his prose,[68] while Yeats and Eliot used a similar theoretical principle to forge Modernism.

Written under the influence of aesthetic ideals that would become unpopular in the wake of the Wilde trial, virtually all that Machen produced from 1895–99 was unpublishable when it was written.[69] Though Machen did take up a position as assistant editor for *Literature* (forerunner to the *Times Literary Supplement*) from 1897–99, he had decided that as far as his 'art' was concerned, he would remove himself from the commercial literary field. This choice was enabled initially by an inheritance that gave him an additional income of £500 a year for about 15 years, freeing him from the necessity to earn a living by writing. From 1905 to 1907 when Machen attempted to resume his literary career in earnest, he was not as keen to popularize his writing as he had been previously. Rather than mediate between the claims of high art and the demands of the literary marketplace as he had done in such productions as *The Great God Pan* and *The Three Impostors*, Machen tried to negotiate the two poles of the literary field in a different way by occupying the opposing poles of the field independently – distinguishing between his journalistic work for the *Academy, T. P.'s Weekly*, and the *Evening News* at the commercial end of the field and his literary work at the high artistic end. His interestedness at one pole of the field enabled his disinterestedness at the other or, as Richards remarked to fellow publisher Alfred Knopf, 'He makes a living by writing for the *Evening News* and does not seem to care what happens to his books.'[70] It was by writing for periodicals, a job he referred to as 'prostitution of the soul',[71] that Machen afforded himself the freedom to be indifferent to the fate his books.

Machen's indifference to the publication of his literary work made him a conundrum to his publishers. Richards, whose publishing centred largely on the production of 'coterie' novels, saw in Machen a potentially profitable writer of such fare. Machen's tales of the 1890s contained elements of the fantasy, horror, and detective genres that had gained in popularity in the Edwardian period. Responding to interest in these genres, Richards urged Machen to re-issue his older work, an appeal that led to the publication of *The House of Souls* (1906), which contained stories from *The Great God Pan* and *The Three Impostors*, as well as unpublished material written in the 1890s. Though willing to publish already-written popularized work, Machen took umbrage at Richards's suggestion that he write more of this kind of fiction. The publisher insisted that 'a fantastic romance in the *genre* of *The Three Impostors*',[72] would be 'a commercial success',[73] but Machen wanted only to produce 'artistic' work, confining his hack work to journalism.

This obstinacy perplexed Richards who described Machen as 'an uncommercial soul, though extraordinarily difficult to handle'.[74] Richards's use of the qualifying 'though' indicates his assumption that 'uncommercial souls' should be easy to handle, presumably because they are grateful to find publishers willing to take them on. In being both 'uncommercial' and 'difficult to handle' Machen went against the grain of Richards's experience. Machen was difficult because, though uncommercial, he demanded 'prohibitive terms' for his work,[75] as though he were a popular writer. At the same time, Machen wanted no costs spared in the presentation of his work. He felt it would sell better presented as 'high art' and complained to publisher Martin Secker about Richards's handling of his work: 'I have always been of the opinion that my books have not been properly handled. They should not be put on the market as ordinary 6/- novels, but rather in the style adopted – I think – for *Marius the Epicurean*: blue boards, white backs and a price like 10/6 net.'[76]

Despite his best efforts, Machen was unable to maintain his separation of commercial and artistic work with any consistency. His hackwork afforded him little time for creative endeavours. As such, *The House of Souls* and *The Hill of Dreams*, both products of the 1890s, were his only works of significance published in the Edwardian period. These publications failed on many levels. They did not establish Machen, as Richards had hoped, as a popular coterie writer in the vein of H. de Vere Stacpoole, Robert Hichens, or Edgar Jepson. They did not garner him the critical acclaim that would establish him among an Edwardian élite that included Joseph Conrad, H. G. Wells, Arnold Bennett, and John Galsworthy, some of whom, like Machen, were products of the 1890s. Finally, they failed to give him the financial freedom necessary to subsidize a full return to the literary life. Still, he struggled on, producing *The Secret Glory*, a work he regarded as 'art', but which would not be published until 1922. Mainly, however, from 1908–14 Machen was fully occupied as a journalist, with little time to pursue the literature that he felt was his true calling.

Machen's re-emergence as a figure in the literary field in 1914 coincided with the beginnings of the period of high Modernism, though he would not be part of this movement. On the one hand, his interest in a mystical and symbolistic aesthetic was antithetical to Poundian Imagism. On the other hand, his literary success in this period would be of the 'lowest' kind in 'high' artistic terms. In the year that Eliot and Pound would meet, a year that also marked the establishment of the Modernist periodicals *Blast* and the *Egoist*, the publication of James Joyce's *Dubliners*, and the serialization of *A Portrait of the Artist as a Young Man*, Machen wrote 'The Bowmen' – a work that would be read by many more people than would read the works of these Modernists that year or for years to come. 'The Bowmen', hackwork produced for the *Evening News*, was a story about the miraculous apparition of St George and an army of bowmen who come to the rescue of English soldiers in battle against the Germans. The story captured the imagination of a nation anxious about the war and, when published in book form, it sold

50,000 copies in three months, 100,000 in a year. Though it was Machen's most successful work, it did not earn him the money necessary to free him from hackwork because the story was the property of the newspaper. It was the paper, therefore, not Machen, that profited from the success of the book. This success would largely determine his subsequent manoeuvrings within the literary field, curtailing his ability to maintain a distinction between his art and his hackwork. While the success of 'The Bowmen' prompted the *Evening News* to ask Machen to write further serials, the publication venue limited the degree to which he could indulge his artistic ideals.

Machen would not be wholly relegated to the ranks of hack writer of newspaper serials for long. If 1914 stood as a defining moment, marking him as a producer of 'low' periodical fiction, a status which placed him in opposition to the 'high' Modernist writers who were establishing themselves in the same year, 1922, the *annus mirabilis* of Modernism, was another significant image-altering moment for Machen. In a year that saw the publication of Joyce's *Ulysses* and Eliot's *Waste Land*, Machen's decidedly non-Modernist work *The Secret Glory* was published. In addition, his major works were being re-issued by Alfred Knopf in America and by Martin Secker in England. Machen had an influential American fan-base, including Vincent Starrett, a newspaper man, bookman, and collector; Robert Hillyer, a Harvard English professor; novelists James Branch Cabell, Ben Hecht, and Carl Van Vechten, and horror writer H. P. Lovecraft.

Donald M. Hassler has described Machen's popularity at this time as part of an anti-Modernist trend in the post-war period, a trend that I have linked to the nostalgia for the *fin de siècle* in this period. Hassler's elaboration of the traditionalist and anti-Modernist *fin-de-siècle* nostalgia of the post-war period focuses on the figure of the book collector. Hassler argues that the book-collecting culture of this period countered a cold, hard, professional, and intellectual Modernism with a soft, sentimental, and romantic nostalgia that valorized amateurism.[77] Where high Modernists rejected their intellectual fathers, proponents of this anti-Modernism were characterized by a 'determination to "face the father" '.[78] Machen garnered a great deal of attention among these book collectors, especially for his *fin-de-siècle* work. Machen's out-of-print works fetched handsome prices throughout the period, an ironic kind of popularity that, like his success with 'The Bowmen', brought Machen no money for himself. It did, however, contribute to his symbolic status among a certain coterie.

In America, Alfred Knopf exploited the nostalgia for the *fin de siècle*, issuing Machen's works in a uniform series of yellow-bound volumes reminiscent of the Decadent *Yellow Book*. And certainly, it was as much the Decadent flavour of his works as their mystical and supernatural elements that attracted a new generation of admirers. Vincent Starrett, for example, titled his study of Machen 'the novelist of ecstasy and sin', while another admirer dubbed him 'the flower-tunicked priest of nightmare'.[79] Though glad of new admirers, Machen continued to disavow his association with Decadence, saying that he had 'no part at all' in the movement.[80] He maintained this stance even as his Decadent 1890s works were gaining favour through the 1920s. The 'products' of the 1890s, he told an admirer in 1925, have 'very little' value: 'I would rather read ... one chapter of Mr Micawber', he continued, 'than all the literature produced between 1890 and 1895'.[81]

Through the Knopf and Secker editions of his works, Machen eventually found the coterie audience that Richards believed he might attract, though he had to come to terms with the fact that his popularity was largely due to his 1890s works. Though aligned with writers of 'low' pulp genres rather than with the Modernist élite, Machen achieved a high status within this sector of the literary field. His tales of mystery, horror, and suspense transcended these genres, according to his admirers, by virtue of their stylistic excellence and because they were ultimately more mystical than horrific. In these respects, Machen was, according to Carl Van Vechten, a writer for the literary connoisseur, not for 'the man in the street' or 'idle bystander' – though such readers, he believed, 'will not find his book[s] lacking in charm'.[82] The paradox of Machen's early career remained with him throughout his life and into posterity as his works continued to challenge the distinctions between high and low art. Is Machen a 'high' writer of 'low' art or a 'low' writer of 'high' art? Ultimately his liminal status deprived him throughout his career both of the rewards due to 'high' artists (literary posterity and symbolic capital) and those due to popular 'low' artists (money).

M. P. Shiel (1865–1947): the mediating Decadent

As in the case of Dowson, Davidson, and Machen, the Wilde scandal and the ensuing backlash against Decadence coincided with a change in literary direction for M. P. Shiel, whose *Prince Zaleski* had earned him the charge of being 'morbid' and 'degenerate'.[83] Initially, Shiel resisted tempering his art to the newly reticent literary values. *Shapes in the Fire*, published in the Keynotes series in November 1896, for example, was more Decadent than *Prince Zaleski*, a work in which Decadence was filtered through a familiar popular literary genre. *Shapes in the Fire*, however, departed from the familiar, 'def[ying] classification' as one reviewer noted.[84] With its stylistic preciosity, eccentric syntax, treatments of death, decay, and rotting, and exotic otherworldly settings, *Shapes in the Fire* took Decadence to an extreme. As one reviewer put it, 'Some of the matter suggests the exclamations of a moon-struck, opium-eating book-worm who was being whirled round the world on a cyclone.'[85] It was likely Shiel's complete departure from familiar popular genres that made *Shapes in the Fire* publishable, particularly for the newly reticent Lane. Though the stories were unmistakably Decadent – reviewers launched the familiar charges of morbidity, perversity, Decadence, affectation, and gruesomeness against the book[86] – the volume was saved from out-and-out attack by what reviewers referred to as its 'obscurity' and 'eccentricity'.[87] Shiel's Decadence in *Shapes in the Fire* was not the deliberately provocative *hypocrite lecteur* type. Nor was it salacious in a manner that would attract a large readership, particularly those susceptible to the pernicious influence of Decadence – women, young persons, and working-class readers. On the contrary, the book required 'patience to wade through [its] involved obscurities and complexities'.[88]

In *Shapes in the Fire*, then, Shiel chose 'high' over 'popular' art, seeking to distance himself from rather than accommodate the wider reading public in the wake of the Wilde trials. This position is endorsed by an essay that appears as an 'interlude' in the collection of stories. Written in dialogue form, like much of Wilde's criticism, Shiel's 'Premier and Maker' presents his views on art, disparaging the novel as art form and expounding the Decadent view that great work may only be recognized by as few as 'five ... cultivated persons'.[89] In his manoeuvrings within the field at this time, Shiel also self-consciously styled himself a literary artist. He ingratiated himself with Lane, for example, insisting on his artistic integrity and deriding his 'old stories of the "tea-cup" realistic sort of which I have grown to feel a little bit ashamed'.[90] He also apologized for his involvement in the production of 'a vile melodramatic novelette' for W.T. Stead and engaged in witty musings on the status of Bodley Head books vis-à-vis the great books of the world.[91] Though Shiel flattered Lane to his face, he disparaged him behind his back, telling his sister, 'These damned little scribblers [Bodley Head writers] think I am one of them, and I am not.'[92] Like Davidson, Shiel thought Lane's coterie a sham and his involvement with it was primarily opportunistic.

It is unclear whether Shiel's break with Lane was due to his sense of his artistic superiority or whether to his view that, in the wake of the Wilde trial, the coterie no longer held the power in the literary field that might do him good. Whether he himself effected the distancing is also unclear. Shiel's snobbish sense of superiority may have concealed his disappointment at not fitting in with this circle as an Irish West Indian with black blood for whom English ways were strange indeed.[93] Though he bragged of having known Robert Louis Stevenson, Oscar Wilde, Pierre Louÿs, and George Egerton, he likely had only the briefest acquaintance with them. He was a fringe figure on the literary scene, though he shared rooms with Dowson in 1898 and was romantically involved for a time with New Woman writer Ella D'Arcy. What is clear, however, is that, after 1897, Shiel's position within the field altered substantially, more so than any of the other Decadents. His high artistic *Shapes in the Fire* would not be representative of his future career. Shiel would go instead to the opposite extreme, immersing himself in the production of popular serialized war novels and tales of imperialist adventure, including *The Yellow Danger* (1898), *The Lord of the Sea* (1901), and *The Yellow Wave* (1905) as well as work in other popular genres including horror, detective, sci-fi, and historical romance. Shiel the decrier of the novel as art form became a writer of serial novels and popular fiction. Though it is true that high-profile writers like H. G. Wells and Arnold Bennett wrote serials, for the most part, serials, like later pulp fiction, were the work of hacks who received neither fame nor literary prestige for the mass-produced fiction they churned out. The move, then, was a risky one for Shiel who aspired to literary posterity and fancied himself a cut above writers such as Arthur Conan Doyle.

Shiel's turn to popular fiction was occasioned by his friendship with Louis Tracy, a writer with whom he would go on to collaborate on numerous stories under the name 'Gordon Holmes'. In 1897 Tracy fell sick and asked Shiel to write instalments of a serial he was working on for *Pearson's Weekly*. Shiel subsequently secured contracts for producing serials from Pearson's and Harmsworth, the most successful publishers of mass-market magazines and newspapers. He continued this work through the Edwardian period and, by his own account, was making up to £3000 a year on serials.[94] Despite his success in writing serials, Shiel was also interested in revising his work for publication in book form. Though serials were often issued in book form after a serial had run, most serial writers did not make revisions. At a time when serial writing often paid far better than novel writing, writers of serials could produce another serial in the time it would take to revise and publish in book form a novel that might not be as popular.

Shiel, however, conceived of the serial and the book as distinct genres, even if the product offered was virtually the same. Where the serial was undeniably hackwork, the novel, in his view, could approach art. At the same time, as Shiel pointed out to Richards, the markets for each were different: 'it is two classes of people who buy book and magazine'.[95] Like Machen, then, Shiel discovered an alternative way to mediate between the claims of high art and the demands of the marketplace. Where Machen earned a livelihood through journalism, pursuing his 'art' independently, Shiel earned a living writing serials while pursuing his 'art' in the novelization of them. He altered his work for book form by giving full play to his eccentric and florid writing style. He called this process making 'real books', an endeavour he characterized as 'trying' in contrast to the 'easy labour' of serial writing.[96] Shiel, then, had a great awareness of his audience, or rather audiences, and crafted his work with respect to its intended audience.

Where most book versions of serials were issued by publishers of cheap fiction such as Hutchinson, Laurie, and Ward, Lock, and Co., Shiel's view of his revised serials as art inclined him to pursue a higher calibre of publisher. Though he would eventually publish with all the above-named publishers, his first choice was always Grant Richards. Richards had been an admirer of Shiel's Bodley Head productions. As one capable of mediating between the high and the popular, Shiel was ideally suited to Richards's aims as a publisher. Shiel approached Richards in the same deliberately unprofessional and dilettantish manner he had used with Lane:

> by some whim of my mind I have a fancy for you as a publisher; so if we
> be mutually just and generous in the money way, it is possible that we
> might strike up a permanent and commonly profitable relation. In making
> me an offer you should not make me a 'business' offer ... but as much as
> you really think you can give; and that I shall probably accept.[97]

Though Shiel's reasons for approaching Richards are obscured in mystification
('by some whim of my mind') he is, I would argue, less interested in money
than in the symbolic capital that an association with Richards, a man of
culture and taste, would bring him. After all, he could easily have
approached publishers more commonly associated with popular fiction, as
he indeed would do after disagreements with Richards. What Shiel sought
from Richards was artistic legitimacy for the 'real books' he made from his
hack serials. In addition, he wanted an educated audience that would take
him out of the obscure realms of the hack writer into the pantheon of the
literary immortals. In later years, for example, Shiel would make much of
critic Jules Claretie's comparison of his novel *The Purple Cloud* with Homer's
Odyssey. Similarly, in his discussion of great writers in 'On Reading' he
brazenly classes himself above Milton, Sophocles, Goethe, Virgil,
Shakespeare, Horace, Bunyan, Petrarch, Boccaccio, and Job.[98]

Shiel's publications with Richards, which he conceived of as high art, sold
poorly, however, and he was unable to attract the educated middlebrow and
highbrow audience that represented Richards's primary market in the
Edwardian period. His books, he admitted to Richards after having issued some
under cheap imprints, 'sell better in cheap form [one or two shilling and six-
penny editions] than in 6/- [six shilling] form'.[99] Though it is difficult to verify
Shiel's claims to popularity in cheap form, he must have made money – at least
for those he called 'the cheap people'[100] – because these publishers continued
to issue his books. Despite his lack of success with Richards and in spite of what
he referred to as his 'unexpected' success in 'cheap form',[101] he persisted in his
pursuit of Richards. Clearly, for Shiel, Richards – as a publisher whose career
was 'marked by the issue of many worthy books, with less pure trash ... than
the others in general'[102] – represented the literary respectability necessary to
ensure his status as a writer of substance. This status was important to Shiel
who ranked himself above the 'cheap people' and those they published.

Shiel's pursuit of Richards was just one of the ways he attempted to
combat his 'low' position within the literary field. Over the years, he balked
at the constraints of his position within the field and of the genres in which
he wrote. Though he accommodated himself to writing popular novels, he
aimed, as he said in his essay 'On Reading',

> to heave the novel just a league or so nearer the sunset from the low
> Daudet–Besant novel where I met it – the modern novel with its lack of

intellectuality, of philosophic intent, its cackle and chaos of cacóphony [*sic*], its music-hall tone of hail-fellow-well-met with its mean readers – positively a wretcheder object to-day than the novels of the Fieldings, Smolletts, themselves people of no particular distinction of intellect.[103]

This intention sometimes led him into difficulties that expose the tensions in his attempts to mediate between his artistic ideals and his financial needs. His novel, *The Last Miracle*, for example – a novel chronicling the end of Christianity and its replacement by a rational religion based on evolutionary principles – was conceived as an artistic work and written 'without the incentive of serial publication'.[104] When it became clear to Shiel that he must, out of financial necessity, make it amenable to serialization, he tried to adapt it. Still, it was too *risqué* for many periodical editors who refused to publish it on the basis of its 'agnostic tone'.[105] As a novel, it would not be published until 1906 and this 'church-cursing book', as Shiel called it, was one of his worst-selling novels.[106] Later in his career, no longer able to obtain contracts for popular serials, Shiel began to fill his works with obscure intellectual and philosophical content, prompting Richards to ask him on one occasion to remove over one hundred pages of 'metaphysical, philosophical, scientific harangues' from a manuscript: 'Excellent sense, I take it', he wrote Shiel, 'but very forbidding to the romantic reader.'[107]

Though Shiel may ultimately have been more successful at popularizing his work than Davidson was, his attempt to resolve tensions between high and popular art prevented him from being either a massively successful bestseller or an acclaimed Modernist of the literary avant-garde. Instead, Shiel was a marginal figure in the Edwardian and Modernist periods. The genres he wrote in made him virtually invisible to the literary élite. Similarly, his appeal among a broad readership was small in comparison with other writers of popular fiction because, according to reviewers of the time, his style proved a hindrance to the average reader. Nothing better illustrates both Shiel's marginal position within the Edwardian literary field and the tensions involved in his attempts to mediate between 'high' and 'low' than the publication of his critical essay 'On Reading', in which he declared himself the greatest writer of all time. It is as much the context as the content that exposes the tensions, for the essay appeared not in the pages of a prominent literary periodical, nor as a published volume on its own (as had Machen's *Hieroglyphics*), but rather as a foreword to his sensational novel *This Knot of Life* (1909).

'On Reading' details Shiel's philosophy of reading and writing as it had evolved since *Shapes in the Fire*. It takes up the questions of why read, what to read, and in what way to read, and is followed by a discussion of great writing. The irony of a critical essay with lengthy and elaborate footnotes appearing in the pages of a popular novel is not lost on Shiel, who addresses the essay in letter form to a Mrs Meade and, tangentially, her neighbours, the ladies of Kensington. His stance in this essay differs from that of his prefatory note in *Shapes in the Fire* of 12 years earlier which was also addressed to a female reader. In the earlier instance, Shiel advises his addressee to skip the critical essay at the centre of the book. It is written for the 'male reader', he writes, and will be 'dull' to her.[108] His preface to the 1909 novel, however, suggests he no longer has a male readership and he is left to share his philosophy with the ladies of Kensington, whose reading habits he denigrates.

In its misogyny, Shiel's view corresponds to the prevailing attitude towards women readers and authors in the *fin-de-siècle* literary field. In other respects, however, his ideas differ substantially from the Decadent high artistic ethos of the 1890s, one that Machen had continued to espouse with a modified Symbolist emphasis in *Hieroglyphics*. Shiel's philosophy, like Davidson's (whom Shiel admired), was strongly pro-science. It was, as he claimed, 'modern'.[109] The 'duty' of the modern reader, he says, 'is to be studious in science' and modern philosophy.[110] Scientists, he insists, are 'better than half the roll of those who have thought themselves writers'[111] and capable of producing 'a book truer, shrewder, closer to the core of Being, than the whole mass and scrap-heap of fiction-books yet scribbled by man'.[112] Though akin to Davidson's philosophy in its scientific emphasis, Shiel's is not as aggressively didactic. The aim of literary art, he declares, is to 'enlarge' the 'reader's consciousness of the truth of things'.[113] At first, the reader will 'follow and learn', but eventually she will be able to 'converse with' and 'controvert' the writer.[114] Far from being typically Decadent or even Edwardian, Shiel's philosophy anticipates Modernist ideas later espoused by Ezra Pound. Like Shiel, Pound sees literary criticism as a science and claims the task of the artist is scientific.[115] Similarly, echoing Shiel on the aim of literary art, he declares that art must be 'true to human consciousness' and that it is 'useful' insofar as it 'maintains the precision and clarity of thought, not merely for the benefit of a few dilettantes and "lovers of literature," but [also] the health of thought outside literary circles and in non-literary existence, in general, individual, and communal life'.[116]

Despite the intellectual seriousness of Shiel's views and their affinity with later Modernist thought, his status as a writer of popular serialized fiction made him invisible to the Modernists. So too, he was silent throughout the heyday of high Modernism, publishing nothing between 1914 and 1923, his only known literary activity in this period being the writing of plays – none of which were produced or published.[117] Save for Virginia Woolf, the supporters of Shiel's Civil List Pension application of 1935 were those who, in canonical terms, represent the B-list of the literary world, writers such as Edward Shanks, J. C. Squire, Lascelles Abercrombie, and others scorned by the high Modernists. Though Shiel never attracted great notice among the literary élite, Rebecca West compared his 'palpitant style' to that of James Joyce.[118] At the same time, Shiel experienced a minor vogue in America in the 1920s and 1930s, profiting from the interest in *fin-de-siècle* writers that had sparked Machen's comeback. Dashiell Hammett called Shiel 'a magician',[119] and Carl Van Vechten brought him to publisher Alfred Knopf's attention in 1923, describing him as 'an important artist' and a 'commercial proposition', sure of 'popular' and 'critical success'.[120] Knopf's issuing of Shiel titles was timely, corresponding with his return to the literary field after a long absence.

Shiel continued writing until his death in 1947, revising works of his earlier period for new audiences, turning his novels into novelettes, and compiling a book of critical essays. Shiel was far more successful at shedding his Decadent image than were his contemporaries Davidson, Dowson, and Machen, even though there was a stylistic continuity between his early and later works. Shiel put his Decadent stylistic affectation to use in twentieth-century popular forms. As a result, he receives more recognition as an Edwardian writer of sci-fi, detective, and adventure stories than as a *fin-de-siècle* Decadent. Like Machen, Shiel appealed to literary connoisseurs, the kind who, as Van Vechten claimed, prided themselves on their 'knowledge of the byways and crannies of exotic literature'.[121] Similarly, his works defy classification in a way that resembles the case of Machen. With Shiel, we are also bound to ask whether he is a 'high' writer of 'low' art or a 'low' writer of 'high' art and to question whether this liminal status is responsible for his relative absence in both canonical literary histories and histories of popular literature. So too, the unclassifiability or 'generic promiscuity' of these writers may account for their critical neglect in a literary history that privileges consistency. Davidson and Dowson have also been subject to traditional literary history's desire for consistency, though in a different respect than Machen and Shiel. Seen as important forerunners of Modernist subjectivity, literary histories have tended to regularize and to make consistent the literary activities of Dowson and Davidson, focusing on their poetry rather than on the novels, plays, and testaments that complicate and make erratic their positions within the 'tradition'.

Ultimately the problem of the Decadents is the problem of Decadence itself – a problem of definition. Where Decadence has a variety of meanings, often contradictory, the Decadents themselves defy classification by the standards of traditional literary history. It has been my intention, throughout this book, to read 'against the grain' of this tradition and to interrogate the place of Decadence and the Decadents within it. For too long, this history has been coloured by myths and clichés, what I have dubbed 'the fictions of Decadence'. Even in much of the ground-breaking contemporary work that has been contributing to the construction of what Lyn Pykett has called 'a "new" *fin de siècle*',[122] Decadence still often figures as 'the weak other of some "strong" literary movement'.[123] It is time that Decadence took its place within this new *fin de siècle* and that the Decadents were recognized not as demonized others in relation to their contemporaries, but as participants in a complex literary field struggling, in Bourdieu's terms, 'to impose the dominant definition of the writer' and 'to delimit the population of those entitled to take part in the struggle to define the writer'.[124]

Notes

Introduction

1. Victor Plarr, *Ernest Dowson 1888–1897: Reminiscences, Unpublished Letters and Marginalia* (New York: Laurence J. Gomme, 1914), p. 22.
2. For an account of the development of ideas about Decadence in nineteenth-century France, see A. E. Carter, *The Idea of Decadence in French Literature 1830–1900* (Toronto: University of Toronto Press, 1958) and R. K. R. Thornton, *The Decadent Dilemma* (London: Arnold, 1983), pp. 15–33.
3. Nicholas White, Introduction, *Against Nature (A rebours)*, trans. Margaret Mauldon (Oxford: Oxford University Press, 1998), p. xiv.
4. N. White, p. xxiv.
5. G. A. Cevasco, *The Breviary of the Decadence: J.-K. Huysmans's* A Rebours *and English Literature* (New York: AMS Press, 2001), p. 13.
6. N. White, pp. xi, xxv.
7. George Moore, *Confessions of a Young Man* (Montreal: McGill-Queens University Press, 1972), p. 169.
8. Arthur Symons, *Figures of Several Centuries* (New York: Dutton, 1916), p. 294. Cevasco's *Breviary of the Decadence* provides an exhaustive account of Huysmans's influence on the British writers. In addition to Moore, Wilde, and Symons, he examines Aubrey Beardsley, Max Beerbohm, John Gray, André Raffalovich, Eric Stenbock, W. B. Yeats, James Joyce, and Evelyn Waugh.
9. Walter Pater, *The Renaissance: Studies in Art and Poetry*, ed. Donald Hill (Berkeley: University of California Press, 1980), p. 189
10. National Vigilance Association, *Pernicious Literature, Documents of Modern Literary Realism*, ed. George G. Becker (Princeton: Princeton University Press, 1963), p. 355.
11. For more detail about the role of circulating libraries and their effect on the novel in Victorian England see Guinevere L. Griest, *Mudie's Circulating Library and the Victorian Novel* (Devon, UK: David and Charles, 1970).
12. These essays are reprinted in abridged form in Sally Ledger and Roger Luckhurst (eds), *The Fin de Siècle: A Reader in Cultural History c. 1800–1900* (Oxford: Oxford University Press, 2000), pp. 111–20; George Moore, *Literature at Nurse; or, Circulating Morals* (New York: Garland, 1978).
13. George Moore, 'Les Décadents', *Court and Society Review* (19 January 1887), pp. 57–8; Havelock Ellis, 'A Note Upon Paul Bourget', initially printed in *Pioneer* magazine in 1889 (*Views and Reviews: A Selection of Uncollected Articles 1884–1932*, first series 1884–1919 [London: Desmond Harmsworth, 1932], pp. 48–60); Richard Le Gallienne, 'Considerations Suggested by Churton Collins' Illustrations of Tennyson', originally appeared in the *Century Guild Hobby Horse (Retrospective Reviews*, vol. 1 [London: Lane, 1896], pp. 19–28); Arthur Symons, 'The Decadent Movement in Literature', *Harper's New Monthly Magazine* 88 (November 1893), pp. 858–67; Lionel Johnson, 'A Note Upon the Practice and Theory of Verse at the Present Time Obtaining in France', *Century Guild Hobby Horse* 6 (1891), pp. 61–6.
14. Bruce Gardiner, *The Rhymers' Club: A Social and Intellectual History* (New York: Garland, 1988), pp. 128, 129.

15. *A Mere Accident* (1887), *Spring Days* (1888), *Mike Fletcher* (1889), and his autobiographical *Confessions of a Young Man* (1888).
16. Stuart Mason provides a thorough documentation of the reception of Wilde's novel and the controversy that ensued (*Art and Morality* [London: Frank Palmer, 1912]).
17. Thornton, p. 42.
18. See, for example, Thomas Bradfield, 'A Dominant Note of Some Recent Fiction', *Westminster Review* 142 (1894), pp. 537–45; 'The Damnation of Decadence', *National Observer* (23 February 1895), pp. 390–1; Janet E. Hogarth, 'Literary Degenerates', *Fortnightly Review* 63 (1895), pp. 586–92; 'Morbid and Unclean Literature', *Whitehall Review* (20 April 1895), p. 13; James Ashcroft Noble, 'The Fiction of Sexuality', *Contemporary Review* 67 (1895), pp. 490–8. Harry Quilter, 'The Gospel of Intensity', *Contemporary Review* (June 1895), pp. 761–82. J. A. Spender, *The New Fiction (a Protest Against Sex-Mania), and Other Papers* (New York: Garland, 1984); Hugh E. M. Stutfield, 'Tommyrotics', *Blackwoods* 179 (June 1895), pp. 833–45.
19. Arthur Symons, *The Symbolist Movement in Literature* (New York: Dutton, 1958), p. 4.
20. Quoted in Karl Beckson, *London in the 1890s: A Cultural History* (New York: Norton, 1992), p. 32.
21. Max Beerbohm, 'Enoch Soames', *Seven Men and Two Others* (Oxford: Oxford University Press, 1980), pp. 3–44. This story was first published in 1916 in the Century magazine before being included in the 1919 collection *Seven Men and Two Others*.
22. Arthur Symons, 'A Literary Causerie', *Savoy* 4 (August 1896), pp. 91–3. This essay was subsequently revised and reprinted as an obituary for Dowson and as the introduction to the Bodley Head edition of his verse; Arthur Symons, 'Aubrey Beardsely: An Essay with a Preface', *The Art of Aubrey Beardsley* (New York: Boni and Liveright, 1918), pp. 15–36. Among the notable memoirs and histories of the 1890s that first appeared in the 1910s and 1920s are Richard Le Gallienne, *The Romantic '90s* (London: Putnam's, 1926); Holbrook Jackson, *The Eighteen Nineties* (New York: Knopf, 1923); and W. G. Blaikie Murdoch, *The Renaissance of the Nineties* (London: De La More Press, 1911).
23. For a discussion of the influence of the 1890s on 1990s popular culture see Philip Hoare's article, 'Symbols of Decay', *Tate: The Art Magazine* 13 (Winter 1997), pp. 22–9. Contemporary films have also sparked the current interest in the period, notably Todd Haynes's film *Velvet Goldmine* (1998), in which Wilde is represented as a progenitor of 1970s glam rock and Baz Luhrmann's *Moulin Rouge* (2001), which juxtaposes late-nineteenth century French Decadent music hall culture with contemporary pop culture. Christopher Dickey's article 'Absinthe's Second Coming' indicates how the reintroduction of absinthe in Britain has also sparked a revival of interest in the Decadents (*Cigar Aficionado* [March/April 2001], 5 September 2005) <http://www.cigaraficionado.com/>. Path: Library; Magazine Archive.
24. The *OED* defines myth as 'a popular conception of a person or thing which exaggerates or idealizes the truth' (definition 2c, *Oxford English Dictionary* (online version), University of Alberta, Edmonton, 4 August 2005, <http:// dictionary. oed.com/>.
25. W. B. Yeats, Introduction, *Oxford Book of Modern Verse: 1892–1935* (Oxford: Oxford University Press, 1936), p. x.
26. W. B. Yeats, *Autobiography* (Garden City, NY: Doubleday, 1958), p. 200.
27. Ibid., p. 208.
28. Quoted in Beckson, *London in the 1890s*, p. 72.

29. Beckson, *London in the 1890s*, p. 71.
30. Karl Beckson, 'Yeats and the Rhymers' Club', *Yeats Studies* 1 (1971), p. 41.
31. Gardiner, *Rhymers'*, 186.
32. From Yeats's *Essays and Introductions*, qtd. in Gardiner, *Rhymers'*, 131.
33. Barbara Charlesworth, *Dark Passages: The Decadent Consciousness in Victorian Literature* (Madison: University of Wisconsin Press, 1965); Graham Hough, *The Last Romantics* (London: Methuen, 1961); Thornton, *Decadent Dilemma*.
34. M. H. Abrams, ed. *The Norton Anthology of English Literature*.vol. 2 (New York: Norton, 1993), p. 1612.
35. Joseph Bristow, Preface, *The Fin-de-Siècle Poem: English Literary Culture and the 1890s*, ed. Joseph Bristow (Columbus, OH: Ohio University Press, 2005), pp. ix–x. This book of essays offers a substantial re-evaluation of the achievements of the Decadents as poets and also illuminates the contributions of women writers to the poetry of this period.
36. John Munro, *The Decadent Poetry of the Eighteen Nineties* (Beirut: American University of Beirut, 1970), pp. 57, 64.
37. Charlesworth, pp. 122, 123.
38. Hough, pp. 202, 204.
39. Regenia Gagnier, *Idylls of the Marketplace: Oscar Wilde and the Victorian Public* (Stanford: Stanford University Press, 1986), p. 144.
40. Regenia Gagnier, 'A Critique of Practical Aesthetics', *Aesthetics and Ideology*, ed. George Levine (New Brunswick, NJ: Rutgers University Press, 1994), pp. 270–6.
41. Abrams, p. 1613.
42. Yeats, *Autobiography*, p. 200.
43. Andreas Huyssen, *After the Great Divide: Modernism, Mass Culture, Postmodernism* (Bloomington: Indiana University Press, 1986), p. viii.
44. Oscar Wilde, *Complete Works of Oscar Wilde* (London: Collins, 1971), p. 1090.
45. The alienated artist was also a theme in much of the Decadent poetry of the period. See, for example, Beckson's discussion in 'Yeats and the Rhymers' Club', pp. 33–5.
46. Numerous critics have commented on the relationship between Decadence and Modernism. In addition to Charlesworth, Hough, Munro, and Thornton, see also J. E. Chamberlin, 'From High Decadence to High Modernism', *Queen's Quarterly* 87 (1980), pp. 591–610; David Weir, *Decadence and the Making of Modernism* (Amherst: University of Massachusetts Press, 1995); Murray G. H. Pittock, *Spectrum of Decadence: The Literature of the 1890s* (London: Routledge, 1993), pp. 175–89; Edmund Wilson, *Axël's Castle: A Study in the Imaginative Literature of 1870–1930* (New York: Norton, 1959); Linda Dowling, *Language and Decadence in the Victorian Fin de Siècle*. Princeton: Princeton University Press, 1986), pp. 244–83.
47. Thornton, p. 200.
48. Charlesworth, pp. 122–23; Munro, p. 73; Hough, pp. 208–12.
49. Hough, p. 215.
50. Julie Codell discusses a number of popular images of the artist including the bohemian (*Victorian Artist: Artists' Lifewritings in Britain ca. 1870–1910* [Cambridge: Cambridge University Press, 2003]). In the Victorian period, she argues, the bohemian was often represented as a bourgeois gentleman as in the works of Charles Dickens and William Makepeace Thackeray (pp. 96–7). At the same time, she insists, there was a 'diabolic, antisocial, and threatening' image of the bohemian as represented in Wilde's *Picture of Dorian Gray* (1890), Morley Roberts's *Immortal Youth* (1896), and George Moore's *A Modern Lover* (1883) (pp. 96, 99). This latter model was certainly what the Decadents drew on in their self-representation.

For more on the artist as dandy see Ellen Moers's excellent study, *The Dandy: Brummell to Beerbohm* (Lincoln: University of Nebraska Press, 1960).

51. Linda Dowling, *Aestheticism and Decadence: A Selected Annotated Bibliography* (New York: Garland, 1977), pp. ix–x.
52. Dowling, *Language and Decadence*, pp. x, xi.
53. See, for example, Talia Schaffer, *The Forgotten Female Aesthetes* (Charlottesville: University Press of Virginia, 2000) and the essays by Annette Federico, Linda K. Hughes, Lisa K. Hamilton, Edward Marx, and Margaret Debelius in Talia Schaffer and Kathy Psomiades, eds, *Women and British Aestheticism* (Charlottesville: University Press of Virginia, 1999).
54. J. Benjamin Townsend, *John Davidson: Poet of Armageddon* (New Haven, CT: Yale University Press, 1961), p. 185.
55. David Cecil, *Max: A Biography of Max Beerbohm* (New York: Atheneum, 1985), p. 92.
56. Gagnier, *Idylls*, p. 3.
57. Jonathan Freedman, *Professions of Taste: Henry James, British Aestheticism, and Commodity Culture* (Stanford, CA: Stanford University Press, 1990); Josephine Guy and Ian Small, *Oscar Wilde's Profession: Writing and the Culture Industry in the Late Nineteenth Century* (Oxford: Oxford University Press, 2000).
58. Laurel Brake, 'Endgames: The Politics of the *Yellow Book* or, Decadence, Gender, and the New Journalism', *Essays and Studies* 48 (1995), pp. 38–64; Margaret Diane Stetz, 'Sex, Lies, and Printed Cloth: Bookselling at the Bodley Head in the Eighteen Nineties', *Victorian Studies* 35.1 (1991), pp. 71–86.
59. Schaffer, *Forgotten Female Aesthetes*, pp. 122–58.
60. Stephen Arata, *Fictions of Loss in the Victorian* fin de siècle (Cambridge: Cambridge University Press, 1996).
61. Weir, pp. 163–91; Brian Stableford, *Glorious Perversity: The Decline and Fall of Literary Decadence* (San Bernadino, CA: Borgo Press, 1998).
62. Gagnier, *Idylls*, p. 65.
63. Ibid.
64. Freedman, *Professions of Taste*, pp. 48–53; Alan Sinfield, *The Wilde Century: Effeminacy, Oscar Wilde and the Queer Moment* (London: Cassell, 1994); Dowling, *Language and Decadence*, p. 234.
65. Dowling, *Aestheticism and Decadence*, p. xiii.
66. John Reed, *Decadent Style* (Athens, OH: Ohio University Press, 1985), pp. 36–40.
67. Thornton, p. 34.
68. Stableford, p. 108.
69. See especially the essays in Schaffer and Psomiades's collection *Women and British Aestheticism*.
70. See Munro, Charlesworth, and Thornton.
71. Wendell V. Harris is an exception here. He has made significant attempts to go beyond the standard texts to consider how Decadence manifested itself in a variety of forms and genres in a larger body of fiction of the period in 'John Lane's Keynotes Series and the Fiction of the 1890's', *PMLA* 83 (1968), pp. 1407–13 and 'Identifying the Decadent Fiction of the 1890s', *English Fiction in Transition* 5,5 (1962), pp. 1–14.
72. James G. Nelson's trilogy of volumes on the Bodley Head, Elkin Mathews, and Leonard Smithers, who were the main publishers of Decadent literature, is an invaluable resource for understanding the complexities of publishing avant-garde literature and the importance of the relationships between late-Victorian writers

and their publishers (*The Early Nineties: A View from the Bodley Head* [Cambridge, MA: Harvard University Press, 1971]; *Elkin Mathews: Publisher to Yeats, Joyce, Pound* [Madison: University of Wisconsin Press, 1989]; *Publisher to the Decadents: Leonard Smithers in the Careers of Beardsley, Wilde, Dowson* [University Park: Pennsylvania State University Press, 2000]).

73. For an account of the variety of conflicting views of Decadence in scholarship, see Weir, pp. 2–13 and Liz Constable, Dennis Denisoff, and Matthew Potolsky's introduction to *Perennial Decay: On the Aesthetics and Politics of Decadence* (Philadelphia: University of Pennsylvania Press, 1999), pp. 2–11. They are particularly troubled by 'disparaging characterizations' of Decadence that 'treat decadence as the weak other of some "strong" literary movement, distinguishing the (good) Aesthetes from the (bad) decadents, the (transcendent) Symbolists from the materialistic decadents', and so on (pp. 4, 7).

74. Weir, p. 10. Richard Gilman's similar claim is that Decadence has a 'purely negative ... existence. It emerges as the underside or logical complement of something else, coerced into taking its place in our vocabularies by the pressure of something that needs an opposite, an enemy. Decadence is a scarecrow, a bogy, a red herring' (Richard Gilman, *Decadence: The Strange Life of an Epithet* [New York: Farrar and Strauss, 1980], p. 159).

75. Gilman, p. 159.

76. Weir, p. 13.

77. Gilman, p. 129.

78. Charles Bernheimer, *Decadent Subjects: The Idea of Decadence in Art, Literature, Philosophy, and Culture of the Fin de Siècle in Europe*, eds T. Jefferson Kline and Naomi Schor (Baltimore: Johns Hopkins University Press, 2002), p. 5.

79. Constable, Denisoff, and Potolsky, p. 12.

80. Gilman, p. 140.

1 The Mystified Class Origins of Decadence

1. Symons, *Symbolist*, p. 4.

2. Moers, p. 287.

3. Ibid., pp. 288–9.

4. Ibid., p. 288.

5. Quoted in Moers, p. 288.

6. Gagnier, *Idylls*, p. 65.

7. Harold Perkin, *The Rise of Professional Society: England Since 1880* (London: Routledge, 1989), p. 78.

8. Ibid., p. 85.

9. Quoted in Perkin, p. 84.

10. The rest of this paragraph draws on Perkin, pp. 120–1.

11. Ibid., p. 120.

12. Ibid., p. 121.

13. Matthew Arnold, *Culture and Anarchy* (New Haven: Yale University Press, 1994), p. 5.

14. Ibid., pp. 34–5.

15. Quoted in Dowling, *The Vulgarization of Art* (Charlottesville: University of Virginia Press, 1996), pp. 40–1.

16. Dowling, *Vulgarization*, p. 41.

17. Quoted in Dowling, *Vulgarization*, p. 41.

18. Freedman, p. 62.
19. The exact dates of the Aesthetic movement are difficult to determine. Those who include Pre-Raphaelitism in the movement, trace its origins to the 1850 publication of the *Germ*. For Ian Small, who regards Pre-Raphaelitism as a distinct phenomenon, Aestheticism originates in the late 1860s in the poetry and criticism of Swinburne (Ian Small, *The Aesthetes: A Sourcebook* [London: Routledge, 1979], p. 1). As to its status as a broad cultural movement rather than a strictly literary or artistic movement most critics agree. For a discussion of the broader cultural manifestations of Aestheticism see Ian Fletcher, 'Some Aspects of Aestheticism', *Twilight of Dawn: Studies in English Literature in Transition*, ed. O. M. Brack (Tucson: University of Arizona Press, 1987), pp. 1–33.
20. Freedman, p. 55.
21. Ibid., p. 60.
22. Dianne Sachko Macleod, *Art and the Victorian Middle Class: Art and the Making of Cultural Identity* (Cambridge: Cambridge University Press, 1996), p. 277.
23. Ibid., pp. 277–8.
24. Freedman, p. 54.
25. Symons, *Symbolist*, p. 4.
26. Ibid.
27. Bourdieu developed his notion of 'habitus' throughout his work, notably in *Distinction: A Social Critique of the Judgement of Taste* (London: Routledge, 1984).
28. Biographical information on the Decadents in the following pages and throughout this book comes from these sources: Richard Ellmann, *Oscar Wilde* (London: Penguin, 1987); Mark Valentine, *Arthur Machen* (Mid Glamorgan, Wales: Seren, 1995); J. Benjamin Townsend, *John Davidson: Poet of Armageddon* (New Haven: Yale University Press, 1961); Arthur Machen, *Things Near and Far* (New York: Knopf, 1923); Karl Beckson, *Arthur Symons: A Life* (Oxford: Clarendon, 1987); Robert Hichens, *Yesterday* (London: Cassell, 1947); Richard Whittington-Egan and Geoffrey Smerdon, *The Quest of the Golden Boy: The Life and Letters of Richard Le Gallienne* (Barre, MA: Barre Publishing Company, 1962); Harold Billings, 'The Shape of Shiel 1865–1896: A Biography of the Early Years', *Shiel in Diverse Hands: A Collection of Essays*, ed. A Reynolds Morse (Cleveland, OH: Reynolds Morse Foundation, 1983), pp. 77–105; David Cecil, *Max: A Biography of Max Beerbohm* (New York: Atheneum, 1985); Jad Adams, *Madder Music, Stronger Wine: The Life of Ernest Dowson, Poet and Decadent* (London: Tauris, 2000); Aubrey Beardsley, *Letters of Aubrey Beardsley*, eds Henry Maas, J. L. Duncan, and W. G. Good (Oxford: Plantin, 1990); Adrian Frazier, *George Moore 1852–1933* (New Haven: Yale University Press, 2000).
29. Whittington-Egan and Smerdon, p. 8.
30. Hichens, *Yesterday*, p. 235.
31. Machen, *Things*, pp. 89–90 and 94.
32. Freedman, p. 55.
33. Walter Pater, *Appreciations With an Essay on Style* (New York: Macmillan, 1906), pp. 14–15.
34. Charles Baudelaire, '*Au Lecteur*' ('To the Reader'), *Les Fleurs du mal*, trans. Richard Howard (Boston: David R. Godine, 1982), pp. 5–6 (English translation); pp. 183–4 (original French).
35. Arata, pp. 44, 49.
36. 'Dilettante', definition 1, *Concise Oxford Dictionary of Current English*, 6th edn (1976).
37. Machen, *Things*, p. 96.

38. George Moore, *Confessions of a Young Man*, ed. Susan Dick (Montreal: McGill-Queen's University Press, 1972), pp. 111, 112.
39. Ibid., p. 84.
40. Dowling, 'The Decadent and the New Woman in the 1890s', *Nineteenth-Century Fiction* 33 (1979), pp. 443–4.
41. Havelock Ellis, 'A Note Upon Paul Bourget', *Views and Reviews: A Selection of Uncollected Articles 1884–1932*, first series 1884–1919 (London: Desmond Harmsworth, 1932), p. 53.
42. Quoted in Ellis, p. 55.
43. Walter Pater, *The Renaissance: Studies in Art and Poetry. The 1893 Text*, ed. Donald Hill (Berkley: University of California Press), p. 189.
44. William Makepeace Thackeray, *The Book of Snobs* (Old Woking, UK: Gresham Books, 1980).
45. Moore, *Confessions*, p. 140.
46. Raymond Williams, *Problems in Materialism and Culture* (London: Verso, 1980), pp. 40–1.
47. François Bédarida, *A Social History of England 1851–1990*, trans. A. S. Forster and Geoffrey Hodgkinson (London: Routledge, 1990), p. 128.
48. Ibid.
49. Ibid.
50. E. Spencer Wellhofer, *Democracy, Capitalism, and Empire in Late-Victorian Britain 1885–1910* (London: Macmillan, 1996), p. 9.
51. For more on these aspects of the British music hall, see Martha Vicinus, *The Industrial Muse: A Study of Nineteenth-Century British Working-Class Literature* (London: Croom Helm, 1974), pp. 238–85; Dagmar Kift, *The Victorian Music Hall: Culture, Class, and Conflict* (Cambridge: Cambridge University Press, 1996); Peter Bailey, 'Custom, Capital, and Culture in the Victorian Music Hall', *Popular Culture and Custom in Nineteenth-Century England*, ed. Robert D. Storch (London: Croom Helm, 1982), pp. 180–208.
52. Dowling gives lengthy consideration to the Decadents' interest in the music hall in *Language and Decadence* (pp. 230–41).
53. Victorien Sardou (1831–1908) was a hugely popular French writer of melodramas and historical plays whose works were frequently performed in translation on the London stage.
54. Moore, *Confessions*, p. 147.
55. Dowling, *Language and Decadence*, p. 237.
56. Jerrold Seigel, *Bohemian Paris: Culture, Politics, and the Boundaries of Bourgeois Life, 1830–1930* (New York: Viking, 1986); Elizabeth Wilson, *Bohemians: The Glamorous Outcasts* (New Brunswick, NJ: Rutgers University Press, 2000); Marilyn Brown, *Gypsies and Other Bohemians: The Myth of the Artist in Nineteenth-Century France* (Ann Arbor, MI: UMI Research Press, 1985); Joanna Richardson, *The Bohemians: La vie de Bohème in Paris, 1830–1914* (South Brunswick, NJ: A. S. Barnes, 1971).
57. Wilson, p. 18.
58. Richardson, p. 11.
59. Arthur Symons, *Studies in Prose and Verse* (London: Dent, 1904), p. 263.
60. See, for example, Arthur Ransome, *Bohemia in London* (London: Swift, 1907); Constance Brandon Margaret Scott, *Old Days in Bohemian London (Recollections of Clement Scott)* (New York: Frederick A. Stokes, 1919); Harry Furniss, *My Bohemian Days* (London: Hurst and Blackett, 1919); George Robert Sims, *My Sixty Years' Recollections of Bohemian London* (London: Eveleigh Nash, 1917); Julius M. Price,

My Bohemian Days in London (London: Laurie, 1914); Phil May, *Mr. Punch in Bohemia; or, the Lighter Side of Literary, Artistic, and Professional Life* (London: Educational Book Co., 1907).

61. 'Bohemian', definition 3, *Oxford English Dictionary* (online version), University of Alberta, Edmonton, 4 August 2005 < http:// dictionary.oed.com./>.
62. Codell, pp. 96–7. See also Christopher Kent's, 'The Idea of Bohemia in Mid-Victorian England'. *Queen's Quarterly* 80 (1973), 360–9 and 'British Bohemia and the Victorian Journalist', *Australasian Victorian Studies Journal* 6 (2000), 25–35.
63. Codell, p. 96.
64. Quoted in Ana Parejo Vadillo's, introduction to *Women Poets and Urban Aestheticism: Passengers of Modernity* (Basingstoke, UK: Palgrave, 2005), p. 37. This book, apart from the introduction, was unavailable to me as I worked on this project. It promises, however, to be an important study of the urban landscape of London in relation to the late-Victorian poetry of women writers. Similarly, Linda Hughes's biography of Graham Tomson, also forthcoming in 2005, provides information about St John's Wood as a bohemian enclave in late-Victorian Britain in *Graham R.: Rosamund Marriott Watson, Woman of Letters* (Columbus, OH: Ohio University Press, 2005).
65. See Gardiner, *Rhymers'* for a discussion of London as a prominent theme in the poetry of the members of the Rhymers' Club (pp. 93–103).
66. Ibid., 93.
67. Quoted in Gardiner, *Rhymers'*, p. 102.
68. Quoted in Gardiner, *Rhymers'*, p. 102.
69. Wilson, p. 65.
70. Pierre Bourdieu, *Rules of Art: Genesis and Structure of the Literary Field*, trans. Susan Emanuel (Stanford, CA: Stanford University Press, 1995), p. 56.
71. Weir, p. xv.
72. Moore, *Confessions*, p. 184.
73. See Wilson, pp. 1–26, M. Brown, pp. 1–17, and Seigel.
74. Weir, p. xv.
75. Rita Felski, *The Gender of Modernity* (Cambridge, MA: Harvard University Press, 1995), p. 99.
76. Freedman, pp. 178, 179.
77. Arata, p. 46.
78. Magali Sarfatti Larson, *The Rise of Professionalism: A Sociological Analysis* (Berkeley: University of California Press, 1977), p. xvii.
79. Pierre Bourdieu, *The Field of Cultural Production* (New York: Columbia University Press, 1983), pp. 75–6.
80. Freedman, pp. 63, 54.
81. Bruce Gardiner, 'Decadence: Its Construction and Contexts', *Southern Review* 18 (1985), p. 36.

2 Decadent Positionings: Decadence and the Literary Field

1. James Ashcroft Noble, 'The Fiction of Sexuality', *Contemporary Review* 67 (1895), pp. 490–1.
2. Moore, *Confessions*, p. 107.

3. For detailed information regarding these aspects of the transformation of the literary field, see Peter Keating, *The Haunted Study: A Social History of the English Novel 1875–1914* (London: Secker and Warburg, 1989) and Richard Altick, *The English Common Reader: A Social History of the Mass Reading Public 1800–1900*, 2nd edn (Columbus, OH: Ohio State University Press).

4. Machen, *Things*, pp. 96, 126.

5. Keating, p. 29.

6. Ibid., pp. 48, 47.

7. Lyn Pykett has argued that concerns about access were the main source of anxiety in most of the literary debates of the 1880s and 1890s – from the romance/realism and 'candour in English fiction' debates to debates over Naturalism, Decadence, and New Woman fiction ('Representing the Real: The English Debate About Naturalism', *Naturalism in the European Novel: New Critical Perspectives*, ed. Brian Nelson [New York: Berg, 1992], pp. 167–88).

8. Huyssen, p. viii.

9. Nigel Cross, *The Common Writer: Life in Nineteenth-Century Grub Street* (Cambridge: Cambridge University Press, 1985), p. 216.

10. Ibid.

11. My characterization of the field as structured around an opposition between the literary élite and producers of popular or mass art is based on Bourdieu's model in *The Field of Cultural Production* (pp. 115–31). For the sake of clarity, however, I use the terms élite and popular where Bourdieu employs the terms sub-field of restricted production and sub-field of large-scale production.

12. Arnold Bennett, *The Truth About an Author* (London: Methuen, 1914), p. 102.

13. Bourdieu, *Field*, p. 42.

14. Marie Corelli, '*Barabbas* – and After', *Idler* (February 1895), p. 134.

15. Marie Corelli, *The Silver Domino* (London: Lamley, 1892), pp. 95–7.

16. Marie Corelli, *The Sorrows of Satan* (Oxford: Oxford University Press, 1998), pp. 125–6; Marie Corelli, *Free Opinions, Freely Expressed on Certain Phases of Modern Social Life and Conduct* (London: Constable, 1905), pp. 252–61 and pp. 245–51.

17. Corelli, *Sorrows*, p. 50.

18. Lyn Pykett, *Engendering Fictions: The English Novel in the Early Twentieth Century* (London: Edward Arnold, 1995), p. 55.

19. Quoted in Peter D. McDonald, *British Literary Culture and Publishing Practice 1880–1914* (Cambridge: Cambridge University Press, 1997), pp. 37–8.

20. George Egerton, *A Leaf From the Yellow Book: The Correspondence of George Egerton*, ed. Terence de Vere White (London: Richards, 1958), pp. 29–30.

21. Spender, *The New Fiction*.

22. *The Autobiography of a Boy* was subsequently published in book form by Elkin Mathews and John Lane in 1894.

23. See Nelson, *Early Nineties*, pp. 107, 108, and 322.

24. See Josephine Guy and Ian Small, *Oscar Wilde's Profession: Writing and the Culture Industry in the Late Nineteenth Century* (Oxford: Oxford University Press, 2000), pp. 57–8.

25. Quoted in Gardiner, *Rhymers'*, p. 85.

26. Ibid., p. 77.

27. Quoted in Desmond Flower and Henry Maas, 'Introduction', *The Letters of Ernest Dowson* (London: Cassell, 1967), p. 4.

28. Ernest Dowson, *The Letters of Ernest Dowson*, eds Desmond Flower and Henry Maas (London: Cassell, 1967), p. 37.

29. Ernest Dowson, *The Letters of Ernest Dowson*, eds Desmond Flower and Henry Maas (London: Cassell, 1967), p. 88.

30. Quoted in Townsend, p. 116.

31. Quoted in A. Reynolds Morse, *The Works of M. P. Shiel Updated*, 2nd edn (Dayton, OH: Morse, 1980), p. 435.

32. Arthur Machen, *A Few Letters from Arthur Machen: Letters to Munson Havens* (Aylesford, UK: Aylesford Press, 1993), p. 32.

33. Ibid.

34. Symons, *Studies*, p. 149.

35. George Allen Cate, 'George Meredith', *Encyclopedia of the 1890s*, ed. G. A. Cevasco (New York: Garland, 1993), p. 391.

36. Beckson, *Arthur Symons*, p. 26.

37. Quoted in Nelson, *Early Nineties*, p. 115.

38. Nicholas Daly, *Modernism, Romance, and the* fin de siècle: *Popular Fiction and British Culture, 1880–1914* (Cambridge: Cambridge University Press, 1999), p. 18.

39. James Ashcroft Noble, review of *Dr Jekyll and Mr Hyde*, *Academy* (23 January 1886), p. 55.

40. Ibid.

41. Arata, p. 47.

42. Symons, *Studies*, p. 77.

43. Dowson, *Letters*, p. 151.

44. Quoted in Christopher Frayling, *Nightmare: The Birth of Horror* (London: BBC, 1996), p. 117.

45. Robert Louis Stevenson, *The Letters of Robert Louis Stevenson*, 6 vols., eds Bradford A. Booth and Ernest Mehew (New Haven: Yale University Press, 1994), vol. 5, p. 171.

46. Dowson, *Letters*, pp. 86, 81.

47. Machen, *Things*, p. 144.

48. Quoted in Morse, p. 436.

49. Guy and Small, p. 66.

50. Cross, p. 206.

51. My discussion of the Bodley Head throughout focuses on Lane's running of the firm from 1894 on. Under Mathews and Lane, the firm focused more on *belles-lettres* and poetry and even though Mathews was a partner in the firm when it inaugurated the *Yellow Book* and began publishing fiction, the firm's turn to Decadence was due, as Nelson notes, to Lane's initiative (Nelson, *Early Nineties*, p. 265).

52. Linda Marie Fritschner, 'William Heinemann Limited', *British Literary Publishing Houses. Dictionary of Literary Biography* 112 (Detroit: Gale, 1991), p. 152.

53. Ernest Dowson, *New Letters from Ernest Dowson*, ed. Desmond Flower (Andoversford, Gloucestershire: Whittington Press, 1984), p. 4.

54. Ibid., p. 6.

55. Stetz, 'Sex, Lies', p. 71.

56. Bourdieu, *Field*, pp. 95–6.

57. Hichens, *Yesterday*, p. 70.

58. Egerton, pp. 26–7.

59. Chalmers Roberts, *William Heinemann, May 18th 1863–October 5th 1920: An Appreciation* (London: printed for private circulation, 1920), p. 5; Frederic Whyte, *William Heinemann: A Memoir* (Garden City, NY: Doubleday, 1929), p. 43.

60. Guy and Small, p. 144. For a detailed account of the Bodley Head's manipulation of the mania for limited editions see Nelson, *Early Nineties*, pp. 77–109.

61. Stetz, 'Sex, Lies', p. 77.

62. 'The Yellow Boot', *Granta* (21 April 1894), p. 271.
63. *Accepted Addresses from Divers Quarters Directed at the Compiler* (London: Bodley Head, 1897), n.p.
64. Stetz 'Sex, Lies', p. 73.
65. See Harris, 'John Lane's Keynotes Series' for a discussion of the series' stylistic innovation (pp. 1409–11).
66. John Sutherland, *The Stanford Companion to Victorian Fiction* (Stanford: Stanford University Press, 1989), p. 258.
67. Quoted in Whyte, p. 63.
68. Ibid.
69. Whyte, p. 43n1.
70. Ibid., p. 203.
71. Stetz, 'Sex, Lies', p. 73.
72. Ibid., p. 84.

3   The Birth of the Decadent in Fiction, 1884–89

1. Keating, p. 79.
2. Stetz, 'Life's "Half-Profits"': Writers and Their Readers in Fiction of the 1890s', *Nineteenth-Century Lives: Essays Presented to Jerome Hamilton Buckley*, eds Laurence S. Lockridge, John Maynard, and Donald D. Stone (Cambridge: Cambridge University Press, 1989), pp. 171–5.
3. Harry Quilter, 'The New Renaissance; or, the Gospel of Intensity', *Macmillans* (September 1880), p. 400.
4. Among the more prominent discussions of Zola and Naturalism in this period were: Andrew Lang's 'Realism and Romance', *Contemporary Review* 52 (1887), pp. 683–93. and 'Emile Zola', *Fortnightly Review* 31 (1882), pp. 439–52; Rider Haggard, 'About Fiction', *Contemporary Review* 51 (1887), pp. 172–180; George Saintsbury, 'The Present State of the Novel II', *A Victorian Art of Fiction*. Compiled by John Charles Olmstead (New York: Garland, 1979), pp. 421–32; Emily Crawford, 'Emile Zola', *Contemporary Review* 55 (1889), pp. 94–113; W. S. Lilly, 'The New Naturalism', *Fortnightly Review* 44 (1885), pp. 240–56; William F. Barry, 'Realism and Decadence in French Fiction', *Heralds of Revolt: Studies in Modern Literature and Dogma* (London: Hodder and Stoughton, 1904), pp. 196–236; Vernon Lee, 'The Moral Teachings of Zola', *Contemporary Review* 63 (1893), 196–212; and the National Vigilance Association, *Pernicious Literature*.
5. Lang, 'Emile Zola', p. 445.
6. Wilde, p. 974.
7. Moore, *Confessions*, p. 173.
8. Ibid., p. 110.
9. Quoted in Phyllis V. Mannocchi, ' "Vernon Lee": A Reintroduction and Primary Bibliography', *English Literature in Transition* 26 (1983), p. 231.
10. Quoted in Peter Gunn, *Vernon Lee/Violet Paget, 1856–1935* (London: Oxford University Press, 1964), p. 98.
11. Review of *Miss Brown*, *Time* (February 1885), p. 212.
12. Vernon Lee, 'A Dialogue on Novels', *Contemporary Review* 48 (1885), p. 397.
13. Ibid., p. 396.
14. Ibid.
15. Vernon Lee, *Miss Brown* (New York: Garland, 1978), vol. 1, p. 274.

16. Lee, *Miss Brown,*, vol. 1, p. 7.
17. Ibid., vol. 1, pp. 7, 8.
18. Ibid., vol. 1, pp. 7–8.
19. Ibid., vol. 1, pp. 293–4.
20. Ibid., vol. 2, p. 93.
21. Ibid., vol. 3, p. 3.
22. Ibid., vol. 3, pp. 4–5.
23. Margaret Diane Stetz, 'Debating Aestheticism From a Feminist Perspective', *Women and British Aestheticism*, eds Talia Schaffer and Kathy Alexis Psomiades, p. 31.
24. Lee, *Miss Brown*, vol. 1, pp. 24, 25.
25. Ibid., vol. 1, p. 26.
26. Ibid., vol. 1, pp. 50–1.
27. Ibid., vol. 1, pp. 122–3.
28. Ibid., vol. 1, p. 218.
29. Stetz, 'Debating Aestheticism', p. 31.
30. Lee, *Miss Brown*, vol. 2, p. 205.
31. Ibid.
32. Ibid., vol. 3, p. 59.
33. Quilter, 'New Renaissance', pp. 392, 393.
34. Cosmo Monkhouse, review of *Miss Brown*, *Academy* (3 January 1885), p. 6.
35. Quoted in Gunn, p. 103.
36. Ibid., p. 104.
37. Ibid., p. 102.
38. Vineta Colby, *Vernon Lee: A Literary Biography* (Charlottesville: University of Virginia Press, 2003), pp. 343–4n4.
39. Quoted in Gunn, p. 104.
40. Henry James, *Henry James: Letters*, vol. 3, ed. James Edel (Cambridge, MA: Belknap Press, 1980), p. 86.
41. Ibid.
42. Quoted in Gunn, p. 103.
43. Gunn, p. 103.
44. Lee, 'Dialogue', p. 395.
45. Quoted in Gunn, p. 102.
46. Review of *Miss Brown*, *Spectator* (13 December 1884), p. 1670.
47. Some recent scholarship has begun to draw attention to Moore's place in the history of Decadence. See the sections on Moore in Weir, Cevasco, and George Schoolfield, *A Baedeker of Decadence: Charting a Literary Fashion, 1884–1927* (New Haven, CT: Yale University Press, 2003).
48. Susan Dick, Introduction, *Confessions of a Young Man*, by George Moore (Montreal: McGill-Queens University Press, 1972), p. 4.
49. Geraint Goodwin, *Conversations with George Moore* (London: Jonathan Cape, 1937), p. 87.
50. Ian Fletcher, *Decadence and the 1890s* (London: Arnold, 1979), p. 12.
51. Dick, p. 2.
52. Gleeson White, review of *Confessions of a Young Man*, *The Artist and Journal of Home Culture* (1 November 1888), p. 349.
53. Arthur Symons, *Memoirs of Arthur Symons: Life and Art in the1890s*, ed. Karl Beckson (University Park: Pennsylvania State University Press, 1977), p. 56.
54. Le Gallienne, *Romantic '90s*, p. 10; Hichens, *Yesterday*, p. 75.
55. Arthur Machen, *Arthur Machen: Selected Letters, the Private Writings of the Master of the Macabre*, eds Roger Dobson, Godfrey Brangham, and R. A. Gilbert (Wellingborough, UK: Aquarian Press, 1988), p. 228.

56. Moore, *Confessions*, p. 191.
57. Frazier, p. 154.
58. Ibid.
59. Quoted in Frazier, p. 165.
60. George Moore, 'Preface' (1917) and 'Preface' (1889), *Confessions of a Young Man* (Montreal: McGill-Queens University Press, 1972), pp. 42, 35.
61. Moore, 'Preface' (1889), 35.
62. Because I am using the first edition of the novel, I refer to the protagonist as Dayne rather than Moore. Otherwise, I see Dayne as Moore, as did 1888 readers of the novel who were 'in the know'. Within months of the book's publication Moore acknowledged that his use of a fictitious name in the first edition was 'a failure of courage which, I must admit, partly spoils the truth of the book' (Quoted in Frazier, p. 165). He changed it to Moore for the second English edition in 1889.
63. Weir, p. 113.
64. Madeleine L. Cazamian, *Le Roman et les idées en Angleterre: L'Anti-intellectualisme et l'esthétisme 1880–1900* (Paris: Faculté des lettres de l'Université de Strasbourg, 1935), p. 377.
65. Moore, *Confessions*, p. 49.
66. Quoted in Moore, *Confessions*, p. 252n1.
67. Pater, *Renaissance*, p. 189.
68. This view dates back to Désiré Nisard's 1834 study of Latin Decadence and has characterized views of Decadence since that time.
69. Moore, *Confessions*, p. 87.
70. Ibid., pp. 138–41.
71. Ibid., p. 108.
72. Ibid., pp. 179–90.
73. Ibid., p. 192.
74. Ibid., p. 150.
75. Ibid., p. 251n2.
76. Jackson, 63; Richard Allen Cave, *A Study of the Novels of George Moore* (Gerrards Cross, UK: Smythe, 1978), p. 107.
77. Quoted in Dick, p. 11.
78. Cave, pp. 106–7. Cave's comments are justified in that they are based on Moore's last revision of the text. Moore became critical of his protagonist as he got older which led him continually to revise and reframe via prefaces the original novel. Elizabeth Grubgeld provides a thorough consideration of Moore's writing and re-writing of himself through his numerous autobiographical works (*George Moore and the Autogenous Self: The Autobiography of Fiction* [Syracuse: Syracuse University Press, 1994]).
79. Moore, *Confessions*, p. 125.
80. Robert Langenfeld, 'A Reconsideration: *Confessions of a Young Man* as Farce'. *Twilight of Dawn: Studies in English Literature in Transition*, ed. O. M. Brack (Tucson: University of Arizona Press, 1987), p. 92.
81. Quoted in Moore, 'Preface' (1904), *Confessions of a Young Man* (Montreal: McGill-Queens University Press, 1972), p. 38.
82. Quoted in Frazier, p. 159.
83. Frazier, p. 165.
84. Review of *Confessions, Hawk* (10 April 1888), p. 172.
85. Ibid.
86. Laurel Brake, *Nineteenth-Century Media and the Construction of Identities* (Basingstoke, UK: Palgrave, 2), p. 272.
87. G. White, p. 349.

88. Review of *Confessions of a Young Man, Athenaeum* (31 March 1888), p. 402.
89. William Sharp, review of *Confessions of a Young Man, Academy* (17 March 1888), p. 184.
90. Review of *Confessions of a Young Man, Vanity Fair* (2 June 1888), p. 322.
91. Ironically, Swan Sonnenschein, the publisher of Moore's *Confessions*, published the *Universal Review* though the firm had no pecuniary interest in the magazine.
92. Robert Buchanan, 'The Modern Young Man as Critic', *Universal Review* 3 (1889), p. 354.
93. Ibid., p. 371. There was, of course, a precedent for using the term 'Cockney' as a term of abuse in literary critical circles. This term had been applied in the early nineteenth century by proponents of the Lake School to describe the London poets – John Keats, Percy Shelley, Leigh Hunt, and William Hazlitt – whose verse they regarded as vulgar, over-emotional, loud, and boisterous. There may be echoes of this kind of critique in Buchanan's use of the term, but overall, given his focus on the music hall, I think he is updating it for a contemporary context.
94. Peter Bailey, 'Custom', pp. 199–200.
95. Buchanan, 'Modern Young Man', p. 371.
96. Ibid.
97. Ibid., p. 362.
98. Ibid., pp. 368–9.
99. Ibid., p. 361.
100. Sinfield, pp. 52–108.
101. Frazier, pp. 165, 169.
102. Robert Buchanan, 'Is Chivalry Still Possible?', *Daily Telegraph* (22 March 1889), p. 5.
103. Buchanan, 'Modern Young Man', p. 372.
104. Quoted in Frazier, p. 184.
105. Frazier, p. 192.
106. The *Pilgrim* is modelled on the *Hawk*, one of the magazines that praised *Confessions*. When Moore wrote *Mike Fletcher*, Moore's brother, Augustus, upon whom Fletcher is partially based, owned the *Hawk*.
107. George Moore, *Mike Fletcher* (London: Ward and Downey, 1889), pp. 39, 39–40.
108. Ibid., pp. 46–52, 118.
109. Quoted in Joseph Hone, *The Life of George Moore* (Westport, CT: Greenwood, 1973), p. 150.
110. Ibid.
111. Review of *Mike Fletcher, Artist and Journal of Home Culture* (1 February 1890), pp. 63, 62.
112. Quoted in Hone, p. 150.
113. Ibid., p. 176.
114. Ibid.
115. Hone, p. 161.
116. Ibid., p. 175.

4   Writing Against Decadence, 1890–97

1. Many studies have argued for Wilde's indebtedness to popular literature in *Dorian Gray*. Among the most interesting are Schaffer's investigation of the influence of Ouida on Wilde and other Aesthetes (pp. 151–8); Gagnier's discussion of the influence of Wilde's experience as editor of *Woman's World* on the novel (*Idylls*, pp. 65–7); and Isobel Murray's comparison of *Dorian Gray* to *The Suicide of*

Sylvester Gray by Wilde's friend, Edward Heron-Allen ('Introduction', *The Picture of Dorian Gray*, ed. Isobel Murray [London: Oxford University Press, 1974], pp. xxi–xxiv).
2. Frazier, p. 194.
3. Pykett also insists on the importance of the anti-Naturalism discourses of the 1880s in shaping the attack on the literary trends of the 1890s: 'the debate about naturalism continued to shape the critical discourse on the novel throughout the nineties and was particularly prominent in the controversies about the New Fiction and the fiction of sex, which were seen by many commentators as the off-spring of naturalism' ('Representing the Real', p. 168). Though she focuses on debates about Naturalism, the same phenomenon can be observed in the case of the discourse against Aestheticism. Compare, for example, Quilter's 1880 attack on Aestheticism, 'The New Renaissance', with his 1895 attack on Decadence, 'The Gospel of Intensity'. Quilter labels both movements 'the gospel of intensity' and describes Decadence as the 'evil result' of Aestheticism (Quilter, 'Gospel of Intensity', p. 763).
4. Mason, p. 27. Beckson also documents the reception of *Dorian Gray* (*Oscar Wilde: The Critical Heritage* [London: Routledge, 1970]). Mason's study, however, provides a better overall view of the controversy over 'art and morality' that the story initiated in the press.
5. Quoted in Mason, p. 116.
6. Quoted in Beckson, *Oscar Wilde*, p. 67.
7. McDonald, p. 37.
8. Mason, p. 36.
9. Hawthorne's and Wharton's essays are reprinted in Mason, pp. 163–85. Details of the special publications of the story are also in Mason, pp. 264–5, 268.
10. National Vigilance Association, pp. 353, 354, 355.
11. Mason, pp. 28, 28, 65, 75.
12. National Vigilance Association, p. 355; Mason, p. 69.
13. National Vigilance Association, p. 357.
14. Mason, p. 76.
15. Ibid., p. 28.
16. Ibid., pp. 28–9.
17. Ibid., pp. 45, 123.
18. Ibid., p. 31.
19. Ibid.
20. Ibid., p. 161.
21. Ibid.
22. Ibid., p. 108.
23. Ibid., p. 28, 65.
24. Ibid., p. 161.
25. Ibid., pp. 28, 65; review of *Picture of Dorian Gray, Pall Mall Budget* (3 July 1890), p. 862.
26. Mason, p. 76.
27. Gagnier, *Idylls*, pp. 61–2.
28. Joseph Bristow, 'Wilde, *Dorian Gray*, and Gross Indecency', *Sexual Sameness: Textual Differences in Lesbian and Gay Writing*, ed. Joseph Bristow (London: Routledge, 1992), pp. 44–5.
29. Montgomery Hyde, *The Trials of Oscar Wilde* (London: Dover, n.d.), p. 114.
30. Sinfield, pp. 104, 105.
31. Ibid., pp. 1–2.

32. Sinfield, p. 95.
33. See, for example, Joseph Bristow's consideration of how Decadence was used by Arthur Symons to promote a heterosexual agenda ('Sterile Ecstasies: The Perversity of the Decadent Movement', *Essays and Studies* 48 [1995], pp. 65–88).
34. Mason, p. 34.
35. Ibid.
36. Sutherland, p. 540.
37. Morley Roberts, *In Low Relief: A Bohemian Transcript* (New York: Appleton, 1890), p. 60.
38. New Woman writing was implicated in the attacks on Decadence in 1895. Spender's 'New Fiction' controversy in the *Westminster Gazette* identified what he called 'the revolting woman' novel as one of three classes of Decadent fiction, the others being the 'defiant man novel' and the 'morbid and lurid' class of novel. Stutfield and Noble also aligned the New Woman and the Decadent in 'Tommyrotics' and 'Fiction of Sexuality'. Some articles focused specifically on women's fiction as degenerate and/or Decadent such as Bradfield's, 'Dominant Note of Some Recent Fiction'; Hogarth's, 'Literary Degenerates'; and William F. Barry, 'Strike of a Sex', *Quarterly Review* 179 (1894), pp. 289–318.
39. Pykett, *Engendering Fictions*, p. 55.
40. Brian Masters, *Now Barabbas Was a Rotter: The Extraordinary Life of Marie Corelli* (London: Hamish Hamilton, 1978), p. 101.
41. Annette Federico, *Idol of Suburbia: Marie Corelli and Late-Victorian Literary Culture* (Charlottesville: University Press of Virginia, 2000), p. 72.
42. I have written elsewhere about the relationship of *Wormwood* to debates about Naturalism, Decadence, degeneration, absinthism, and Francophobia. See Kirsten MacLeod, Introduction, *Wormwood*, ed. Kirsten MacLeod (Peterborough, ON: Broadview, 2004), pp. 9–55 and Kirsten MacLeod, 'Marie Corelli and *fin-de-siècle* Francophobia: "The Absinthe Trail of French Art" ', *English Literature in Transition* 43 (2000), pp. 66–82.
43. Marie Corelli, letter to George Bentley, 8 September 1890, Corelli Collection, General Collection (Beinecke Rare Book and Manuscript Library, Yale University, New Haven, CT).
44. Marie Corelli, *Wormwood: A Drama of Paris* (Peterborough, ON: Broadview, 2004), p. 74.
45. Ibid., pp. 61–2.
46. Marie Corelli, *Sorrows*, p. 139.
47. Ibid., p. 6.
48. Corelli, *Free Opinions*, p. 251.
49. Corelli, *Sorrows*, p. 39.
50. Marie Corelli, letter to John Lane, March 1900, John Lane Company Records (Harry Ransom Center, University of Texas, Austin, TX).
51. Corelli, *Wormwood*, p. 61.
52. Ibid., p. 62.
53. Ibid., p. 66.
54. Ibid., p. 67. The dedication translates as, 'to the absintheurs of Paris, these braggarts of depravity who are the shame and despair of their country'.
55. Marie Corelli, letter to George Bentley, 28 August 1890, Corelli Collection, General Collection (Beinecke Rare Book and Manuscript Library, Yale University, New Haven, CT). Corelli's letters to Bentley throughout her writing of *Wormwood*

are filled with accounts of news stories she has read about absinthe addiction and with expressions of her earnest desire to draw attention to the problem.

56. Marie Corelli, letter to George Bentley [12 June 1890], Corelli Collection, General Collection (Beinecke Rare Book and Manuscript Library, Yale University, New Haven, CT).
57. Federico, pp. 72, 73.
58. Corelli, *Wormwood*, p. 74.
59. Mason, p. 33.
60. Federico, p. 74.
61. Corelli, *Wormwood*, pp. 173–4.
62. Ibid., p. 109n2.
63. Federico, p. 75.
64. Marie Corelli, letter to George Bentley, 2 January 1889, Corelli Collection, General Collection (Beinecke Rare Book and Manuscript Library, Yale University, New Haven, CT).
65. Review of *Wormwood*, *Graphic* (29 November 1890), p. 624.
66. Review of *Wormwood*, *Literary World* (17 January 1891), p. 21.
67. Ibid., p. 22.
68. Quoted in advertisement for *Wormwood*, *Academy* (13 December 1890), p. 554.
69. Sutherland, p. 6.
70. Review of *Wormwood*, *Athenaeum* (15 November 1890), p. 661.
71. J. Barrow Allen, review of *Wormwood*, *Academy* (29 November 1890), p. 500.
72. Reviews of *Wormwood*, *Pall Mall Gazette* (27 November 1890), p. 3; *Times* (23 January 1891), p. 13.
73. Corelli herself did not interpret these as positive reviews. Rather, she thought they damned with faint praise. Of the *Athenaeum* review she commented to Bentley, 'it struck me as a strange one – and a more or less useless one, purposely arranged so *as to be* useless' (Marie Corelli, letter to George Bentley, 15 November 1890, Corelli Collection, General Collection [Beinecke Rare Book and Manuscript Library, Yale University, New Haven, CT]).
74. Diderik Roll-Hansen, *The Academy 1869–1879: Victorian Intellectuals in Revolt* (Copenhagen: Rosenkilde and Bagger, 1957), pp. 210–11.
75. Saintsbury, p. 431.
76. Edmund Gosse, 'The Tyranny of the Novel', *A Victorian Art of Fiction*, compiled by John Charles Olmsted (New York: Garland, 1979), p. 528.
77. Ellis, p. 59.
78. Hubert Crackanthorpe, 'Reticence in Literature: Some Roundabout Remarks', *Yellow Book* 2 (1894), p. 266.
79. Dowling, 'Decadent', p. 436.
80. Quoted in Stutfield, p. 840.
81. Bradfield, p. 543.
82. Sutherland, p. 258.
83. See Spender, p. 83.
84. Corelli, *Sorrows*, p. 29.
85. Sarah Grand, *Selected Letters*, Vol. 2 of *Sex, Social Purity and Sarah Grand*, eds Ann Heilmann and Stephanie Forward (London: Routledge, 2000), p. 53.
86. Teresa Mangum, *Married, Middlebrow and Militant: Sarah Grand and the New Woman Novel* (Ann Arbor: University of Michigan Press, 1998), p. 145.
87. Ibid., p. 150.
88. Ibid., pp. 150–3.

89. Sarah Grand, *The Beth Book: Being a Study of the Life of Elizabeth Caldwell Maclure, a Woman of Genius* (London: Virago, 1980), p. 367.
90. Ibid., p. 374.
91. Ibid., p. 455.
92. Ibid., p. 475.
93. Ibid., p. 477.
94. Ibid., p. 460.
95. Ibid., p. 376.
96. Ibid., p. 371.
97. Ibid.
98. Ibid., p. 423.
99. Ibid., p. 476.
100. Ibid., p. 457.
101. Ibid.
102. Ibid., p. 476.
103. Ibid., p. 460.
104. Ibid., pp. 460–1.
105. Ibid., p. 452.
106. Ibid., p. 376.
107. Ibid., p. 518.
108. Mangum, p. 185.
109. Lyn Pykett, *'Improper' Feminine: The Women's Sensation Novel and New Woman Writing* (London: Routledge, 1992), p. 186.
110. Grand, *Journalistic Writings and Contemporary Reception*. Vol. 1 of *Sex, Social Purity and Sarah Grand*, eds Ann Heilmann and Stephanie Forward (London: Routledge, 2000), p. 477.
111. Ibid., p. 473.
112. Ibid., pp. 475. 469.
113. Grand, *Selected Letters*, p. 62.
114. Review of *Beth Book*, *Academy* (13 November 1897), p. 393.
115. Grand, *Journalistic Writings*, p. 470.
116. Ibid.
117. Ibid., pp. 470–1.
118. Ibid., p. 471.
119. Ibid.
120. Ibid.
121. Ibid.

5   Decadent Fiction Before the Keynotes Series

1. The *Century Guild Hobby Horse* was largely an organ for the Arts and Crafts movement that appealed to a readership interested in Pre-Raphaelitism, medievalism, Aestheticism, the Renaissance, Pater, Symbolism, Decadence, and uranianism. The *Artist and Journal of Home Culture* had similar interests, though with a greater interest in Decadence specifically. For more on these magazines, see Ian Fletcher 'Decadence and the Little Magazines' (*Decadence and the 1890s*, ed. Ian Fletcher [London: Arnold, 1979], pp. 173–202). The *Pioneer*'s interests were more social than aesthetic. It was a progressive periodical published by the Pioneer Club to promote the discussion of social, literary, and philosophical issues (Lesley Hall, e-mail to author, October 1998).

2. Ellis, p. 52.
3. Symons, 'Decadent Movement', p. 858.
4. Ellis, p. 51.
5. Symons, 'Decadent Movement', p. 859.
6. Ellis, p. 60.
7. Ibid., p. 59.
8. Ibid., p. 60.
9. Ibid., pp. 59–60.
10. Henley, a popular writer, to Decadent friend and collaborator Trenchard in Robert Hichens, 'The Collaborators', *The Folly of Eustace*, by Robert Hichens (London: Heinemann, 1896), p. 120.
11. Richard Bleiler, 'Robert S. Hichens', *Late-Victorian and Edwardian British Novelists, First Series, Dictionary of Literary Biography* 153 (Detroit: Gale, 1995), p. 108.
12. N.O. B., review of *Flames*, *Echo* (26 March 1897), p. 1.
13. Hichens, 'Collaborators', p. 119.
14. Ibid., pp. 117, 118, 119.
15. Ibid., p. 118.
16. Ibid., p. 120.
17. Ibid., p. 119.
18. Ibid., p. 120.
19. Ibid., pp. 120–1.
20. Ibid., p. 121.
21. Arthur Moore (no relation to George Moore), was from a prominent family of painters, which included John C. Moore, Henry Moore, RA, and Albert Moore. Moore earned his living primarily as a solicitor, though he and Dowson collaborated on four novels: *Felix Martyr* (unpublished), *The Passion of Dr Ludovicus* (unpublished), *A Comedy of Masks* (1893), and *Adrian Rome* (1899). The manuscripts of *Felix Martyr* and *The Passion of Dr Ludovicus* have not been traced and the only information on them is contained in Dowson's letters.
22. Dowson, *Letters*, p. 152.
23. Ibid., pp. 151, 152.
24. Ibid., p. 151. Walter Besant and James Rice collaborated on a number of highly successful novels from the 1870s up to Rice's death in 1882 (Sutherland, pp. 59–61, 533). W. E. Norris was a popular writer of light romances, mostly dealing with fashionable society (Sutherland, p. 468).
25. Schaffer, p. 151.
26. Review of *Comedy of Masks*, *Critic* (17 February 1894), p. 109.
27. Review of *Comedy of Masks*, *Graphic* (14 October 1893), p. 54.
28. Review of *Comedy of Masks*, *Daily Chronicle* (4 October 1893), p. 3.
29. Review of *Comedy of Masks*, *Academy* (18 November 1893), p. 435.
30. Review of *Comedy of Masks*, *National Observer* (14 October 1893), p. 469.
31. Dowson, *Letters*, p. 151.
32. Review of *Comedy of Masks*, *Pall Mall Gazette* (27 November 1893), p. 4.
33. Review of *Comedy of Masks*, *Daily Chronicle*, p. 3.
34. Ibid.
35. Lang, 'Realism', p. 688.
36. Quoted in Dowson, *Letters*, p. 10. Flower and Maas contextualize these comments, explaining that they are a response to the last lines of Schreiner's preface, which reads: 'Sadly he must squeeze the colour from his brush, and dip it into the *grey pigments* [Dowson's emphasis] around him. He must paint what lies before him.'

In his note, Dowson describes this method as the 'greater method' and proceeds with the comments on the novel form that I have quoted.

37. Dowson, *Letters*, p. 33.
38. Ibid.
39. Ibid., p. 151.
40. Ibid., p. 154.
41. Ibid., p. 167.
42. Ibid., p. 151.
43. Review of *Comedy of Masks, Daily Chronicle*, p. 3.
44. 'Shade', *Synonym Finder*, ed. J. I. Rodale (Emmaus, PA: Rodale Books, 1961).
45. Dowson, *Letters*, p. 122.
46. Ernest Dowson and Arthur Moore, *A Comedy of Masks*, 2nd edn (London: Heinemann, 1894), p. 28.
47. Dowson, *Letters*, p. 153.
48. Dowson and Moore were working on their novel at the same time as Corelli, in the summer of 1890, though the publication of *Wormwood* would precede *A Comedy of Masks* by three years. Bentley, who published Corelli's novel in 1890 would reject Dowson and Moore's in 1892.
49. Dowson and Moore, pp. 28, 29.
50. Ibid., p. 33.
51. Dowson, *Letters*, p. 153.
52. Dowson and Moore, p. 33.
53. Ibid.
54. Dowson, *Letters*, p. 81.
55. Ibid., 154.
56. Dowson and Moore, p. 33.
57. Ibid.
58. Ibid.
59. Robert Sherard, *The Real Oscar Wilde* (London: Laurie, 1916), p. 81.
60. Weir, p. 13.
61. Ibid., p. 15.
62. John Davidson, *The North Wall* (New York: Garland, 1978), p. 9.
63. Ibid., p. 10.
64. Ibid., pp. 10–11.
65. Ibid., p. 10. Davidson here anticipates Wilde's reflections in the 'Decay of Lying' concerning the relationship between art and life.
66. Ibid., p. 12.
67. Ibid., p. 126.
68. Ibid., p. 10.
69. Ibid., p. 145.
70. This chapter was not included in the 1891 version of the novel, which was re-titled *A Practical Novelist*. This omission obviously has a significant impact on the effect of the book, making it more conventional in style.
71. Davidson, *North Wall*, p. 147.
72. Ibid.
73. Ibid., pp. 148, 151, 152.
74. Ibid., pp. 147–50.
75. Ibid., p. 150.
76. Ibid., p. 136.
77. Ibid.

78. Ibid., p. 145.
79. Ibid., p. 151.
80. Quoted in Townsend, p. 379.
81. John Davidson, *Selected Poems and Prose of John Davidson*, ed. John Sloan (Oxford: Clarendon Press, 1995), p. 192.
82. Quoted in Townsend, p. 141.
83. Pierre Bourdieu, *Rules*, pp. 259, 260.
84. Davidson, *Selected Poems*, p. 182.
85. See Brake, 'Endgames', and Stetz, 'Sex, Lies'.
86. R. D. Brown, 'The Bodley Head Press: Some Bibliographical Extrapolations', *Bibliographical Society of America Papers* 61 (1967), p. 39.

6 'Keynotes' of Decadence, 1894–95

1. R. D. Brown, p. 39. Though Mathews was still a partner when *The Yellow Book* and the Keynotes series began, both of these projects were, as Nelson argues, Lane's ideas (*Early Nineties*, p. 265). As such, I focus on Lane in my discussion of the Bodley Head's promotion of Decadence.
2. The popularity of Bodley Head publications must be put into context. Very few sold 10,000 copies, a sales figure that Keating cites as standard for popular authors, and they certainly never sold the 50,000 copies that constituted a 'best-seller' in this period (Keating, p. 424).
3. Stutfield, p. 834.
4. Spender, p. 105; 'Morbid and Unclean Literature', p. 13.
5. George Moore, for example, attacked women readers, the writers who wrote for them, and the circulating libraries' that catered to them in *Literature at Nurse; or, Circulating Morals*. Shiel similarly complained of women's reading tastes and their preferences for 'bad' and 'unnovel' novels, while Machen held them responsible for sensational journalism (Shiel, 'On Reading', *This Knot of Life*, by M. P. Shiel [London: Everett, 1909], p. 14; Machen, *Things*, p. 126).
6. 'Morbid and Unclean Literature', p. 13.
7. Stutfield, p. 841.
8. Pykett, 'Representing the Real', p. 175.
9. Wilde, p. 1205.
10. Noble, 'Fiction', p. 491.
11. 'Damnation of Decadence', p. 391.
12. Ibid., p. 390.
13. Machen, 'Introduction', *Great God Pan* (London: Simpkin, Marshall, Hamilton, Kent, 1916), p. xix. Some of *The Great God Pan* appeared in the short-lived magazine the *Whirlwind* in 1890.
14. Machen, *The Great God Pan and the Inmost Light* (London: Lane, 1894), p. 3.
15. Ibid., p. 16.
16. Machen, *Things*, p. 96.
17. Ibid., p. 55.
18. This contradictory logic worked well for Machen in 1923 when he published his memoirs. At this time, his works were being re-issued and he was experiencing a minor vogue, particularly among high-profile literary types in America. This élite fan base implied that his economic failure must be read as proof of artistic martyrdom rather than the undesirable alternative: that is, that Machen was, quite simply, a bad writer.

19. Valentine, p. 19.
20. William Francis Gekle, *Arthur Machen: Weaver of Fantasy* (Millbrook, NY: Round Table Press, 1949), p. 43.
21. John Gawsworth, unpublished ts. of biography of Arthur Machen, Armstrong Collection (Harry Ransom Center, University of Texas, Austin, TX), p. 162.
22. Review of *Great God Pan, Daily Free Press* (Aberdeen) (17 December 1894), p. 2.
23. Ibid.
24. Gawsworth, p. 150
25. Machen, *Great God Pan*, pp. 112–13.
26. Ibid., p. 114.
27. Ibid., p. 155.
28. Ibid., p. 136.
29. Ibid., p. 155.
30. Ibid., pp. 18, 19.
31. Ibid., p. 162.
32. Ibid., p. 37.
33. Ibid., p. 116.
34. Ibid., p. 137.
35. Ibid., pp. 137–8.
36. Ibid., p. 62.
37. Felski, p. 99.
38. Ibid.
39. Review of *The Great God Pan, The Guardian*, quoted in Machen, *Precious Balms* (Horam, UK: Friends of Arthur Machen and Tartarus Press, 1999), p. 8. *Precious Balms* is a published collection, compiled by Machen, of reviews of his works.
40. Review of *Great God Pan, Belfast News Letter*, quoted in Machen, *Precious Balms*, p. 2.
41. Review of *Great God Pan, Cork Examiner*, quoted in Machen, *Precious Balms*, p. 8.
42. Reviews of *Great God Pan, Yorkshire Post* (16 January 1895), p. 3; *Whitehall Review* (15 December 1894), p. 18.
43. Review of *Great God Pan, Academy* (25 February 1895), p. 166.
44. Review of *Great God Pan, Weekly Sun* (30 December 1894), p. 2.
45. Review of *Great God Pan, Guardian*, quoted in Machen, *Precious Balms*, p. 7.
46. Review of *Great God Pan, Literary World* (12 January 1895), p. 7.
47. Reviews of *Great God Pan, Westminster Gazette* (4 January 1895), p. 3; *Yorkshire Post*, p. 2.
48. Reviews of *Great God Pan, Athenaeum* (23 March 1895), p. 375; *Lady's Pictorial*, quoted in Machen, *Precious Balms*, p. 7.
49. Review of *Great God Pan, Whitehall Review*, p. 18.
50. Reviews of *Great God Pan, Literary News* (February 1895), p. 44; *Weekly Sun*, p. 2; *Lady's Pictorial*, quoted in Machen, *Precious Balms*, p. 7.
51. Reviews of *Great God Pan, Scotsman* (17 December 1894), p. 3; *Yorkshire Post*, p. 3; *Manchester Guardian*, quoted in Machen, *Precious Balms*, p. 4.
52. Reviews of *Great God Pan, Pall Mall Gazette* (15 December 1894), p. 4; *Literary World*, p. 7.
53. Review of *Great God Pan, Lady's Pictorial*, quoted in Machen, *Precious Balms*, p. 7.
54. Review of *Great God Pan, Whitehall Review*, p. 18.
55. Spender, p. 101.
56. For more on Machen's symbolic notion of 'realism' see his essay on Poe, 'The Supreme Realist', in *The Glorious Mystery* (Chicago: Covici-McGee, 1924).

57. Susan J. Navarette, *The Shape of Fear: Horror and the Fin de Siècle Culture of Decadence* (Lexington: University Press of Kentucky, 1998), p. 6.
58. Ibid., p. 188.
59. Review of *Great God Pan*, *Literary News*, p. 44.
60. Dowling, *Language and Decadence*, pp. xi–xii.
61. Ibid., p. 62. See also Kelly Hurley, *The Gothic Body: Sexuality, Materialism, and Degeneration at the Fin de Siècle* (Cambridge: Cambridge University Press, 1996), pp. 12–14.
62. Navarette, p. 211.
63. Dowling, *Language and Decadence*, p. xv.
64. Ibid., p. 104.
65. Hichens, 'Collaborators', p. 120.
66. Dowson, *Letters*, p. 152.
67. Mason, pp. 80–1.
68. Wilde, p. 17.
69. Machen, *Great God Pan*, p. 18.
70. Ibid., p. 28.
71. Ibid., p. 92.
72. Ibid., p. 18.
73. Review of *Great God Pan*, *Literary World*, p. 7.
74. Review of *Great God Pan*, *Manchester Guardian*, quoted in Machen, *Precious Balms*, p. 4.
75. Reviews of *Great God Pan*, *Westminster Gazette*, p. 2; *Echo* (18 January 1895), p. 1.
76. Review of *Great God Pan*, *Lady's Pictorial*, quoted in Machen, *Precious Balms*, p. 7.
77. Review of *Great God Pan*, *Westminster Gazette*, p. 2.
78. Review of *Great God Pan*, *Observer*, quoted in Machen, *Precious Balms*, p. 1.
79. Review of *Great God Pan*, *Woman* (9 January 1895), p. 7.
80. Review of *Great God Pan*, *Observer*, quoted in Machen, *Precious Balms*, p. 1.
81. Spender, p. 101.
82. M. P. Shiel, *Prince Zaleski* (London: Lane, 1895), pp. 3–4.
83. Ibid., pp. 4–5.
84. Review of *Prince Zaleski*, *Vanity Fair Literary Supplement* (13 June 1895), p. i.
85. Reviews of *Prince Zaleski*, *Times* (20 April 1895), p. 8; *Vanity Fair Literary Supplement*, p. ii.
86. Joseph Bell, review of *Adventures of Sherlock Holmes*, quoted in Richard Lancelyn Green, 'Introduction', *The Adventures of Sherlock Holmes* (Oxford: Oxford University Press, 1994), pp. xxx–xxxi.
87. Review of *Prince Zaleski*, *Times*, 8.
88. M.P. Shiel, letter to Gussie Shiel, 30 April 1895, Shiel Collection (Harry Ransom Center, University of Texas, Austin, TX).
89. Shiel, *Prince Zaleski*, pp. 1–2.
90. Quoted in Morse, p. 514.
91. Review of *Prince Zaleski*, *Speaker* (9 March 1895), p. 278.
92. Ibid.
93. Review of *Prince Zaleski*, *Vanity Fair Literary Supplement*, p. i.
94. Review of *Prince Zaleski*, *Athenaeum* (23 March 1895), pp. 375, 375–6.
95. Review of *Prince Zaleski*, *Guardian* (19 June 1895), p. 917.
96. 'Guardian', *Waterloo Directory of English Periodicals and Newspapers: 1800–1900*. 2nd series, ed. John S. North <http://www.victorianperiodicals.com/series2/>.

97. Shiel, *Prince Zaleski*, p. 4.
98. Larson, p. xvii.
99. Review of *Prince Zaleski, Times*, p. 8.
100. Shiel, *Prince Zaleski*, pp. 28–9.
101. Ibid., p. 143.
102. Ibid., p. 145.
103. Ibid., p. 147.
104. Ibid., pp. 32–3.
105. Ibid., pp. 30, 31.
106. Review of *Prince Zaleski, Guardian*, p. 917.
107. Shiel, *Prince Zaleski*, p. 18; quoted in *Guardian*, p. 917.
108. Reviews of *Prince Zaleski, National Observer* (16 March 1895), p. 482; *Academy* (13 April 1895), p. 312.
109. Review of *Prince Zaleski, Guardian*, p. 917.
110. Ibid.

7   Decadence in the Shadow of the Wilde Trials and Beyond

1. Symons, 'Decadent Movement', p. 867.
2. Wesley Sweetser, *Arthur Machen* (New York: Twayne, 1964), pp. 156–8.
3. Moore, *Confessions*, p. 35.
4. Arthur Machen, 'Introduction', *Hill of Dreams* (New York: Knopf, 1923), p. viii.
5. Moore, *Confessions*, p. 192.
6. Dowling, *Language and Decadence*, p. 154.
7. Ibid., p. 160.
8. Arthur Machen, *The Hill of Dreams* (New York: Knopf, 1923), p. 308.
9. Dowling, *Language and Decadence*, p. 160.
10. Machen, *Hill of Dreams*, p. 174.
11. Ibid., pp. 245–6.
12. Ibid., pp. 301.
13. Wilde, p. 17.
14. Stutfield, p. 843.
15. Hyde, p. 110.
16. Ibid.
17. Ibid., p. 116.
18. 'Art', *Westminster Gazette* (6 April 1895), p. 1.
19. 'Concerning a Misused Term; viz., "Art" as Recently Applied to a Certain Form of Literature', *Punch* (13 April 1895), p. 177.
20. 'A Philistine Paean; Or, the Triumph of the Timid One', *Punch* (11 May 1895), p. 222.
21. Ibid.
22. Untitled, *National Observer* (6 April 1895), p. 547.
23. Quoted in Jonathan Goodman, *The Oscar Wilde File* (London: Allen, 1988), p. 78.
24. 'Art', p. 1.
25. Nelson, *Publisher*, p. 58.
26. Arthur Machen, letter to John Lane, 29 June 1895, John Lane Company Records (Harry Ransom Center, University of Texas, Austin, TX).
27. Ibid.
28. Arthur Machen, letter to John Lane, 11 July 1895, John Lane Company Records (Harry Ransom Center, University of Texas, Austin, TX).

29. Egerton, pp. 41–2.
30. Nelson, *Publisher*, p. 59.
31. James Nelson, 'Leonard Smithers', *British Literary Publishing Houses, 1881–1965, Dictionary of Literary Biography* 112 (Detroit: Gale, 1991), p. 316.
32. In his reader's report for Lane on Symons's *London Lights*, John Davidson wrote, 'Ten years ago it would have been to risk a sojourn in Holloway to publish "To One in Alienation" ... "Leves Amores" ... "White Heliotrope" ' (John Davidson, Reader's report, Walpole Collection [Bodleian Library, Oxford University, Oxford], n.p.). Though Nelson indicates that Symons withdrew his book from Lane over his anger at Beardsley's dismissal from the *Yellow Book*, Lane was no doubt relieved at not having to publish it, particularly given the tenor of Davidson's comments, which were written before Wilde's imprisonment (Nelson, *Publisher*, p. 63).
33. Beardsley, p. 148.
34. Quoted in Nelson, *Publisher*, p. 61.
35. It is significant that the cautious Richards attracted the Decadent writers of fiction to his firm, whereas the more daring Smithers attracted the poets. Fiction writers as producers of a fairly popular genre, are far more affected by fluctuations in demand for their work than are poets who, except in a very few instances, do not sell in anywhere near the kind of numbers that would make them vulnerable to public disapproval. Symons, Yeats, and Dowson were, therefore, in a better position to thumb their noses at the British public and join the rebellious Smithers than were Machen, Shiel, and Egerton who opted for the more conservative Richards.
36. Dowson, *Letters*, p. 362.
37. Ella D'Arcy, *Some Letters to John Lane*, ed. Alan Anderson (Edinburgh: Tragara Press, 1990), pp. 19–20.
38. Arthur Machen, letter to John Lane, 5 June 1895, John Lane Company Records (Harry Ransom Center, University of Texas, Austin, TX).
39. B. A. Crackanthorpe, letter to John Lane, [1895], John Lane Company Records (Harry Ransom Center, University of Texas, Austin, TX).
40. John Batchelor, *The Edwardian Novelists* (London: Duckworth, 1982), p. 119.
41. McDonald analyses Bennett's artistic self-fashioning and his manoeuvrings within all realms of the literary field in *British Literary Culture and Publishing Practice* (pp. 68–117).
42. Batchelor dates the beginning of the Edwardian period from Wilde's fall in 1895 (p. 2). Burdett traces it to Wilde's death in 1900 (See Hunter, *Edwardian Fiction*, [Cambridge, MA: Harvard University Press, 1982], p. 13), while Hunter argues for 1901, the beginning of Edward's reign, though he acknowledges there is a strong claim for dating it from 1897 (pp. vii, 155).
43. Hunter, p. viii.
44. Sandra Kemp, Charlotte Mitchell, and David Trotter, *Edwardian Fiction: An Oxford Companion.* Oxford: Oxford University Press, 1997), pp. x, xvii.
45. Hunter, p. 47.
46. Kemp, Mitchell, and Trotter, p. xvii.
47. William Greenslade, *Degeneration, Culture, and the Novel 1880–1940* (Cambridge: Cambridge University Press, 1994), p. 131. Greenslade discusses the use of these terms in the reception of the Post-Impressionist exhibition of 1910–11 (pp. 129–33).
48. For the reception history of *The Waste Land* see Michael Grant (ed.), *T. S. Eliot: The Critical Heritage* (London: Routledge, 1982), pp. 17–22 and pp. 134–212.

49. Review of *Shapes in the Fire*, *Weekly Sun* (13 December 1896), p. 2.
50. Review of *Shapes in the Fire*, *Academy* (9 January 1897), p. 43.
51. Michael Levenson, *A Genealogy of Modernism: A Study of the English Literary Doctrine 1908–1922* (Cambridge: Cambridge University Press, 1984), p. 123.
52. For an account of Pound's involvement in writing the introduction to Johnson's poems, see Nelson, *Elkin Mathews*, pp. 154–6.
53. Quoted in Julian Symons, *Makers of the New: The Revolution in Literature 1912–1939* (London: Andre Deutsch, 1987), p. 114.
54. For more on twentieth-century Decadence see Martin Green, *Children of the Sun: A Narrative of 'Decadence' in England After 1918* (New York: Wideview Books, 1980) and Ellis Hanson, *Decadence and Catholicism* (Cambridge, MA: Harvard University Press, 1997), 345–64.
55. Theodore Wratislaw, letter to Elkin Mathews, 13 March 1914, Walpole Collection (Bodleian Library, Oxford University, Oxford).
56. Murdoch, pp. 82, 83.
57. Ezra Pound, 'Hugh Selwyn Mauberley', *Selected Poems* (London: Faber, 1948), p. 177.
58. Eric Homberger (ed.) documents Pound's critical reception and the hostility he encountered in the British literary scene in *Ezra Pound: The Critical Heritage* (London: Routledge, 1972).
59. Machen, *Few Letters*, p. 27.
60. M. P. Shiel, letter to Edgar Meyerstein, 29 August 1935, Shiel Collection (Harry Ransom Center, University of Texas, Austin, TX).
61. Quoted in Morse, p. 435.
62. For a different view of the relationship between old and new avant-gardes and Modernists and anti-Modernists in this period see Marysa Demoor, ' "Not with a bang but a whimper" ' (*Cambridge Quarterly* 30, 3 [2001], pp. 233–56). In this article, Demoor examines the correspondence of turn-of-the-century writer Lucy Clifford from 1919 to 1929 to illustrate 'a painful period of transition, a handing over of the symbolic capital by one generation to another' (p. 234).

8   The Afterlife of the Decadents or, Life After Decadence

1. Jackson, p. 131.
2. Flower and Maas, p. 3.
3. Yeats, *Autobiography*, p. 200.
4. Plarr, p. 99
5. Vincent O'Sullivan, *Aspects of Wilde* (New York: Holt, [1936]), p. 118.
6. Nelson, *Publisher*, p. 122.
7. Ibid., p. 72.
8. Dowson, *Letters*, p. 372.
9. Symons, 'A Literary Causerie', pp. 91, 92.
10. Ibid., p. 93.
11. Dowson, *Letters*, p. 371.
12. Thornton, p. 83. See also Chris Snodgrass, 'Ernest Dowson and Schopenhauer: Life Imitating Art in the Victorian Decadence', *Victorians Institute Journal* 21 (1993), pp. 1–46. Here Snodgrass argues that Dowson 'was willing to endorse certain dubious (even flatly inaccurate) depictions of himself, as long as they reinforced Schopenhauren self-ravaging futility but did not directly feature the concomitant emphasis on "contaminating" disease (p. 34).
13. Dowson, *Letters*, p. 372.

14. Murdoch, p. 76.
15. Quoted in Christopher Ricks (ed.), *Inventions of the March Hare: Poems 1909–1917 by T. S. Eliot* (London: Faber and Faber, 1996), p. 394.
16. Ezra Pound, 'Lionel Johnson', *Literary Essays of Ezra Pound*, ed. T. S. Eliot (London: Faber, 1954), pp. 363, 367.
17. A. R. Orage, *Readers and Writers: 1917–1921* (London: Allen and Unwin, 1922), p. 174.
18. Ibid.
19. Ibid.
20. Ibid., p. 175.
21. See Townsend, pp. 1–28.
22. Yeats, *Autobiography*, p. 211.
23. Townsend, pp. 178–9.
24. Davidson, *Selected Poems*, p. 182.
25. Ibid., p. 187.
26. Ibid.
27. Ibid.
28. Townsend, p. 287.
29. Ibid., p. 187.
30. Ibid., pp. 291, 292.
31. Bourdieu, *Field*, p. 94.
32. Townsend, p. 422.
33. Virginia Woolf, 'John Davidson', *Times Literary Supplement* (16 August 1917), p. 390.
34. For Pound's reception history see Homberger.
35. Davidson, *Testament of a Vivisector* (London: Richards, 1901), p. 5.
36. Davidson, *Testament of an Empire-Builder* (London: Richards, 1902), pp. 7, 8.
37. Ibid., p. 13.
38. Quoted in Townsend, p. 374.
39. Filson Young, letter to Grant Richards, 15 October 1906, Richards Archives (University of Illinois at Urbana-Champaign, microfilm copy at the Bodleian Library, Oxford University, Oxford).
40. Quoted in Townsend, p. 365.
41. Filson Young, letter to Grant Richards, 5 September 1906, Richards Archives (University of Illinois at Urbana-Champaign, microfilm copy at the Bodleian Library, Oxford University, Oxford).
42. Quoted in Mary O'Connor, *John Davidson* (Edinburgh: Scottish Academic Press, 1987), p. 91.
43. John Sloan, introduction, *Selected Poems and Prose of John Davidson*, ed. John Sloan (Oxford: Clarendon, 1995), p. ix.
44. Woolf, p. 390.
45. Quoted in Ricks, p. 394.
46. T. S. Eliot, 'Preface', *John Davidson: A Selection of his Poems*, ed. Maurice Lindsay (London: Hutchinson, 1961), p. xii.
47. Machen, letter to John Lane, 5 June 1895.
48. Arthur Machen, letter to John Lane, 29 June 1895, John Lane Company Records (Harry Ransom Center, University of Texas, Austin, TX).
49. My account of this incident is culled from letters Machen wrote to Lane (7 June 1895 and 17 June 1895, John Lane Company Records [Harry Ransom Center, University of Texas, Austin, TX]) and to Richard Garnett (7 June 1895, Machen Collection [Harry Ransom Center, University of Texas, Austin, TX]) and from Gawsworth's

unpublished biography of Machen which suggests that Smithers was also involved. For Smithers's role in the publication see Nelson, *Publisher*, pp. 36 and 403n3.

50. Machen, letter to Richard Garnett.

51. Machen, letter to John Lane, 17 June 1895.

52. Machen, letter to John Lane, 29 June 1895. Machen's use of the term 'quilter' refers to Harry Quilter, author of a recent attack on Decadence, 'The Gospel of Intensity'.

53. Bourdieu, *Field*, p. 15.

54. Machen, *Arthur Machen*, p. 229.

55. Gawsworth, pp. 177–8.

56. Grant Richards, letter to Arthur Machen, 6 March 1902, Richards Archives (University of Illinois at Urbana-Champaign, microfilm copy at the Bodleian Library, Oxford University, Oxford).

57. Machen, 'Notes on *The Hill of Dreams*', *Arthur Machen: A Bibliography*, by Henry Danielson (London: Henry Danielson, 1923), p. 39.

58. The novel was first published in magazine form in 1904 in *Horlicks Magazine*. Its appearance in this unlikely publication put out by the Horlicks malted milk company was due to the intervention of Machen's friend and fellow dabbler in things occult, A. E. Waite, who served as a director on the board of the company. Waite convinced the board to finance a magazine that he used as a vehicle for his interest in the occult (Aidan Reynolds and William Charlton, *Arthur Machen: An Account of His Life and Works* [London: Richards Press, 1963], p. 53).

59. Review of *Hill of Dreams*, *Outlook* (9 March 1907), p. 317.

60. Reviews of *Hill of Dreams*, *Birmingham Gazette and Express*, (28 March 1907), p. 4; *Birmingham Post*, quoted in Machen, *Precious Balms*, p. 93.

61. Reviews of *Hill of Dreams*, *Birmingham Gazette and Express*, (28 March 1907), p. 4; *Morning Post* (22 April 1907), p. 2; *Daily Chronicle* (19 March 1907), p. 3.

62. Review of *Hill of Dreams*, *Nation* (11 July 1907), p. 37.

63. Machen would likely have taken exception to the comparison with Symons for though their aesthetic theories coincide in their mystical, romantic, anti-realist, and anti-materialist emphases, they find their ideals in different sources. Symons finds his in nineteenth-century French Literature, while Machen finds his in Dickens, Cervantes, Rabelais, and the American writer Mary Wilkins. Indeed, in what may well be a response to Symons (Machen began composing *Hieroglyphics* the year that Symons's work was published), Machen insists that eighteenth- and nineteenth-century French literature is 'second-rate' (Machen, *Hieroglyphics* [London: Richards, 1902], p. 174).

64. Symons, *Symbolist Movement*, p. 3.

65. Machen, *Hieroglyphics*, p. 11.

66. Ibid., pp. 11, 51.

67. Review of *Hieroglyphics*, *Glasgow Herald*, quoted in Machen, *Precious Balms*, p. 29.

68. Machen, *Precious Balms*, pp. 69, 60.

69. *Ornaments in Jade*, written in 1897, was published in 1924; 'The White People' and 'A Fragment of Life', written in 1899, were published in 1906; 'The Red Hand', written in 1895, was published in 1906.

70. Grant Richards, letter to Alfred Knopf, 25 February 1921, Richards Archives (University of Illinois at Urbana-Champaign, microfilm copy at the Bodleian Library, Oxford University, Oxford).

71. Quoted in Sweetser, p. 36.

72. Grant Richards, letter to Arthur Machen, 27 August 1906, Richards Archives (University of Illinois at Urbana-Champaign, microfilm copy at the Bodleian Library, Oxford University, Oxford).

73. Grant Richards, letter to Arthur Machen, 28 August 1906, Richards Archives (University of Illinois at Urbana-Champaign, microfilm copy at the Bodleian Library, Oxford University, Oxford).

74. Grant Richards, letter to Filson Young, 30 August 1906, Richards Archives (University of Illinois at Urbana-Champaign, microfilm copy at the Bodleian Library, Oxford University, Oxford).

75. Ibid.

76. Machen, *Arthur Machen*, p. 230.

77. Donald M. Hassler, 'Arthur Machen and Genre: Filial and Fannish Alternatives'. *Extrapolation* 33, 2 (1992), pp. 118–22.

78. Ibid., p. 119.

79. Quoted in Roger Dobson, 'Preface', *Arthur Machen, Selected Letters: The Private Writings of the Master of the Macabre* (Chatham, UK: Aquarius Press, 1988), p. 6.

80. Machen, 'Introduction', *Great God Pan*, p. vii.

81. Machen, *Few Letters*, p. 33.

82. Carl Van Vechten, *Excavations: A Book of Advocacies* (New York: Knopf, 1926), pp. 162, 164.

83. Reviews of *Prince Zaleski, Academy*, p. 312; *Guardian*, p. 917.

84. Review of *Shapes in the Fire, Scotsman* (26 November 1896), p. 8.

85. Review of *Shapes in the Fire, Weekly Sun*, p. 2.

86. Reviews of *Shapes in the Fire, The Critic* (17 April 1897), p. 270; *Scotsman*, p. 8; *Weekly Sun*, p. 2.

87. Reviews of *Shapes in the Fire, The Critic*, p. 270; *Academy*, p. 43.

88. Review of *Shapes in the Fire, The Critic*, p. 270.

89. M. P. Shiel, *Shapes in the Fire, Being a Mid-winter Night's Entertainment in Two Parts and an Interlude* (New York: Garland 1977), pp. 134 and 165–6.

90. M. P. Shiel, letter to John Lane, 9 August 1894, John Lane Company Records (Harry Ransom Center, University of Texas, Austin, TX).

91. M. P. Shiel, letters to John Lane, 21 February 1895 and 16 January 1895, John Lane Company Records (Harry Ransom Center, University of Texas, Austin, TX).

92. M. P. Shiel, letter to Gussie Shiel.

93. Though Shiel publicly concealed his racial difference, he was still a subject of curiosity to his peers. Machen recalled a parlour game played at his literary gatherings in the 1890s in which the object was to guess Shiel's race (Machen, *Arthur Machen*, p. 50).

94. Shiel, 'About Myself', *The Works of M. P. Shiel Updated*, 2nd edn (Dayton, OH: Reynolds Morse Foundation, 1980), p. 420. This claim is probably exaggerated. His letters to Richards are filled with pleas for money and, in a letter supporting his application to the Royal Literary Fund, Richards expressed his belief that Shiel had 'always been poor: often very poor' (Grant Richards, letter to Llewellyn Roberts, 20 September 1914, Royal Literary Fund Archives on microfilm [British Library, London]). If ever he did make this much money on serials, it was likely for a brief period early in the century.

95. M. P. Shiel, letter to Grant Richards, 25 March 1898, Richards Archives (University of Illinois at Urbana-Champaign, microfilm copy at the Bodleian Library, Oxford University, Oxford).

96. Shiel, 'About Myself', p. 420.

97. M. P. Shiel, letter to Grant Richards, 9 March 1898, Richards Archives (University of Illinois at Urbana-Champaign, microfilm copy at the Bodleian Library, Oxford University, Oxford).

98. Shiel, 'On Reading', pp. 52–7. After analysing the greatest writers in the categories of matter, expression, harmony, and tone, Shiel concludes that either the Jehovist

('if he was at all a harmonist') or he himself (if the Jehovist was not a harmonist) is the greatest writer overall.

99. M. P. Shiel, letter to Grant Richards, 4 July 1911, Richards Archives (University of Illinois at Urbana-Champaign, microfilm copy at the Bodleian Library, Oxford University, Oxford).

100. M. P. Shiel, letter to Grant Richards, June 1922, Richards Archives (University of Illinois at Urbana-Champaign, microfilm copy at the Bodleian Library, Oxford University, Oxford).

101. M. P. Shiel, letter to Grant Richards, 4 July 1911.

102. M. P. Shiel, letter to Grant Richards, 8 November 1926, Richards Archives (University of Illinois at Urbana-Champaign, microfilm copy at the Bodleian Library, Oxford University, Oxford).

103. Shiel, 'On Reading', p. 76.

104. M. P. Shiel, letter to Grant Richards, [March 1899], Richards Archives (University of Illinois at Urbana-Champaign, microfilm copy at the Bodleian Library, Oxford University, Oxford).

105. M. P. Shiel, letter to Grant Richards, 11 February 1900, Richards Archives (University of Illinois at Urbana-Champaign, microfilm copy at the Bodleian Library, Oxford University, Oxford).

106. M. P. Shiel, letter to Grant Richards, 24th October 1913, Richards Archives (University of Illinois at Urbana-Champaign, microfilm copy at the Bodleian Library, Oxford University, Oxford).

107. Grant Richards, letter to M. P. Shiel, 13 May 1925, Richards Archives (University of Illinois at Urbana-Champaign, microfilm copy at the Bodleian Library, Oxford University, Oxford).

108. Shiel, *Shapes in the Fire*, p. vi.

109. Shiel, 'On Reading', p. 37.

110. Ibid.

111. Ibid., p. 23.

112. Ibid., p. 20.

113. Ibid., p. 37.

114. Ibid.

115. Ezra Pound, 'How to Read', p. 19 and 'The Serious Artist', p. 46 (*Literary Essays of Ezra Pound*, ed. T. S. Eliot).

116. Pound, 'How to Read', p. 22.

117. Shiel's activities during these years are difficult to trace. He spent about 18 months in prison and is also said to have served as a translator during the war. He married a well-off woman in about 1918 and may have been financially secure enough to try his hand at play-writing.

118. Rebecca West, press clipping from a review in the *Daily Telegraph*, Richards Archives (University of Illinois at Urbana-Champaign, microfilm copy at the Bodleian Library, Oxford University, Oxford).

119. Quoted in Don Herron, 'Mysteries of M. P. Shiel', *Shiel in Diverse Hands: A Collection of Essays*, ed. A. Reynolds Morse (Cleveland, OH: Reynolds Morse Foundation, 1983), p. 179.

120. Carl Van Vechten, *Letters of Carl Van Vechten*, ed. Bruce Kellner (New Haven, CT: Yale University Press, 1987), p. 56.

121. Van Vechten, *Excavations*, p. 149.

122. Pykett, 'Introduction', *Reading Fin de Siècle Fictions* (London: Longman, 1996), p. 3.

123. Constable, Denisoff, and Potolsky., p. 7.

124. Bourdieu, *Field*, p. 42.

References

Abrams, Meyer Howard, ed. *The Norton Anthology of English Literature*. 2nd volume (New York: Norton, 1993).

Accepted Addresses from Divers Quarters Directed at the Compiler (London: Bodley Head, 1897).

Adams, Jad. *Madder Music, Stronger Wine: The Life of Ernest Dowson, Poet and Decadent* (London: Tauris, 2000).

Advertisement for *Wormwood. Academy* (13 December 1890), 554.

Allen, J. Barrow. Rev. of *Wormwood*, by Marie Corelli. *Academy* (29 November 1890), 500–1.

Altick, Richard. *The English Common Reader: A Social History of the Mass Reading Public 1800–1900*. 2nd edn (Columbus: Ohio State University Press, 1998).

Arata, Stephen. *Fictions of Loss in the Victorian fin de siècle* (Cambridge: Cambridge University Press, 1996).

Arnold, Matthew. *Culture and Anarchy* (New Haven, CT: Yale University Press, 1994).

'Art'. *Westminster Gazette* (6 April 1895), 1.

Bailey, Peter. 'Custom, Capital, and Culture in the Victorian Music Hall'. *Popular Culture and Custom in Nineteenth-Century England*. Ed. Robert D. Storch (London: Croom Helm, 1982), 180–208.

Barry, William F. 'Realism and Decadence in French Fiction'. 1890. *Heralds of Revolt: Studies in Modern Literature and Dogma* (London: Hodder and Stoughton, 1904), 196–236.

——. 'The Strike of a Sex'. *Quarterly Review* 179 (1894), 289–318.

Batchelor, John. *The Edwardian Novelists* (London: Duckworth, 1982).

Baudelaire, Charles. *Les Fleurs du mal*. Trans. Richard Howard (Boston: David R. Godine, 1982).

Beardsley, Aubrey. *The Letters of Aubrey Beardsley*. Eds Henry Maas, J. L. Duncan, and W. G. Good (Oxford: Plantin, 1990).

Beckson, Karl. *Arthur Symons: A Life* (Oxford: Clarendon, 1987).

——. *London in the 1890s: A Cultural History* (New York: Norton, 1992).

——, ed. *Oscar Wilde: The Critical Heritage* (London: Routledge, 1970).

——. 'Yeats and the Rhymers' Club'. *Yeats Studies* 1 (1971), 20–41.

Bédarida, François. *A Social History of England 1851–1990*. Trans. A. S. Forster and Geoffrey Hodgkinson (London: Routledge, 1990).

Beerbohm, Max. 'Enoch Soames'. *Seven Men and Two Others* (Oxford: Oxford University Press, 1980), 3–44.

Bennett, Arnold. *The Truth About an Author* (London: Methuen, 1914).

Bernheimer, Charles. *Decadent Subjects: The Idea of Decadence in Art, Literature, Philosophy, and Culture of the Fin de Siècle in Europe*. Eds T. Jefferson Kline and Naomi Schor (Baltimore, MD: Johns Hopkins University Press, 2002).

Rev. of *The Beth Book*, by Sarah Grand. *Academy* (13 November 1897), 393.

Billings, Harold. 'The Shape of Shiel 1865–1896: A Biography of the Early Years'. *Shiel in Diverse Hands: A Collection of Essays*. Ed. A Reynolds Morse (Cleveland, OH: Reynolds Morse Foundation, 1983), 77–105.

Bleiler, Richard. 'Robert S. Hichens'. *Late-Victorian and Edwardian British Novelists, First Series. Dictionary of Literary Biography* 153 (Detroit: Gale, 1995), 106–19.

'Bohemian.' Def. 3. *Oxford English Dictionary* (online version), 3 September 2005, <http://dictionary.oed.com/>.

Bourdieu, Pierre. *Distinction: A Social Critique of the Judgement of Taste* (London: Routledge, 1984).

——. *The Field of Cultural Production* (New York: Columbia University Press, 1983).

——. *The Rules of Art: Genesis and Structure of the Literary Field*. Trans. Susan Emanuel (Stanford: Stanford University Press, 1995).

Bradfield, Thomas. 'A Dominant Note of Some Recent Fiction'. *Westminster Review* 142 (1894), 537–45.

Brake, Laurel. *Nineteenth-Century Media and the Construction of Identities* (Basingstoke, UK: Palgrave, 2000).

——. 'Endgames: The Politics of the *Yellow Book* or, Decadence, Gender, and the New Journalism'. *Essays and Studies* 48 (1995), 38–64.

Bristow, Joseph. Preface. *The* Fin-de-Siècle *Poem: English Literary Culture and the 1890s*. Ed. Joseph Bristow (Columbus: Ohio University Press, 2005), pp. ix– xvii.

——. ''Sterile Ecstasies': The Perversity of the Decadent Movement'. *Essays and Studies* 48 (1995), 65–88.

——. 'Wilde, *Dorian Gray*, and Gross Indecency'. *Sexual Sameness: Textual Differences in Lesbian and Gay Writing*. Ed. Joseph Bristow (London: Routledge, 1992), 44– 63.

Brown, Marilyn. *Gypsies and Other Bohemians: The Myth of the Artist in Nineteenth-Century France* (Ann Arbor: University of Michigan Research Press, 1985).

Brown, R. D. 'The Bodley Head Press: Some Bibliographical Extrapolations'. *Bibliographical Society of America Papers* 61 (1967), 39–50.

Buchanan, Robert. 'Is Chivalry Still Possible?' *Daily Telegraph* (22 March 1889), 5.

——. 'The Modern Young Man as Critic'. *Universal Review* 3 (1889), 353–72.

Carter, Alfred Edward. *The Idea of Decadence in French Literature 1830–1900* (Toronto: University of Toronto Press, 1958).

Cate, George Allen. 'George Meredith'. *Encyclopaedia of the 1890s*. Ed. G. A. Cevasco. (New York: Garland, 1993).

Cave, Richard Allen. *A Study of the Novels of George Moore*. (Gerrards Cross, UK: Smythe, 1978).

Cazamian, Madeleine L. *Le Roman et les idées en Angleterre: L'Anti-intellectualisme et l'esthétisme 1880–1900* (Paris: Faculté des lettres de l'Université de Strasbourg, 1935).

Cecil, David. *Max: A Biography of Max Beerbohm* (New York: Atheneum, 1985).

Cevasco, George A. *The Breviary of the Decadence: J.-K. Huysmans's* A Rebours *and English Literature* (New York: AMS Press, 2001).

Chamberlin, James Edward. 'From High Decadence to High Modernism'. *Queen's Quarterly* 87 (1980), 591–610.

Charlesworth, Barbara. *Dark Passages: The Decadent Consciousness in Victorian Literature* (Madison: University of Wisconsin Press, 1965).

Codell, Julie F. *The Victorian Artist: Artists' Lifewritings in Britain c. 1870–1910*. (Cambridge: Cambridge University Press, 2003).

Colby, Vineta. *Vernon Lee: A Literary Biography* (Charlottesville: University of Virginia Press, 2003).

Rev. of *A Comedy of Masks*, by Ernest Dowson and Arthur Moore. *Academy* (18 November 1893), 435.

——. *Critic* (17 February 1894), 109.

——. *Daily Chronicle* (4 October 1893), 3.

——. *Graphic* (14 October 1893), 54.

——. *National Observer* (14 October 1893), 569.

Rev. *Pall Mall Gazette* (27 November 1893), 4.

'Concerning a Misused Term; viz., "Art" as Recently Applied to a Certain Form of Literature'. *Punch* (13 April 1895), 177.

Rev. of *Confessions of a Young Man*, by George Moore. *Athenaeum* (31 March 1888), 402.

——. *The Hawk* (10 April 1888), 172–3.

——. *Vanity Fair* (2 June 1888), 322.

Constable, Liz, Dennis Denisoff, and Matthew Potolsky. 'Introduction'. *Perennial Decay: On the Aesthetics and Politics of Decadence*. Eds Liz Constable, Dennis Denisoff, and Matthew Potolsky (Philadelphia: University of Pennsylvania Press, 1999), 1–32.

——, eds. *Perennial Decay: On the Aesthetics and Politics of Decadence* (Philadelphia: University of Pennsylvania Press, 1999).

Corelli, Marie. '*Barabbas* – and After'. *Idler* (February 1895), 120–34.

——. *Free Opinions Freely Expressed on Certain Phases of Modern Social Life and Conduct* (London: Constable, 1905).

——. Letter to John Lane, March 1900. John Lane Company Records (Harry Ransom Center, University of Texas, Austin, TX).

——. Letter to George Bentley. 2 January 1889. Corelli Collection, General Collection (Beinecke Rare Book and Manuscript Library, Yale University, New Haven, CT).

——. Letter to George Bentley. [12 June 1890]. Corelli Collection, General Collection (Beinecke Rare Book and Manuscript Library, Yale University, New Haven, CT).

——. Letter to George Bentley. 28 August 1890. Corelli Collection, General Collection (Beinecke Rare Book and Manuscript Library, Yale University, New Haven, CT).

——. Letter to George Bentley. 8 September 1890. Corelli Collection, General Collection (Beinecke Rare Book and Manuscript Library, Yale University, New Haven, CT).

——. Letter to George Bentley. 15 November 1890. Corelli Collection, General Collection (Beinecke Rare Book and Manuscript Library, Yale University, New Haven, CT).

——. *The Silver Domino* (London: Lamley, 1892).

——. *The Sorrows of Satan* (Oxford: Oxford University Press, 1998).

——. *Wormwood: A Drama of Paris*. 1890. Ed. Kirsten MacLeod (Peterborough, ON: Broadview Press, 2004).

Crackanthorpe, Blanche Althea. Letter to John Lane [1895]. John Lane Company Records (Harry Ransom Center, University of Texas, Austin, TX).

Crackanthorpe, Hubert. 'Reticence in Literature: Some Roundabout Remarks'. *Yellow Book* 2 (1894), 259–69.

Crawford, Emily. 'Emile Zola'. *Contemporary Review* 55 (1889), 94–113.

Cross, Nigel. *The Common Writer: Life in Nineteenth-Century Grub Street* (Cambridge: Cambridge University Press, 1985).

Daly, Nicholas. *Modernism, Romance, and the* Fin de Siècle: *Popular Fiction and British Culture, 1880–1914* (Cambridge: Cambridge University Press, 1999).

'The Damnation of Decadence'. *National Observer* (23 February 1895), 390–1.

D'Arcy, Ella. *Some Letters to John Lane*. Ed. Alan Anderson (Edinburgh: Tragara Press, 1990).

Davidson, John. *The North Wall* (New York: Garland, 1978).

——. Reader's Report on *London Nights*, by Arthur Symons. Walpole Collection (Bodleian Library, Oxford University, Oxford).

——. *Selected Poems and Prose of John Davidson*. Ed. John Sloan (Oxford: Clarendon Press, 1995).

——. *Testament of an Empire-Builder* (London: Richards, 1902).

Davidson, John. *Testament of a Vivisector* (London: Richards, 1901).

Demoor, Marysa. ' "Not with a Bang but a Whimper": Lucy Clifford's Correspondence, 1919–1929'. *Cambridge Quarterly* 30, 3 (2001), 233–56.

Dick, Susan. 'Introduction'. *Confessions of a Young Man*, by George Moore. Ed. Susan Dick (Montreal: McGill-Queen's University Press, 1972), 1–22.

Dickey, Christopher. 'Absinthe's Second Coming'. *Cigar Aficionado* (March/April 2001), 5 September 2005 <http://www.cigaraficionado.com/>. Path: Library; Magazine Archive.

'Dilettante'. *Concise Oxford Dictionary of Current English*. 6th edn, 1976.

Dobson, Roger. 'Preface'. *Arthur Machen, Selected Letters: The Private Writings of the Master of the Macabre* (Chatham, UK: Aquarius Press, 1988), 5–8.

Dowling, Linda. *Aestheticism and Decadence: A Selected Annotated Bibliography* (New York: Garland, 1977).

——. 'The Decadent and the New Woman in the 1890s'. *Nineteenth-Century Fiction* 33 (1979), 434–53.

——. *Language and Decadence in the Victorian Fin de Siècle* (Princeton, NJ: Princeton University Press, 1986).

——. *The Vulgarization of Art* (Charlottesville: University of Virginia Press, 1996).

Dowson, Ernest. *The Letters of Ernest Dowson*. Eds Desmond Flower and Henry Maas (London: Cassell, 1967).

——. *New Letters from Ernest Dowson*. Ed. Desmond Flower (Andoversford, Gloucestershire: Whittington Press, 1984).

—— and Arthur Moore. *A Comedy of Masks*. 2nd edn (London: Heinemann, 1894).

Eckersley, Adrian. 'A Theme in the Early Works of Arthur Machen: Degeneration'. *English Literature in Transition* 35 (1992), 277–87.

Egerton, George. *A Leaf from the Yellow Book: The Correspondence of George Egerton*. Ed. Terence de Vere White (London: Richards, 1958).

Eliot, T.S. 'Preface'. *John Davidson: A Selection of his Poems*. Ed. Maurice Lindsay (London: Hutchinson, 1961).

Ellis, Havelock. 'A Note Upon Paul Bourget'. 1889. *Views and Reviews: A Selection of Uncollected Articles 1884–1932. First Series 1884–1919* (London: Desmond Harmsworth, 1932), 48–60.

Ellmann, Richard. *Oscar Wilde* (London: Penguin, 1987).

Federico, Annette R. *Idol of Suburbia: Marie Corelli and Late-Victorian Literary Culture* (Charlottesville: University Press of Virginia, 2000).

Ferguson, Christine. 'Decadence as Scientific Fulfillment'. *Proceedings of Modern Languages Association* 117 (2002), 465–78.

Felski, Rita. *The Gender of Modernity* (Cambridge, MA: Harvard University Press, 1995).

Fletcher, Ian. *Decadence and the 1890s* (London: Arnold, 1979).

——. 'Decadence and the Little Magazines'. *Decadence and the 1890s*. Ed. Ian Fletcher (London: Arnold, 1979), 173–202.

——. 'Some Aspects of Aestheticism'. *Twilight of Dawn: Studies in English Literature in Transition*. Ed. O. M. Brack (Tucson: University of Arizona Press, 1987), 1–33.

Flower, Desmond and Henry Maas. 'Introduction'. *The Letters of Ernest Dowson*. (London: Cassell, 1967), 3–8.

Frayling, Christopher. *Nightmare: The Birth of Horror* (London: BBC, 1996).

Frazier, Adrian. *George Moore 1852–1933* (New Haven, CT: Yale University Press, 2000).

Freedman, Jonathan. *Professions of Taste: Henry James, British Aestheticism, and Commodity Culture* (Stanford, CA: Stanford University Press, 1990).

Fritschner, Linda Marie. 'William Heinemann Limited'. *British Literary Publishing Houses. Dictionary of Literary Biography* 112 (Detroit: Gale, 199), 151–7.

Furniss, Harry. *My Bohemian Days* (London: Hurst and Blackett, 1919).

Gagnier, Regenia. 'A Critique of Practical Aesthetics'. *Aesthetics and Ideology*. Ed. George Levine (New Brunswick, NJ: Rutgers University Press, 1994), 264–80.

——. *Idylls of the Marketplace: Oscar Wilde and the Victorian Public* (Stanford, CA: Stanford University Press, 1986).

Gardiner, Bruce. 'Decadence: Its Construction and Contexts'. *Southern Review* 18 (1985), 22–43.

——. *The Rhymers' Club: A Social and Intellectual History* (New York: Garland, 1988).

Gawsworth, John. Unpublished ts. of biography of Arthur Machen. Armstrong Collection (Harry Ransom Center, University of Texas, Austin, TX).

Gekle, William Francis. *Arthur Machen: Weaver of Fantasy* (Millbrook, NY: Round Table P, 1949).

Gilman, Richard. *Decadence: The Strange Life of an Epithet* (New York: Farrar and Strauss, 1980).

Goodman, Jonathan, compiler. *The Oscar Wilde File* (London: Allen, 1988).

Goodwin, Geraint. *Conversations with George Moore* (London: Jonathan Cape, 1937).

Gosse, Edmund. 'The Tyranny of the Novel'. *A Victorian Art of Fiction*. Compiler John Charles Olmsted (New York: Garland, 1979), 521–33.

Grand, Sarah. *The Beth Book: Being a Study of the Life of Elizabeth Caldwell Maclure, a Woman of Genius* (London: Virago, 1980).

——. *Journalistic Writings and Contemporary Reception*. Vol. 1 of *Sex, Social Purity and Sarah Grand*. Eds Ann Heilmann and Stephanie Forward (London: Routledge, 2000).

——. *Selected Letters*. Vol. 2 of *Sex, Social Purity and Sarah Grand*. Eds Ann Heilmann and Stephanie Forward (London: Routledge, 2000).

Grant, Michael, ed. *T. S. Eliot: The Critical Heritage* (London: Routledge, 1982).

Rev. of *The Great God Pan*, by Arthur Machen. *Academy* (25 February 1895), 166–7.

——. *Athenaeum* (23 March 1895), 375.

——. *Daily Free Press* (Aberdeen) (17 December 1894), 2.

——. *Echo* (18 January 1895), 1.

——. *Literary News* (February 1895), 44.

——. *Literary World* (12 January 1895), 7.

——. *Pall Mall Gazette* (15 December 1894), 4.

——. *Scotsman* (17 December 1894), 3.

——. *Weekly Sun* (30 December 1894), 2.

——. *Westminster Gazette* (4 January 1895), 2.

——. *Whitehall Review* (15 December 1894), 18.

——. *Woman* (9 January 1895), 7.

——. *Yorkshire Post* (16 January 1895), 3.

Green, Martin. *Children of the Sun: A Narrative of 'Decadence' in England after 1918* (New York: Wideview Books, 1980).

Green, Richard Lancelyn. 'Introduction'. *The Adventures of Sherlock Holmes*. Arthur Conan Doyle (Oxford: Oxford University Press, 1994), pp. xi–xxxv.

Greenslade, William. *Degeneration, Culture and the Novel: 1880–1940* (Cambridge: Cambridge University Press, 1994).

Griest, Guinevere L. *Mudie's Circulating Library and the Victorian Novel* (Devon, UK: David and Charles, 1970).

Grubgeld, Elizabeth. *George Moore and the Autogenous Self: The Autobiography of Fiction* (Syracuse, NY: Syracuse University Press, 1994).

'The Guardian'. *Waterloo Directory of English Periodicals and Newspapers: 1800–1900*. 2nd series. Ed. John S. North. http://www.victorianperiodicals.com/series2/.

Gunn, Peter. *Vernon Lee/Violet Paget, 1856–1935* (London: Oxford University Press, 1964).

Guy, Josephine and Ian Small. *Oscar Wilde's Profession: Writing and the Culture Industry in the Late Nineteenth Century* (Oxford: Oxford University Press, 2000).

Haggard, H. Rider. 'About Fiction'. *Contemporary Review* 51 (1887), 172–80.

Hall, Lesley. E-mail to the author. October 1998.

Hanson, Ellis. *Decadence and Catholicism* (Cambridge, MA: Harvard University Press, 1997).

Harris, Wendell V. 'Identifying the Decadent Fiction of the 1890s'. *English Fiction in Transition* 5,5 (1962), 1–14.

——. John Lane's Keynotes Series and the Fiction of the 1890's'. *Proceedings of the Modern Language Association* 83 (1968), 1407–13.

Hassler, Donald M. 'Arthur Machen and Genre: Filial and Fannish Alternatives'. *Extrapolation* 33,2 (1992), 115–27.

Herron, Don. 'The Mysteries of M. P. Shiel'. *Shiel in Diverse Hands: A Collection of Essays*. Ed. A. Reynolds Morse (Cleveland, OH: Reynolds Morse Foundation, 1983), 179–93.

Hichens, Robert. 'The Collaborators'. *The Folly of Eustace*, by Robert Hichens (London: Heinemann, 1896), 117–46.

——. *Yesterday* (London: Cassell, 1947).

Rev. of *The Hill of Dreams*, by Arthur Machen. *Birmingham Gazette and Express* (28 March 1907), 4.

——. *Daily Chronicle* (19 March 1907), 3.

——. *Morning Post* (22 April 1907), 2.

——. *Nation* (11 July 1907), 37.

——. *Outlook* (9 March 1907), 317.

Hoare, Philip. 'Symbols of Decay'. *Tate: The Art Magazine* 13 (Winter 1997), 22–9.

Hogarth, Janet E. 'Literary Degenerates'. *Fortnightly Review* 63 (1895), 586–92.

Homberger, Eric, ed. *Ezra Pound: The Critical Heritage* (London: Routledge, 1972).

Hone, Joseph. *The Life of George Moore*. 1936 (Westport, CT: Greenwood, 1973).

Hough, Graham. *The Last Romantics* (London: Methuen, 1961).

Hughes, Linda K. *Graham R.: Rosamund Marriott Watson, Woman of Letters* (Columbus: Ohio University Press, 2005).

Hunter, Jefferson. *Edwardian Fiction* (Cambridge, MA: Harvard University Press, 1982).

Hurley, Kelly. *The Gothic Body: Sexuality, Materialism, and Degeneration at the* Fin de Siècle (Cambridge: Cambridge University Press, 1996).

Huyssen, Andreas. *After the Great Divide: Modernism, Mass Culture, Postmodernism*. (Bloomington: Indiana University Press, 1986).

Hyde, Montgomery. *The Trials of Oscar Wilde* (London: Dover, n.d.).

Jackson, Holbrook. *The Eighteen-Nineties: A Review of Art and Ideas at the Close of the Nineteenth Century* (New York: Capricorn, 1966).

James, Henry. *Henry James: Letters*. Vol. 3, 1883–1895. Ed. James Edel (Cambridge, MA: Belknap Press, 1980).

Johnson, Lionel. 'A Note Upon the Practice and Theory of Verse at the Present Time Obtaining in France', *Century Guild Hobby Horse* 6 (1891), 61–6.

Keating, Peter. *The Haunted Study: A Social History of the English Novel 1875–1914*. (London: Secker and Warburg, 1989).

Kemp, Sandra, Charlotte Mitchell, and David Trotter. *Edwardian Fiction: An Oxford Companion* (Oxford: Oxford University Press, 1997).

Kent, Christopher. 'British Bohemia and the Victorian Journalist'. *Australasian Victorian Studies Journal* 6 (2000), 25–35.

——. 'The Idea of Bohemia in Mid-Victorian England'. *Queen's Quarterly* 80 (1973), 360–9.

Kift, Dagmar. *The Victorian Music Hall: Culture, Class, and Conflict* (Cambridge: Cambridge University Press, 1996).

Lang, Andrew. 'Emile Zola'. *Fortnightly Review* 31 (1882), 439–52.

——. 'Realism and Romance'. *Contemporary Review* 52 (1887), 683–93.

Langenfeld, Robert. 'A Reconsideration: *Confessions of a Young Man* as Farce'. *Twilight of Dawn: Studies in English Literature in Transition*. Ed. O. M. Brack (Tucson: University of Arizona Press, 1987), 91–110.

Larson, Magali Sarfatti. *The Rise of Professionalism: A Sociological Analysis* (Berkeley: University of California Press, 1977).

Ledger, Sally and Roger Luckhurst, eds. *The* Fin de Siècle: *A Reader in Cultural History c. 1800–1900* (Oxford: Oxford University Press, 2000).

Ledger, Sally and Scott McCracken, eds. *Cultural Politics at the* Fin de Siècle. (Cambridge: Cambridge University Press, 1995).

Le Gallienne, Richard. 'Considerations Suggested by Churton Collins' Illustrations of Tennyson'. *Retrospective Reviews*. Vol. 1 (London: Lane, 1896), 19–28.

——. *The Romantic '90s* (London: Putnam's, 1926).

Lee, Vernon. 'A Dialogue on Novels'. *Contemporary Review* 48 (1885), 378–401.

——. *Miss Brown*. 3 vols (New York: Garland, 1978).

——. 'The Moral Teaching of Zola'. *Contemporary Review* 63 (1893), 196–212.

Levenson, Michael. *A Genealogy of Modernism: A Study of the English Literary Doctrine 1908–1922* (Cambridge: Cambridge University Press, 1984).

Lilly, William Samuel. 'The New Naturalism'. *Fortnightly Review* 44 (1885), 240–56.

Machen, Arthur. *Arthur Machen: Selected Letters, the Private Writings of the Master of the Macabre*. Eds Roger Dobson, Godfrey Brangham, and R. A. Gilbert (Wellingborough, UK: Aquarian Press, 1988).

——. *A Few Letters from Arthur Machen: Letters to Munson Havens* (Aylesford, UK: Aylesford Press, 1993).

——. *The Glorious Mystery* (Chicago: Covici-McGee, 1924).

——. *The Great God Pan and the Inmost Light* (London: Lane, 1894).

——. *Hieroglyphics* (London: Richards, 1902).

——. *The Hill of Dreams* (New York: Knopf, 1923).

——. 'Introduction'. *The Great God Pan* (London: Simpkin, Marshall, Hamilton, Kent, 1916), pp. vii–xxiii.

——. 'Introduction'. *The Hill of Dreams* (New York: Knopf, 1923), pp. v–xiv.

——. Letter to John Lane, 5 June 1895. John Lane Company Records (Harry Ransom Center, University of Texas, Austin, TX).

——. Letter to John Lane, 7 June 1895. John Lane Company Records (Harry Ransom Center, University of Texas, Austin, TX).

——. Letter to John Lane, 17 June 1895. John Lane Company Records (Harry Ransom Center, University of Texas, Austin, TX).

——. Letter to John Lane, 29 June 1895. John Lane Company Records (Harry Ransom Center, University of Texas, Austin, TX).

——. Letter to John Lane, 11 July 1895. John Lane Company Records (Harry Ransom Center, University of Texas, Austin, TX).

——. Letter to Richard Garnett. 7 June 1895. Machen Collection (Harry Ransom Center, University of Texas, Austin, TX).

Machen, Arthur. 'Notes on *The Hill of Dreams'*. *Arthur Machen: A Bibliography*, by Henry Danielson (London: Henry Danielson, 1923), 39–42.

——. *Precious Balms* (Horam, UK: Friends of Arthur Machen and Tartarus Press, 1999).

——. *Things Near and Far* (New York: Knopf, 1923).

Macleod, Dianne Sachko. *Art and the Victorian Middle Class: Art and the Making of Cultural Identity* (Cambridge: Cambridge University Press, 1996).

MacLeod, Kirsten. 'Introduction'. *Wormwood: A Drama of Paris*, by Marie Corelli. Ed. Kirsten MacLeod (Peterborough, ON: Broadview Press, 2004) 9–55.

——. 'Marie Corelli and *Fin-de-Siècle* Francophobia: The Absinthe Trail of French Art'.*English Literature in Transition* 43 (2000), 66–82.

Mangum, Teresa. *Married, Middlebrow and Militant: Sarah Grand and the New Woman Novel* (Ann Arbor: University of Michigan Press, 1998).

Mannocchi, Phyllis F. ' "Vernon Lee": A Reintroduction and Primary Bibliography'. *English Literature in Transition* 26 (1983), 231–67.

Mason, Stuart. *Oscar Wilde: Art and Morality* (London: Frank Palmer, 1912).

Masters, Brian. *Now Barabbas Was a Rotter: The Extraordinary Life of Marie Corelli.* (London: Hamish Hamilton, 1978).

May, Phil. *Mr Punch in Bohemia; or, the Lighter Side of Literary, Artistic, and Professional Life* (London: Educational Book Co., 1907).

McDonald, Peter D. *British Literary Culture and Publishing Practice 1880–1914.* (Cambridge: Cambridge University Press, 1997).

Rev. of *Mike Fletcher*, by George Moore. *The Artist and Journal of Home Culture* (1 February 1890), 62–3.

Rev. of *Miss Brown*, by Vernon Lee. *Spectator* (13 December 1884), 1670.

——. *Time* (February 1885), 207–14.

Moers, Ellen. *The Dandy: Brummell to Beerbohm* (Lincoln: University of Nebraska Press, 1960).

Monkhouse, Cosmo. Rev. of *Miss Brown*, by Vernon Lee. *Academy* (3 January 1885), 6–7.

Moore, George. *Confessions of a Young Man.* (Montreal: McGill-Queen's University Press, 1972).

——. 'Les Decadents'. *Court and Society Review* (19 January 1887), 57–8.

——. *Literature at Nurse; or, Circulating Morals* (New York: Garland, 1978).

——. *Mike Fletcher.* London: Ward and Downey, 1889.

——. 'Preface' (1889). *Confessions of a Young Man* (Montreal: McGill-Queens University Press, 1972), 35–6.

——. 'Preface' (1904). *Confessions of a Young Man* (Montreal: McGill-Queens University Press, 1972), 6–7.

——. 'Preface' (1917). *Confessions of a Young Man* (Montreal: McGill-Queens University Press, 1972), 41–5.

'Morbid and Unclean Literature'. *Whitehall Review* (20 April 1895), 13.

Morse, A. Reynolds. *The Works of M. P. Shiel Updated*. 2nd edn (Dayton, OH: Morse, 1980).

Munro, John. *The Decadent Poetry of the Eighteen Nineties* (Beirut: American University of Beirut, 1970).

Murdoch, W. G. Blaikie. *The Renaissance of the Nineties* (London: De La More Press, 1911).

Murray, Isobel. 'Introduction'. *The Picture of Dorian Gray*, by Oscar Wilde. Ed. Isobel Murray (London: Oxford University Press, 1974), pp. vii–xxvi.

'Myth'. Def. 2c. *Oxford English Dictionary* (online version), 3 August 2005 <http://dictionary.oed.com/>).

National Vigilance Association. *Pernicious Literature. Debate in the House of Commons. Trial and Conviction for Sale of Zola's Novels. With Opinions of the Press.* 1889. Ed. George G. Becker. *Documents of Modern Literary Realism* (Princeton, NJ: Princeton University Press, 1963), 351–82.

Navarette, Susan J. *The Shape of Fear: Horror and the* Fin de Siècle *Culture of Decadence* (Lexington: University Press of Kentucky, 1998).

Nelson, James A. *The Early Nineties: A View from the Bodley Head* (Cambridge, MA: Harvard University Press, 1971).

——. *Elkin Mathews: Publisher to Yeats, Joyce, Pound* (Madison: University of Wisconsin Press, 1989).

——. 'Leonard Smithers'. *British Literary Publishing Houses, 1881–1965. Dictionary of Literary Biography* 112 (Detroit: Gale, 1991), 315–18.

——. *Publisher to the Decadents: Leonard Smithers in the Careers of Beardsley, Wilde, Dowson* (University Park: Pennsylvania State University Press, 2000).

'N. O. B.' Rev. of *Flames* by Robert Hichens. *Echo* (26 March 1897), 1.

Noble, James Ashcroft. 'The Fiction of Sexuality'. *Contemporary Review* 67 (1895), 490–8.

——. Rev. of *Dr Jekyll and Mr Hyde*, by Robert Louis Stevenson. *Academy* (23 January 1886), 55.

O'Connor, Mary. *John Davidson* (Edinburgh: Scottish Academic Press, 1987).

Orage, Alfred Richard. *Readers and Writers: 1917–1921* (London: Allen and Unwin, 1922).

O'Sullivan, Vincent. *Aspects of Wilde* (New York: Holt, [1936]).

Pater, Walter. *Appreciations with an Essay on Style* (New York: Macmillan, 1906).

——. *The Renaissance: Studies in Art and Poetry. The 1893 Text.* Ed. Donald Hill. (Berkeley: University of California Press, 1980).

Perkin, Harold. *The Rise of Professional Society: England Since 1880* (London: Routledge, 1989).

'A Philistine Paean; Or, the Triumph of the Timid One'. *Punch* (11 May 1895), 222.

Rev. of *The Picture of Dorian Gray*, by Oscar Wilde. *Pall Mall Budget* (3 July 1890), 862.

Pittock, Murray G. H. *Spectrum of Decadence: The Literature of the 1890s* (London: Routledge, 1993).

Plarr, Victor. *Ernest Dowson: Reminiscences, Unpublished Letters, and Marginalia* (New York: Laurence J. Gomme, 1914).

Pound, Ezra. 'How to Read'. [1927 or 1928]. *Literary Essays of Ezra Pound.* Ed. T. S. Eliot (London: Faber, 1954), 15–40.

——. 'Hugh Selwyn Mauberley'. 1919. *Selected Poems* (London: Faber, 1948), 173–87.

——. 'Lionel Johnson'. 1915. *Literary Essays of Ezra Pound.* Ed. T. S. Eliot (London: Faber, 1954), 361–70.

——. 'The Serious Artist'. 1913. *Literary Essays of Ezra Pound.* Ed. T. S. Eliot (London: Faber, 1954), 41–57.

Price, Julius M. *My Bohemian Days in London* (London: Laurie, 1914).

Rev. of *Prince Zaleski*, by M. P. Shiel. *Academy* (13 April 1895), 312.

——. *Athenaeum* (23 March 1895), 376.

——. *Guardian* (19 June 1895), 917.

——. *National Observer* (16 March 1895), 481–2.

——. *Speaker* (9 March 1895), 278.

——. *Times* (20 April 1895), 8.

——. *Vanity Fair Literary Supplement* (13 June 1895), pp. i–ii.

Pykett, Lyn. *Engendering Fictions: The English Novel in the Early Twentieth Century.* (London: Edward Arnold, 1995).

——. *The 'Improper' Feminine: The Women's Sensation Novel and New Woman Writing.* (London: Routledge, 1992).

——. 'Introduction'. *Reading* Fin de Siècle *Fictions* (London: Longman, 1996).

——. 'Representing the Real: The English Debate about Naturalism'. *Naturalism in the European Novel: New Critical Perspectives.* Ed. Brian Nelson (New York: Berg, 1992), 167–88.

——, ed. *Reading* Fin de Siècle *Fictions* (London: Longman, 1996).

Quilter, Harry. 'The Gospel of Intensity'. *Contemporary Review* (June 1895), 761–82.

——. 'The New Renaissance; or, the Gospel of Intensity'. *Macmillans* (September 1880), 391–400.

Ransome, Arthur. *Bohemia in London* (London: Swift, 1907).

Reed, John R. *Decadent Style* (Athens, OH: Ohio University Press, 1985).

Reynolds, Aidan and William Charlton. *Arthur Machen: An Account of His Life and Works* (London: Richards Press, 1963).

Richards, Grant. Letter to Alfred Knopf. 25 February 1921. Richards Archives (University of Illinois at Urbana-Champaign, microfilm copy at the Bodleian Library, Oxford University, Oxford).

——. Letter to Arthur Machen. 6 March 1902. Richards Archives (University of Illinois at Urbana-Champaign, microfilm copy at the Bodleian Library, Oxford University, Oxford).

——. Letter to Arthur Machen. 27 August 1906. Richards Archives (University of Illinois at Urbana-Champaign, microfilm copy at the Bodleian Library, Oxford University, Oxford).

——. Letter to Arthur Machen. 28 August 1906. Richards Archives (University of Illinois at Urbana-Champaign, microfilm copy at the Bodleian Library, Oxford University, Oxford).

——. Letter to Filson Young. 30 August 1906. Richards Archives (University of Illinois at Urbana-Champaign, microfilm copy at the Bodleian Library, Oxford University, Oxford).

——. Letter to Llewellyn Roberts. 20 September 1914. Royal Literary Fund Archives on microfilm (British Library, London).

Richardson, Joanna. *The Bohemians: La vie de Bohème in Paris, 1830–1914* (South Brunswick, NJ: A. S. Barnes, 1971).

Ricks, Christopher, ed. *Inventions of the March Hare: Poems 1909–1917 by T. S. Eliot.* (London: Faber and Faber, 1996).

Robbins, Ruth. 'Vernon Lee: Decadent Woman?' Fin de Siècle/Fin du Globe: *Fears and Fantasies of the Late Nineteenth Century.* Ed. John Stokes (London: Macmillan, 1992), 139–61.

Roberts, Chalmers. *William Heinemann, May 18th, 1863–October 5th, 1920: An Appreciation* (London: printed for private circulation, 1920).

Roberts, Morley. *In Low Relief: A Bohemian Transcript* (New York: Appleton, 1890).

Roll-Hansen, Diderik. *The Academy 1869–1879: Victorian Intellectuals in Revolt.* (Copenhagen: Rosenkilde and Bagger, 1957).

Saintsbury, George. 'The Present State of the Novel. II'. *A Victorian Art of Fiction.* Compiler John Charles Olmsted (New York: Garland, 1979), 421–32.

Schaffer, Talia. *The Forgotten Female Aesthetes* (Charlottesville: University Press of Virginia, 2000).

Schaffer, and Kathy Alexis Psomiades, eds. *Women and British Aestheticism* (Charlottesville: University Press of Virginia, 1999).

Schoolfield, George. *A Baedeker of Decadence: Charting a Literary Fashion, 1884–1927* (New Haven, CT: Yale University Press, 2003).

Scott, Constance Brandon Margaret. *Old Days in Bohemian London (Recollections of Clement Scott)* (New York: Frederick A. Stokes, 1919).

Seigel, Jerrold. *Bohemian Paris: Culture, Politics, and the Boundaries of Bourgeois Life, 1830–1930* (New York: Viking, 1986).

'Shade'. *The Synonym Finder*. Ed. J. I. Rodale (Emmaus, PA: Rodale Books, 1961).

Rev. of *Shapes in the Fire*, by M. P. Shiel. *Academy* (9 January 1897), 43.

——. *Critic* (17 April 1897), 270.

——. *Scotsman* (26 November 1896), 8.

——. *Weekly Sun* (13 December 1896), 2.

Sharp, William. Rev. of *Confessions of a Young Man*, by George Moore. *Academy* (17 March 1888), 184–5.

Sherard, Robert. *The Real Oscar Wilde* (London: Laurie, 1916).

Shiel, Mathew Phipps. 'About Myself'. [1929]. *The Works of M. P. Shiel Updated*. 2nd edn (Dayton, OH: Reynolds Morse Foundation, 1980), 417–22.

——. Letter to Edgar Meyerstein. 29 August 1935. Shiel Collection (Harry Ransom Center, University of Texas, Austin, TX).

——. Letter to Grant Richards. 9 March 1898. Richards Archives (University of Illinois at Urbana-Champaign, microfilm copy at the Bodleian Library, Oxford University, Oxford).

——. Letter to Grant Richards. 25 March 1898. Richards Archives (University of Illinois at Urbana-Champaign, microfilm copy at the Bodleian Library, Oxford University, Oxford).

——. Letter to Grant Richards. [March 1899]. Richards Archives (University of Illinois at Urbana-Champaign, microfilm copy at the Bodleian Library, Oxford University, Oxford).

——. Letter to Grant Richards. 11 February 1900. Richards Archives (University of Illinois at Urbana-Champaign, microfilm copy at the Bodleian Library, Oxford University, Oxford).

——. Letter to Grant Richards. 4 July 1911. Richards Archives (University of Illinois at Urbana-Champaign, microfilm copy at the Bodleian Library, Oxford University, Oxford).

——. Letter to Grant Richards. 24 October 1913. Richards Archives (University of Illinois at Urbana-Champaign, microfilm copy at the Bodleian Library, Oxford University, Oxford).

——. Letter to Grant Richards. June 1922. Richards Archives (University of Illinois at Urbana-Champaign, microfilm copy at the Bodleian Library, Oxford University, Oxford).

——. Letter to Grant Richards. 13 May 1925. Richards Archives (University of Illinois at Urbana-Champaign, microfilm copy at the Bodleian Library, Oxford University, Oxford).

——. Letter to Grant Richards. 8 November 1926. Richards Archives (University of Illinois at Urbana-Champaign, microfilm copy at the Bodleian Library, Oxford University, Oxford).

——. Letter to Gussie Shiel. 30 April 1895. Shiel Collection (Harry Ransom Center, University of Texas, Austin, TX).

Shiel, Mathew Phipps. Letter to John Lane. 9 August 1894. John Lane Company Records (Harry Ransom Center, University of Texas, Austin, TX).

——. Letter to John Lane. 16 January 1895. John Lane Company Records (Harry Ransom Center, University of Texas, Austin, TX).

——. Letter to John Lane. 21 February 1895. John Lane Company Records (Harry Ransom Center, University of Texas, Austin, TX).

——. 'On Reading'. *This Knot of Life* (London: Everett, 1909), 9–80.

——. *Prince Zaleski* (London: Lane, 1895).

——. *Shapes in the Fire: Being a Mid-winter Night's Entertainment in Two Parts and an Interlude* (New York: Garland 1977).

Sims, George Robert. *My Life: Sixty Years' Recollections of Bohemian London* (London: Eveleigh Nash, 1917).

Sinfield, Alan. *The Wilde Century: Effeminacy, Oscar Wilde and the Queer Moment* (London: Cassell, 1994).

Sloan, John. 'Introduction'. *Selected Poems and Prose of John Davidson*. Ed. John Sloan (Oxford: Clarendon, 1995), pp. ix–xxiii.

Small, Ian. *The Aesthetes: A Sourcebook* (London: Routledge, 1979).

Snodgrass, Chris. Aesthetic Memory's Cul-de-sac: The Art of Ernest Dowson'. *English Literature in Transition* 35 (1992), 26–53.

——. 'Decadent Mythmaking: Arthur Symons on Aubrey Beardsley and Salomé'. *Victorian Poetry* 28 (1990), 61–109.

——. 'Decadent Parodies: Aubrey Beardsley's Caricature of Meaning'. Fin de Siècle/Fin du Globe: *Fears and Fantasies of the Late Nineteenth Century*. Ed. John Stokes (New York: St Martin's, 1992), 178–209.

——. 'Ernest Dowson and Schopenhauer: Life Imitating Art in the Victorian Decadence'. *Victorians Institute Journal* 21 (1993), 1–46.

——. 'Ernest Dowson's Aesthetics of Contamination'. *English Literature in Transition* 26 (1983), 162–74.

Spender, John Alfred. *The New Fiction (a Protest Against Sex-Mania), and Other Papers* (New York: Garland, 1984).

Stableford, Brian. *Glorious Perversity: The Decline and Fall of Literary Decadence* (San Bernadino, CA: Borgo Press, 1998).

Stetz, Margaret Diane. 'Debating Aestheticism from a Feminist Perspective'. *Women and British Aestheticism*. Eds Talia Schaffer and Kathy Alexis Psomiades. (Charlottesville: University of Virginia Press, 1999), 25–43.

——. 'Sex, Lies, and Printed Cloth: Bookselling at the Bodley Head in the Eighteen Nineties'. *Victorian Studies* 35,1 (1991), 71–86.

——. 'Life's "Half-Profits": Writers and their Readers in Fiction of the 1890s'. *Nineteenth-Century Lives: Essays Presented to Jerome Hamilton Buckley*. Eds Laurence S. Lockridge, John Maynard, and Donald D. Stone (Cambridge: Cambridge University Press, 1989), 169–87.

Stevenson, Robert Louis. *The Letters of Robert Louis Stevenson*. 6 vols. Eds Bradford A. Booth and Ernest Mehew (New Haven, CT: Yale University Press, 1994).

Stutfield, Hugh E. M. 'Tommyrotics'. *Blackwoods* 179 (June 1895), 833–45.

Sutherland, John. *The Stanford Companion to Victorian Fiction* (Stanford: Stanford University Press, 1989).

Sweetser, Wesley. *Arthur Machen* (New York: Twayne, 1964).

Symons, Arthur. 'Aubrey Beardsley': An Essay With a Preface'. *The Art of Aubrey Beardsley* (New York: Boni and Liveright, 1918), 15–36.

Symons, 'The Decadent Movement in Literature'. *Harper's New Monthly Magazine* 88 (November 1893), 858–67.

——. *Figures of Several Centuries* (New York: Dutton, 1916).

——. 'A Literary Causerie'. *Savoy* 4 (August 1896), 91–3.

——. *Memoirs of Arthur Symons: Life and Art in the1890s*. Ed. Karl Beckson (University Park: Pennsylvania State University Press, 1977).

——. *Studies in Prose and Verse* (London: Dent, 1904).

——. *The Symbolist Movement in Literature* (New York: Dutton, 1958).

Symons, Julian. *Makers of the New: The Revolution in Literature 1912–1939* (London: Andre Deutsch, 1987).

Thackeray, William Makepeace. *The Book of Snobs* (Old Woking, UK: Gresham Books, 1980).

Thornton, Robert Kelsey Rought. *The Decadent Dilemma* (London: Edward Arnold, 1983).

Townsend, J. Benjamin. *John Davidson: Poet of Armageddon* (New Haven, CT: Yale University Press, 1961).

Untitled. *National Observer* (6 April 1895), 547.

Vadillo, Ana Parejo. *Women Poets and Urban Aestheticism: Passengers of Modernity*. (Basingstoke, UK: Palgrave, 2005).

Valentine, Mark. *Arthur Machen* (Mid Glamorgan, Wales: Seren, 1995).

Van Vechten, Carl. *Excavations: A Book of Advocacies* (New York: Knopf, 1926).

——. *Letters of Carl Van Vechten*. Ed. Bruce Kellner (New Haven, CT: Yale University Press, 1987).

Vicinus, Martha. *The Industrial Muse: A Study of Nineteenth Century British Working Class Literature* (London: Croom Helm, 1974).

Weir, David. *Decadence and the Making of Modernism* (Amherst: University of Massachusetts Press, 1995).

Wellhofer, E. Spencer. *Democracy, Capitalism, and Empire in Late-Victorian Britain 1885–1910* (London: Macmillan, 1996).

West, Rebecca. Press clipping from a review in the *Daily Telegraph*, Richards Archives (University of Illinois at Urbana-Champaign, microfilm copy at the Bodleian Library, Oxford University, Oxford).

White, Gleeson. Rev. of *Confessions of a Young Man*, by George Moore. *The Artist and Journal of Home Culture* (1 November 1888), 348–50.

White, Nicholas. Introduction. *Against Nature (A rebours)*. Trans. Margaret Mauldon (Oxford: Oxford University Press, 1998), pp. vii–xxvi.

Whittington-Egan, Richard and Geoffrey Smerdon. *The Quest of the Golden Boy: The Life and Letters of Richard Le Gallienne* (Barre, MA: Barre Publishing Company, 1962).

Whyte, Frederic. *William Heinemann: A Memoir* (Garden City, NY: Doubleday, 1929).

Wilde, Oscar. *Complete Works of Oscar Wilde* (London: Collins, 1971).

Williams, Raymond. *Problems in Materialism and Culture* (London: Verso, 1980).

Wilson, Edmund. *Axël's Castle: A Study in the Imaginative Literature of 1870–1930* (New York: Norton, 1959).

Wilson, Elizabeth. *Bohemians: The Glamorous Outcasts* (New Brunswick, NJ: Rutgers University Press, 2000).

Woolf, Virginia. 'John Davidson'. *Times Literary Supplement* (16 August 1917), 390.

Rev. of *Wormwood*, by Marie Corelli. *Athenaeum* (15 November 1890), 661.

——. *Graphic* (29 November 1890), 624.

——. *Literary World* (17 January 1891), 21–2.

——. *Pall Mall Gazette* (27 November 1890), 3.

Rev. *Times* (23 January 1891), 13.

Wratislaw, Theodore. Letter to Elkin Mathews. 13 March 1914. Walpole Collection (Bodleian Library, Oxford University, Oxford).

Yeats, W. B. Introduction. *Oxford Book of Modern Verse: 1892–1935* (Oxford: Oxford University Press, 1936), pp. v–xlii.

——. *The Autobiography of William Butler Yeats* (Garden City, NY: Doubleday, 1958).

'The Yellow Boot'. *Granta* (21 April 21 1894), 271–5.

Zatlin, Linda Gertner. *Aubrey Beardsley and Victorian Sexual Politics* (Oxford: Oxford University Press, 1990).

——. *Beardsley, Japonisme and the Perversion of the Victorian Ideal* (Cambridge: Cambridge University Press, 1997).

Index